BACK AND FORTH

DILLON BANCROFT

Looking to Connect?

Check out my LinkTree! It has all the links to my social media and website. Please make sure to sign up for the newsletter so you can stay in the know about exciting and upcoming releases!

Email: dillon@dillonbancroft.com
LinkTree: https://linktr.ee/dillon.bancroft
Website: www.dillonbancroft.com

One

I expect the chick in the mirror to be someone different. Maybe I expect her to be somebody who *wants* to be here, or at least someone who dabbed on a little concealer on the purple bags under her eyes before she got to the studio. But no, the woman who sits before me is miserable. Well, not *miserable,* but like, she could use a double shot of espresso and an uninterrupted nap.

The chick is me, unfortunately, and I could use the uninterrupted nap. Hair and makeup are crammed into this tiny shoebox dressing room because I'm not *that* famous anymore and they try their best to iron waves into my frizzy, honey-colored hair, and erase the purple bags under my eyes.

Yes. Ava Reid, the very actress who gave the bird to her successful acting career to raise a family and to hide from the press, agreed to participate in a tell-all interview to broadcast to the world that she *wasn't* the woman who "trapped" Grayson Wentworth into a loveless marriage. Oh, and to promote the new movie that was coming out.

God, I don't want to be here.

But Gray was the one who encouraged me to do it. "Tell the world what really happened! It's time to take back the narrative!"

It was an empowering moment when he first mentioned it, I'll admit, but now that I'm doing it, it doesn't seem like the best idea. I've been out of the game for thirteen years now. While Gray crooked his finger to any panty-hosed legs that meandered his way, I stayed home, raising our children to not be entitled assholes.

I don't regret it for a single minute. Our children, Ethan and Alice, are possibly the *only* good that came out of my marriage with Gray. They're great kids and my whole reason for living. I wouldn't trade my thirteen-year hiatus for anything.

The door to the dressing room opens dramatically with Gray wildly grinning at me through the mirror.

"Juanita, Russell, she looks amazing, but you need to go." I frown because Russell isn't even halfway finished with my face. "Are you ready for this?"

"No. Why are we doing this? You and I are friends now and our children are happy with our dynamic. Isn't that enough?"

He sighs and pulls up a folding chair from behind the door.

"Of course it's enough. But... I tanked your career." He's not wrong about that. Directors refused to work with me because of Gray's image. Because of Gray's promiscuity during our marriage, I was painted as the woman who trapped him in a marriage with children he didn't want. None of it was true. Gray is an amazing father, and our children were very much planned. And since Gray has been America's favorite heartthrob since he was a teenager, his fans made sure to drag my name through the mud. I refuse to be a diva, so it was a no-brainer to take a step back.

"Gray..."

"I didn't correct anyone about the rumors, Ava. You singlehandedly raised our children. They're only great human beings because of you."

"Stop it. You're a great father. They're half you, so that means some of their greatness comes from you."

The way his smile falters isn't wasted on me, but there isn't a lot of time to dwell on that. I'll save it for a rainy day.

"You're coming out of retirement, and it's only right that you get to set the record straight. I'll be within eye shot the entire time; I promise. I'm even slated to sit down and confirm everything. I have your back this time. I'm sorry I let you down before."

Gray is my friend. He was my first true love, my first and only husband, and the father of my children. If I didn't see him as a brother right now, I'd kiss him.

Age has done him well. His dark brown hair is now peppered with gray, and his laugh lines accentuate his denim blue eyes.

"Get Russell back in here. If I'm going to do this, I may as well look pretty." He chuckles as he stands up and replaces the folding chair behind the door.

"You're always pretty. Knock 'em dead. Pull no punches. Set the media on fire." Russell reenters the room and stares me down, like I'm equally a colossal disappointment and boring as hell.

"We'll need to contour."

I'm on the set of *Great Morning Chicago*. They've dedicated a whole hour and a half interview for me. Honestly, I don't even know what I could talk about for an hour and a half. My workout regime, maybe? Ha! If half-assed pushups are what America wants to know about me, have at it. I can take the heat from the internet trolls for that.

Sunny Brauer, who is just as sunny as her name, waves frantically at me with a megawatt smile. Jane, my publicist, groans next to me.

"She can't be that chipper all the time, can she?" Jane whispers.

"Hm, it looks like it. Be glad you're not the one in the spotlight."

Jane snorts as we approach Sunny to the stage they're using for the interview. A black leather armchair is separated from a black leather sofa by a white coffee table. Home.

"Ava Reid! I'm sorry to fan girl, but I am your *biggest* fan! I'm so ecstatic that I get to be the one who gets to sit down with you today!" *It's an hour and a half of your life, Reid. Just get the damn thing done.*

"It's so nice to meet you, Sunny! I've been watching you on my TV for years!" No, I haven't. The only thing my TV is used for is to watch Disney movies and the Hallmark Channel.

"I received the line of questioning from the PA's, but I'll just need a final copy before Ms. Reid takes a seat," Jane remarks.

"Oh, of course!" She turns around and picks up a yellow—*of course*—folder and hands it over to Jane. "Everything you need should be in there. I understand that you spoke with production about the questions we cannot ask."

"Yes, we're all set there. I'll review these one more time and I'll let production know." Jane walks away and starts to read over the questions as she walks. Sunny grins and motions for me to take a seat on the black sofa.

"This is nerve-wracking. I haven't done this in so long."

"Oh, don't worry about it. We'll answer the tough questions first. I know the reason you're here is to set the record straight about Grayson. I never believed those silly rumors about you trapping him."

I laugh. "Thank you. It's nice to hear that."

"Anyway, this will be in front of a live audience. Let me know if you need a break, we can cut to commercial, although, the break can't be long. It'll be just enough time to consult with your team."

Great. I don't have a problem talking about Gray's infidelity. It was excruciating back then, but now we've come so far. We're friends now.

"Quiet on the set!" I look around for Jane, who gives me a thumbs up. Tess, my best friend, and producer of *Great Morning Chicago*, joins Jane to watch the interview. I find Gray in the wings as promised. He's camera ready in case he needs to make an appearance. The set grows eerily quiet.

It's showtime, girl. Deep breath in, deep breath out.

"We knew her as the little girl on the TV Show, *Growing Up*. With her wild curls and mischievous smile, we watched as Ava Reid grew from a four-year-old child to beautiful teen star. She starred in several movies alongside actors like George Clooney and Bruce Willis. When we thought she would be a teenaged burnout, she proved us wrong in the TV Show, *The Elite.* She was always the picture of grace and poise, never showing her emotions when her love life was put under the microscope. She landed the starring role in *Congregation* and fell in love with her future ex-husband, Grayson Wentworth. Today, I sit with Ava Reid to dive into every aspect of her life. To set the record straight. To fix broken hearts." Psh. Broken hearts. I don't see any. "Ava Reid, thank you so much for sitting with us today."

"Thank you, Sunny. I'm so happy to be here." I *could* be neck-deep in my bathtub with a glass of rosé, thank you very much.

"I just saw your Instagram post from last night of you and your kids making a blanket fort and watching *Finding Dory.* That looked so fun!"

"Oh, they hated every minute of it," I laugh, "I'm just an embarrassing mom, clinging to their childhood."

"Oh, I don't believe that. That's something they'll remember for a lifetime!"

"I hope so. It's important to Gray and me that they have these childhood memories."

"Well, let's jump right into it, shall we? How did you know you wanted to be an actress?" Easy. Peasy.

"Well, it took me a while to figure it out, honestly. It was just a fun thing for me to do when I was a kid, but after *Growing Up*, and getting the role of Bea in *The Elite,* I realized I wanted to make it a career instead of just a hobby. I loved getting to step into somebody else's shoes. And in Bea's case, the shoes were fancy and gorgeous." Sunny laughs. I look for Gray and Jane in the wings to put my racing heart at ease.

"You were so young when you starred in *Growing Up.* Do you think you had to grow up quickly because you were constantly surrounded by adults?"

"Anyone in this industry has to grow up quickly. I love my *Growing Up* family something fierce. When I was four years old, they tried so hard to give me a childhood. They knew my relationship even then with my mother wasn't the greatest. They'd play games on set with me, and they'd help me memorize my lines. I know that isn't the case in similar shows, but I'm so fortunate to have found a family in them."

"Are you still close with that cast?"

I weakly smile. "Yes. To this day, I can still rely on them to be my family. When Gray and I divorced, they were there every step of the way with me."

"You were eleven when the series ended. How did you feel when the network pulled the plug?"

"I was devastated," I laugh. "I had spent almost every day for seven years with these people and it felt like the rug was being pulled out from under me. Looking back, though, it was the right move. We told every story we needed to tell. It also opened a lot of doors for me later on."

"What did you do after?"

"I went to public school. I begged my mother for some semblance of a normal childhood."

Sunny grins and turns my attention to the monitor that shows a picture of me with Tyler Smith at our eighth grade dance. I giggle into my hand.

"My eighth grade dance!"

"Grayson insisted this get shown to you. Why do you think that?"

"He used to tell me that this was his favorite version of me. Carefree, confident, fearless..." Except I was *so* nervous for this dance. Tyler only asked me because I was somewhat famous, but he made sure I had a good time.

My best friend Tess showed me how to "dance." And when I say "dance" I mean, how to grind and shake my ass. Those were the days.

"In *The Elite*, your character Beatrice 'Bea' Hamilton was the daughter of a President of the United States who didn't receive a lot of love or attention. How did you prepare yourself for this role?"

"It wasn't difficult, to say the least. I had an acting coach that helped me to hone my feelings of abandonment and neglect from my mother. President and Mrs. Hamilton had children to get him to the presidency. Bea and Michael were props, and that was that."

"Was it worth it?"

"It's hard to say. I mean, it made the show amazing, and it won so many Golden Globes and Emmys. But, in the same breath, I was throwing my own trauma into my acting. The whole country was front and center to my coping mechanism."

Again, my attention is brought to the screen to show me walking down Rodeo Drive in Los Angeles, hand in hand with Ben Crawford.

"Tell me about Ben Crawford."

I smile to myself. Ben Crawford is the sweetest man alive. I would have been lucky to end up with him, but alas, stardom.

"Ben's character was Bea's love interest in *The Elite*. Naturally, I fell for him quickly."

"But you didn't date right away?"

Laughing, I shake my head and bury my face in my hands. "No. I was embarrassed to tell him how I felt." The audience and Sunny laughed. "I was fifteen and had such a huge crush on him. I didn't know how to articulate my feelings to him."

"But it worked out in the end!"

"Yes, it did." Sweet Ben Crawford. Always my knight in shining armor. "He was very sweet. I'd always manage to choke on my tongue when we would be in between scenes. Finally, when we finished filming season two, he told me he was taking me to dinner."

"Did you love him?" Sunny asks knowingly.

Of course I did. Who *wouldn't* love Ben Crawford? I place my hand over my heart and sneak a glance at Gray, who scowls at me.

"Very much. He's the epitome of a perfect first boyfriend."

"During your time together, the media was involved in almost every aspect of your relationship. Is that what led to the demise of your relationship with Ben?"

"No. The media had us broken up at least a dozen times and none of it was true. We were already spending so much time together, and because of work, we were always together. No, the demise of our relationship presented itself as an offer for a role of a lifetime. He was written off *The Elite*, and he promptly moved to Vancouver for filming. We were both minors and vacations to Vancouver twice a month weren't realistic. It just couldn't continue." I frown.

What would it have been like to marry Ben? I mean, I'm not blind, nor am I an idiot. I follow him on social media. I see that beautiful, leggy, blonde he's already made into a mother. He would've been perfect.

When he received the offer, he wasn't going to take it. He wanted to stay with me and see where our relationship went. But even at sixteen, our relationship lasted for only a year, and I didn't want him to resent me.

My eyes itch. I miss Ben. But platonically. It would've never worked out, I know that. I wouldn't have Ethan or Alice—and that, right there, is why I don't regret a single minute of my existence or anything in between. Including everything that happened with Gray.

"Are you getting a little dusty there, Ava?"

I giggle. "A little. Ben was amazing. He's been such a great friend over the years and thinking back to that time makes me a little sad."

"Let's move onto *Congregation*. This was your first motion picture that went on to win three Oscars. What about the script made you want the role?"

"I just felt that this was a story that hasn't been told before. We see the stories about dysfunctional churches on the news all the time. But putting an actual story to it—to live the lives of these parishioners, to make us care about these characters—I wanted to be a part of that."

"And of course, it's where you met your future ex-husband, Grayson Wentworth."

I turn to the wings to find Gray watching me intently, silently urging me to tell the truth.

How ironic.

"Was it love at first sight?"

"Kind of. We met at our chemistry screening. I had seen Gray at a few premieres, but we never spoke a word to each other. Our chemistry was palpable from the very beginning. He was charming and handsome—the perfect rebound for my broken heart."

"You were eighteen, correct? You and Ben had been broken up for two years at that point."

"Yes, but Ben was my first love, Sunny. I didn't think my world would turn right side up ever again." The audience laughs at my nervous laughter. "Anyway, I don't think I'd call it love at first sight. Of course, by the end of that screening, I already had named our children."

Sunny's chest bounces with laughter.

I shift uncomfortably because this is the part where I dig into one of the most painful areas of my life.

"Like Ben, you and Grayson didn't date until after you were done filming. Why is that?"

My gaze finds Gray's once again. I take a deep breath and revel in the kindness of his stare. "I didn't want to ruin the chemistry we had. We were so young and all it would take is one bad argument or," *premature mashing of genitals,* "a breakup that would ruin the movie. I wasn't willing to throw this opportunity of a lifetime away just because America's Heart Throb was much cuter in person."

"That sounds...painful." I giggle.

"It was certainly painful for Gray." From my peripherals, I see him shake his head. "All kidding aside, it was painful for me too. We were friends first and foremost. I enjoyed spending every free minute with him, and it didn't even need to be romantic. I think that's why when we finally divorced, it was that much more painful. I lost my husband, but I also lost my best friend."

"I think my whole generation ascended into heaven when you *finally* debuted your relationship on the red carpet for the first time. I was 'shipping the two of you together before 'shipping' was even a thing.'"

Oh, God.

"We were already together for a year by then." There are hushed whispers in the audience. It's nice to know that I can still be a little unpredictable. Sunny's eyebrows furrow.

"But I have here that you started dating a week before the premiere..."

"That's what we told everyone. We became official the day we finished shooting. Gray took me to this tin can diner at the edge of town and we ordered an unhealthy amount of burgers, fries, and milkshakes. You know, the stuff you aren't allowed to have while filming." My heart aches. It's my favorite memory with him. And up until now, it was the only memory the two of us shared that the entire world didn't know about.

"He was really sweet. He told me that he was already in love with me. And then he kissed me while two truckers watched." Gray's booming laugh makes me crack a grin. The cameras briefly show Gray laughing next to Tess and Jane.

"How did you *not* get caught by the media?"

Guilt twists my stomach.

"We became skilled in hiding the relationship. And unfortunately, we both got good at hiding it. Gray paid off the whole diner not to talk. But after that, we were pretty much shut-ins. Our publicists worked together to keep it on the down-low. Occasionally, just to throw things off, we orchestrated 'sightings' with other celebrities. Ben even agreed to be caught seen with me."

"But *why* did you feel the need to hide it?"

This time, I laugh without humor. I could answer bitterly, but it isn't Sunny's fault.

"We wanted uninterrupted time to be together. We had a long break in between filming *Congregation* and our next projects. And, well, it wasn't anybody else's business. Like I said before, there was a tabloid every week that broke Ben and me up and sometimes, yeah, caused some doubt in our relationship. There were tabloids of Gray sleeping around *even then* that weren't remotely true. We wanted to take the time to build the trust in our relationship."

Sunny scowls at me while my insides churn.

"Knowing what you know now, especially of all the confirmed reports of the infidelity in your marriage that *he* caused, do you *really* think he wasn't sleeping around back then?"

I shake my head. I'm not naïve. Not like I was back then.

"Gray admitted to cheating on me after we got married. He told me of every single affair. He could have hidden that, denied all the rumors, paid people off—but he didn't. He was honest. So, when he tells me that he didn't sleep around in earlier relationships, I believe him. He's never given me a reason not to believe him."

I can already tell this is going to be a social media shit storm. Ava Reid is a human doormat. Ava Reid is a naïve idiot. Ava Reid is oblivious.

"That doesn't make him honorable. If I ever needed to know something—especially about the cheating—all I ever had to do was ask."

Sunny shifts uncomfortably and then looks into the camera. "I would love to talk to you about this further, Ava. When we come back, we will dive into the most talked about celebrity failed marriage."

I cringe when we're given the all-clear.

Ignoring Sunny completely, I jump up and move towards Gray, Tess, and Jane. "I fucked up already, didn't I?"

Jane isn't hearing me because she's already on the social media hunt. She scowls as she scrolls, making my heart race a mile a minute. Shit. I shouldn't have said that.

"Hey. You're doing great." Gray reaches for my hand and squeezes. "This is your story. Don't let perception dictate how you interview. You're setting the record straight."

Yeah, taking back the narrative. All that other bullshit.

"You're doing great, Ava," Jane finally pipes up. "We have the social media under control. Don't worry about a thing."

I take a deep breath and wrap my arms around Gray. My ear rests up against his chest and I time my breathing to the slow 'thump' of his heart.

"Go finish it. It's going to be okay." I nod and release him. I trudge back to the black armchair and slowly lower myself into it, smiling at Sunny.

I'm pretty sure I've disappointed her. But that doesn't matter. I've spent the majority of the last thirteen years at odds with Gray. He shattered my heart into a million pieces. I didn't have a choice *but* to co-parent with him. It's a lot of trust and forgiveness.

"Quiet on the set!" Sunny hesitantly glances over to me and gives me a tight-lipped smile.

"Welcome back. We're with Ava Reid, America's Sweetheart. Before we went to commercial, we talked about the early days of her relationship with Grayson Wentworth."

Sunny brings my attention to the monitor in front of me, to a picture that makes me feel warm and fuzzy inside. Baby Ethan, with his two-toothed smile and chubby cheeks, grins back at me.

"This is your oldest son, Ethan. You had him at twenty-one, just eight months after you married Grayson. Was Ethan the reason you married?"

"No. We knew we wanted to have children sooner rather than later. Both of our children were planned. We were going to start trying after we got married, but Ethan surprised us a month before."

I stare into Ethan's blue eyes and smile nostalgically. My fiercest protector. My buddy.

"How was Grayson in those early years as a husband and father?"

"He was—*is*—an amazing father. I couldn't breastfeed with either of my children. I just couldn't produce what was needed, so we exclusively formula-fed. Gray got up with me every three hours. He would make the bottle and then made sure I was comfortable while I fed Ethan. Sometimes, Gray would wake up with him and would let me sleep." My heart twists with anxiety. What changed? He was perfect then.

"And as a husband?"

I sigh. "That first year with Ethan was eye-opening. There was no denying Gray loved his son—or that he loved me. But I think there was always a nagging feeling in the back of my head that maybe he didn't think all of this through."

"What do you mean?"

"You have to understand that Gray was raised by a single mother. His father up and left when he was six years old and never made a point to make contact after that. I *know* that he wanted a full, nuclear family. Now that we're friends, we've talked about this at great extent. He loved me. I was his first true love—somebody who he could see spending the rest of his life with. But with that, he—*we*—skipped a lot of steps in between. You're supposed to play the field in your twenties, not settle down and have children a month after you get married.

"In this profession, your job has you falling in love every single project. Gray has a big heart. He fell in love with his co-stars *so* easily."

"And how did that affect you?"

Isn't it obvious? How would this affect *anyone?* It killed me. My forever was being flushed down the toilet without a second glance.

"The first time, I thought it was just a fluke. We just had a baby, and he was sorry about cheating on me. I was devastated. How could he just 'forget' us in that moment? How could he not think about his wife and son at home? How could he not think of the consequences? Was it something I did or didn't do? Was I less attractive now that he bagged me and knocked me up?"

Gray gives me a reassuring nod. It's time to show America the ugly side of Grayson Wentworth.

Two

Ava

Now

"He didn't come home one night while filming *Retribution*. Ethan was a year old and was sleeping through the night. I fell asleep on the couch, waiting for him. I woke up around three in the morning and he wasn't home. I didn't have any missed calls or text messages, so naturally, I panicked. I started calling around. The director said that he left at seven for the day. I called around to jails and hospitals and I couldn't find him. An hour later, he snuck in."

I close my eyes to banish the tears. That was the night I knew my marriage was doomed.

"He told me everything. He snuck away with his co-star, Lucy Rodriguez, and got a room for the night. I didn't hear it from the media, which is a small mercy, I suppose, but it stung, nonetheless."

"What happened after that? There was the whole controversy of her faking her pregnancy with him six years ago. I mean, for a while there, we all thought Lucy was going to be moving into your house and snatching up your family."

That's what it seemed like to me too. Lucy has her issues. We're a lot alike. We both tried to "fix" Gray, and it blew up in our faces spectacularly. At least *I* didn't fake a pregnancy.

"He was sorry. But he still was in love with Lucy *and* me. We went to counseling. We were adamant on trying to fix this."

"And then Alice arrived."

My beautiful blonde-haired beauty with her cute dimples and a sweet smile appears on the monitor. My twin.

"Things were better. He broke it off with Lucy and took some time off from acting. We talked about having Alice with our therapist. She wasn't so sure it was a good time to be thinking about that, because there was still a lot of fear on my part regarding Gray's infidelity. He couldn't take time off forever, and I'd never allow him not to follow his passion. But we talked about it and Alice was wanted. We would figure out the rest later."

"Is Alice a daddy's girl?" The question takes me by surprise, though it shouldn't.

Not to the right person.

The thought alone is a gut punch. I glance up to the camera, and then to Gray, who is waiting expectantly for me to answer.

The truth is, my kids aren't stupid. They saw firsthand how Gray destroyed my self-esteem. Kids at school would make fun of them for their dad being on the news, or if they'd see me crying out of nowhere. There has been some distance in their relationship with Gray, especially over the last six years.

"Alice is more of a mommy's girl," I reluctantly answer, even though it isn't even remotely true.

"We've seen a ton of photos circulating the time Alice was born. It was mostly pictures of Grayson taking both children out for walks and you aren't anywhere to be found."

Unintentionally, I give the biggest Liz Lemon eye roll and pinch the bridge of my nose. All right. I'm done being polite.

"Gray was decent enough to give me breaks. He wasn't as attentive as he was when Ethan was born. I was up doing the feedings and he'd occasionally change a diaper. I put my career on hold to be home with my children. Alice was a colicky baby. She'd cry for hours on end and have terrible ear infections. I needed a break. Gray taking the kids out to play at the playground was not a sign of our marriage deteriorating." But it was. I was desperately grasping for any shred of hope that he would wake up and see all his slack I was picking up.

I wanted him to notice me.

"Tell me about Kaitlin Connor."

Kaitlin Connor. The woman who couldn't take no for an answer. She tried *so* hard to break us up, to get him to leave us. There was even a one-month period she lived in our guest room. Hearing the headboard rhythmically bang against the wall was soul crushing.

"She was just another co-star Gray fell in love with."

Sunny shakes her head.

"They were caught together for over a year."

I shrug carelessly and grind my teeth.

"That one hurt, honestly. The icing on the cake was she was living in our guest room while her house was being worked on. The media painted me to be the woman who trapped him in a loveless marriage with kids he didn't want. It was so far from the truth. Gray... he confused love and lust. Kaitlin Connor was just another woman in a long line of women who Gray was sure he was in love with."

"But a whole year," Sunny flounders. "You must believe he was in love maybe just a little bit, right?"

"No. I don't believe it. Because he cheated on her."

"With you?"

I giggle.

"With me, with Lucy Rodriguez, Jennifer Harrington, Missy Jones, and Haley Marie Angiers."

For comfort, I look to Gray, who wears a melancholy grimace. He's come so far. He's not the playboy he used to be.

"And then after that, it wasn't about love anymore."

"What was it about then?"

"Filling a void."

"What void was that?"

"His roaring twenties." I chuckle. "He resented our marriage. He resented me for trying to work it out. As far as he was concerned, he could sleep with *anyone* who crooked her finger, but he still wanted the family he had."

"But... *why* did you stay with him through all of that? If it were me, I would've been gone after Lucy Rodriguez."

"I made a vow." The audience groans. More ammo for social media. "I vowed that I would love him through sickness and health, through good times and bad. We have two children together. I was determined to make it work. We owed our children that."

"Why didn't you come back to Hollywood when the divorce was final?"

"Directors didn't want to work with me because of the negative press that surrounded me due to Gray's philandering. And I learned later that out of spite, Gray took on multiple projects that took him out of the country. So, I stayed home with the kids. I was a ghostwriter on a lot of the shows you watch today. I guest star if there are openings. I was 'back' in Hollywood, just not in the same capacity as I was."

"What happened to you after the divorce? There weren't any reports or sightings of you dating anyone. You have divorced seven years ago. Did you *seriously* not get close with anyone? Not even a string-free hook up?"

"How is that any of your business?" The words fall out of my mouth faster than I can catch my temper. "My personal life is just that, personal. Would you have asked Gray that if I was the one who was sleeping around?" *Shut up! You need this!*

Sunny bumbles about, flipping through her notecards. Who would ask such an asinine question?

"There wasn't anyone after Gray," I spit poisonously. "Not that it's up for discussion. If there were someone worth mentioning, I would've told the world by now." My deepest, darkest secret weighs heavily on my heart. The lies come to me so easily. If I lie, the further away from the truth I get. The faster I get away from his memory.

"When did you start seeing Brandon Wentworth?" She's not so sunny anymore. In fact, her tone changes like she's gloating.

My heart stops beating in my chest.

The world stops spinning on its axis.

"What?"

The final blow?

The picture of Brandon and I kissing in the barn of his mother's house. His arm wrapped around my waist, his free hand fisting my hair, his lips pressed up against mine.

Tears are there before I even know what's happening.

Suck it up.

"Ava? When did you start seeing your brother-in-law?"

I rip my gaze from Sunny. This is *not* how I wanted Gray to find out. I scan the wings until I land on a pair of rainforest green eyes.

I was wrong. This is the final blow.

And he's angry.

Brandon Wentworth, my dirty little secret is here in the flesh. And still, my heart calls to him as if he didn't tear my world apart.

"When we return, we will sit down with Ava Reid and Brandon Wentworth to rehash their unconventional relationship."

Three

Ava

Now

We're given the all-clear, and I jump out of my seat. Sunny calls after me, but I don't miss a beat. I push past Brandon; the Adonis I should've steered clear of. I ignore the way his brown hair no longer falls into his eyes and the way his arms are much bigger than the last time I laid eyes on him.

Fucking Brandon.

I storm down the hallway with Jane and Tess following close behind. Where the hell is Gray?

My lungs scream like I'm submerged in water. The second the sun and cool air hit my face, I feel like I can breathe—barely.

"Ava—"

"What the *fuck*, Tess!"

"I swear, babe, I didn't say anything!"

"The picture. How did they get the picture?"

"Social media is blowing up about this. We need context we need—"

"Jane, you're not helping," Tess snaps.

Jane finally looks up from her phone and blinks between Tess and me.

"Ava, is any of this true?" She asks timidly.

I wish it weren't. I wish I never asked him for help. I wish I never kissed him. Oh my god! How is this happening? I was so careful!

"Yes," I say in a whisper. Jane swallows and nods.

"I know you don't want to go back in there, but we *have* to. You're too far into this interview—it's all live. Social media is painting you into a corner again. We *have* to see this through. There's too much riding on this," Jane frets. There's too much riding on this interview for *all of us.*

She's right, damn it. I can't just leave—not with this bombshell.

"Where's Gray?" I ask, scanning the small alcove for him.

Tess shifts her weight from foot to foot and glances around the lot. "I don't know. As soon as they put the picture up, he bolted."

I sink to the ground, ruining Russell's makeup. This can't be happening!

"I'll find Gray, Ava. Okay? I'll fix it." I look to Tess and sigh.

"You can't fix it, Tess." Deep breath in, deep breath out. "I can't believe he's here. I can't believe Gray has to find out like this." Tess sinks next to me and rests her head on the brick wall behind us.

"It's just Brandon. No matter what went down, I can guarantee he won't do anything to hurt you."

"Did you know about this?" I ask.

She sadly shakes her head.

"I wasn't privy to those meetings because of our relationship. I swear, if I were allowed to be a part of this, I would've put a stop to it, I promise."

How did this happen?

"I'll finish it. Let's just get it over with." I scramble to my feet and dust myself off. Tess rubs the smudged eyeliner from under my eyes and smiles.

"You've got this," she encourages with a reassuring squeeze.

I muster all the courage I can scrape up and march back into the studio. I walk through the halls while the crew stares at me. I reach the stage and Gray is just gone. Where the black armchair I was sitting in, now sits a longer black sofa. Brandon sits tall and stoic on the end of the couch farthest away from Sunny.

Sunny looks like she's going to faint. Brandon broods, refusing to acknowledge the audience or the crew. Until, of course, I walk into the room. Like Gray, the hair at his temples is graying. Unlike Gray, Brandon shares their mother's eyes. He's an easygoing guy. You'd never guess that by looking at him now. Right now, he looks so angry that he'd Hulk Smash the building down.

I swallow my tears and plop down on the sofa next to him.

"Great, you're back! Now, I just want to—"

"If you wanted to see me, Ave, all you had to do was call," he interrupts and completely disregards Sunny. I arch my eyebrow and turn to him for the first time in six years. I hate how his voice still makes my heart flutter.

"Did you have us followed this entire time? Was this the long con, Brand? Gray didn't humiliate me enough, so you swoop in to finish the job?"

"That's bullshit and you know it," he sneers. "*I* respected *your* wishes to keep it secret."

"Oh really? It was my wish to keep us a secret. Last time I checked, *Brand,* you wanted to keep it a secret. You went after your brother's ex-wife—"

"Like it wasn't mutual," he snaps.

It was mutual, damn it. I cross my arms in some tacky attempt to comfort myself and scan the wings until I land on *her*.

Fucking Ellen.

"How does this surprise me?" I whisper, not particularly to Brandon, but more to myself. She stands defensively where Gray stood, glaring at me with her perky high pony that attempts to contain her wild, strawberry blonde hair. "God, she didn't even wait until the body was cold..." I smirk and give her a finger wave.

Ellen rolls her eyes and storms down the hallway.

Bye, bitch.

"Leave her alone," Brandon warns.

"That's a low blow," I say quietly. "Bringing her here. Dangling her in front of me. It's a real Grayson Wentworth move, don't you think?" He grinds his teeth, his jaw ticks, and he drops his gaze. Score one for Ava Reid.

"Um, we're ready to start..." Satisfaction washes over me now that Sunny is less chipper and uncomfortable.

I close my eyes and take a deep breath.

"We're back with Ava Reid and Brandon Wentworth." They show the picture of us again. I *wish* that every time I look at it—at us—I didn't feel like I'm being hit by a Mack truck. I wish that my heart didn't constantly seek comfort from him, even after he walked away.

"Did you have an affair with your brother-in-law while you were married to Grayson?"

"No. Gray and I had already been divorced for two years before Brandon and I started seeing each other." It's like the day after he left all over again. Grief is that gut punch I never wanted or asked for. And him sitting next to me is just salt in the wound.

"Judging by your reaction, Ava, things ended on bad terms."

Flashes of Ellen standing naked in the doorway of Brandon's apartment enter my mind. The TV commercials of him entering that stupid game show shadow that memory. They were so much alike, and I didn't fucking see it.

Brandon was the one between him and Gray, who had a moral compass—or so I thought. He was kind and actually cared—

Oh, God.

I'm an idiot.

That was Gray in the beginning. How could I have been so blind?

"It ended on strange terms," Brandon answers for me. For a second, I'm glad he still has my back. But *I'm* the one who is supposed to take back the narrative. This is *my* story.

"Take me back six years ago. How did this all start?"

Four

Ava

Then

We're a broken record. Every year since Alice was born, two days after Thanksgiving, we both get deathly ill. Okay, I'm exaggerating just a little bit, but the sentiment remains the same. Tess and her husband, Jordan, are vacationing in New York, and Gray has dropped off the face of the Earth.

Awesome.

I've shamefully allowed my eight-year-old son to take care of us—only by letting him pour us Gatorade and water. But now, at nearly nine-thirty at night, Alice and I spoon on the couch while we watch Ethan's pick of the night, *Teenage Mutant Ninja Turtles*.

Panera Bread has been our restaurant of choice since it hurts to get up and they'll deliver soup on-demand. Plus, Ethan can indulge in his favorite mac and cheese. Mother of the year, I know. I play the cards I've been dealt like a fucking lady.

Alice's honey-colored curls fall into her eyes while she quietly snores next to me. It feels like five pounds of rocks sit in the center of my head. I reach over and place my hand on Alice's forehead, so hot like she's been in an oven.

Too hot.

Pushing myself into a sitting position and trying hard not to disturb Alice.

"Mom, what are you doing?" Ethan asks, sitting up in alert.

"Lay down, baby. I'm just going to get the thermometer."

"But I can do it."

"Ethan, honey, be a kid and watch your movie. I've got this." Barely. I shuffle from the couch into the kitchen and grab the thermometer off the counter and shuffle back. I'm a granny.

I gently shake Alice awake and slip the thermometer in her mouth. The numbers jump up so effortlessly. It continues climbing over one hundred degrees Fahrenheit without slowing down. It stops on 104 and I nearly burst into tears.

"Okay. Ethan, babe, go get your shoes and your coat on. Bring your Gameboy."

"Where are we going?" Alice asks in a raspy voice. My eyes sweep over Alice. She looks so pale, so fragile.

"We're going to the hospital, baby. We're going to get the doctors to take care of you."

"It's a Nintendo Switch, *not* a Gameboy," Ethan informs me. "We're not in the nineties anymore, mom."

Ugh, thank you for that.

"Shoes and coat, buddy. Chop chop." I shuffle to the front door, pull on my coat and my UGGS and grab Alice's coat and her cute pink cowboy boots and shuffle back to the couch.

Alice is a sack of potatoes. I hoist her up and pray that the second I can hold her up is enough time to get one of her arms through the sleeve of her coat before she falls flat onto the couch cushion again.

Ethan, sensing my struggle and watching me fight this losing battle, walks over and helps me lift his sister so I can get the other arm through the sleeve. I zip her up and push her boots on. For good measure, I wrap her like a burrito with the blanket from the couch.

The icy air feels like razor blades against my skin. I hold my baby close to me while we descend the stairs that lead up to the house.

I should've joined a gym. Thirty minutes of cardio or strength training a day could do me wonders right now. But no, I chose to make chocolate chip cookies and bathe with pink wine every night.

I regret it now.

Ethan opens the car door for Alice. I get her in and buckled up. Ethan races to the other side and buckles in. I thank the gods that there isn't frost on the windshield. I get in the car and start it up. I nearly cry when the a/c vents start-up and only push out cold air, despite the fact I cranked the heat up.

I call Gray again, and of course, it goes to voicemail. Fucking typical. And he's *People's* Dad of the Year? Fuck off.

The heat finally kicks on five minutes into our trip. The hospital is twenty minutes from our little house, but without the traffic, we get there much quicker.

Being that I look like I'm homeless, I don't get many stares when we enter the waiting room. I set Ethan and Alice up in the chairs where I can see them and fill out the arrival paperwork. There are maybe three other people here.

I trudge back to the chairs and have Alice sit in my lap. Her hair smells like strawberries and it tickles my nose. Ethan sits quietly with his headphones on and plays his games while we wait for Alice to be called for triage.

Her light snores should make me happy, but in reality, I'm scared. She had Tylenol over an hour ago. Her fever shouldn't be that high, and now I'm completely alone. I have nobody to help me through this.

"Alice Wentworth!" Our little party scrambles to our feet and I carry Alice into the triage room. The nurse takes her temperature and asks me questions about the last time she took medication, when the fever spiked, yadda, yadda, yadda.

She directs us back to the chairs and assures us that Alice will be admitted tonight and someone will be here in a moment to escort us back. I should've brought my own blanket. My teeth chatter together in the coolness of the sterile hospital air.

"Hello Wentworth family, my name is Gina and I'm your nurse today." I look up to the sweet, motherly woman in purple scrubs and force a smile.

"Hi. I'm Ava, this is Alice and Ethan." Gina grins at both of my children, but then motions for me to follow her.

"She needs to be admitted, but Ethan can't come into the room with us. We can only allow one visitor."

I want to cry.

"I would send him home if I could, but it's only me. I can't get a hold of their father; my best friend is out of town… I don't have a choice."

Gina gives me a tight-lipped smile and reassuringly squeezes my arm.

"It's hospital policy. Tell you what. Try your husband again and if he doesn't answer, we'll see who we can speak with to bend the rules."

Husband.

I nod and find a corner of the room and dial Gray once again.

"Holy shit, Ava—what could you possibly want?"

His voice makes me want to sucker punch him through a window. What could I possibly want? Oh, I don't know, help? A co-parent who actually does their job!

"Alice is getting admitted into the hospital." I hear the rustling of sheets, the muted whispers, and a groan.

"What do you mean she's getting admitted into the hospital?"

"She has a fever that isn't breaking—look, I don't ask you for *anything*, but I need you to pick Ethan up. They won't allow him into the room—"

"I'm in Australia, Ava. I can't pick him up."

Volcanoes.

Geysers.

Hordes of angry bees.

How else can I describe myself right now?

"How are you in Australia? You didn't tell me you were leaving the country! You have children, Gray!"

"I'm on location, calm down."

"Don't tell me to calm down! Tess and Jordan are in New York—what am I supposed to do, Gray? We have an agreement that you are supposed to give me a heads up if you leave for a location so I can make other arrangements so that things like *this* don't happen!"

I'm a screaming lunatic, earning stares from the other people in the waiting room. I don't fucking care. I'm giving Grayson Wentworth a piece of my mind that's long overdue.

"I'm sorry—"

"This is so irresponsible. I'm one person, Gray. You may not love me anymore, but if you love our children like you claim you do, you'd stop doing *stupid shit* like this!" Gray huffs.

"I'm sorry, okay?" *Not okay.* "Brandon flew in last night. You can probably call him and see if he can hang out with E for a while."

He doesn't even get a chance to say anything else because I end the call. I'm so sick of the "I'm sorry's" and the deadbeat attitude. But Brandon...

He's a different horse. I'm not entirely sure how they have the same parents. Brandon is polite and attentive. Gray is abrasive and a sack of shit. Over the course of my relationship with Gray, my relationship with Brandon was skin-deep at best. We small talked and did movie nights when he was married to his ex-wife, but we never had any heart to hearts or deep, philosophical conversations.

Hovering over his name in my contacts, I glance over at the kids who sit nicely with Gina and take a deep breath.

"Ave?" His voice is gravelly, like I just woke him up. It gives my poor heart made of cactus a jolt. "Is everything all right?" He's also the only person who calls me "Ave."

"Hey, Brand," my voice shakes.

"What's going on? Where are you?"

"I'm at the hospital. Alice is really sick, and they want to admit her, and they won't let Ethan in the room and Gray is in freakin' Australia, Tess and Jordan are in New York—"

"Hey, it's okay. I'm glad you called. What hospital are you at? I can hang out with Ethan for a while if you want me to." His voice is so soothing.

"La Grange Memorial."

"Okay. I'm on my way. I'm just leaving my place now, okay?"

"Yeah, okay." I end the call and trudge back over to my little family and sit down.

"E, baby. Uncle Brandon is going to come by and pick you up, okay?" He furrows his dark eyebrows and glances at Alice.

"But, I don't want to leave you and Alice." I pull him into a bear hug and drop a kiss on the crown of his head.

"I know you don't. But you can't come into the room because we don't want you getting sick. You've done so much for us already, baby. Tonight, you can sleep in your own bed and I'm sure Uncle Brandon will play some football in the yard with you…"

Ethan isn't convinced whatsoever, but he doesn't say anything else. Gina sits with Alice and asks her questions about school and what her favorite candy is.

It's thirty minutes before the front doors of the ER see any action. I catch sight of Brandon as he strolls through the front doors and catches sight of our little pow-wow.

Holy crap, he's pretty. Even though he's wearing a coat, his biceps are well-defined and squeezable. And those green eyes? I could lose myself in that rainforest.

"Hey gorgeous," he coos, crouching down in front of Alice and grinning.

"Hi, Uncle Brand."

"I'm sorry you're feeling yucky." She shrugs, her eyes showing barely any life. He turns to Ethan and offers a fist bump. "How are you doing, buddy?"

"Are you going to spend the night?"

Brandon nods, his smile never leaves his face.

"Yeah. We can throw the football around in your front yard when we wake up tomorrow."

Sometimes I feel like a horrible mother. Especially when Ethan breaks into the widest grin I've ever seen on him. My serious little boy has been the man of the house since the news reports of Gray's philandering were on every channel. He's the kind of kid who comes right home after school and does his homework right away and then hounds his sister until she finishes hers.

So yeah, when his face lights up at the prospect of football in the front yard, the mom guilt takes over.

Finally, his gaze moves to me. His smile falters for a moment as if he realizes that my homeless look is because I'm knocking on death's door but doesn't want to freak my kids out.

"Hey, Ave. Let's talk for a minute." I stand up and lead Brandon into the corner of the room—not to make out.

"Thanks for coming. I don't know what I would've done if you didn't pick up."

He squeezes my shoulder and nods. "I'm happy to help. Listen, please don't take this the wrong way, but you look terrible."

I laugh. Partially out of hysteria, partially out of exhaustion.

"Yeah, well..." I shrug. I don't want to tell him I don't have anyone to look after me, so I swallow my words. "I'll be fine. It's nothing Nyquil can't fix." He scowls.

"Ave—"

"I can give you some money for food. He has to be back to school on Monday, so hopefully, we won't be here long. I'll keep you posted, but maybe we can set up FaceTime dates every night, so Ethan doesn't feel like I abandoned him?"

"Of course—"

"Ethan knows where everything is. I just washed the sheets yesterday, so I'm sorry...you'll have to make the bed yourself. Help yourself to anything and just...keep me posted, okay?"

Brandon looks over his shoulder, checking on the kids who are preoccupied with Gina's stethoscope. "Everything is going to be okay. We'll hang out. We'll play out in the yard and maybe I'll take him out for pizza or something. But being that you're going to be in the hospital, maybe you could take the time to rest." I purse my lips.

"I really look like shit, don't I?"

The corners of his mouth twitch but shakes his head. Nice save.

"It's going to be okay. I promise. We'll try not to destroy the house." I glance at him warily, which earns me a laugh. "I'm kidding."

"Let me get you the key." He follows me back to the kids and I fish around my purse for my keys. I spin the key off the ring and place it into his open hand. I crouch beside Ethan and throw my arms around him. "I'll FaceTime you tomorrow. Be good, okay?" Ethan gives me a knowing look and nods. He knows. I know. He's a good kid.

"I'll miss you, mom."

"I'll miss you too, baby. See you later." Ethan hops off the chair and shrugs his coat back on. Brandon offers me his hand to help me stand up. Once I'm vertical and woozy, Brandon lets go of my hand and grins.

"I'll text you in the morning. Feel better, Alice!"

Gina ushers us past the double doors once I stop blubbering about leaving Ethan. We're brought into the children's wing and Alice is redressed in a gown and then covered with two warm blankets.

They start IVs and hook her up to all sorts of machines. Meanwhile, I'm useless and helpless in a chair right beside her bed, clinging onto any strand of consciousness I can grab.

"Sweetheart? Mrs. Wentworth?" I'm too delirious to correct Alice's sweet nurse. I can't answer her verbally. I'm tired. "Alice has her own room tonight, so you can take the extra bed. I'll go grab some warm blankets for you." She helps me out of the chair and into my bed and slips my shoes off for me. She gives me a sincere smile and heads out the door. I reach into my purse and grab the Nyquil I slipped in before we left the house. I measure out my dose and shoot it back.

Then, I let the sleep take me.

Alice remains in the hospital for two days. We've FaceTimed Ethan and Brandon as often as our bodies allowed us and they had a grand old time. I still feel like hell. Alice's nurse has been kind enough to hang out with Alice while I self-medicate with whatever *Vicks* has to offer.

But now, we *finally* get to go home. We're handed our discharge papers and we're sent on our way. Alice is perky, but still under the weather. And if I'm right—which I always am—when I look behind me, when I reach a red light, she'll be out like a light.

It's nearly five o'clock in the evening. Here's to hoping Brandon and Ethan completely pigged out and have a ton of leftovers from takeout so I don't have to make anything.

Please!

I pull into my driveway thirty minutes later. We ascend the stairs quietly, and when we open the door, there's not a soul in sight. I set my purse on the entryway table while Alice races out the back door to the sounds of grunts and laughter in the backyard. I cross the living room and peer out the back window to see Brandon and Ethan throwing the football around. Alice settles in a chair on the deck while she watches her brother play. Brandon gives her that gorgeous megawatt grin and waves at her. I step away from the window and collapse promptly on the couch.

I shiver from the cool air of the house and place a throw pillow over my eyes. The back door opens, and the kids jabber to each other like they've been away from each other for eons. But that slowly dissipates to their rooms.

"Hey, Ave. You still alive?"

"Barely," I grumble. He pulls the pillow off my face, and suddenly I feel his warm lips on my forehead. My eyes fly open.

"Still running a fever. Why don't you go upstairs and take a bath or take a nap? I can hang out with the kids and order in dinner or something."

"Did you just take my temperature by kissing my forehead?" I ask in mock horror.

He laughs.

"It always worked for my momma. She was never wrong." I groan. "Seriously. Go upstairs. Do what you need to do. I don't mind sticking around."

It's so tempting. I can see myself sinking into my bathtub and taking the longest nap I can, but I can't put off my mothering anymore. I can't ask Brandon to step in when there's much to do.

"Thanks, Brand, but you should go. You've been here for two days—"

"Lady, I already told you I don't mind. Go. I promise we won't burn the house down."

When will I ever have this chance again? With Gray currently on location, my chances of a weekend alone are nil.

"Ugh. Fine. I won't be long, I promise. Just make sure Ethan does his homework. He had a little before he went on Thanksgiving break."

He nods. "See ya in a bit," I grunt so disgustingly when I sit up and launch myself off the couch. My joints pop when I stretch, but it doesn't alleviate any of my body aches. I trudge up the black spiral staircase that leads up to my room. Brandon stays put and watches me ascend the staircase with an unreadable expression that makes my heart race. I close the door behind me and breathe a sigh of relief.

I strip out of my clothes almost instantly. I stumble and shiver into the bathroom and turn on the hot tap as high as it will go.

I ignore the bath bomb I've been *dying* to use since Tess gave it to me for my birthday a few weeks ago and sink in while the scalding water envelopes me. One of these days, I'll spring for one of those tubs Meredith Gray described: cover the boobs and the knees. What a world.

My eyes droop closed.

I remember when the kids were little, Gray would offer to watch them so I could do something like this. But when I would light my candles and throw in a bath bomb, it would only take five minutes for the kids to either cry or bang on the door for me to come out. Gray would be off, talking on the phone to one of the women he'd be seeing.

Is it bad *that's* what I'm waiting for? That when my aching head rests against the cool porcelain and the hot water laps over me, I wait for the crying and the banging like an old friend?

But they never come. Instead, my mind visits waterfalls and vacant meadows. In these places, my head doesn't weigh a ton and I can breathe through both of my nostrils. Remember when I could do that, breathe through my nose? I took it for granted. Why did I do that? I want to smell things again.

My attention is grabbed by the most unattractive, unladylike snore and my eyes fly open. I scan the bathroom for the intruder, but I'm completely alone. I'm the guilty party.

My bath water is lukewarm, which means I've been dreaming for a while. I pull the plug and stand up. I wrap myself in a fluffy towel and pad to my bedroom, throwing on the most socially unacceptable clothing I have. Thank you, baggy sweatpants and ugly gray Harvard sweatshirt.

I attempt to brush out my hair, but it's been in a bun for the last... four days. Once that is somewhat presentable, I make my way downstairs. When I open my bedroom door, I'm hit with the most amazing smell. It's tomatoey and oniony. Heaven. My stomach growls. I see my two children sitting at the table opposite each other.

Ethan sits in his seat with an open notebook. I descend the stairs and sit down on the bottom step and watch this all play out. Alice watches her brother while she colors in another open notebook. Brandon is at my stove stirring something.

"What does 'synonym' mean?" Ethan asks.

"A synonym is a word that has the same meaning for another word. So, if I were to ask you what a synonym for 'big' is, what would you say?"

"Um, large?" Ethan replies.

"Enormous!" Alice shouts with a giggle.

"Right, exactly!" Brandon chuckles.

"So...how do you spell it?"

Brandon laughs.

"When I was your age and I didn't know how to spell a word, your grandmother would tell me to look it up in a dictionary."

"We don't have a dictionary so..."

Chuckling, Brandon turns to him with his toothy grin and crosses his arms across his chest. "S-y-n-o-n-y-m. And I will be buying you a dictionary for Christmas."

I take this opportunity to make my presence known by standing up and walking into the kitchen. I drop a kiss on Alice's head and occupy the seat next to her. Ethan's eyes light up and Brandon turns off the stove.

"Hey, killer! Feelin' any better?"

I scoff. "A little, thank you. Did you cook?" He nods and fills a bowl with the reddish soup. He takes some cilantro leaves from the windowsill and places them on top, and then places the bowl in front of me.

"I hope you don't mind, but you had almost everything I needed. I didn't put any cheese in it. I thought it would be better if you didn't for the congestion." I spoon a little into my mouth and nearly keel over. I can die happy now. This is better than anything Panera could make for me. No offense. I'll see you next week, Panera.

"I don't mind. This is good, Brand. You made this? Like, you got ingredients from my pantry and made all this?" He nods as he fills the other bowls.

"My momma used to make this for me when I was sick. It worked every time." What? Gray has never told me this before. I mean, granted, he's had his issues with his mother—with his whole childhood, honestly. But this is a sweet childhood memory. Why wouldn't he ever bring that up? I watch the kids inspect the soup. Brandon sits next to Ethan and digs right in. I fully expect them to turn their noses up at it and ask for chicken nuggets instead, but they eat it without complaint.

Interesting.

We eat and Alice interrogates Brandon with questions about football. Well, not football *per se*, mostly about the cheerleaders. He doesn't have much to say about them, but it's been, what, four years since he and Kayla divorced? What's he doing now?

The kids finish up their dinner and pack away their homework and doodles. Ethan wants to show Alice his progress on one of those stupid Roblox games, so he brings her into his room.

Brandon is up immediately. He scoops up the kids' bowls and I reluctantly give him mine when I'm finished. He immediately starts washing and placing them in the dishwasher.

What is this? Why is he doing this?

"Ave? You all right?" My gaze meets his.

"You don't have to do that. I can clean up."

"Don't worry about it. I don't mind."

I don't mind. Brandon's mantra. How is it that two Wentworth's—brothers, at that—are so different?

"How are you feeling? I can stay overnight if you want to sleep in. I could bring Ethan to school…"

"Oh…thank you. No, the bath and the nap were plenty. But I could use some company if you wanted to hang out for a bit. I realize you've been here for a while, and you probably want to go home—"

"Would you be up for a movie? Or maybe a cup of coffee and a chat?" My dry, unattractive, chapped lips quirk into a genuine smile.

"A movie sounds great. Any requests?"

"I wouldn't say no to a good ol' action thriller. One that threads in American History. One that stars Nicholas Cage..."

"*National Treasure*. You want to watch *National Treasure?*"

He nods enthusiastically. "Don't make fun! *He's* the national treasure!"

Giggling, I step out of the dining room and burrow into the couch and cover up to my chin with a blanket. I reach for the remote and queue up National Treasure.

"So, what have you been up to?" I call out. I hear him turn off the sink and open the fridge.

"Football, mostly. I've been doing some charity work here and there—not enough, but I do what I can. How about you?"

He returns to the living room and sets a cold water bottle in front of me before collapsing on the other side of the couch.

"I'm doing some writing—guest starring here and there. Auditioning some, but not a lot."

He covers up with the blanket that drapes over the cushions. I sip the water that he gave me and give one final stretch before pressing play.

I catch him giving me a wary stare.

"I'm sorry if it seemed like I chose sides when everything went down with Gray." I shrug, mostly because I hadn't given it a lot of thought before now.

"It's okay. I know you were traveling a lot—"

"No. I stayed away because I didn't want to rock the boat. I love my brother, but he's an asshole and I *hate* the way he treated you and the kids. I wasn't sure if you hated *all* of us."

"At that time? I don't know. I think I was more embarrassed than anything. There was so much going on. I mean, when I signed on the dotted line, I knew I'd be a single mom without help from him. I probably would have died a thousand deaths if you would have asked to help out right after the divorce was final."

He smirks thoughtfully and rests his head on the pillow.

"Are you proud, Ave?"

Yes.

"Maybe a little bit." I sigh.

"Ethan was really good, by the way. We spent a lot of time outside and then we went out to dinner on Sunday night. He's a great kid. He was really worried about the two of you." My heart warms at Ethan's gigantic heart. He's the best kid.

"I missed him," I admit. "But I'm glad he was able to be a kid. He's always so serious. A true man of the house." And here comes the guilt.

"Ave, if it's all right with you, I'd like to help out a little bit more."

I sit up so fast my head spins. "What?"

"I don't get to see Ethan and Alice often. When I do, it's always at one of my games and Gray usually leaves with them right after. Not to mention, he has the rift with my mom—she hasn't seen them since they were little."

More guilt.

I love Beverly. If you saw her and Gray together, you would never know Gray didn't get along with her. Bev is from a farming family in Texas. She works hard for her money and was skeptical of Gray following his father's footsteps in the world of show business.

And...well...she was always kind to me. She sent over baked goods when the news of Gray's philandering broke. I was never blamed as the woman who trapped him. She understood. She sent me cards and well wishes.

And in return, I totally forgot to set up a visiting schedule for my children to spend time with their grandmother.

Mother of the year.

"Even if it's just to hang out with them while you go grab a cup of coffee or something. I love them. I probably won't have kids of my own...I'd like to spoil my niece and nephew."

I heave a big sigh.

"Okay."

His eyes light up. I'm pretty sure he was expecting a fight. "I have a hard time giving up control, Brand. It's always been the three of us—occasionally the peppering of Gray." *Only* when they were babies.

"Would it make you feel better if I promise not to take away your control? I can hang out with them while you're around. I promise to be respectful."

If this were Gray, he wouldn't give a rat's ass if I was worried about giving up control. He'd force my hand and then I'd spend the whole day worrying about my babies.

How are they so different? Why do I feel so secure and trusting for Brandon and not for Gray? Gray is their father, for fuck's sake!

"I trust you."

He smiles in surprise. Damn it, I surprise even myself! It has to be the NyQuil. I can't be held responsible for what's coming out of my mouth right now.

He's so pretty.

"I know we were never really close, but I'd like it if we could be friends."

My smile never seems to leave my face.

"I'd like that."

He grins so boyishly and turns his attention to the TV. I press play on the remote and snuggle in. I glance over to Brandon, who is so enthralled in the opening credits. He isn't even paying me any attention. I admire his chestnut hair falling into his forest green eyes. His bulging biceps hug my teal throw pillow close to his chest.

And that smile...

I'm fucked.

Five

Brandon

Now

She finishes the story of that night. The night I made myself comfortable on her couch and begged her to let me spend time with Ethan and Alice—to spend time with her. And yet here I am, so completely enraged and enamored by her all at the same time. It's sickening.

"So, it wasn't just a one-night stand then. You had a friendship first." Sunny looks at us for answers, but Ava isn't cracking. I look at her. This is her interview, not mine. I didn't even know she'd be here.

"We were friends first," I reply quietly, dropping my gaze. "We didn't go looking for each other. Our relationship just kind of...happened." I glance over at her. She refuses to look at me, or Sunny—not even the camera. She finds a spot. A blank spot on the wall and stares. Her eyes fill up with tears. She has no reason to cry. She broke *my* heart.

"Ava? Do you have anything to add?" We're greeted by silence.

Say something!

I need answers! I need to know why she threw us away so easily!

"He made it easy to trust again," she says, almost in a whisper. More tears escape her eyes. She squeezes them shut so tight and emits a sob. Brandon from six years ago wants to pull her close and fight her demons. It's so tempting.

She's gorgeous.

And that makes me angry.

Brandon from now wants her to keep crying. She has no idea how horribly she fucked me over.

Fuck her!

"I'm sorry. I need a break," Ava murmurs. Sunny gets the crew to cut to commercial and as soon as we're clear, Ava jumps up and heads over to Tess and her publicist.

I didn't come here for her. I was told that *Great Morning Chicago* wanted to talk about my charity that launches tomorrow. Color me surprised when I see the former love of my life sitting in front of a camera, absolutely dumbfounded, staring at a picture of the two of us.

She's a great fucking actor, I'll give her that.

Sunny asks me a question, but I ignore her. I stand up and start down the hallway as Ellen stormed off before this line of questioning. I reach for my phone and dial Gray's number. He's still an asshole, but he's my brother and I love him. He didn't deserve to find out like this.

"This is Grayson Wentworth. Leave a message."

I sigh.

"Gray, I'm sorry. Let's just talk, man. We weren't trying to hurt you..." No matter how much I try to lessen what Ave and I were, it just sounds like more excuses. "Call me back, please?" I hang up and reach the dressing room we were given. Ellen sits on the ugly, burnt orange sofa and scrolls through her social media.

Ellen...she wasn't supposed to happen, either. We've been together almost four years now. She got me through the ugly times after Ava. She brought me confidence and love. She didn't take the hurt away...not completely. But she saved my life.

"Hey," I say from the door jam. She gives me a sidelong glance and remains silent. "Thank you for being here with me. I know this is awkward." She sighs and throws her phone on the sofa.

"It *is* awkward," she sighs. "But I'm here for you. She broke your heart and now you have to salvage your relationship with your brother." I should feel guilty about Gray, but I just...don't. When we were kids, we were close. But the second he had an ounce of fame; I was the scum on the bottom of his shoe. I was an embarrassment.

Falling for his ex-wife was unplanned. But I loved her. The kind of love that settles deep into your bones and squeezes until you feel numb inside.

"If this makes you uncomfortable, you don't have to stay. I'd appreciate it if you stayed, but I won't force you to."

She stands up and snakes her arms around my waist and pulls me close.

"Mr. Wentworth, Ms. Reid is requesting a longer break. There is a spread in the green room if you and your guest are hungry." Ellen groans.

"Thank you," I say to the production assistant. "Are you hungry?"

Ellen shrugs.

"Yeah, I could eat." I kiss the crown of her head and reach for her hand.

We walk hand in hand to the green room. It's a modest spread. Mostly pastries, fruit, and cheese. There's a small table with eggs and bacon, but I'm not sure how long that's been sitting out. I'm not going to embarrass myself on camera.

We go through the line and Ellen fills up her plate. I load mine only with grapes because I'm sick to my stomach. I sit down with Ellen and glance around the room.

Ava isn't anywhere to be found, nor is Gray. Are they conspiring together?

I'm being paranoid.

Ellen goes on and on about something at work, but I can't seem to focus on her. I watch the door, ready to pounce on anyone close to the situation. How did the media find out? Why are they bringing it up six years later?

Tess materializes at the door and scans the room. Her gaze locks onto mine, and she purses her lips. This woman, the Tess of right now, is a stranger to me. She's in best friend mode. She'll kill for Ava. I know she would. It doesn't matter that her husband used to be my teammate and best friend. She motions for me to follow her. I excuse myself and race to the door.

She stands just outside, raking her hand through her wildly curly black hair. "Have you seen Gray?" she asks.

"No, I haven't."

She frowns and sinks to the floor. "How did this happen, Brand? Why are you doing this six years later?"

I sink next to her and sigh.

"I don't know. I swear I had nothing to do with this." I glance around to make sure Ellen isn't near. It still hurts her when I'm honest about my feelings for Ava. "She broke my heart, Tess. I was content with never having to see her again."

Tess whips her head to me. "Don't start that bullshit with me, Brand. You didn't see her when you destroyed her life." She jumps up and dusts herself off.

What the fuck is she talking about? *I* destroyed *her* life?

"It's probably best you stay away from her unless you're on camera. She's dealing with enough."

When everything went down, Jordan refused to talk to me. He believed Ava's lies and washed his hands of me without even hearing my side of the story.

I step back into the green room and sit back in my place with Ellen. She went from stuffing her face a few minutes ago to angrily picking at her fruit.

"What did *she* want?"

"She was just wondering if I knew where Gray was." She nods, but doesn't meet my eyes. She infamously doesn't get along with Tess. And before Tess, it was Ava. Ava was terrified that Ellen and I were a thing. I mean, we weren't then. But now?

She's pretty. And nice.

"She's just trying to protect that *cow*."

Involuntarily, my spine locks straight, and rage fires in my belly. "She's not a cow," I murmur.

But obviously, that isn't the right thing to say about your ex-girlfriend to your current girlfriend, because fire erupts in her eyes.

"Don't defend her," she snaps. "She ruined your life, Brandon!" People around us stare as the theatrics of Ellen Wilson begin to make a scene.

"She's the mother of my niece and nephew, Ellen," I reply quietly. She's much more than that. She once was the keeper of my secrets. She was the one who understood me and held my heart in her delicate hands. She was my best friend.

I'm angry at her. I'm so angry that she walked into my life and blew it up while she snuck out. But when Ellen calls her a cow, that hurts me.

Why?

"And how often do you see those kids?" The blows just keep on coming. I just didn't expect them from her. "We don't need to stay here. Let's just go. We can go order in, watch a movie, and forget this ever happened."

I stare at her in disbelief. I haven't had answers for six years. There's no fucking way I'm turning back now.

"I know this is uncomfortable for you so you can leave if you want," I tell her quietly, so the other people around here stop staring. "But I haven't had closure. I need to know answers." Ellen stares at me darkly.

"This is wrong. I love you, Brandon, but you're hurting me. She doesn't matter to you anymore." I reach for her hand, but she pulls away quickly.

"I'm sorry. But I'm staying." She rolls her eyes and shoots up, allowing her metal chair to scrape against the concrete.

Great. Now everyone can't take their eyes off us.

She storms off and a wave of relief washes over me.

I need a moment of peace without her criticizing anything and everything.

I love her, but she isn't the most understanding person in the world. She *hates* Ava. She isn't on the best of terms with my mother...

But she saved my life. I can never thank her enough for that.

The silence she gives me by walking right now is welcome. The PA who found me earlier stops me when I start to walk back to my dressing room.

"They need you back on set, Mr. Wentworth." I sigh and head back that way.

I look around for my brother, but still can't find him. I bet he left. He's probably holed up at his fancy mansion with some other woman by now.

The set comes into view when I turn the corner. Ava sits on the sofa quietly, politely listening to Sunny, but when she catches sight of me, her armor cracks. Her icy cornflower blue eyes narrow and her body stiffens. I set her teeth on edge.

I just want this to be over with. I want her to tell me why she left me so that I can move on with my life.

I take my place on the opposite end of the couch. Our limbs don't touch, nor do we dare look at each other.

We're counted in. Sunny welcomes the audience back and then turns to us.

"We covered some difficult topics before we went to break. Ava, are you ready to continue?"

"Yes. I'm ready."

"All right." Sunny turns to me. "Brandon. After that night. What happened next?"

Six

Brandon

Then

She was exhausted that night. We only watched twenty minutes of *National Treasure* before she passed out. Hard. Mouth wide open, unattractive snoring, drool dripping out of her mouth, hard. And still, she's easily the most beautiful woman I've ever laid eyes on. I carried her upstairs and made sure she was comfortable and set out her DayQuil and a glass of water for her when she woke up. I made sure to turn up the heat on the thermostat before I left.

She texted me a quick, 'thanks' the following morning, but it's been a week and it's been radio silent. It's six o'clock and I'm *supposed* to be at the hotel with the team before tomorrow's game, but I find myself punching in the code to her front gate and parking next to her little blue Honda.

I skip up the front steps of the steep staircase and ring the doorbell. The kids call for her but don't come near the door.

Good kids.

A *thud* echoes from inside.

"Ow, *fuck!*" I chuckle at Ava's muffled curse and I'm greeted with her holding her foot and scowling up at me.

"Brand, hey! Come in." She hobbles to the side and allows me entry to... chaos. Blue, red, and green plastic storage bins take over most of the square footage downstairs. The Christmas tree is up, and the kids decorate until they see me. They abandon their task and come barreling towards me, enveloping me in the hugs I've missed out on for so many years.

"Hey, guys!" I squeeze them back until they start squealing from squeezing hard.

"What are you doing here?" Alice demands.

"I thought we could hang out for a bit."

"Can we play football?" Ethan asks.

"Will you cook for us again?" Alice asks.

"Give Uncle Brand a minute." She hesitantly smiles at me. "Really? You came all the way out here to hang?"

I nod and reach down to pick up Alice and place her on my shoulders.

"Are you okay with that? I thought we could order in pizza and play some board games or something."

"Mom said we can make s'mores in the fire pit tonight!" Ethan chimes in.

S'mores. Fire. Perfect.

"We'd be happy to have you for s'mores. I'll go ahead and order some pizza. You two finish up the tree and then we can put all the bins back in the garage." Ava gives Alice the classic "mom look," and walks into the kitchen. I take Alice off my shoulders and place her on the floor.

"Okay. You two finish the tree, I'll start stacking boxes." They hurry off excitedly and scan the room.

So many boxes. So much *fucking* glitter.

The banister of the spiral staircase is decorated in lit garland with fake red cardinals and frosted greenery. An extensive Christmas village is placed meticulously on the entryway table with the white fluff you use to make pillows.

Every inch of the downstairs is decorated for Christmas. Even the couch has seasonally appropriate throw pillows. I don't miss the mantle above the fireplace, though. Four Christmas-colored stockings with characters from *Rudolph the Red-Nosed Reindeer* line the mantle neatly. Including Gray's. Does he even spend the holidays with them anymore?

I stack all the boxes next to the front door, giving me four neat stacks. Holy shit. And this is *just* Christmas? Does she have shit like this for all the other seasons? She walks back in and eyes the stacks.

"Oh, you didn't have to do that. I could've managed."

"I'm happy to help. You have muscle until about midnight, so take advantage while you have it."

She snickers and opens the front door. "Well, load me up. If we work together, we might have these put all away before the pizza gets here."

The most she can hold is two, so I load her up appropriately. I take as much as I can and by the time we make our second trip, we just give up completely and she throws the boxes down from the landing while I catch them and put them away.

Teamwork.

Fifteen minutes later, I'm throwing the football to Ethan and then eventually to Alice. We teach her hand placement and then she throws like a pro. I'm amazed at how athletic she is. She uses her freakishly long legs and jets past me for a touchdown while I try not to trip over her.

"You're going down, Uncle Brand!" she shouts from across the yard.

"I don't think so, gorgeous!"

Ethan rolls his eyes. "Just hike the ball, Alice!" I chuckle as she crouches down, butt high up in the air and her hands on the ball. She hikes it to Ethan, and he comes barreling towards me. Just when I think he's going to fake left, he drops the ball and launches himself at my chest.

Fuck.

The bigger they are, the harder they fall. It's true, and it hurts. Ethan is eight and I feel like I've just been tackled by a fourteen-year-old. He laughs and is truly pleased with himself.

"Told ya," he taunts, just as Alice picks up the ball and races past us and pegging it in my endzone.

"Yeah. You got me, buddy." I cough like my rib punctured my lung.

"Hey, weirdos! Pizza's here!" Ava shouts from the deck.

"You got saved by Mom." I manage to get up into a sitting position and scoff.

"How did she save me? She came out *after* you tackled me."

"Because Alice was going to tackle you next." I groan.

"You guys are mean. Maybe I won't come back."

Ethan giggles. Actually giggles. "Yeah right. You said you wanted to hang. You like us."

The little shit is right. I like them. I love them. I grumble as I pull myself up. The kids and I race up the steps and have the kids sit down while I help Ava get food on their plates and get them their drinks.

I sit next to Ava, and I'm enchanted by their family dynamic. Alice tells us stories about her friends at school and only eats half of her pizza, which she gets scolded for...by Ethan.

Last week, when Ave and I watched the movie together, she mentioned that Ethan was the man of the house. And boy, was she right. He scolds his sister for talking much and not eating. He asks his mother if she's had enough pizza and if he can get her any more.

I also see a lot of Gray in Alice. She's boisterous like he is. She tries so damn hard to get me to laugh—it's endearing.

My leg touches Ava's, and I don't dare move it. I enjoy being close to her. If she realizes this, she doesn't make it known.

After dinner, she grabs the leftover pizza boxes and shoves them into the fridge. She tells Ethan to grab the s'mores components and to bring them to the firepit. She grabs a stack of blankets from the couch and motions for me to follow her outside. We ditch the blankets on the Adirondack chairs that surround the fire pit and then walk to the garage.

"So, you're spending your Saturday night with lil' ol' us tonight?" She asks, pulling firewood out of its place and into my arms.

"Why is that so hard to believe?" I ask with a chuckle. She shrugs so nonchalantly, almost like no matter what I say, she won't believe it.

"I'm projecting a little bit, so for that, I'm sorry. This was supposed to be Gray's weekend with them, and he took a job in Australia, so I'm a little pissy." She grabs a box of tumbleweeds and sighs. "It's just taken me by surprise that you're wanting to hang out with us tonight when their own father doesn't want to."

Gray is an asshole.

He doesn't deserve her. Or them.

I don't know why I'm so fucking surprised though. Our father was the same way. He didn't give a damn and Gray is falling directly into his footsteps.

"He's awful company, anyway," I tease to lighten the mood. She laughs and shrugs. She exits the garage, not giving me a second glance. "Ave…" She stops dead in her tracks and turns around slowly.

"I don't want to make this a bad night, Brand. I'm sorry I brought it up, but I don't want to talk about him tonight."

Me either.

"You don't have to tell me twice."

She grins and continues her journey back to the kids. Ethan and Alice have already doled out the graham crackers on paper plates and have placed them on our chairs. As we approach, they place chocolate bars on each plate.

We build the fire in tandem, just as the sun sinks behind the horizon. The kids settle into their chairs, and once we get the fire just right, Ava and I settle into ours. She passes me a roasting stick and a bag of marshmallows. Alice scoots her chair right next to mine and rests her cheek on my arm.

Why have I stayed away from them for so long? Why didn't I ask Gray to see them more?

"The trick is to get it super black. Then they're the best," she whispers.

"I agree. I like my marshmallows really gooey." Alice giggles.

The twinkle lights turn on and envelope us in a warm glow. I try not to look at Ava, but I can't help it. She's too busy watching the fire to realize I'm staring at her like a creeper, but I digress. She's a sight for sore eyes.

Unlike last week, she doesn't look like death warmed over. Her beautiful honey locks are tied into a high ponytail but actually brushed through. Her cornflower-blue eyes show life, and the rosy color in her cheeks is back. Last week was scary. Last week, she was pale almost to the point of turning green.

She wears a cream-colored, oversized sweater and dark blue skinny jeans that I swear are painted on. I admire the brown thigh-high boots she wears. If she was wearing them before, I don't remember it. Which is a damn shame because she wears them so damn well.

Our gazes meet.

Shit! Busted.

The corners of her mouth twitch, but then she looks away to talk to Ethan. Alice's marshmallow catches on fire, and she squeals in delight as I try to put it out.

Yep. Alice Wentworth is a pyro. If this house goes up in flames within the next few days, I know who to ask.

We munch on our s'mores and the kids trade ghost stories. Ethan's is more of a psychological thriller, very Hitchcock of him. Alice's is more...gory. Very Quentin Tarantino.

She has such an imagination, and I'd be interested to live a day in her head, just to see how she thinks.

The kids jabber on, but I'm more captivated by the fire. I'm surrounded by two kids I'd die for, and Ava Reid. The woman I've been crushing on for so long it's inappropriate.

I got into *The Elite* late. Like when the series was over. She always held herself with such grace and poise. She could be wearing a clown suit and she'd still be the most beautiful woman in the room.

And then, *Congregation* happened. She met Gray and fell in love.

I wish I met her first.

She's your sister-in-law. Stop it!

Alice crawls into my lap and rests her head on my left arm. Ava throws me a blanket and I cover us both with it.

Does she do this with Gray? I can't see Gray as the cuddling type.

I glance across the fire to see Ethan laying sideways in his chair and watching the fire with heavy eyelids. He's a fighter, and he's not going to leave his mom alone outside.

"So, you have a game tomorrow?" Ava asks quietly.

"Yeah, at noon."

"Are you nervous?"

I ponder her question for a minute. I'm older, so games like this don't get me nervous anymore.

"No, not nervous. Maybe a little anxious. It gets worse when we get closer to the game." Her eyes fall to Alice and a melancholy smile spreads across her lips.

"Do you have any rituals? Like the day before a game?"

"Well, I'm supposed to be in a hotel right now."

Her eyes widen.

"Oh, I'm so sorry. You can leave if you need to. I'm sorry we kept you so long."

I shake my head. "I have a curfew, but I'm one of the older ones, so they don't worry about me so much. Usually what they do is have everyone stay in a hotel downtown and then we get bussed over to Soldier Field in the morning. But the night before, they usually stuff us with enough protein for a week's worth of calories, and then we fall on our faces because we're so exhausted from practicing all week." I shrug. "This is a much better ritual."

Her eyes bore into the side of my skull, so I meet her gaze.

"She's never done that with anyone," she admits softly, with just a hint of jealousy. "She's never been very affectionate."

"Well, I'm honored to be the first. I'm glad someone enjoys my ugly mug." She laughs and rolls her eyes.

"You don't need to go fishing, Brand. We both know you're not ugly."

Ava Reid thinks I'm sexy.

"You think so?"

She rolls her eyes and attempts to hide her beautiful smile.

The crackling of the fire is our soundtrack for the evening. And so are Alice's small snores.

"How's Kayla?" My ex-wife is not a taboo subject for me. But bringing her up makes me instinctually look at Ethan.

We were still married when Ethan was born. My relationship with Gray was still strained, but he wanted to show off his pride and joy, so he invited me to the hospital. When I married Kayla, we agreed not to have kids.

My dream was to be in the NFL. I wanted to travel and not having anything tie me down. Kayla was different. I mean, she's my agent, and pathetically my best friend, still. So, wherever I traveled, so did she.

That was, until, I held Ethan in my arms.

Nine pounds of Wentworth came out of Ava; yet, I was holding this tiny person in my arms and suddenly, my world was kicked off its axis. I remember the small smile that spread across his lips, although Gray insisted it was gas. He smiled at me. He took a hold of my heart—and threw my other visions of how my life was supposed to go out the window.

I wanted kids. Kayla didn't.

We're no longer married, but we're still friends.

"She's good. I don't know if you saw, but she plays for the other team now." Ava quirks an eyebrow and shakes her head.

"I saw her with her wife a few weeks ago. We said 'hey,' but that was about it. I hope she's doing well. She was always a fun time."

"She's doing all right. She's enjoying life. Her wife, Cassie, is fantastic. They make each other very happy."

"And what about you? Are you seeing anyone?" She asks quietly.

I glance over at her and smirk. She doesn't cower under my intense stare. Instead, she stares right back at me, eyes narrowed, the corners of her mouth twitching.

"No. I'm not seeing anyone."

"Mom, I'm tired," Ethan announces groggily.

Her gaze holds mine for a strong ten seconds, but then she glances to Ethan.

"Okay, buddy. Let's go to bed," she replies softly.

I stand up with Alice and follow the couple inside. Ethan trudges behind Ava and looks back to make sure I'm still following with Alice. Once inside, Ava points me to the room directly down the hall that I assume is Alice's.

The room is painted a soft pink. A frog lamp next to her bed glows in the dark when I set her down. After taking off her shoes and covering her up, I can't help but smile.

She's a tomboy through and through. But she's girly too. She sleeps like a rock and doesn't even budge when I turn off the light.

"Goodnight, Alice," I whisper, slowly closing the door behind me. Ethan's door is now closed, so I assume Ava has already beaten me outside. The early December air bites on the exposed skin on my neck.

She's in the same chair, bundled up in a blanket, now with a glass of wine that sits on the arm of the chair. Her gaze is trained on the fire, but as I approach closer, she watches my every step in her direction.

I reclaim my chair and scoot the tiniest inch towards her and cover up with the blanket that once covered Alice. It's warmed only by the fire, but I bring the softness to my face and breathe in Ava's mango scent.

"I brought you out a beer," she says, reaching beside her and passing it over to me. I twist the cap off and take a pull of the dark amber liquid. I shouldn't be drinking this. I have to do my job tomorrow, but there's a big pit of anxiety in my stomach. Ava Reid makes me nervous, and I need to take the edge off.

"Thank you." She grins and tucks her plump, pink bottom lip into her perfect teeth. "Are *you* seeing anyone?"

She giggles. "No. There's no room in my life for that."

Damn.

Not that I should be looking.

She's my sister-in-law.

My *ex*-sister-in-law.

Fuck it. I'm looking.

When I don't answer, she sighs. "People know too much about me. I have a whole Wikipedia page dedicated to my life and if some guy comes across it, he'll change his behavior or his general likes and dislikes to match mine. That doesn't sound like a fun time. I don't want to date myself, Brand."

"There are men who don't consult the internet about a girl he likes, you know." She tilts her head back and laughs.

"Even still. If I ever came across that unicorn, I have kids."

"And?"

"That's not an attractive quality! Nobody wants an instant family." She purses her lips together and thinks for a moment. "Nobody would want to compete with Gray. Not that there would be a competition. I mean, my time in the limelight is practically nonexistent, now. But throw in 'Ava Reid's new mystery man' can't stand her because she compares him to her one true love, Grayson Wentworth." She gives me a thumbs down and frowns. "Trust me. There isn't anyone alive who would want to be humiliated that publicly."

I would.

Except I couldn't care less about Gray.

If there was ever an opportunity that I got to get to know her better, there wouldn't be a competition. I'm not cocky. I'm not. But I know how to treat a woman. And Ava...she's absolute perfection.

"You've dated children, Ave." She scowls at me. "If a man can't see that you're a package deal, then they're not it. How can they *not* fall in love with Ethan and Alice,?"

She shrugs. "I don't know. They're amazing and funny. Honestly, I don't think Ethan would allow it. He'd just give the guy the beady eye until he's intimidated enough to drive home."

I chuckle. "Yeah, I could see that. He's the best."

She grins and sips her wine, avoiding my gaze.

"Can I ask you something kind of personal?"

I glance over at her warily. I'm an open book. I have no skeletons in my closet, no scandals for the media to cling to for easy ratings. "Sure."

"Why don't you and Gray get along?"

I lied. This is my one skeleton.

"Other than he's a selfish asshole? It's a long story. But the *Cliffs Notes* version is because he blames my mom for our dad leaving. It wasn't her fault, but Gray is my father reincarnated. And I hate my dad, so..."

"I worked with your dad once. Shortly after Gray and I married. He avoided me like the plague. Then, Gray came to visit on set and your dad refused to come out of his trailer. I'm not sticking up for Gray at all. I believe in your analysis of him, but it seemed to break his heart."

"My dad isn't a good person. Gray worships the ground he walks on, but he doesn't know what kind of person he is." I sigh. I don't want to talk about this anymore.

My dad is a major pain point. He's an abusive prick that nearly killed my mom. Gray doesn't know that because I protected him from it. I only know about it by accident. I walked in on him beating her senseless.

I was ten years old. I was just a runt, but I was able to pull him off of her. I called the police, but he was long gone by then. Mom spent a few days in the hospital while Gray and I stayed with our grandparents. He remained blissfully ignorant, while I almost lost the one woman who gave a damn about us.

"You've overcome him though. At least, that's what it looks like to me. I won't make you talk about it if you don't want to. I won't make you relive your trauma."

I don't know if I've overcome him. I've pushed him to the back of my mind. I don't want to talk about Preston Alan Wentworth II tonight. I want to sit with Ava and flirt a little bit.

I shouldn't, though. I mean, Gray's an asshole and we hardly talk anymore, but that's still his ex-wife. It doesn't matter that I wish I met her first. He's still my brother. She's still my sister-in-law.

But damn.

"Alice is very athletic," I observe. Ava blinks and then realizes I'm using Alice as a distraction. She sighs and nods.

"She gives Ethan a run for his money, that's for sure. She's fearless, which I think is a curse and a blessing."

"She'll give you gray hair, I promise you that."

Ava laughs.

"I'm sure she will. I'm terrified I won't survive her. She's so headstrong and so unbelievably independent. I fear the day she starts sneaking boys in the house."

The thought alone breaks my heart a little bit, but at the same time, it makes me chuckle.

"He'd have to get past Ethan first. But she's beautiful like you are—so you and Ethan will have a long line of douche bags to battle." Upon calling her beautiful, her gaze snaps to mine. Her pulse is visible in her neck from the glow of the fire and races just a little bit faster.

"He'll be her worst nightmare." She giggles and lets the blanket fall to her waist. Involuntarily, my gaze falls to her open jacket. She's every man's wet dream. Her jacket shows her cream sweater underneath and that hint of cleavage.

Stop it!

"Tell me something nobody knows about you."

She purses her lips and closes her eyes. "I'm a pretty open book, Brand." She squints one eye open and grins.

"Pretend we don't know each other, then. Pretend that I don't know what TV is and I'm meeting you for the first time." Anything to get her mind off of me staring at her.

"Umm." She sighs. "Oh! When I was fifteen, there was this abandoned house down the street where I lived. It reminded me of the house in *Edward Scissorhands.* Anyway, I convinced Tess and another friend to come spend the night in there with me."

I raise my eyebrows.

"You broke and entered?" She giggles and nods enthusiastically.

"I grabbed a sleeping bag and spent the night on the second story. The floors were rotting so badly that the staircase collapsed. I was so convinced that I was going to come into contact with a ghost or a demon or something. The one friend chickened out, but Tess and I still spent the night. I was scared out of my wits, but I so badly wanted some paranormal activity. We were out of our minds." She laughs and stares directly into my soul. "Needless to say, there was no paranormal activity, and Tess's parents had to come with a ladder the next morning so we could get down safely."

"Holy crap, Ave. I bet her parents were pissed."

"They were," she laughs. "I'm nobody's wallflower. I saw a challenge, and I followed through with it. Now, I'm sure that's all going to bite me in the ass when Alice gets to be that age."

"It would be well deserved," I quip, earning me a light punch on the arm from her. "I'm just saying—you probably took ten years off of Tess's mother's life!"

Her giggle is music to my ears. It's nice to see her genuinely smile for once—and that I'm the reason for it.

"What about you? I'm *positive* your mother didn't find you to be the golden boy everyone believes you to be."

"How dare you! I was an angel," I say in mock hurt. I was *so* the opposite. And she knows that.

"Mmmhm, I recall a few stories of you and petty theft."

"Um, excuse me, stealing my own shit doesn't qualify as petty theft." She giggles.

"Go on, Mr. Wentworth, tell me something I don't know about you."

I like you.

I wish I met you first.

You've been my every fantasy for so fucking long.

"I can remember every single dream I've ever had." Especially when Ava Reid is involved.

"Bullshit."

"I'm serious! I dream every single night. There is a reason I don't usually have cheese before bed. It gives me nightmares." She stares at me for a long minute, sizing me up.

"You mean to tell me that since you had pizza for dinner tonight, you'll have a nightmare?"

"I'll pay you a hundred bucks and a high five, I'm right. And since I'm a little anxious, I guarantee that I'll have some nightmare about a sinkhole swallowing me up while I'm on the field." She holds her hand out as to shake my hand. I grasp hers tightly and shake.

"You're on, Wentworth. Tomorrow, before your game or after—whenever, call me and share your dream with me in detail."

There's a short moment of a pang of guilt that settles in my stomach, but it disappears quickly. She's giving me permission to call her, and it has nothing to do with the kids.

"It's a date."

Her eyes bore into mine. My heart hammers in my chest as she attempts to uncover my secrets without speaking a word. I might be obvious, but I don't give a damn if she knows I'm attracted to her. In another world, another life, she'd be *mine*.

She poorly tries to hide her smile, which only makes me more confident. She has the power to end whatever *this* is and send me packing, but it seems to me she's enjoying this.

"Pass me the marshmallows. I need another s'more." I pass her the skewer and the bag of marshmallows while she breaks apart the graham crackers and gets her chocolate prepared. "Sometimes I wonder if I'm fucking all of this up." She sighs. "When you picked Ethan up from the hospital last week and he asked you to play out in the yard, I'd never seen him smile so big. He's my man-child. I try to force him to have a childhood, to play with his friends...but he's so worried about Alice and me. I think I made him grow up fast."

I shake my head.

"There are just some kids who are built to be so much more than they are. It wouldn't have mattered if you and Gray stayed together. He still would've been on your ass whether or not Gray was in the picture." I grin. "He's a great kid. And yeah, he'll probably need some reminding that he needs to be a kid every now and then. But he *played* with me today. He smiled and messed around. You've been dealt a shitty hand of cards, but you're killing this mom thing, Ave."

She pulls her marshmallow out of the fire and sandwiches it in between her graham crackers and stares at it like it's the most riveting thing in the world.

"There was a time before we separated when I knew it was over. I wanted to call your mom and ask her how she got through it." She finally meets my gaze and worries with her bottom lip. "I chickened out. Mostly because I didn't want her to convince me to stay with him, and just a minuscule part of me wanted him to love me back." She sighs. "Your mom is probably the coolest woman on the planet. I didn't want her to be disappointed in me."

Beverly Wentworth isn't that kind of person. Especially after my father, she buried herself to help other women. And it wasn't that Gray was physically abusing Ava, but he *was* openly humiliating her. Mom would've told her to leave.

"I don't want you to think we just sit around and talk about you all the time, but my mom isn't disappointed in you." Her breath hitches in her throat. "We saw what he was doing. We saw the women he was with all over the tabloids. He never talked to us about it, but mom always worried about you. She didn't want to rock the boat—especially if you thought that all of us Wentworth's are the same. It's been two years since you've signed on the dotted line, Ave. She was waiting to talk to you when you felt like you were ready. If you didn't reach out by the beginning of the new year, she would've tracked you down."

And she would've blown up her phone, email, and social media accounts. Mom loves the woman my brother tried to tie himself down to. But she wasn't going to make herself a burden. Ava sighs.

"I'll call her, I promise. But it's nice to hear that she doesn't hate me." She doesn't respond, but takes a small bite of her s'more and watches the fire.

We talk for two hours. She tells me about the screenplay she's working on and the thirty auditions she's been on in the last month. I tell her about my life in the NFL and the charity I'm working on in my head. She promises to donate whenever I decide to make it a reality, but I won't ever ask her to.

Her laugh is music. Unlike the alarm that blares on my phone, telling me I need to haul ass back to the hotel.

I help her put out the fire and bring our trash and the blankets back up to the house. She walks me over to the door and wraps her arms around my torso. Her honey-colored hair that smells like mangos tickles my nose.

"Thanks for coming to hang out with us. The kids enjoyed it."

"What about you?"

She steps back and I miss the way her heart raced against mine.

"I enjoyed it too. I'm glad we're friends."

Friends.

It tastes like acid in my mouth, but I have to take what I'm given.

"Me too. I hope you know you can call me whenever...especially if you need help with the kids." She smiles and opens the door for me.

"Good luck tomorrow. We'll be watching."

"Goodnight, Ave. Lock up behind me." I start down the steps and wave as she watches me through the window. Ava and I will probably never happen. There's much baggage on both sides. She once married my brother and mothered my niece and nephew. But there's a stupidly optimistic voice in my brain that tells me to keep trying.

So, I will.

Seven

Ava

Then

Brandon was at our house every Saturday leading up to Christmas. While we haven't had much time for any more philosophical conversations, he has stayed after the kids went to bed and watched movies with me. He is the killer of ugly bugs and wild bedtime stories.

Christmas came and went without much fanfare. Gray was still in Australia but FaceTimed with the kids on Christmas morning. We spent time with Tess's parents and grandparents and filled up on too much ham and cheesy potatoes.

And with the new year came a wave of badassery and confidence. So, I called up my agent and told him Ava Reid is making a comeback. I read for a director I worked with previously, Jason Evans, last week. I felt good about it, but now it's been a whole seven days and I still haven't heard anything. Chin up. Things can be worse.

Like standing behind *this* guy at the check-out counter at the grocery store trying to get lucky with the unwilling cashier. The box of Hamburger Helper refuses to be rung up. He hits on her while he slides his credit card through the reader, and it gives me the tiniest bit of satisfaction when it gets declined. He stammers for a bit and fumbles for his phone.

"I got it." Before he can say anything, I insert my card into the chip reader and pay for his boxed dinner for the night. He refuses to look at me, murmurs a thank you, and gets out of my sight.

While she rings up my groceries, my phone vibrates in my pocket. Grocery store etiquette be damned. I answer my phone and dodge the glare of the old bitch behind me.

"Ava, hey. It's Jason." Oh shit. It's happening! Ava Reid is making her comeback!

"Hey, Jason. How are you?"

"I'm good. Listen, I wanted to thank you so much for coming in to read for us last week."

"Oh, thanks for seeing me. I had some ideas to bring her to life—"

"Ava, stop." I glance up to the cashier who is done ringing me up and the bagger has placed my groceries in my cart. I pay and try to get out of here. I know that tone of his voice. "Look, I wanted to reach out to you because we're friends. We're going in a different direction."

"What?"

Jason sighs. "We're filming exclusively in Wilmington, North Carolina. I know you take an active part in your children's lives...how would that work out for you?" It wouldn't.

"I mean, I could talk to Gray—"

"No, Ava." He sighs. "I know for a fact Grayson just signed another deal, and he's in Australia. There's no possible way this could work out."

"I feel like there's another reason here, Jason. I need to know."

"I love you, and I love working with you. I need you to know that. *But,* this project is already on shaky ground. I know you and Grayson aren't very friendly anymore...we can't have any bad press. And that means for your personal life too."

My stomach feels so hollow that I want to barf. I reach my car and throw the trunk open.

"Well, I certainly don't want to be a problem for you, Jason. Thanks for letting me know."

"Please, this isn't personal. I hope this doesn't ruin our working relationship." What fucking working relationship?

"No, of course not. Thanks for letting me read for the part. It was a good exercise." I swiftly hang up. "Asshole."

Once again, Grayson Wentworth finds another way to fuck up my life. It's only one reading. One audition. Somebody will want to work with me.

I hope.

I load my groceries and hop into my car. Gray *finally* came home and is taking the kids for the weekend, which means I have a whole weekend to myself. I wonder what wallowing I can get into this weekend.

I *should* see what Tess is up to since these weekends are so few nowadays. I hop into the front seat and dial her number.

"Hey, you! What's up?"

"Just leaving the grocery store now. The kids are with Gray for the weekend, so I had to stock up on more wine."

Tess giggles.

"You are positively wild. Babycakes?"

"Yes, darling?"

"When was the last time you took your vagina in to get serviced?" My laugh gets stuck in my throat, leaving me to give the whole town of La Grange a show of my choking on my stupid embarrassment. "That long, huh?"

"Yes. It's been a long time. Thanks for that reminder."

"Like, how long are we talking?"

"Um...I don't know. After Alice was born, I guess."

"*Ava Lucille Reid!* That girl is six years old!"

"I know..." Shoot me now. I'm embarrassed enough that my last romp was my mother fucking ex-husband. What with the overall heartbreak of the failed marriage and being a single mother, there hasn't been time for me to have wild trysts. My vagina is probably reminiscent of the Sahara Desert, but you don't hear me complaining about it.

Except that I am.

God, I haven't been touched in forever. No hurried kisses in coat closets, no necking, and certainly not any over the clothes groping.

I'm sexually repressed with my only relief as my battery-operated boyfriend while I think about my brother-in-law.

Stop it!

"Let's go out tonight. Jordan is getting ready for the playoffs, so he's been training hard all day. He'll be flat on his face by the time he steps foot into our room. It'll be fun. I can be your wing woman. I'll find you a nice guy who will be deliciously naughty with you, preferably in the bathroom, and then we can get drunk and eat mozzarella sticks."

"You should be an artist, Tess."

"Gross, I can't draw."

"But you can certainly paint a picture." I love my best friend. She's been with me since we were kids. She's the sister I never had.

"What do you say? We can even be back at my place by midnight if you strike out—which isn't likely."

I haven't been out in forever. I've lived exclusively in long-sleeved shirts and the same pair of sweatpants for the last few weeks. It'll be nice to slut up a bit.

"Okay. Fine. I'll go dump my groceries and start getting ready. I'll meet you at your place in a bit."

"See ya soon, hooker!"

I grin as she kills the call, and conveniently it's when I'm turning onto my street.

Tonight is the night I put the vibrator away and lose my inhibitions with a guy I don't know and who possibly doesn't care about who I am. And...maybe that'll satisfy my taste for Brandon.

I'm not dumb. Falling for Brandon is career suicide. It can't ever happen, no matter how much I'd like to take him for a spin.

He's nice.

And he genuinely enjoys hanging out with my kids.

God damn it! Why is it that I always find myself attracted to men who aren't available?

Who is this *babe*!? I stare at myself in the mirror like some imposter is staring back at me. I haven't been out since before Alice, but *damn*—I've still got it!

I'm embarrassed to admit how much time I spent on Tik Tok this afternoon as I researched how to take care of my curls, but on the other hand, the research paid off and my curls aren't frizzy, but well defined and sleek. My blue eyes pop from my smoky eyeshadow. I wear my little black dress—pre-Alice—and slide on some strappy heels.

For the first time in forever, I feel *good*. I look *good*. I don't have to worry about the kids tonight, thank God. With one quick glance in the mirror, I take a deep breath and grab my clutch.

It takes me an hour to drive into the city where Tess and Jordan live. I park in the visitor parking in the attached garage and take the elevator up to her floor. I never used to have to knock, but I, unfortunately, know that Jordan has a healthy sexual appetite and I have walked in on them one too many times. So I knock.

Jordan, the six and a half foot giant, answers the door with a tired grin.

"Hey, Ava. Good to see you." He steps aside so I can come in. I step into their foyer and accept Jordan's hug.

"Good to see you, Jordo. I was told you were going to be flat on your face." He laughs and leans up against the door.

"Heading there. But I wanted to make sure you ladies got out okay. You're stealing my boob pillow away from me." I love that Tess found Jordan. He's a Chicago Bear, and they met when she scheduled him for an interview with *Great Morning Chicago* four years ago. I think it was love at first sight. You can't meet Tess and *not* fall in love.

Tess walks into the foyer with the *click-click-click* of her heels. She wears a strapless purple dress and impossibly high Louboutin's which makes me feel like a hobbit. Her wildly curly black tresses are ironed straight and pinned up on one side like a true fifties icon. Gosh. I love my best friend.

"Yes! Look at you! You look gorgeous! There's no way you're striking out tonight!"

Jordan hungrily sweeps his eyes over his wife and yanks her into him. She squeals and playfully swats him on the arm.

"You look beautiful, babe. You should reconsider staying."

"Not a chance, cowboy. Ava needs to get laid, so I help Ava get laid. Don't wait up for us."

"Be careful, both of you." He looks from me to Tess. "Text me when you get there, okay? Don't leave your drinks unattended and definitely don't leave with anyone who gives Tess the murder vibes."

I mock salute.

"I'll keep her safe, I promise. See you later. But hopefully not." I wink and reach for the door. Jordan whispers into Tess's ear and kisses her forehead.

With an Uber already ordered, we take the elevator down to the ground floor and meet Grace, our driver, in front of the building.

"I feel like we need a signal," Tess says, turning in her seat to lock gazes with me. "If you end up finding someone you want to go home with, I mean."

"I could just text you."

"You're no fun. It's just straight to business with you. I need some foreplay, Ava." I snort as Grace pulls up to *Crease.*

"Foreplay with your husband. My ex-husband has Hollywood terrified and reluctant to work with me. Tonight, I'm all about the business. I need a good romp so that I know what my vagina feels like again." Tess frowns.

"What?" We hop out of the car and we're escorted straight in. We find a table and order a round of shots.

"Jason Evans called this afternoon. He said the project I read for was already on shaky ground and they didn't want my bad press to overshadow it." I shrug. "It is what it is. It's one director and I have plans to continue. I'm not letting Gray steamroll me into *only* being a mother." Tess scrunches her nose.

"He's an asshole. I'm sorry, babe. Let's get drunk and order some food. I already see that group of guys staring you down." I turn my head to see a small line of men on the other side of the bar staring at us.

They're all attractive. No murder vibes, so that's a plus. We start our shots and order some mozzarella sticks because Tess promised.

"Hm, it looks like they're circling other women. Maybe try deep throating a mozzarella stick."

"You're disgusting." Tess laughs and pushes another round of shots. Two shot Ava is mellow. But I don't want to be mellow right now. I want confidence and maybe better flirting tactics. How does one even flirt nowadays? I probably can't get away with, "I find your tractor sexy, sir."

Yeah.

That didn't even work back when I was single either.

After three shots, we find ourselves on the dance floor. I dance along to "Despacito" while Tess's hands slide over my hips.

When was the last time I was this free? My movements are fluid and my hips roll against Tess.

"You're beautiful!" I turn around when I realize it isn't Tess's hands on me anymore. He's at least six feet tall with dark hair that is illuminated by the blue lighting.

"Thanks!"

He's athletic, but not like Brandon.

Stop it!

"Woah, okay. I'm sorry. I didn't know you had a man." Did I say that out loud? I shrug. Whatever. Plenty of fish in the sea. Or in this club.

Where's Tess?

The guy backs away from me and finds some other bimbo to dance with. Tess waves at me from the bar, so I follow.

"What was wrong with him? He seemed nice." I will *not* be telling her that he wasn't muscular like Brandon.

"I don't know. We just didn't vibe."

"I saw you earlier when you were sitting down with your friend. You're a sight for sore eyes." I glance to my left to the Adonis standing next to me. "Can I buy you a drink?" Tess's chair scrapes against the floor, and she flits to the dance floor.

"Sure." He takes the vacant seat and flags the bartender down. He's sort of tall. He has a pretty face, and he looks toned.

"I'm Brian."

"Veronica. Nice to meet you." Yeah, I'm not opening that can of worms with my real name. I'm Victoria—no, Veronica—for the night. What is Veronica like? The bartender places a fruity drink in front of me and I nearly cry. I'm not a fruity drink kind of gal. But Veronica is. I start sipping as he drones on about how he watched me move on the dance floor.

"What's your story, Veronica?" Single. Two children. Sexually repressed. Nope. That's Ava. Not Veronica.

"I work in finance." I can already tell he's checked out of this conversation. Men like him don't like women who threaten to be smarter than them—let alone take residence in a career that's exclusively male-driven. "My friend is taking me out for a girls' night because I had a shitty week." He nods and sips on his scotch.

"Oh yeah? Seems like you need to let off a little steam."

"Wanna dance?" I ask. He nods enthusiastically and while he helps me up, I sip down the rest of my drink. I'm a little dizzy, but the alcohol coursing through my system is a welcome distraction.

Brian's handsy. He grips my ass a few times while we dance, and luckily, Tess comes to my rescue when he starts groping my breasts. I never gave permission to touch. We dance together and sneak back to the bar for more drinks.

I wish Brandon were here.

He thinks I don't notice him staring at me when we're together. My heart slams against my chest when I picture his hands sliding down my hips, groping them possessively. He's that devilish kind of handsome, the kind us mothers warn our daughters about. But he's so damn kind that it erases that danger from him.

If I called him right now, would he dance with me? Can he feel the sexual tension in the air whenever we're together? Tess excuses herself to the bathroom while I fumble for my phone in my clutch.

I'm gonna tell him I like him. I'll let him kiss me if he wants to because sober Ava is an asshole who doesn't like Victoria having fun. What is one night going to do to our relationship, anyway? He can still hang out with the kids. He's nice and he won't make it weird.

I tap his name on my phone and bring the ringing to my ear.

"Ave? You all right?"

"No, not Ave. Not tonight. Tonight, I'm Vivienne." I think he's in bed. I hear the rustling of sheets and a groan.

"Where are you?"

"I'm at a club. Totally not like me, right?" He chuckles.

"Right."

"I think you're handsome, Brand. Do you want to dance with me?"

"Are you drunk?"

"Psh. A little bit. We did some shots when we got here, and then Brian got me a stupid girly drink. But I couldn't be rude, so I drank it all and then we danced, but then Tess scared him away because he got handsy."

"Who's Brian? He sounds like a douche canoe."

"Douche canoe," I repeat and cackle. Tess still hasn't made it back from the bathroom, so I'm counting on the fact there's a long line. I think she would talk me out of this. "He was nice I guess, but Jordan told me not to go home with anyone who gave Tess the murder vibes." I shrug, not that he can see it. "I'd bet all of my alimony that he was going to whack me in the alleyway when he was done fucking me." Brandon chokes on something.

"Holy shit, Ave. You're totally wasted. Where are you?"

"If I tell you, will you dance with me?"

He groans. "It sounds like you need a pot of strong coffee. Are you at least drinking water? It's important you stay hydrated."

"Relax, *mom*, I'm fine. This isn't my first rodeo." I totally have *not* been drinking water. "I saw you staring at my boobs the other night at the fire pit. I have a nice set."

"I'm coming to get you. Where are you?"

"*Creasseeee*. Near the loop. Come dance with me, Brand. I'll even let you touch my pretty titties."

"You are so crass."

"But you want to, don't you?" When he doesn't answer, I giggle. "Fuck Victoria tonight, Brand. She needs a night to be free."

"I'm on my way, okay? Don't leave the club. Don't go into the alley with that douchebag. I'm calling Jordan to pick up Tess."

"Oh, don't be a party pooper. The kids are with Gray and it's the one night I get to be Veronica. Let me be Victoria, Brand."

"I thought you were Vivienne."

"Who the fuck cares! Veronica, Vivienne, and Victoria all need a night to unwind and get fucked senseless. I'll be on the dance floor. Come find me when you get here." I drop my phone back into my clutch and make my way back to the dance floor. I dance with the people who blink black and white to the rave lighting. Tess finds me and frowns.

"Jordan's on his way to get me. He said you called a friend?"

"I did! Veronica is getting fucked by someone she shouldn't!"

"Who's Veronica?"

"*Victoria*—whatever. I can't keep my aliases straight anymore. He'll be here in a few minutes. You don't need to stick around." She laughs and twirls me.

"We didn't even need to go out tonight if you called a friend, hussy!"

"Whatever! I look good. I'm going to go do things that would make Gray blush!" We're here for two song changes when Tess gets the text that Jordan is here.

"Be careful, okay? Is your friend close?" I glance around the room and just when I find a pair of rainforest green eyes scanning the room for me, the air is stolen from my lungs.

"Yeah, he's here. I'll see you tomorrow!" I shout over the music. Our gazes lock and I start heading in his direction. Even in just a black button-down shirt and dark jeans, he looks bitable. How do you get muscles like that? How do you maintain that at his age?

We meet halfway, and I snake my arms around his waist.

"You came."

"Let's get out of here. I'll make you something to eat."

"You promised a dance, Brand. I even told you I'd let you touch my boobs." His eyes darken and his pupils dilate. Shit. He could fuck me right here and I'd be a-okay with that.

"One dance."

Eight

Brandon

I am *not* taking advantage of her while she's drunk. But she's stronger than she looks. She drags me onto the dance floor, into the throng of people who gyrate against each other. I can't dance to save my life, but it's like the DJ can read my mind and switches to a slower song. I place my hands on her waist and will my heart to stop racing.

Her arms snake against mine and meet at the back of my neck. I love the black dress she wears. It clings in all the right places and shows off her supple cleavage. She closes the space between us and rests her head on my chest. The music is so loud I can barely hear myself think. Not that I need to. I already know she's gorgeous and if my brother caught us like this, he would start a shitstorm. But this is nice.

She said those things drunk. She saw me staring at her a few weeks ago, and she isn't even mad about it. I hold her in my arms and wish this was a different time, a different place, different circumstances. But I have to take what I can get. I'll take her back home and let her sleep this off.

The song ends and I manage to talk her into going back to my apartment. We walk hand in hand to my car that's parked in a nearby garage just a few steps away from the club. She gives me the bedroom eyes and reaches over and places her perfectly manicured hand on my leg.

"So tense, Brand." Yeah, because I'm in public with my sister-in-law and she's drunk off her ass. Also, I want to do things with her and I know I can't.

I'm not a stranger to women. After Kayla, I've been well acquainted with women who didn't necessarily want any attachments. It's been over a month since I've gotten busy with someone, and this succubus sitting in my passenger seat is making it so fucking difficult to keep a straight head.

Brew coffee.

Maybe stop for a burger.

Do something that will help her sober up.

"Are you hungry, Ave?"

"Not for food." I groan. I glance over at her and wince when she grins. "Live a little. How often are we alone like this?"

Just every night when the kids go to bed. But she's right. Ethan and Alice are at Gray's house.

"I could go for some coffee. What about you?"

She scrunches her nose and shakes her head.

"If I knew better, I'd think you were trying to sober me up." Yep. Bingo.

"Do you want to be with me this way? How many drinks have you had?"

She shrugs nonchalantly. "I don't know. I had a few shots and a stupid daiquiri."

"Will you remember this in the morning?"

Her grin is wiped clean off her face.

"Don't ruin this for me, okay? I haven't gotten lucky since after Alice was born. Tonight is the night I drown my sorrows and go home with someone I shouldn't."

It's not happening. She brings her long arms over her head and stretches. At least she's tired. At least I won't have to wrestle her into bed and hold the door closed until she fell asleep.

"Let me make something clear to you, especially since you won't remember this in the morning: I like you. I know it's taboo and I want to do things with you that adults do in the dark hours. But you bet your pretty ass that I would want you to remember it." She swallows, her Adam's apple bobbing.

"Yeah? What are you like, Brand? You don't seem like the kind of man who makes slow, sweet love." I'm not. And I know what she's doing. She's trying to rev me up. My cock hardens and presses painfully against my zipper. It's fucking working.

"That's for sober Ava to find out."

She scoffs. "Damn. I thought I had you there."

I chuckle.

Baby goats.

Babies.

Mrs. Trunchbull.

Anything to get the swelling to go down.

"Nice try. Maybe when you wake up tomorrow morning and you still feel the same way, we can...do something." I pull into the garage and park the car next to the elevators.

"I don't know about that. Sober Ava is a prude. You could have had your way with me tonight." I groan.

Pressing her up against walls and ripping her clothes off is exactly what I would've done if she was sober. But I'm unfortunately a gentleman, and my momma taught me better.

We enter the elevator bay and I jam the up button and wait for the doors to open. She steps closer to me, snaking her arm around my waist and resting her head on my chest. Her mango scented hair wafts up my nose. I'd love to run my fingers through it, give it a firm, but gentle pull. But she spent a lot of time on her hair. I won't mess it up.

Lucky for us, the elevator is empty when it arrives. I send it to the twenty-first floor and play with the ends of her hair. She shivers and buries her face in my side. My hands itch to hold her the way I did when we danced. All of this could be distorted in the worst of ways. I avoid the cameras in the elevator, and I realize that she's doing the same. So many clues we're dropping, and people could pick up on it so quickly.

I hate my brother, but I'd *hate* for him to see this.

When the elevator reaches my floor, I grasp her hand tightly and race through the hallway to my apartment. These newer Chicago apartments for the rich and famous are equipped with some of the best security. Instead of sinking a key into a lock, I just hold a key fob to the door, and it unlocks automatically.

I open the door for Ava and usher her inside, closing and locking it tightly behind me. She hesitantly walks through the foyer and looks around my clean walls with very few pictures.

"Make yourself at home. I'll go start some coffee." We walk through the foyer into the open floor plan, right into the kitchen. As she walks, she lightly touches each surface and looks around. I head into the kitchen and start a pot of coffee. She takes a quick peek into the living room, but as if she doesn't want to be left alone, she turns back into the kitchen and hoists herself up onto the island.

"This is a big place for someone who claims to never be here." I weakly smile. Because I've spent the last month at her house.

"My mom stays here occasionally. And sometimes I let my friends crash if they've had much to drink." I look her straight in the eye and chuckle when her cheeks flush. "But you're right. This is a lot of space for one single guy."

"It's really nice."

"We can have our coffee on the balcony if you want. I have a pretty good view of Lake Shore Drive."

"You sure know how to wine and dine a gal." I chuckle and pull down to mugs from the cabinet above the coffee maker.

"Are you hungry? I can make you a grilled cheese or something?"

"No, but thank you. Coffee should be good. I'll go back to seducing you when we're dangerously dangling over Chicago."

She is going to be the death of me. Mark my words, I am not going to survive Ava Reid.

We pour our coffee and then I lead her out onto the balcony and sit her on the out of place porch swing. I'm a Texas boy through and through. If I was going to live in some hoity-toity luxury apartment in downtown Chicago, I was going to bring a piece of home with me regardless of what my neighbors thought of it. And on nights like tonight, I'm fucking glad I did.

Ava's eyes scan the city below her. The streetlights twinkle in her eyes, and a small smile spreads across her cheeks. She brings the black mug up to her lips and sips her coffee. She scoots as close as she can to me so that we're touching from shoulder to ankle.

"This is an incredible view, Brand. I'm insanely jealous."

"Thank you. It has nothing on your cute treehouse, but I'm lucky I bought in when the price was fair."

"My treehouse isn't *cute*. My treehouse is spectacular, thank you very much. It was literally a fight to the death on who got it during the divorce." She turns her head to me and grins. "I won. I found that house on accident and I begged Gray to live there. He wanted something grander. I wanted something that felt like home. I don't lose, Brandon."

I chuckle. No, she doesn't. I'm glad Gray didn't win it. I've had some fun times in that house and none of it was even sexual.

"A literal fight to the death, eh? Who died? You or Gray?" She rolls her eyes and nudges me in the ribs with her elbow.

"Jerk. Anyway, he was spiteful and tried to take it away from me, but the judge was familiar with our circumstances. She saw all the evidence of him never being around, so I got the house, a timeshare with the kids, but it feels like I have full custody." She shrugs and looks into my eyes. "Sober Ava would never admit this, but Vivienne will. I regret Gray. I don't regret our kids, so I guess no matter what hand of cards I was dealt, I was always meant to be a mom to *them*. But I so badly wish that I could've had them without Gray."

Me too. I wish I met her first. I wish those kids were *mine.*

"He's an asshole."

She snickers and nods. "A gaping asshole. But they're getting older, and they see who is there for them. He's starting to learn the hard way that he can't buy their affection. Remember how I said Alice didn't cuddle up to anyone?" I nod. I feel the ghost of Alice in my arms, snoring against my chest. The very reason I wanted kids—to warm my cold, dead heart. Alice crawled up into my lap that night and wormed her way into my heart. "She never got along with Gray. Whenever he held her, she would cry until he passed her off to anyone else. She's six years old and barely talks about him." She sets her mug on the ground and cuddles into me, taking in my scent. Thank *God* I put on deodorant before I left to pick her up.

"Why were you out tonight?" I ask gently.

Her face falls.

"I read for a part last week for a director I worked with previously. He called me back today and told me my reputation was the plague and didn't want me anywhere near his project. It hurt my feelings a little bit. And then Tess was trying to get me laid. So that's what tonight was about. Just a break." My fingers trace little circles on her arm.

"You were going to sleep with some stranger?" She giggles.

"Yeah, I was. It's a burden being Ava Reid all the time. Tonight, I was the three V's."

"Veronica...Victoria...Vivica?"

"*Vivienne.*" She giggles. "I can't keep them straight anymore. I told Brian Victoria, I think. By the end of the night, I think I was all three. It was nice not having to be me. Sober Ava's a bore."

"Sober Ava is *not* a bore. She's level-headed." She rolls her eyes and shakes her head, and then looks up to me with a heated look in her eyes.

"Do you really feel something for me, Brand? Because ever since you came to pick up Ethan from the hospital that night, I find my ovaries screaming whenever you're around."

I choke on my coffee.

Do I be honest with her now and have her forget everything tomorrow? Do I be honorable and change the subject? It doesn't matter which way I choose. I'm fucked either way. I'm breaking a sacred code to my brother, but I don't care. I don't give a flying fuck what he thinks about this.

"I know that when I'm around you, I feel a need to be as close to you as you'll allow. Sometimes I want to kiss you hello and goodbye. More recently, I've wanted to cuddle up with you on the couch when we watch our movies..."

"Only sometimes? Bullshit."

I chuckle. "Fine. All the time. But I don't want to cause trouble for you."

"Kiss me, Brandon. Sober Ava has been wanting you to for a long time now. She wanted to kiss you at the fire pit and last weekend when you killed a roach for her."

A war fires off in my head. I want to. *Damn it,* I want to so badly. What's just a kiss? It doesn't have to go any further than this. I sigh and place my hand on her cheek. Her eyes flutter closed as she inches closer to me, finally pressing her lips to mine. Her sweet tongue taps my bottom lip for entrance. Her free hand reaches around and threads in my hair.

I want to set my mug down. But my brain doesn't allow me to. Logic just made his way into the picture and forces me to break away from her.

"Ave..."

She sighs.

"Can't blame a girl for trying." She snickers and stands up. "Well, this obviously isn't going to go any further, no matter how much I want it to. If it's cool with you, I'm going to crash on your couch because I don't think I'm in any shape to walk back to Tess's house."

"You don't have to sleep on the couch. You can crash in the guest room."

"How about your room?" She wriggles her eyebrows suggestively, eliciting a pained chuckle from me.

"You can take my room. I can take the guest room."

"Prude." I stand up and swipe her mug up from the ground and follow her inside. She waits for me in the kitchen when I place the mugs in the sink. My bed is comfortable and made especially for athletes. So, while she gets the best sleep of her life tonight, I'll be miserable on the lumpy guest mattress. I lace my fingers with hers and lead her into my room.

"Help yourself to my clothes if you don't want to sleep in your dress tonight, and the shower is all yours."

"Will you join me?" She gives me a mischievous grin and presses on to the bathroom. She already knows the answer, she's just waiting for me to cave.

"Goodnight, Ave. I'll see you in the morning."

"Goodnight, Brand!" She calls from the bathroom. I sigh and reluctantly close the door behind me. I *want* to go back in there. I want to wrestle between the sheets with her. I want to wash her hair and take off the dark makeup she left the house with.

But all I'm left with is a painful erection and Handgela to relieve it. I prefer Ava—or any of the V's to relieve it.

The guest room is pretty small, no bigger than Alice's room at the treehouse, but my momma decorated it to remind me of home. I take off my shirt and jeans and crawl in between the sheets and sigh. I hope she remembers tonight. She told me a lot. She told me she liked and wanted me just as much as I wanted her.

This is so wrong.

But maybe I can frame it to Sober Ava in such a way that she'd agree to one dinner. Or at least to cuddle up on the couch together.

Being with me can't be that repulsive. She might rip my heart out if she isn't open to it. But the three V's seemed open to it.

Tomorrow's a new day. Tomorrow I'll make Sober Ava mine.

Nine

Ava

Can your jaw fuse shut if you've clenched it tight all night? There isn't much noise around me, but the sunlight filters through the floor-to-ceiling windows and throws my stomach into overdrive. I want to hurl. I want to purge all the alcohol I drank last night. But I don't necessarily want to vomit. My dress is cute, damn it, and I don't want to have to throw it away.

I have a most disgusting case of dry mouth and no matter how much I swallow, no saliva reproduces. My eyes flutter open as I take in my unfamiliar surroundings. Tess doesn't have these magnificent windows. The bed is massive and keeps me cool, even though I'm bundled up in a thick down blanket.

Brian got me a daiquiri. That, I remember. Then what? Tess and I danced. I vaguely remember calling someone. God, I *hope* it wasn't Gray. How humiliating would that be? How fast would that end up on the tabloids? I can see it now: *Ava Reid—Child Star Turned Hot Mess Express*. I hope I was careful enough that I didn't get any unwanted attention. I untangle myself from the blanket and swing my legs over the bed, and my feet touch the frigid marble flooring.

My stomach revolts at standing upright. I quickly rush to the bathroom and empty the contents of my stomach into the stranger's sparkly clean toilet. No skid marks, so I guess that counts for something. After flushing, I go to the sink and wash my face.

Who did I call?

I close my eyes hard and think back as hard as I can. *"I think you're handsome, Brand. Do you want to dance with me?"*

Oh no.

No.

No.

No.

No.

No!

I didn't sleep with my brother-in-law. *Please* tell me I didn't sleep with him! Looking into the mirror, the makeup I carefully painted on last night is gone, and my perfectly styled hair is matted from the bed. Sex hair! *Sex hair!* Oh my god.

Ava Reid, you dirty slut!

I'm not even wearing my own clothes!

I blame the three V's. Those horny bitches! This is why I don't go out. This is why I don't drink! What the hell was I thinking? How is this going to play out? I quickly shuck the oversized white t-shirt that is practically a dress off of me and squeal when there is absolutely nothing underneath it. Shit!

I find my dress, shoes, and undergarments in a pile near the shower. I quickly dress, throw my hair into a messy bun, and grab my shoes. I don't want to see him. I'm humiliated. I threw myself at my brother-in-law last night!

Where was Tess? Why didn't she stop me?

When I reach the room, I grab my phone and then press my ear to the door to see if there are any signs of life outside of it. Except for the hum of the air conditioning, I don't hear a thing. With my heels in my hands, I carefully open the door and pray it doesn't creak. I pad through the living room and through the foyer. No sign of Brandon anywhere, thank God! I slip out the front door and quietly pull the door closed and turning the handle back in place without a peep. From my phone, I order an Uber to take me back to Tess's house.

When the elevator arrives, I slip my heels back on and take a deep, cleansing breath.

This is bad. Death con level bad. Did I sleep with him?

Flashes like a movie filter through my brain. There was the porch swing—that much I remember. He made me coffee. And then...I told him to kiss me! Shit. Shit. Shit. Shit. Shit. This is bad.

I get a text that the Uber is downstairs waiting for me. I step out of the elevator and don't even bother glancing at the doorman when I sneak out. I hop into the green Nissan and try to pull my shit together before I sneak back into Tess's apartment. I've never done the walk of shame before. There was never a need to.

What do I tell Tess? What happens if Brandon tells Jordan when they go to practice later? I craft my parting speech to my career in my head while I'm whisked away to Tess's house. Within twenty minutes, I'm dropped outside of Tess's building. I manage to find my keys in my clutch and get her key ready. I plan on sneaking in and disappearing into their guest room until I hear them milling around and making breakfast. I'll tell them I snuck in around three.

This all feels like an out-of-body experience. It's like I'm on autopilot and my body is doing the work for me while I freak out in my head. I take the elevator and my rational side knows exactly where to go.

I could burst into tears. I can't have Brandon. There won't be a soul who'd want to work with me ever again. Gray would throw the world's largest and loudest tantrum. My label of "Trap Artist" will quickly get changed to "Slut." I know the three V's told him my deepest, darkest secrets. Those bitches can never keep their traps shut. I vaguely remember telling him about my screaming ovaries...

God damn it!

When I reach Tess's door, I quietly sink my key into the lock and quietly crack the door open wide enough to allow me to slip in, and quietly close the door behind me. I lock it without making any noise.

I could be a burglar in another life if I wasn't so afraid of cops. I slip my heels off and tiptoe through the foyer.

"Well good morning, gorgeous!"

I shriek in reply and drop my heels. Tess sits at the island wearing her glasses and sipping her coffee with a plate of scrambled eggs and bacon in front of her.

"I hate you. You're a jerk, Tessie."

She cackles and motions for me to grab a seat next to her. Jordan grins from the kitchen and pours me a mug of coffee.

"Have you ever done the walk of shame before, Goody Two Shoes? I have to say, this is so flattering on you. I hope he fucked you good and proper."

Jordan makes an uncomfortable noise and turns around so he doesn't look at me.

"Who?" Please tell me she doesn't know who she's talking about.

"The guy you left with! I didn't get a good look at him, but he was tall and muscly." And kind.

"Um. If he did, I don't remember it. I'm never drinking again." Jordan places a plate of eggs, bacon, and toast in front of me. It sends my stomach into a tailspin and I want to barf.

"Eat it. I know you probably want to hurl, but it'll help, I promise," he says kindly and with a wink. Jordan is the brother I never had. He's sweet, and he treats me like a sister.

"Thanks." I glance back over to Tess, who watches me expectantly.

"Did he kiss you goodbye?"

"No. I snuck out." Gray would die if he ever found out about this.

"Geez! You're supposed to endure the awkward the next morning."

Jordan frowns.

"It worries me you know the proper procedures for hookups, baby." This time, I giggle when Tess's face falls.

"I had a past before I met you, Jordo. I'm not apologizing for it."

"Yeah, yeah, I know. Feminism, pay gap, burning of the bras. I know." He kisses her on the crown of her head. "I still don't like hearing about it. It makes me want to hit someone." I giggle into my coffee.

I force-feed myself the eggs and I can barely stomach the bacon. But he was right. I'm feeling a lot better. Tess and I do the breakfast dishes while Jordan gets ready to go to practice.

Brandon doesn't seem like the kind of guy who will pretend this didn't happen. It gives me some kind of relief that I know he'll be at practice most of the day. It gives me time to prepare a long speech about how this could never happen again and pretend I'm indifferent.

Except, I *want* to do naughty things with him. It's not practical, I know this. I know what it would mean for me to be an active participant in an affair that could *never* happen. I sigh. Why did I marry Grayson Wentworth? Why couldn't I meet his nice, attractive older brother first?

Tess and I spend the morning watching a movie. Though she begs me to stay for lunch, I know I need to get home. I have kids who come home tomorrow and a potential run-in I don't want to deal with.

I stop at Panera on my way home and grab some soup and a sandwich. I don't eat it right away, because I still feel like I could vomit my guts up, but then I clean up the living room and the kitchen.

I cut up fruit and bag it up so they're at the ready for the kids. I take a shower and dress in mom appropriate clothing and catch up on the laundry. Finally, I take a minute to eat. With *Supernatural* on in the background, I nibble on my sandwich and relax on the couch.

It's weird not to hear my children bicker in the background or the sounds of their games blaring from their rooms. Every mother needs a break every now and then. This is the first one I've had in a really long time, but I find myself missing them. I hope they're having fun. I pray that their father didn't just shuttle them back to his house and sit them in front of the TV.

I *should* work on the screenplay that's collecting dust on my hard drive. But I'd rather watch Sam and Dean Winchester save the world with the best music ever. If this screenplay ever saw the light of day, this could be a new beginning for me. I could produce my own movies and not have to worry about being rejected because of my stupid ex-husband.

After my late lunch, I don't do much of anything. I post a little on social media and crack open a book. My stomach is feeling a lot better. What I *really* want to do is sink into my bathtub—sans wine—and use that bath bomb.

But that gets thrown out the window when I see Brandon's truck from the living room window.

Showtime.

I didn't prepare a speech. I don't know how I'm going to talk my way out of this. Maybe he won't want to mess up our friendship either. Maybe we can awkwardly laugh about this and pretend last night didn't happen. I don't even know if I slept with him. There's no phantom ache in my nether regions, so I have to assume nothing happened.

But I begged him to kiss me. So maybe he just has a pencil dick and I kicked him out of his own room.

Not likely.

I nearly jump out of my skin when he knocks on the door. I'm expecting him, and I'm expecting this to get ugly. He deserves a woman who can give him everything he wants. I can't. My reputation is already damaged. I have to provide for my babies. He may have a panty-dropping smile and a sharp tongue, but my reputation will be blown to smithereens if I entertain this any further.

I shyly open the door and offer him a hesitant smile. He grins and pecks me on the cheek. Why do I swoon so much around him? How are he and Gray so different? I always had to go to war for Gray's affection. Brandon doles it out for free.

He's dressed casually. White t-shirt, blue jeans, and some converse. Even when he's not trying to be sexy, he's fucking sexy.

Damn it.

"Hey." My voice doesn't even sound like me. I'm not meek. I speak my mind especially when people don't want to hear my opinions. But right now, I'm terrified. I don't want to lose Brandon just because I can't be with him.

"Hey. How are you?"

"Living the dream."

You're an idiot.

Cringing, I shut the door behind him and step into the kitchen. I need something to do with my hands or to distract myself from wanting to jump into his arms.

"Do you want to watch a movie?" I call out to him. From the bar in the kitchen, he walks into the living room like it's second nature. He glances at me curiously as if to say, "What are you doing?"

"Sure. I was hoping we could talk."

Nope.

"Oh? About what?"

He visibly flinches. Off to a *great* start.

"Do you need help in there? I could make the popcorn..."

I'm the master of procrastination. The longer I stay in the kitchen, the longer I put that "talk" off. Brandon, on the other hand, is the master of telepathy. He's somehow noticed how uncomfortable I am and tries to change the atmosphere. Doesn't he know I'm the world's worst cooler?

"Oh, thanks. I got it." We stare at each other in the most non-confrontational way. He shoves his hands in his pockets while he narrows his eyes in confusion.

"Ave?"

"Hmm?"

"Are you going to make the popcorn?" I quickly turn around to hide my embarrassment. I'm much more suave when he isn't around.

But there's something about him that makes me act like a teenager with a crush.

"Mmhm." I disappear into the pantry. "Stop being weird," I whisper to myself. And now I'm talking to myself. "Any requests on the movie? We could watch *Top Gun* or *Clue*. I'm biased. I'd rather watch *Clue*." I step out of the pantry and walk right into his chest on a scream.

Chuckling, he steadies me on my feet. "You all right, killer? You're acting weird."

"Living the dream." I groan at my repeated phrase. *This* is why I never make the first move on anyone. My awkwardness gets me in trouble every single time.

He sighs and drops his arms.

"You're acting weird. I think we should talk about last night." I don't need a mirror to tell me the color has drained from my face. Pushing past him, I take the popcorn bag out of the cellophane and toss it into the microwave.

"Brand..."

"Nothing happened, Ave, if that's what you're worried about." I don't miss the disappointment in his voice, or in his eyes, when my face relaxes with relief.

"Um, it's not that I don't want to...with you...it's just...messy."

His lips quirk lazily into a crooked smile.

"The three V's didn't seem to have a problem with voicing their deepest desires."

Oh god.

"The three V's..." I'm never drinking again. "They said a lot last night."

"Like how your ovaries scream whenever I'm around."

Yep. That was the phrase I used.

How was I ever married? How do I have children?

"It was cute."

"Um, no. It definitely wasn't cute." When the microwave goes off and I pull out a bag of hot popcorn, I pour it into a bowl and motion for him to follow me out to the living room. He grabs two beers, though. Just the sight of that Guinness sends my stomach into a tailspin. "So, *Clue?* It's a cult classic. Tim Curry is the most amazing man on the planet. We don't deserve him, you know."

He swiftly grabs the remote out of my hand and crashes to the couch.

"Let's talk."

Let's not.

"I feel something for you. Every time I'm here, I want to hug you. I want to cuddle with you on the couch and kiss you sometimes. You cuss like a sailor, but it's so endearing that I don't even mind it. I want to take you to dinner and hang out with your kids. What do you think about giving us a shot?"

My body stiffens at the "I want to take you to dinner" comment. I miss the days before my reputation was sullied. I miss the days when he could've asked me this and I wouldn't even give it a second thought.

"Brand...this can't happen."

He stares at me in disbelief.

"Right now, I'm a villain in Hollywood. I trapped Gray into a loveless marriage and saddled him with kids he didn't want. I'm a social pariah. If you throw in...*this,* it's a recipe for a disaster. I won't ever work again. I can't risk that."

He points the remote at the TV and puts on *Clue.* He's done talking about this for now. He stews next to me. He doesn't drink his beer or pick at the popcorn. His eyes face the screen, but he isn't watching the movie.

In a perfect world, I could stand in front of the audience and tell them what really happened with Gray. I could date his brother without the image of keeping it in the family or dating him just to spite Gray.

This, unfortunately, isn't a perfect world. I'm standing in the middle of a shitstorm that is Grayson Wentworth. I'm an innocent bystander getting caught up in his tornado. The aftermath is scary. Until Alice turns eighteen, I'm stuck with him for that much longer. And that means not doing stupid shit like dating his brother.

Halfway through the movie, Brandon gets up and bounds to the kitchen. He paces back and forth before deciding to go outside. Grabbing my UGGS and my coat, I race outside to follow him.

Contain it. Make sure he isn't petty like his brother.

He sits in front of the unlit fire pit with his index fingers steepled under his chin. He stares ahead like he sees right through me. I've been around Brandon long enough to know that when he needs to think, he comes outside. It's like the artificial air doesn't allow all the circuits in his brain to fire at the correct speed.

I drop into the chair next to him and wait for the shouting.

"You *have* to stop letting Gray run your life," he says quietly.

I think I'd rather have the shouting. This disappointment in his voice is much worse.

"He doesn't run my life, Brand." Sighing, I turn my body to face him. "My whole career revolves around people liking me. The more people like me, the more jobs I'm considered for. That's my livelihood. That's how I provide for my babies. You don't think I want to be with you? I don't remember what it's like to be touched by a man who *wants* to. Gray has never looked at me the way you do. Nobody has. If I would have gone home with anyone else last night, I would've made bad decisions. The man I could've gone home with wouldn't give a shit about consent. We'd do the deed, and I'd hate myself in the morning for it."

"Then stop acting, Ave! At some point, you have to ask yourself if worrying about what other people think about you is good for your mental health!"

"Quit acting? Then what? Quit football, Brand!" His glare rips through me like daggers. "I *love* acting. I *love* my job. I couldn't imagine doing anything else. I'm not going to quit my job just because you think I'm pretty."

Well, *that* was the wrong thing to say.

"It's more than that, come on. You're smarter than that."

My teeth grind together. The man is stubborn. He thinks he's always right. I guess that's how he and his brother are alike.

"Look, I know this isn't what you want to hear, but us being together is a horrible idea. You may not care about perception, but I do. My kids come first every single time, Brand. I will not take away their livelihood, no matter how much I want to fall into bed with you."

Standing, I start towards back the warmth of my treehouse. His hand wraps around my wrist and spins me around to face him. His nostrils flare and for a moment, I steel myself to accept the name-calling and criticism.

"What are you doing now, Ava? What was the last role you had?"

The truth is, I haven't had a starring role in forever. Him throwing it in my face like that is a punch to the gut.

"I'm auditioning." I rip my wrist out of his grasp. "I'm going inside. I'll make us a pot of coffee and then we can talk about this where it's warm." He laughs without humor.

"Do what you want." Shrugging like it doesn't bother me, I trudge through the icy grass and up the steep stairs to the deck. It bothers the hell out of me that he isn't looking at this from my perspective.

What a caveman!

Quit acting? I'm not going to rely on a man to take care of us when I'm perfectly capable of taking care of the three of us myself. My husband cheated on me multiple times while I was stuck at home waking up every three hours and entertaining a toddler. There has always been one person looking out for the three of us. That person wasn't Brandon Wentworth.

I angrily measure out the coffee into the filter and fill the reservoir up. Why does he get to be the angry one? He's asking much of me. He's asking me to give up my career to be with him.

What if it doesn't work out?

The back door opens, but I don't bother glancing in his direction. He walks so heavy-footed, it's intimidating.

"I meant what I said about wanting to help out with the kids." I set the pot down and turn to face him. He towers over me by a foot, and though he wears an angry scowl, I refuse to give him the upper hand. "You told me how you felt about me last night—"

"I was drunk!"

"A drunk person's an honest person." I purse my lips. I fucking hate the three V's and their big mouths. "I can't be around you if we aren't going to be doing something about our chemistry."

Oh, brother.

"I'll see you around, Ave."

Ten

Brandon

Now

"Rejection must have stung," Sunny says seriously. It did. I knew Ava was always going to be the one that I'd hate myself for not trying to make *something* happen. She was everything I was looking for in a woman: kind, compassionate, and relatively drama-free. Boy, was I wrong.

"At that moment it did. The most frustrating thing was that I knew she wanted to be with me." I glance down at Ava, who stares past the camera to that same blank spot on the wall.

She tries so hard to keep her cool, but the tips of her ears redden. Which means either Sunny or I are about to get an earful.

Thinking better of talking to Ava, she turns her gaze to me and smiles sweetly. "Isn't there some kind of guy code not to steal your brother's girl?"

Ava scoffs and smirks.

"Yes. However, she was no longer my brother's girl." Her perfectly sculpted eyebrow lifts to the sky.

"So, I was just fair game then? You didn't care how Gray would react?"

"No, Ava, I didn't care." I look back to Sunny. "A man who loves a woman immediately switches on to protector mode. Gray was a jerk to her, to put it mildly. All the infidelity, the harsh words, the ghosting...no. I didn't give one flying you-know-what if he found out about us. I wanted to protect them."

"Why?" Sunny asks.

The audience watches on with bated breath. There's not much to tell, really.

"It's no secret Gray and I have been at odds our entire lives. It was seriously dumb luck that I fell in love with his ex-wife." Shrugging, I shift my attention to Ava. Her brows are furrowed and if this were a cartoon, I could see the steam billowing out of her ears. "You say I couldn't have loved you then. It was too early. But I *was* in love with you. I was willing to put everything on the line if it meant I got to be with you."

The audience reacts with an "aw," but Ava doesn't see it that way.

"Isn't that adorable," she seethes. "You claim you were in love with me then, but you *still* showed your true colors at the end, didn't you?" She turns to Sunny. "You should've been there. It would have made for great TV."

Rolling my eyes, I continue with my explanation. "As soon as I pulled out of her driveway, I wanted to turn right around and go back inside."

"But you didn't." She crosses her arms across her chest and leans all the way back until her back is flush against the back of the sofa.

"No. You weren't listening with an open mind. Like it or not, Reid, you aren't the easiest person to talk to. You *always* assume you're right, even if you're wrong, and you don't trust worth a damn."

"Ha!" She cackles. "I wonder why!"

"Ava, how did you feel after he left?"

She considers her words carefully before speaking. "I wanted what he was selling. What woman wouldn't? Back then, I put trust into him when I couldn't do that with anyone else. My kids adored him, he was friends with my friends, he was in the process of setting up the Live Oaks Foundation—he was the whole package. Smart, attractive, kind..." she frowns as the tears well up in her eyes.

Blinking them away and wiping the excess with her index finger, she sighs.

"Yet, you said no," Sunny assumes, trying to fill in the blanks we're all wondering about.

"I'm not the villain the media has painted me to be. Gray proposed to *me*. It wasn't the other way around. I didn't trap him in a marriage he didn't want. We wanted kids together, so I gave him kids. They were wanted no matter how many women like Lucy Rodriguez or Katie Jensen try to give their two cents on a man they don't even *know*." She sniffles and accepts a tissue from Sunny. "If I threw my inhibitions to the wind and said yes to Brandon and went public, I would've been crucified. I can take it. I grew up in this industry. I know how awful people can be to each other. What I couldn't handle was the ridicule my children would've received."

I straighten up.

I didn't think about the kids.

"Tell me about that."

"When *you all* were calling me every name under the sun, Gold digger, Trap Artist, Whore, the children at Ethan's school were merciless. Parents talked about us in which their kids would overhear. They'd tease Ethan until the kid snapped and took care of business."

That's my boy...

"I'd get calls from the school about fights he was in. My son has always taken this unspoken vow that he protects his women. Even at five years old, he was so serious. Always listening to the gossip, always at the ready to protect my feelings." She sadly smiles. "What kind of mother would I have been if I had put them through that again?"

"So, you put your happiness aside for your children, not your career," Sunny clarifies.

"Everything I do is for my children, Sunny. When I became a mother, it meant putting all my selfish notions on the back burner. Brandon would have been perfect had he not been Gray's brother."

"How do you feel about that, Brandon?"

Is this a shrink session?

"I knew about the ridicule Ethan received. I didn't know it *then,* which is why I was so insistent." I stare at Ava in a new light. She'll never throw her kids under the bus, yet when she was pushed into a corner, she does.

"What happened next?"

It's my favorite part of the whole story.

"It's what I think about when I remember what happens next. It's the bravest thing I've ever done. There was a party." She looks at me with pure, unaltered hatred. "When I think about us, I think about that stupid party."

"You came for me."

"Yeah. 'Cause I was stupid."

Eleven

Brandon

Then

We lost in the second round of the playoffs. As soul-crushing as it is, it's also a relief. For a month or two, we can eat whatever the hell we want without any repercussions, just as long as we're prepared to work our asses off to get back to where we were.

The last two weeks have been miserable. My Saturdays have been empty and boring and have forced me to spend time with my childhood best friend, Ellen Wilson. I use the term "best friend" loosely. She's a friend. But she's from home, and sometimes you just need that dose of home when you can't physically go there.

She's the team's physical therapist. After she graduated from college, she networked her ass off and got in good with general management, and voila, she has a job. She's a natural flirt, though I don't see the appeal. She's nice. She's loyal and kind of pretty.

She's no Ava Reid.

Stop it!

After the season ends, Jordan opens up his apartment for the team and crew to come over and pig out. Which means Jordan orders entire menus from every restaurant in a ten-mile radius so that Tess can eat like a real human being. I'm all the way in Lake Forest where Ellen lives, because she doesn't have a car and relies solely on public transportation, and she asked.

She sits in the front seat with her converse lazily placed on the dash while she scrolls through her social media. It's a quiet drive, one I'm finding myself taking more and more to get some serenity outside of the city.

"Do you mind if I crash at your house tonight if I don't go home with anyone?" She asks absentmindedly.

Frowning, I nod.

"That's fine. I'm leaving early in the morning, so the door will lock automatically when you leave. Just text me and let me know when you leave." *So, I don't have to be there.*

"Okay. Where are you going?"

"Just for a drive. I want to clear my head."

"Want some company? I could use some time outside of the city for a day."

No.

"Thanks, but no. I want to go by myself." She frowns and opens the bag of potato chips that was sitting at her feet. They *were* for the party. She's never been a considerate person.

Jordan's apartment building is fancier than mine. They have a valet, where mine does not. I gratefully hand my keys over to the valet and lead Ellen through the building. She loops her arm through mine and gropes my bicep possessively.

Partying isn't my thing. I hate crowds, even though I know all these people. All of my friends' wives will be here and ask me how I'm still single. Ellen is painfully shy, which means she'll be my shadow for the entire night.

I should've stayed home.

But I didn't because I knew Tess would be there and I could casually ask her about Ava.

How is she doing? Does she hate me for losing my cool? Did she tell Tess about the fight?

Ramirez and Philips join us in the elevator. They flirt with Ellen, though she doesn't show much interest in them. I watch as the digital numbers change so fucking slow until they reach their floor.

Jordan is from money. I've heard Tess joking that if they ever got divorced, the only thing she'd take from Jordan was his trust fund. He's not a stereotypical rich kid. His mother is some honored neurosurgeon, and his father does something with hedge funds. What I know about all of the Archer's I've personally met, they're all hardworking. Jordan has two bachelor's degrees: one in Biology, one in Environmental Engineering. If football didn't work out for him, he would've been set.

The people line the hallway, talking and sipping from red plastic cups. I worry that he pisses off his neighbors when he throws parties like this, but I think they get paid a nice sum for their trouble.

It's not my business.

The foyer is overflowing with people. We push our way in and make the obligatory rounds to our teammates. The kitchen is bursting at the seams with women standing around Tess's island. There's food on every available surface and drinks outside.

"Brandon!" Tess shrieks. I turn towards her voice and grin, but the sight I see makes me want to vomit.

Ava's here.

Is she here for me? She *never* comes to these.

Her sad eyes sweep over me and stop at Ellen's hand so comfortably in the crook of my arm.

It's not what it looks like!

It doesn't matter because some guy's wife asks her a question and steals her attention. Like it didn't even bother her, she pastes on her best smile and answers enthusiastically.

"I was beginning to think you didn't want to hang out with me!" She throws her arms around me, and her wild black curls tickle my nose. She smiles politely at Ellen, though I know for a fact they *hate* each other.

"Sorry. I had to go to Lake Forest to get Ellen."

"Welcome, Ellen. Make yourself at home." Glancing back at me, she winks. "Jordo's out on the balcony. He's making burgers."

Why!?

Stealing one last look at Ava before I reluctantly make my way outside to the twenty-degree weather. How does a grill even work in this weather? Why didn't he just *buy* burgers?

"There he is!" Jordan's shout makes the twenty guys cheer as we close the sliding glass door behind us. Thankfully, Ellen *finally* detaches herself from me and lowers the zipper on her coat, showing her supple cleavage. She must have not gotten the memo about the weather. She parks herself on a lawn chair with Jose Goode, her most recent conquest.

Jordan waves me over as he flips a burger. "You could have bought burgers, you know? You ordered from every single restaurant—"

"I had meat that was going to go bad tomorrow if I didn't make it today."

Definitely not eating a burger.

"Have I told you that I hate Chicago?"

"No, you don't." He's still salty that his home team of the New York Giants didn't draft him as a rookie.

"You're right. I don't. At least it's not New York." He's a New York boy through and through. He talks wild shit about his home state, yet the guy doesn't stop bitching about Chicago-style pizza.

"This is some turnout."

He shrugs nonchalantly. "Not as much as last year, but that's okay. I'm going to need all you fuckers to get out of here by ten because I have a date with my wife and my bed. Simultaneously."

I roll my eyes. Always the joker.

"I won't stay long. I plan on falling on my face once I get home." And so I can drive past Ava's house to make sure she got home okay.

"Hey, I meant to ask you...how did you know Tessie needed to be picked up from the club the other night?"

They don't know.

Be cool, jackass.

"Ava called. She said she was drunk and needed a place to crash." Lie. Kind of. Jordan's eyes widen to the size of saucers. He closes the lid.

"Bro, you didn't."

I didn't.

"Relax. It's not what you think."

"Dude, she's your sister-in-law!" His whisper shouting would be comical if it were directed at someone else. Curious glances get thrown our way, including from Ellen.

"Nothing happened, so stop freaking out!"

"Jordo!" Tess's voice sounds off from the sliding glass door.

"And don't tell Tess. I don't think Ava told her."

"There is something wrong with you."

I chuckle as Tess and Ava approach. Tess wears a bright smile, whereas Ava is more cautious.

"The babes are hungry, babe. Hurry up."

"How! There is so much food in there!"

Ava's eyes meet mine. I offer her a simple smile. I wish we were telepathic. I'd apologize for being an ass without embarrassing her in front of everyone here. Her chapped lips form into a small smile.

"Well, they want your burgers," she says slowly, looking from me to Ava. Clearing her throat, she grabs Jordan's arm. "Come on."

"The burgers!"

"I got it," I assure him. He doesn't want my assurances. He just glares and allows himself to be dragged inside by his wife. "Hi, Ave."

"Hey, Brand."

She approaches the grill quietly and leans against the banister. She pulls her coat tighter and throws her hood up. Even looking like the Michelin man, she's sexy.

"How are you doing?" She asks softly.

"Not bad. Where are the kids?"

"Gray took them to Wisconsin Dells for the weekend."

Must be fun getting to be the fun parent.

"That sounds fun. I bet they were excited."

She giggles nervously.

"I don't know about that. Alice is a different breed. She'll drive him up the wall just because it's fun and Ethan…"

Doesn't want to be there. I got it.

"I'm happy you're here." I ignore the glare Ellen throws my way. She *hates* Ava. Mostly because I think she believes the tabloids, but also out of loyalty for Gray. She refuses to see the monster he is.

"Yeah? I was worried. I thought maybe you'd yell at me some more." She flashes a playful grin and faces the city. The free strands of her hair get tousled by the chilling breeze. This picture reminds me so much of the night we spent on my balcony. Only this time, she's sober.

I take the patties off the grill and hand them over to Thompson, who brings them inside. "I'm sorry I yelled at you. When I don't get what I want, I tend to be irrational."

She commands the city just by existing.

"If you weren't Gray's brother, we wouldn't be having this conversation." I step into her personal space. Her pert nose is just inches from my chest. I'll do anything to have her. Even if it means we keep it between us for now.

"What if we kept it a secret?"

"That sounds like a recipe for disaster." I itch to hold her hand in mine, though I resist. I won't embarrass her. That's something Gray would do.

"It gives us time to explore *this* without media scrutiny. It gives us the opportunity to slowly ease the kids into the idea. I promise you love and kindness. I'm not my brother. We're *leagues* away from each other. I know how to treat women."

She scoffs.

"You're so sure I'll fall in love with you?" She confidently smirks and rolls her eyes.

"It would be mutual, I promise."

"Men all over the world promise love and rainbows and sunshine. He'll whisper sweet nothings and empty promises into her ear. He'll pound his chest, show the world that she's *his*. The second things get just a little domestic, he'll 'forget' to text her back. He'll tell her she looks prettier with makeup. And in a month when she finally believes those sweet nothings and empty promises, he'll bang her one last time for good measure and disappear."

We're toe to toe. She has to tilt her head up to look at me.

"Ave," I drawl in a dangerously low tone, "I've been around you for *over* a month. I played with your son for two days while you stayed in the hospital with your daughter. You came back home in the same clothes you went to the hospital with. You passed out on the couch, mouth wide open, snoring that would wake the dead, and snot dripping down your nose and I'm *still* here." Her breath hitches in her throat. My eyes sweep her body and see her pulse quickening in her neck.

I shove my hands in my pockets because I long to push her hair out of her face and cradle her head in my hands.

"I don't believe in sweet nothings. My promises are never empty. I've literally seen you at your worst, and I am *begging* you to spend some time with me. We can be discreet. I promise I won't ever leak anything to anyone. I love your kids. I..." *Shut up!* "I care about you. There would have to be an end date because I'm *not* ashamed to be with you. But for a while, we can keep it between us."

"Brand, can you grab me a beer?" Ellen appears at my side, again looping her arm in mine. Our trance is broken. She licks her dry lips and then smiles at Ellen.

"Hi, Ellen. It's great to see you! How are you doing?"

Ellen grimaces.

"Great, thanks for asking." She turns back to me. "Can you get me a beer, please?" She whines.

This is where I prove myself.

"There's a fresh case inside. I'm hanging out with Ava." My eyes never leave Ava's. It's like an intense staring contest and nobody's allowed into our bubble. She slinks away with an ugly scowl.

"Is that a thing?" she asks, quickly glancing at her and back at me.

"What? No."

"She has a thing for you."

I hope not.

She laughs without a care in the world.

"No, she doesn't. She's just shy."

"Well, you walked in with her. You looked cozy." She faces the city again. The sunlight looks so damn good on her.

What is it about the outdoors that makes us so brave around each other? She's normally so guarded. I'm enjoying this free version of her.

"We came together, but we didn't come *together*. She needed a ride."

"*Hey!*" Tess's voice echoes off the nearby buildings. "The cupcakes are here! Get inside!" She backs up from the balcony and grins.

"Will you think about it?" Her breath is visible when she sighs. Hey, if I'm wearing her down, that's a good sign. I can work with this. I can get her to agree.

"Maybe. See ya around, Brand."

Twelve

Ava

Then

Tess slingshots me into the master bedroom and closes and locks the door behind her. "Spill." I collapse onto her bed and stare at the patterns from her textured ceiling. She will *never* let me live this down.

"There's nothing to spill, Tessie." She snorts.

"Nice try. Spill. I want all the dirty details. You're not getting out of this." She grunts as she splays out next to me. Our heads lie side by side. Her black curls tangle with my honey-colored curls. "You were practically dry humping out there. We all saw it."

My stomach drops.

"Well, not all of us. But Jordan and I definitely noticed. It's not *nothing.*"

"He helped me out with Ethan when Alice was admitted to the hospital. And then he said he wanted to spend more time with the kids since he doesn't get to, so he's come over every Saturday."

Except for the last two.

"He's hot," she muses.

"Very."

"But you're leaving out the details. I want to know *everything.*" I heave a big sigh. She's going to beat it out of me, regardless.

So, I tell her. I tell her about the couch and how he tucked me into bed and did my dishes. I tell her about the hours long conversation in front of the fire pit and how he's come over every Saturday and played with the kids and watched movies with me. I told her about the roach he killed for me in the bathroom.

"Wait, so was he the one you called that night at the club?" As ridiculous as I was that night, it still makes me smile. He was such a gentleman. He ignored all my advances and my not-so-subtle 'you make my ovaries scream whenever you're around' comments. "How did I *not* recognize him!?"

She giggles into my shoulder.

"But then things got bad. He came over the next day. He wanted to be with me, and I turned him down."

Tess shoots up. "Why?"

"Come on, Tessie, he's my brother-in-law. It's career suicide!"

"He isn't your brother-in-law anymore!" She sighs dramatically and lies on the bed again. "I know Gray hurt you in the most painful way, babe, but Brandon isn't like him. I never vouch for Jordo's friends, but I can personally vouch for him. He'd never hurt you."

"But that doesn't change the fact I'll never grace the silver screen ever again."

"Actresses make comebacks all the time. Look at Winona Ryder. Vanessa Williams. Drew Barrymore! They've all had scandals. They took time away from the spotlight and came back stronger than ever. Close your eyes."

Groaning, I oblige. I'm exhausted, number one. Tess invited me over yesterday and let slip the team was coming over tonight for the party. I wanted to see him.

"Now. Imagine that we're eighty-five. We're sitting in our rocking chairs in front of the little cottage we buy with Jordan's trust fund. Ethan serves us lemonade; Alice smuggles us some special brownies."

"Why is my baby giving us pot?"

"Focus! You look back on your life, okay? You see your children, your successful career, me, Jordan—it's a happy life. Do you regret not giving Brandon a shot? Are you content living out the rest of your life with me?"

The simple answer is yes. I'd regret not giving him a chance. The complicated answer—maybe. What happens if he breaks my heart? What happens if he hurts me way worse than Gray ever did?

"I'm always content living my life with you. We have a codependent relationship. But...yeah. I think I'd regret it." She grins. "When we were talking outside, he said we could keep it a secret."

She props herself up on her elbow and looks down at me with a frown.

"He wants to keep you a secret?"

"No. He wants to go public and tell the world. I can't do that to Ethan again. I can't subject him to more ridicule. *But* it could be a way to ease into it. See where it goes, and if it's more, then go public?"

"You're a hot mess express."

I giggle. There has never been a truer story.

"I could always insert myself into your marriage. I think you're pretty. Besides, you guys have the room for the kids."

"As much as I'd *love* that, Brandon is clearly the better choice. You're always welcome into our marriage, babycakes, but only as a last resort." We're silent for a beat. "Besides, your vagina will thank you in the long run."

His proposal is attractive. But how do I even break this to the kids? It's not fair to ask them to keep a secret of this magnitude. And what if it doesn't work out? He's asking me to jump off a cliff on the promise he's on the ground with a big fluffy mattress to catch me. What happens if this goes to shit and I miss the mattress completely?

This part of Tess's life is unchartered territory for me. I'm her best friend, her sister from another mister, but the women of the Chicago Bears are...different. They have their significant others. I envy the way she seems to fall into place anywhere she goes. She laughs with her fellow wives while I navigate their apartment, just sort of watching everything from afar.

Ellen watches me like a hawk. She doesn't have any claim over him, yet she eyes me like I'm a giant homewrecker waiting to swoop in and take her man. I don't know where it all went wrong with us. I feel like I was on her radar long before I met her. When Gray brought me home to meet his mother, Ellen happened to be there. She wouldn't give me the time of day, and *only* talked with Bev or Gray until Brandon and Kayla arrived. They were only dating then, but it was getting serious.

I offer her a small smile, in which she scoffs and turns her attention back to the beefy guy sitting next to her.

Whatever.

Not everyone is going to like me. That's what we're taught in the biz, right?

I find Jordan in the kitchen, tidying up and throwing things away. I grab the empty beer bottles next to the kitchen sink and help him get the kitchen back in order. When he's satisfied, he opens his arms in invitation.

I'm an only child. The closest thing I had to a sister was Tess. When Tess and Jordan got together, I gained a brother. He watches out for me and occasionally jokes about us being a throuple.

I wrap my arms around his torso and smile against his chest.

"I'm glad you decided to come over today."

"Yeah, me. Thanks for inviting me." He leans against the counter. The rooms buzz with excited chatter and. The clacking of the foosball table in the living room echoes off the baren walls.

"I think you have all the delivery boys fighting against each other to feed the elusive Tess Archer."

He laughs.

"My baby says to order everything, so I order everything. And she was sick of eating baked chicken and boiled broccoli. She's a trooper."

Tess's obnoxious laugh floats into the kitchen. She throws her arms around both of us and giggles.

"This is a pretty picture, isn't it? Tessie invited me into your marriage, Jordo. I hope you're ready for another three mouths to feed," I tease. He stares at Tess in disbelief.

"You asked her to be in our marriage *without* me?"

Tess cackles.

"Nice try, Reid. I said you could only join in as a last resort. We all know who you *really* want to sleep with."

Jordan looks at me seriously.

"Who?"

"The linebacker who's staring at her from the corner of the living room." As one, Jordan and I both look in that direction. Sure enough, Brandon is staring at me with hungry eyes. Ellen is telling him a story, but he isn't listening to a single word she's saying.

Electrocution. Not like the whole body electrocution, but when you accidentally shock yourself when you're closing your car door in the cold. That's what his stare feels like. He's egging me on to say "yes." He's so damn cocky that I'm going to fall in love with him.

And I will. I have no doubt I will.

He's a mind reader, I'm sure of it. He knows I've made *the* decision and he's done spending his time here. He stalks over, leaving Ellen mid-sentence. He approaches our small group, eyes boring into mine. You can cut the sexual tension with a butterknife.

"Thanks for having us over. I'm heading out."

"Oh! What a coincidence! Maybe you can walk Ava out to her car. She's being a wuss and wants to leave early too." She's an asshole.

"I can walk you to your car," he offers politely. We're not dumb. He's not walking me to my car. He's walking me to *his*. We *all* know what's going down when we step outside their front door.

"Thank you," I murmur.

Tess winks at me, then presses a noisy kiss on Jordan's cheek. We turn and walk to the front door. We don't dare look in anyone's direction. Right now, the heat is on. I have twenty-four hours before Gray and the kids get home.

I haven't been touched by a man who genuinely cares about me in six years. The hallway buzzes with outliers who drink sloppily from their red plastic cups. We share the elevator with one other person, though he doesn't suspect a damn thing. Since Jordan is one of the elites, there are cameras everywhere. I keep my eyes ahead, focused on Brandon's reflection behind me in the gold-plated elevator doors. His eyes hold a promise of an unforgettable time, one that I may end up regretting in the long run. The wedges I wear on my feet are the only support I have for not falling flat on my face.

The three of us are let off on the ground floor. Our elevator guest soars past us without a second glance. I'm more cautious. I pull the hood of my coat over my head and stay out of sight from the cameras. All I'm missing is a pair of Jackie O sunglasses and I'm a stereotypical incognito actress, hiding away from the world.

Brandon stays a few paces behind me until we reach the valet outside. He stays with the valet to hold his attention. Once his black mustang whips around the corner and pulls up in front of me is when he rejoins me.

"Relax," he whispers, his lips on the shell of my ear. Can he feel how rigid I am? Does he know the repercussions that hang in the balance? He opens the car door for me and holds my hand until I'm buckled in safely. The warm air from the air conditioner blasts in my face. He hops into the driver's seat, and I close my eyes to his masculine scent of Old Spice and sandalwood filling the car.

He holds my hand in his, tracing small circles on the inside of my knee.

I'm going home with Brandon Wentworth.

He listens to country music, but I won't hold that against him. In fact, I'm grateful that I can focus on Josh Gracin's deep voice and singing about big brass beds and lying clocks. Really, it's the first act of what's to come. He hums along with a hint of a smile on his face.

I vaguely remember his apartment. He doesn't have a valet like Jordan, but he *does* have a reserved parking spot in the garage. I don't even remember him turning into traffic or driving down Lake Shore Drive. When we're parked, he helps me out of the car and laces his fingers with mine. He jams the "up" button with his thumb and pulls me into his chest.

He drops my hood and strokes my hair. If it were his choice, we'd be starting here. He'd claim me in the elevator, the hallway, even the car. He's a gentleman tonight. Maybe some other time, when the world isn't watching and waiting for me to royally fuck up. I wrap my arms around his torso and walk backward into the elevators when the doors invite us in.

The digital numbers that flash what floor we're on flash painfully slow. His touch finds the exposed skin on the back of my neck, making me shudder and erupt in goosebumps. Finally, we're let off at his floor.

He pulls me quickly down the hallway. He holds his fob up to his door and flings it open. The foyer looks familiar. It's almost sterile. Like he didn't put any thought into it—

"Do you want this Ave?" He asks, shoving me up against the door. Heat pools low in my belly. The butterflies are in a frenzy. I nod in reply. I'm inept to form complete and coherent sentences. "I need the words, baby."

"Yes," I whisper.

It's the magic word.

It's the skeleton key.

It's the secret password.

He crashes his lips to mine and lifts me, my legs wrapping around him. His lips assault every inch of exposed skin on my neck. He doesn't need his eyes to see, yet he carries me into the kitchen without opening them once and setting me down on his pristine countertop. I shrug off my coat and his hands roam, eager to touch me. I clumsily reach for the zipper of his coat, crying out when the damn thing won't go down. He chuckles and offers an assist.

His white, long-sleeved shirt sticks to his body and outlines every ridge. It looks even better on the floor.

A gasp escapes my lips as I drink in the beauty in front of me. Eight abs, I counted. Pecs with a deep valley in between. His natural olive complexion looks darker against his pale walls.

He carefully slips off my shoes, and my jeans fall into a heap on the floor with his shirt. His hands roam my naked thighs until he hooks his fingers into my panties. With one quick tug, he rips them off me and stuffs them into his pocket.

"You won't be getting those back, Ave." He cockily smirks at me.

"Wear them. Frame them. Throw them away. I don't care." I don't recognize the breathiness of my voice, or the moan he pulls from my lips when he traces my throbbing core. He spreads my legs and laps me up from top to bottom.

Ho. Lee. Shit.

He wraps my squirming legs around his head and slides a finger inside of my soaked folds.

"You're so sweet, Ave." My fingers thread in his hair. I'm on sensory overload, the coolness of his granite countertops against the bare flesh of my ass, Brandon's tongue teasing my clit, his thrusting fingers tapping that sweet spot.

It's enough to undo me.

"Brandon, stop. I'm going to come."

"Come in my mouth. This isn't the end, baby."

I explode like a rocket. My body writhes as my orgasm fills his mouth.

My body shakes when he stands up. Without hesitation, he pulls my blouse over my head. He's the first man besides Gray that has seen my post baby body. I want to cover up, to hide the stretch marks and the small pouch I wish would go away.

His eyes sweep over me, hungrily. As fast as I hold my breath for him to see me this way, it eases my fear when he smiles at me.

"You are absolutely beautiful."

"You are too," my voice cracks.

Shut up. I haven't had sex in six years. You'd cry too.

He kisses me. Gently at first, but then his tongue begs for entrance. I taste myself on his tongue. It's strange, but sexy all at the same time. My clumsy fingers find his belt and undo it. His button and zipper open with ease, and when I tug his jeans and briefs down, his dick springs free.

My eyes widen. He seeps from want, begging me to relieve the ache that builds inside of him. My hand wraps around his length. His breath explodes against the side of my head.

"I've dreamed of this, Ava." He groans as I pick up the pace. "You're perfect." I slide off the counter and kneel to my knees. I take him in my mouth, my tongue raking up his length and swirling at the tip. "Fuck fuck fuck fuck *fuuccccckkkkkkk.*" Brandon always has the upper hand, but right now, the power is all mine. His thighs contract, threatening to explode in my mouth. "Stop. Not yet." He pulls me up to stand, then lifts me by the globes of my ass and carries me into his bedroom.

All that connects us is our lips. My core pulses against his taut abs. He gently lays me flat on the bed, spreads my legs, and sinks inside of me.

My skin tingles at the penetration. He's big, and I haven't had a romp in six years. He's essentially fucking a born-again virgin. Sensing my hesitation, he stops moving and gives me a minute to adjust.

His beautiful eyes that remind me of the rainforest bore into mine. He wears a content smile and kisses my forehead.

"I'm not letting you go," he promises. "I'm here to catch you." He resumes his movements. He slides in and out of me, slowly at first, until I remember what my vagina feels like.

"You feel so good," I whimper.

I'm a mewling mess as his hips piston faster. My hands wrap in the sheets, ripping the fitted sheet off the bed and bunching up at my head.

"Brand, hurry. I'm going to come!" There's barely a warning. No flashing lights or oncoming trains. I explode around him before he's finished.

"Fuck!" He roars, finally finishing. I have an IUD. I'm not worried about him finishing inside of me. He crashes on top of me, kissing my forehead, my nose, my lips. He sighs sleepily with a smile. "You're a siren. *My* siren. I had every intention of going through every ugly scenario with you until we were blue in the face. We weren't going to do *this* tonight."

Giggling, I kiss his lips. "I could die a happy woman if it was my time to go right now, Brand." Sighing, he rolls off me and pulls me into him as his little spoon.

"You're not allowed to die. Not until we do *this* ten thousand more times." I sigh. Not out of frustration or sadness. No. For the first time, I sigh dreamily. Out of contentment.

Damn.

Thirteen

Brandon

Then

Ava Reid is a living work of art. If I could commission a picture of her coming undone and hang it up above my bed, I totally would. And as much as she's art, she's also a bed hog. And the snoring isn't exclusive to being sick.

She's a bed hog of the highest order. Limbs stretch out to all corners of the bed. And I have a king! The other thing I've noticed besides her hogging the bed, she's also a cuddler. Whenever I would move, she would move. She craved my warmth.

She's a fucking space heater.

We made love at least a dozen more times. I've had her on every surface of my bedroom.

My body is still stuck on the sleep schedule I had during the regular season. While she snores away at seven in the morning, I've already been awake for two hours. Seven o'clock is my limit. The sun is already shining through the windows and my stomach is protesting being horizontal any longer.

I gently untangle my limbs from hers. I pull on my trusty pair of gray sweatpants and I creep out to the living room without her moving an inch. My heart is given a jolt when I find Ellen at the island, sipping coffee and leafing through a magazine.

I forgot she was spending the night.

"Good morning."

She glances up at me and grins sleepily.

"Mornin' Brand. Sleep good?"

Perfect. The best sleep I've had in years.

"I did, thanks. You?"

"Mmhm." The magazine is more interesting.

Breakfast is usually healthy shit. A lot of egg whites, spinach, protein, and veggies. I won't bore Ava with my usual fare but opt for something more wholesome. I grab the pancake mix from the pantry and the eggs and bacon from the fridge.

"Hungry?" *Say no.*

"Mm. I could eat. Do you want some help?" She asks politely.

I'm *definitely* not asking her to help make breakfast for Ava, a woman I *know* she hates. I politely decline and prep the bacon to go into the oven. "What do you think about going back to Texas for a week or two? I haven't seen my folks in forever, and I could go with you to visit Bev..." Texas seems like a dream.

I'd want Ava and the kids to join me. I already know how that conversation is going to go. There will be a ton of self-hatred and big, bold, *no's*. My mom hasn't seen the kids since they were little and contrary to what the fox in my bed thinks, my mom still loves her.

"Hm, I don't know. You should go regardless of what I decide, though. Getting out of Chicago would be a nice distraction, don't you think?"

She nods and grins excitedly.

"Are you still going on your drive today?"

Drive?

"What?" She furrows her brows.

"You said you were going on a drive to clear your head today. Want some company?" Right. Because I lied to her and told her I was going to go for a drive so I wouldn't have to hang out with her. *And* so I could drive around Ava's house.

"Oh, right. Yes, I'm still going. No, but thank you for offering. I'm sure you have better shit to do anyway." *Please.*

"I was going to do some shopping while I'm in the city. Then I have to get ready for tomorrow so I can set up the schedule for appointments."

The oven shrieks after ten minutes. I flip the strips of bacon over and pray Ava doesn't walk into this awkwardness. I scramble eggs, pour batter into the pan and within ten more minutes, I have a complete breakfast prepared. Ellen helps herself and talks with her mouth full about Philips asking her to go home with him.

I praise the gods and curse them at the same time when my bedroom door creaks open. She wears the sweater I wore last night, and her bare, long, lean, snow-white legs steal my breath away.

She's a vision. Her makeup from yesterday is smudged, though it looks...edgy. Perfect. Amazing. My clothes were meant to be worn by her. I mean, fair's fair. I took her panties; she could take my sweater. She grins at me until Ellen grabs her attention. She utters an "eek!" and considers turning back into my room.

"Morning, Ave," I call out. Deciding against hiding, she reluctantly walks my way and kisses me on the cheek as she nears.

"Morning, Brand." She glances at Ellen, who only stares daggers back. She needs to cool it. Isn't it exhausting being so angry all the time? "Good morning, Ellen. Did you sleep well?"

Did she hear us?

"Great. Thanks." Ellen's dagger eyes meet mine. "I have to go. See you later." She disappears into the guest room for a moment, then storms out of the apartment fully dressed with a dramatic slamming of the door.

Ava scoffs.

"You sure that's not a thing?"

I chuckle and kiss her lips.

"It's not a thing. Also, I made you breakfast." She glances over to the stove in surprise. I don't think she's had someone make her breakfast in a long time.

"That's sweet of you. Thank you!" I pile up her plate and seat her in the seat next to the one Ellen occupied.

"Last night was fun." She giggles into a forkful of scrambled eggs.

"Which time?"

"All of them." Her cheeks flush. "You don't believe me?"

"They were all fun." She smiles dreamily and sits back in her chair before turning to me.

"What are your plans for today?" She's thoughtful for a moment. She slides my mug of coffee away from me and brings the rim to her lip, slowly sipping.

"The kids aren't home until later. I was just going to veg. Do you have any plans?" Her.

"I plan to hang out with you. We could stay here. We could go for a drive. We could go to your house…" Just don't shut me out.

"Let's stay here. I have to leave by three, so I can be home in time for the kids."

We eat our breakfast slowly as she wakes up. She helps me with the breakfast dishes, but somewhere in between washing the dishes and placing them in the dishwasher, we lose the rest of our clothes. She's insatiable, and I'm not complaining.

The sultry tones of Led Zeppelin serenade us in the shower. My lady is a classic rock kind of gal. She sings—*horribly*—along with ZZ Top and Eric Clapton. My bodywash smells like it belongs on her skin. My shampoo and conditioner don't smell like the mangos her hair always smells like, but it does the job.

The shower spray hangs in her lashes. Her smile is contagious. And the way she relaxes into me while I lather her hair in shampoo is porn worthy.

"Are you enjoying yourself, Ave?"

"Very much so. Why would I ever wash my hair again when I have you to do it for me?" I'd wash her hair any time. I rinse my hands and they find their place on the globes of her ass. She leans back, not breaking our connection, and allows the water to wash away the suds.

When was the last time she allowed herself to feel this free?

"There has probably been one other time I felt like...this. It was shortly after Ethan was born before everything went to shit." She grins and pulls herself back into me. Her hands skim over my arms and squeeze.

"What do you feel like?" She shrugs.

"I don't know how to describe it. I just know that I'm happy, and I'm stoked we're doing this."

Chuckling, I turn her around and work the conditioner into her hair. "Will you tell Tess?"

"Yeah, probably. They know we left together. And I think it might be a good idea if we each had a person who knows." Turning again, she lets the shower spray wash the conditioner out.

"And what about the kids?"

It was one of the things I couldn't stop thinking about last night. Ethan will murder me, I'm sure of it. His job is to protect his mom and I'm breaking a shit ton of rules by being with her without talking to him first.

I'm more scared of him than I am of Gray, and I'm not fucking ashamed of that.

"I can't keep that secret from them. It wouldn't be fair."

"So maybe we tell them over dinner. I could come over next weekend. You won't be doing this alone, Ave. I'm here *with* you every step of the way." Her smile falters when she looks at me.

"And the end date?"

Sooner rather than later.

"Maybe it's something we keep checking in with each other. I'm not going to set a date and expect you to conform." I cradle her head in my hands. Her eyes shine with emotion like I just made her the happiest woman in the world. "I'm not ashamed to be with you, Ava. Gray shouldn't be a part of the equation. I want to make you happy because you make *me* happy." Her lips quirk into a smile.

"You make me happy," she replies quietly. "Brand?"

"Hmm?"

"Take me to bed."

Fourteen

Ava

"So that was it? He offers to keep the relationship a secret and you just dove in headfirst?" Sunny asks in disbelief.

I know. I sound so fucking desperate, yet here I am.

"I came to the party knowing he'd be there. I didn't want us going separate ways when I'd finally found someone who didn't care about the weight my name held. I wouldn't have said yes if there wasn't some condition of discretion. I was still trying to revive my career."

"Okay...so you keep the relationship a secret. How is it possible you weren't caught?"

"I've hidden relationships my entire career. Ben and I didn't go public for a few weeks, Gray and I went a whole year of keeping it between us. That part was easy. We were homebodies anyway. Not much changed except Brandon was a lot more affectionate."

"We were aware of the cameras. It wasn't like we could go out to dinner without being noticed. If we were caught together *once*, it would've been on the front page of every tabloid," I reason.

Sunny reshuffles her note cards. Gray is still not here.

"We're going to take a short break. When we return, we will continue to dissect the relationship between Ava Reid and her brother-in-law, Brandon Wentworth."

I wish they would stop calling him that. He was my former brother-in-law, if anything. We're given the all-clear. I leave the studio and reach for my phone. Ethan's name flashes on the screen.

"Mom, just leave the interview. He's an asshole and isn't worth it." I love my sweet boy. I sweep into my dressing room and close the door.

"Go to class, baby. I can't leave the interview, and I would *love* not to get any calls from school that you're skipping class."

He laughs. "Are you doing all right? Maybe I can get Uncle Jordan to pick me up and bring me to the studio? I can keep you company..."

"No, but thank you for the offer. Stay in school. It's your only job, E. Stay in school, learn something. I'll see you when you get home from school." We hang up, and I sink into the chair in front of the mirror. I try Gray again, but only get voicemail. I leave another pleading message for him to come back so I can profusely apologize.

I don't bother looking through social media. It's a battlefield I'm not ready to cross just yet. There's a light knock on the door, and Tess materializes inside, locking us in. She sits on the chair behind me and smiles at me through the mirror.

"How are you doing, Gorgeous?"

"I'm hanging in there. Have you heard from Gray?" She shakes her head sadly.

"I'm blacklisted from upstairs. I'm not allowed up and everyone's on a gag order not to talk to me. *But* I did check in with the front gate and they said he hasn't left. So, he's here."

Groaning, I rake my hand through my hair, messing up the curls Juanita spent so much time perfecting.

"I can't believe this is happening. He must be so angry."

"I'm sure he's hurt, but he's changed. Gray always had the potential to be the man you needed him to be, even though it's not romantic. You guys have been through so much together. This is just a speedbump."

God, I hope so. The last six years have been excruciating. He was my rock. He finally became a parent.

I sigh.

"That was a lot you uncovered just now. You didn't tell me some of that," Tess soothes.

"He made me fall in love with him." She's out of her seat before the first tear falls. She wraps her arms around me. "I wanted to be with him, so I made it happen. But why didn't I see the signs? They were all right there in front of me..."

"Babe..." She sighs. "You're doing amazing. I would've broken down in the beginning if this were happening to me. You are so strong. I'm so incredibly proud of you."

I stare at the sister to my soul through the mirror. We're opposites in every single way. She's loud, where I prefer to be quiet. Her jet-black hair is a nice contrast to my honey-colored locks. She's outspoken, where I'm a stark observer.

"Is there still room for me in the throuple?" She giggles in my ear and kisses my temple.

"You're the only one we'd ever consider. There's always room for you in our marriage, babycakes."

We're told I need to get back to the stage. I pull on any strand of courage I can muster. Tess and I walk hand in hand back to the stage. When the bright lights blind us, I notice a new body next to Jane. She towers over Jane by at least five inches. She talks fast and concisely. She speaks a language Jane knows fluently.

Her platinum blonde hair is messy and piled on the top of her head like she's just rolled out of bed. When she feels our presence, she turns ever so slightly to reveal the massive baby bump.

Kayla.

She doesn't smile, but she doesn't look angry to see me, either. She nods to me and then turns her attention back to Jane. I join Brandon on the sofa. He seems more resigned. He watches his ex-wife with worry. I wonder how far along she is. At least nine months? She looks like she's ready to pop.

"I thought she didn't want children," I offer softly.

He shrugs. "Cassie makes her happy. When you find your *someone,* your preconceived notions are nonexistent at that point. They're having a boy, by the way." My heart squeezes. I thought he was my *someone.* I was horribly, horribly wrong.

"She looks great. I'm glad she's happy." Jealous of her, but happy, nonetheless. Sunny sits back down, ignoring us completely.

"How did you get that picture?" I ask her. She keeps her eyes on her notes. She doesn't have much of a poker face, I've noticed. So, she does what any woman would do when she's uncomfortable: she distracts herself with something else.

"We got it from an anonymous source," she replies matter-of-factly.

"Who was it? This interview is *so* unsanctioned. I know for a fact this line of questioning was not on the list of questions that was given to my publicist. I have a right to know where you got this information." Her hands shake.

"Look, Ms. Reid, I can't give you that information. Your people have already got in touch with our legal team. I can tell you for sure that your legal team is involved. We're moving ahead with the interview, but I cannot give up the source."

Un-fucking-believable.

We *have* to go through with the interview. Too much shit has been uncovered without and context or lack of information.

I hope Gray is okay. I hope this doesn't ruin the friendly relationship we've forged over the years. We've *finally* got life on track.

"Quiet on the set!"

My stomach somersaults at what comes next. My babies were never supposed to be a part of this. And now, they're going to be put front and center. It's part of the story, after all.

"And we're back! When we left, we talked about the relationship starting in secrecy. You were going to tell your kids, but you weren't going to tell Grayson. Why is that?"

"He wouldn't have taken it well," I offer softly. Obviously, he isn't here. Though, I don't blame him. This is a shitty way of finding out. "I was scared he'd leak it to the press and paint it in a way that made me look like I was dating his brother out of spite."

"Were you?" She challenges.

"Absolutely not. It was real." I close my eyes in frustration. "It was real for me, anyway."

Brandon scoffs.

"Yeah, right," he mutters.

"What happened next?"

"Dinner. It always starts with dinner." I reply softly.

Fifteen

Brandon

Then

It has taken every morsel of willpower for me not to go over to her house every single night this week. The best I could get was phone calls every night when the kids went to bed. I'm genuinely concerned with how tonight is going to go.

I suspect Alice will be the one to be the most accepting of this change. She's my little best friend, my partner in crime. I would be lying if I said I wasn't worried about Ethan. Truth be told, I'm *terrified.* You read that right. Brandon Wentworth, thirty-three years old, two sixty-seven, is terrified of an eight-year-old.

We planned every detail. Ava is making dinner. We were going to introduce this as gently as possible. She told me not to dress up even though I want to make a good first impression *on an eight-year-old.* So, I go with a long-sleeved shirt and jeans. I bring a football along just in case Ethan wants to play. Or, if he decides to beat the shit out of me, I can throw it at him to give me a head start to run.

I'm being ridiculous.

I knock on the door with a football in one hand and a bouquet of pink roses in the other hand. The kids call for their mother. This time, there is no tripping over boxes and muffled curses. Instead, I'm greeted by a blonde beauty wearing a simple cotton black dress and a wide smile. She's a sight for sore eyes, especially since I haven't seen her in a week.

"Hey, Brand. Come on in." She steps aside and allows me into the warmth of her treehouse. The kids race over in excitement. I toss the football over to Ethan and grin at Alice.

"Are those pretty flowers for me?" Alice asks. She's her mother's twin, except for Gray's wild imagination.

"They are for you *and* your mom." I hand the bouquet over to Ava, who blushes instantly, and I scoop up Alice in my arms. She giggles into my neck and wraps me in a tight hug.

"I missed you, Uncle Brand." I missed her. It's weird being around them for so long and then missing an objectively long chunk of time. I swear Ethan's grown another inch or two.

"Thanks, Brand. They're beautiful." She turns to Ethan. "Maybe you can ask Uncle Brand if he'd like something to drink?" Ethan smirks and tosses the football on the couch.

"We have water, pop, or milk." His mischievous smile dares me to ask him for a beer.

"Water would be great. Thanks, buddy." He disappears into the kitchen while I set Alice on the floor. Without warning, Ava closes the distance between us and wraps her arms around me, her head resting on my chest.

The mango scent of her hair tickles my nose. I missed her.

Ethan returns with a glass of water. "Water was a good choice. It's best you hydrate now."

Was that a threat? I'm pretty sure that was a threat. I ruffle his hair.

"Thanks, buddy. Ave, can I help with anything?"

"Sure. I could use some help dressing the salad." She turns to the kids. "Go put something on the TV. I'll call you when dinner is ready." They don't need to be told twice. They race each other to the couch. Ethan wins the remote, but once Alice starts pouting, he hands the remote over with a huff.

Ava winks at me and motions for me to follow her. Stepping into the kitchen, I eye the bowl of *dressed* salad on the counter. She grabs my wrist and pulls me into the pantry. She kisses me hurriedly and grins when she has to wipe off some of her lipstick that lingers on my lips.

"I missed you, Brand."

"I missed you too, baby." I kiss her again. This might be our last if Ethan doesn't kill me tonight.

"Come on, they're going to come looking for us if they don't hear us talking in the kitchen." She winks and steps out. I wish I could be confident like she is. I help her set the table. I've been around long enough which kid likes which plate and their preferred dinner drinks. She pulls a lasagna out of the oven when the timer goes off and sets it on the stove to sit for a minute.

We call the kids into the dining room and sit at the kitchen table like we've been doing this for years. We each take a kid's plate and place a slice of piping hot lasagna and salad. We don't eat it because it's good for us, we eat it to set a good example.

Ava and I are seated next to each other. We sit touching from shoulder to ankle. I don't dare move because I like feeling her body against mine.

"I never got to ask you guys. How were the Dells? Did you have fun?" The mood immediately dampens. Ethan's good mood sours.

"Ethan got in trouble with Lucy," Alice explains.

"Who's Lucy?"

"Dad's girlfriend." I glance over to Ava, who shrugs.

"I didn't think he was seeing anyone," I reply glumly.

"I didn't either. It wasn't discussed with me when they left." She frowns. "There was an incident...Gray said Lucy was talking to Ethan, and he ignored her." Ethan rolls his eyes and groans.

"I ignored her because she was saying mean things about you. She said I was too much like you, so I stopped listening to her. I'm not sorry about it."

"I'm getting two very different stories. But regardless, we respect adults, correct?" He nods slowly but doesn't believe it whatsoever.

Where was Gray throughout all of this?

I change the subject. This is supposed to be a good night. We're celebrating the news and inviting in a good thing. "What did you learn at school this week?" I ask.

"Multiplication tables," Ethan announces. "I'm trying to win mathematician of the class."

"Oh? What's that?" Ava asks.

"Basically, every Friday we get a test with fifty questions on it. We have five minutes to complete as many problems as we can before time runs out. Whoever gets the most correct answers, wins mathematician of the class."

"Hmm. Interesting. Tell me more," I encourage him.

Ethan shrugs and stuffs salad into his mouth.

"If we win, we get to have lunch with the teacher."

Bingo.

"That's the prize? You get to eat lunch with your teacher?" Ava asks in disbelief.

"Yeah. While the rest of the class eats lunch in the cafeteria, I get to go back in the classroom and eat with the teacher." Oh my god.

Ava arches an eyebrow and sets her fork down. "Why do you want to eat alone with Ms. Collins?"

His cheeks flush. Much like his mother, he hides his true feelings.

"She's nice to me, okay? She says I'm smart!" On a huff, Ava resumes eating.

"I had a crush on the office assistant in my elementary school when I was your age." His eyes widen. "I used to pick the wildflowers behind Nana's house and bring them in to her every day."

Ethan moves forward and slightly lowers his voice. "Did that work?"

"Oh my god, that's enough of that," Ava groans.

I chuckle.

"No, it didn't. She was married."

"Damn," Ethan grumbles.

"Ethan!" I love this kid. He is my favorite person on the planet.

"What about you, Miss Alice? What have you learned at school this week?"

"We made the solar system using recycled materials. I got to paint Mars!" Her lasagna is half gone, but her salad remains untouched.

"That's awesome, gorgeous! What do you know about Mars?" She's practically standing up in her seat. The kid vibrates with excitement and word vomit.

"We send rovers to collect samples and rocks and stuff. Ethan, maybe you can buy Ms. Collins a rock from Mars with the lunch money you've been saving."

Oh shit.

Ethan sinks in his seat, glares at Alice, and avoids Ava's glare.

"What do you mean with the lunch money you've been saving?" *Now* is the time Alice keeps her mouth shut. Nobody talks. I reach for her hand under the table for comfort, but she slaps me away.

"I've been giving you money for lunch, and you've been socking it away? For what? You haven't been eating at school?"

"Mom, relax." Oh, no, buddy! Ava's eyes flare.

"Start talking."

He sighs dramatically.

"I haven't been going hungry at school. I've been making my lunch every morning and putting it in my backpack."

"How much money have you saved?" Ava demands.

He pushes the folds of the lasagna around, avoiding his mother's gaze.

"Like, twenty dollars." She groans.

"Why were you saving it?"

He refuses to answer that one. I mean, it's obvious. Note to self: Don't tell secrets to Alice. She will dime you out no matter what.

"Perfect. That will cover the groceries you've been using." He grumbles and threatens Alice under his breath. "Baby, I love you so much."

Ethan gets embarrassed so easily.

"I love you, Mom."

"You will make someone incredibly happy one day. Someone *your own age.* I'm supposed to be the love of your life forever."

He screws up his face like he just sucked on a lemon. He's not touching that statement with a ten-foot pole. That's smart.

The kids finish their dinner. Alice monopolizes the conversation by telling us about her dance recital and some kid named Mitchell in her class that she *does not* have a crush on.

What I'm gathering here is that Alice is the life of the party. She'll give us a run for our money when she hits those teenage years.

We clear the table and pass out dessert plates. Ava brings out a chocolate cream pie and sets it on the table. The kids pick up on something immediately when she sits down and doesn't make a move for the knife.

"So, we wanted to talk to you guys about something..." Ethan watches his mom curiously, then snaps his eyes to me. He holds my gaze and narrows his eyes. "Do you remember when Daddy and I were getting divorced, and we talked about the different kinds of families?" I catch Alice nodding in my peripherals, but I don't break my connection to Ethan. He's sensing the danger. I just need to prove I'm not a threat.

"Yeah..." Alice drawls with fear.

"Well, you see, when parents divorce, they sometimes find other people to be happy with. Like dad is with Lucy now and I'm..." Ethan's eyes leave mine and narrow at his mother's. Ava can't get the words out. She licks her lips nervously. "Listen, I..."

"I care about your mom," I blurt. Alice squeals in delight, where Ethan looks at me like I just stole the twenty dollars he was saving for his teacher. "I think your mom is smart and beautiful. I want to kiss her sometimes if that's all right with you."

Alice talks a mile a minute, but I can't focus on her right now. I'm busy trying to telepathically comfort my nephew.

"Do you guys have any questions?" Ava asks nervously. "Ethan? Do you have any questions?"

"I want to talk to Uncle Brand." Oh god. "Alone."

"No, I think it's best if we all talk about this together," Ava states, trying to get the conversation back on topic.

"Would you like to talk outside?" I ask.

He nods once and stands up.

"No, I don't like this. We're going to talk this out. The four of us." Ava tries to intervene, but he's never going to respect *this* if he doesn't get his two cents in. Especially not when he could potentially hurt his mother.

Ethan ignores her and grabs his coat off the coat rack.

"I promise I'll be respectful, Mom. I won't even punch him that hard."

"Absolutely not," she snaps. She turns to me. "Brandon, no. I don't like this."

"His beef is with me, Ave, not you. We'll talk outside. We won't be long, I promise."

"You said you wouldn't make me give up my control," she snaps. I kiss her temple in comfort.

"It's going to be okay. I'm not making you give up your control. He wants to talk to me man to man."

Her eyes swim with tears.

"You have a five-minute limit, Ethan. Not a second more. Do you understand?" Ethan nods and flicks the deck lights on. I squeeze her hand in reassurance. I step out onto the deck into the frigid air, closing the door behind me. He's already trotting down the steps. I follow him closely. He crosses the yard and sits in Ava's seat next to the fire pit.

I follow his lead, but I don't dare speak the first word. This is his show. I'm following his lead.

"Are you going to make her cry?" His question catches me off guard. I'm expecting accusations and heated words.

"No, buddy. I'm not going to intentionally make her cry."

He nods seriously and stares at me sternly.

"Dad wasn't nice to her. He doesn't see what she does. He doesn't appreciate her. He...he dated other women."

"I know. I saw what he did to her. I'm not the same, Ethan. Your dad is my brother, but we're nothing alike."

"How do I know that?" I feel like I'm talking to a teenager. I hate Gray for making a man out of Ethan at such a young age. I hate him for ghosting them like this.

"There's this unspoken rule in this society that tells us we have to get married, and then have kids. Everything else should fall together after that." He's *eight!* "Anyway, I think with your dad...he tried to live up to that rule. He tried to do the right thing, but his judgment was cloudy. He loved your mom, but not enough to be with her forever."

I don't want to talk shit about his dad to him. Ethan is beyond his years, he understands more than he lets on.

"And you want to be with her forever?"

Yes.

"I think your mom is my *someone*. I want to make her happy. You, Alice, your mom...you're a package deal. I love you and Alice so much, E. I want to make you happy too." He glances up towards the house. Ava watches us from the window in genuine terror.

I don't think I've ever seen Ethan cry. With the exception of when he was a baby, he hasn't cried in my presence. Yet when he looks up at me after my proclamations of being a family—a real one, his eyes swim with tears.

"You have to protect her heart, Uncle Brand. Dad didn't. *I've* been the one protecting her heart. You have to be better than him. You have to promise to be better than him." A sob rips through him, tearing my soul to shreds. I crouch on the ground and open my arms to hug him.

"I'll protect her heart, Ethan, I promise." Ethan stands and falls into my arms. He sobs into my neck, squeezing my heart so tight it makes me sick. "I don't care what other people say. It's okay to cry. I'll take care of her, I promise. I'll protect you and Alice."

A watery, "Okay," is the only relief of the night. My poor buddy. He lets go of me and wipes his eyes.

"Do you need a minute?" He shakes his head.

"Let's go back inside. She'll get mad at us if we stay here any longer." We stand up and brush the dirt off our knees. Ava waits for us on the deck, barefoot. As we ascend the stairs, Ethan grins and pulls his mom into a hug.

"I love you, Mom." Her sad eyes warm.

"I love you, baby. More than you could ever know." We step inside, back into the warmth. The chocolate pie is cut, and Alice is already done with her first slice. Her mouth is covered in chocolate and whipped cream.

"Okay. Now. Does anybody have questions?" Ava asks.

"Will you be our dad now?" Alice asks.

I choke on my saliva and Alice's bold questions.

"No, sweetheart. I'm still your uncle." Her face falls slightly but is excited about the prospect of what this new relationship means for us all.

"Are you going to tell dad?" Ethan asks warily. I reach for Ava's hand on the table.

"No, not right away. Uncle Brand and I are still trying to get to know each other a little better before we tell dad."

"Yeah, that's a good idea. I won't tell him." He zones out, mentally preparing himself of what's to come.

"I won't tell him either," Alice announces.

"Look guys, this is a big secret to keep, and I know it isn't fair to ask you to keep it. If you want to tell your dad, that is totally fine." Alice grimaces.

"He'd have to actually *talk to me* for me to tell him." Yikes.

The questions have died down, so I take the opportunity to clear the table and start on the dishes. I have no doubt Ava worried about this all day, not to mention cleaning the house from top to bottom. The least I can do is do the dishes so she can go to bed at a decent hour.

She sweeps into the kitchen and wraps her arms around my torso. Alice and Ethan cuddle up on the couch.

"That went well."

I grin and steal a kiss from her.

"It did. I was certain Ethan was going to beat the piss out of me outside."

She groans and shrinks her arms back. She hops up onto the counter next to the sink and rests her head against the cabinet.

"What did he say out there?"

Bro code. Snitches get stitches.

"That's confidential information, baby." I zip my lips and throw away the key. She rolls her eyes and glances into the dishwater.

"You know...this is sexy."

"Me doing your dishes does it for you? Maybe I should buy a webcam, start charging by the dish."

"Oh brother. Don't quit your day job to become a comedian, Brand."

I chuckle and place another dish into the dishwasher. "You laugh, but there are women all over the world who have to do their own dishes on top of having full-time jobs and being mothers. This is sexy. A man who *wants* to take care of his woman is sexy."

I grin and step in between her legs.

"I'm going to take care of you, Ave. Doing the dishes is part of it. Now. Go hang out with your kids so I can finish up." She loops her arms around my neck and presses me against her lips. My hands are damp and soapy, so I avoid touching her dress, though I yearn to hold her hips.

I swallow her sigh and pull away slowly. "Fine, you win. Don't take long. Ethan wants to play football with you."

It takes me ten minutes for me to finish up. Ethan helps me track down the dish detergent. I run the dishwasher, wipe down the counters and table, and wrap up the rest of the lasagna and place it back in the refrigerator.

The four of us bundle up in our winter clothes and head out to the backyard. Ava doesn't play, though she watches from the deck. Ethan and Alice team up and tire me out within fifteen minutes. My joints and muscles are warmed up and ready for the next tackle.

Alice hasn't grown into her long limbs yet, so she's clumsy. Ethan, on the other hand, is solid. It hurts when he tackles me. They call me old at least forty times before our game is over. Ava calls us inside and puts on a movie that knocks the kids out in the first ten minutes.

She grins mischievously and motions for me to follow her upstairs. I slip my shoes off, so my footsteps don't echo off the spiral staircase.

Ava's room is not what I imagined for her. She has a modest king-sized bed in sheets that I imagine are a million-thread count. Her furniture matches and is all painted distressed white. She pulls me into bed with her and rests her head on my shoulder.

"I want you to spend the night," she starts softly, but it wouldn't be a good idea. Not yet anyway.

"We'll work up to it. I don't want to make them uncomfortable." She sighs against me.

"Thank you...you know. For keeping this between us for a little bit. I know it's not what you wanted, but you have no idea what it means to me." My hand splays out on her lower back. Her voice is shaky with emotion. That's how I know I'm doing the right thing. She isn't embarrassed by me, but she's cautious about how it will affect the kids.

"Don't thank me for that, Ave. We're doing what's best for us right now." We'll figure the rest out later.

"You were right about one thing," she yawns.

"Yeah? What's that?"

"I'm falling for you." I kiss her forehead.

"Me too, Ave."

Sixteen

Ava

For the next month and a half, Brandon is a regular at our house. He's home for dinner every night and helps with homework. If there's enough time, they'll play outside. Over the weekend, he does my yard work even though I insist I've hired a company that does this all for me.

Alice is his shadow. If he's pulling weeds, she's right there next to him wearing my garden gloves and a ballcap. If he's playing football with Ethan, she's right there with him, tackling him until he falls to the ground.

This is what I was hoping for: a seamless transition. Nobody's hurt, nobody feels neglected. Everything is as it should be.

During the day, Brandon works on his charity, The Live Oaks Foundation, and keeps his workout schedule so he doesn't have to work double-time when the preseason starts up. While the kids are at school, I blitz auditions. I must have read for forty directors in the last month. I don't know if any of them will pan out, but I'm cautiously optimistic.

One face I see almost everywhere I go is Ellen. She calls Brandon multiple times a day and shows up at his house unannounced at weird times. Gray is back in Australia which has made our stays in Brand's apartment next to nothing.

I miss him when he isn't around. We spend hours on the phone when the kids go to bed. Sometimes when I'm lucky, he'll stay over an extra hour or two before he reluctantly walks out my front door.

Today has been the day I've been dreading since I found the note from Alice's teacher in her backpack last week. They want a conference. I tried to get Gray to attend via video conference, but *of course,* he can't. I can't rely on the guy to wipe his own ass if I left him to his own devices, let alone attend a conference for his child.

Alice is the one I always have to worry about. She's boisterous and talks a mile a minute. She has trouble focusing.

That's what they said. *"Alice is a bright girl. She is friendly and compassionate, but she is also a distraction to the class. She talks to everyone around her. She hasn't been completing her classwork. She loves making people laugh, which I'm sure will suit her later on in life, but as of right now she's the class clown. Can I ask where Mr. Wentworth is? Will he be joining us today? Please look at this disturbing journal entry Alice wrote about her father..."*

It went like that.

Gray died a fiery death in a train wreck. There were no survivors. You know, part of me is impressed that her mind can imagine something so complex and...riveting.

I'm a terrible mom.

But things could be worse. I could be a horrible and neglectful father.

Speaking of...

I don't give a rat's ass what time it is in Australia. I call him. The phone rings and rings until I get voicemail, but that doesn't perturb me. I call again. This time, he picks up on the second ring.

He's learning!

"Hi Ava," he grumbles.

Great. Maybe he's too tired to argue with me.

"Got a minute? I just got out of Alice's conference with her teacher." He moans and groans and eventually shuffles out of bed to somewhere else.

"Fine. Make it quick."

"She's not taking school seriously. She's been labeled the class clown and is distracting the rest of the class."

"I wasn't a great student either. I don't think it's fair to hold that against her." And *this* is why I'm the primary parent.

"We can't let her get away with this, Gray. She's in first grade and already making terrible choices. She wrote a story about you, by the way. You die in a train wreck." I'm met with a painful silence. Maybe this will be the wake-up call he desperately needs to rejoin the land of co-parenting.

"What?"

"You were on a train with Lucy. There was a bomb in your suitcase, and it went off. There were no survivors on the train." My girl is going to be a writer one day. Mark my words.

"She's really mad about the Dells, huh?"

"They both are."

"He was outright ignoring her when she was talking to him, Ava. I'm not sorry for delegating the discipline to Lucy. I won't apologize for that."

"Firstly, Lucy isn't his parent. She shouldn't have any part in discipline. Secondly, I'm getting two different stories, but we're not talking about Ethan right now. Alice has an obvious need for you to be around, Gray. She barely talks about you. She dreads having to go to your house. She plotted your demise on a school assignment!"

"That's because you poison her against me!"

"Don't you dare start that bullshit with me. I am nothing but encouraging when it comes to you, not that you fucking deserve it. She needs more than just the one-minute slice of time you give her when you video call. She needs more than you picking her up from our house and sitting her in front of the TV and leaving her like that the whole weekend. This is a cry for help. I need you to do your job as a co-parent and help me out!"

He roars and throws something on his end. Whatever it is, it is. I can hear it when I pull the phone away from my ear.

"Where do you get off with your self-righteous, holier than thou attitude, huh? I'm working my ass off! You like the child support and alimony I pay to you every month? You force me into these situations!"

"Are you fucking serious!? The child support is for your *children,* asswipe! And the alimony was put in place because you couldn't wait to run your mouth how I trapped you in a marriage you didn't want! You ruined my career and here you are thinking you're doing *me* a favor! Fuck you, Gray! If you don't want to claim your fatherhood, that's fine with me. I can make the change!"

"It's been a while since you got laid, hasn't it?" It was actually last night, jerk. "I swear to god you *love* to be a bitch. Do you like it when I yell at you, Ava? Does that do it for you? Do you need me to hire an escort so you can get lucky tonight?"

And that's enough of that.

I hang up as I scream my frustration out. The administration of the kids' school should get a kick out of the security footage of me yelling into my phone.

Here's my advice: don't have children with a man who has offered to purchase the services of an escort on more than one occasion.

What did I ever *see* in him?

I leave the school parking lot in a huff. It would be my pleasure if I never had to set eyes on Grayson Wentworth ever again. I threaten him to take full custody, but we both know I won't ever follow through with it. It's not good for the kids. As much as he's a pain in the ass, he loves his kids.

Probably.

My phone rings off the hook for the next hour. Brandon continues to text me to ask me how the conference went, and Ben blows up my phone like we're still dating. I'm lying in my bed when I finally give up.

"Hi, Ben."

"God finally! Have you seen the news?" Nope. And I don't plan on turning my TV on either.

"No. What's going on?"

"You're trending. Are you really threatening to take full custody of the kids?" Wow. He stooped to that level.

"No! And he knows that. It's not true. We got into a stupid fight and he's just throwing a tantrum." Because he's a child.

"You need to get on this, babe. Quick." I wish he'd stop calling me that. We haven't been together in eons.

"Is that why you called? You wanted to throw my crappy life in my face?" He chuckles nervously.

"No, jerk. I was calling to see if you wanted to catch up. But since you're in *that* mood, I don't want to now."

"Is that so? Well, then, Mr. Crawford. It's been a pleasure."

"Wait! No! I was kidding." Whomp, there it is. "You still there?"

"I'm here. What's up?"

"I bagged a girl. Her name's Camille. We met in France last year." *Of course* they did. "Anyway, she's moving here in a few months, and I'd love it if you would meet her."

Pass.

"Sure thing. Name a time and a place and I promise to be there."

He sighs. "There's also another reason why I was calling." There always is.

"Okay…"

"So you know that director, Jason Evans?" I already don't like where this is going. "He has been spreading some rumors that you're desperate for work. Is that true? Can I help you in any way?"

I shouldn't have gotten out of bed today. When my alarm went off, I should've thrown it against the wall and buried my face in my pillow. Instead, I got out of bed, *like a responsible adult,* and got my kids ready for school.

"I'm fine, Ben. But thanks for telling me. I read for a part for him, and he turned me down. I know he's chummy with Gray, so they're probably in cahoots. Nothing my PR team can't fix." I cover myself in my blankets. I have four hours before I have to get the kids, and as soon as I can get Ben off the phone, I'm going back to bed.

"I didn't call you to be a Debbie Downer, but there's talk about you almost everywhere. Gray's got his hooks in deep."

That tracks.

"I guess. Hey, it's been nice catching up with you, but I need to go. I'll talk to you later, Ben." I hang up before he can say anything else.

I can't bring myself to text Brandon back. He'll be so disappointed that Alice isn't doing well in school. He'll want to kill Gray for hurting her, and I just don't have the energy to keep the peace.

To seal in this crappy day, my agent, Nick, calls right after I hang up with Ben. I'm not opening this can of worms. I send it to voicemail and pray he has something good to give me when I wake up.

My bed sinks and a pair of strong arms wrap around my waist. He kisses my exposed shoulder and becomes my big spoon. His presence is a welcome one.

"You had me worried, Ave. You didn't answer any of my texts."

"I'm sorry. I had a shitty day, so I put myself back to bed."

His breath feathers the back of my neck, and his hand strokes my arm.

"Did her conference go that bad?"

I frown as a fresh wave of tears takes over me.

"That's part of it. The conference went okay. It's sort of what we expected. She's a good kid but loves to talk, but it turns into a distraction for the class. She isn't doing her classwork, but her tests and homework are perfect." I sigh. "Then she wrote a journal entry that involved Gray dying in a train wreck. So of course, I called him to talk about it and it went *fucking* spectacular." I sob into my pillow.

I refuse to let Brandon see me like this. I'm an ugly crier. Right now, I have a time-sensitive voicemail from my agent that I *know* will be terrible news and I just can't take it right now. I'm tired of being the strong one. It's somebody else's turn.

"He died in a train wreck?"

"Via bomb in his suitcase. Oh, and Lucy was with him. There were no survivors."

He chuckles, though it's no laughing matter.

"Where does she come up with that shit?" Beats the hell out of me!

"I don't know. But it's a concern with her teacher. At what point do I consult a child psychologist?" I feel him shrug next to me. His fingertips feather my arm, making my eyes droop.

"I don't think it would hurt. Honestly, the shrink could probably back you up if this ends up going to court." I close my eyes in frustration. I forgot about the news. And I also forgot to get in touch with my PR team. The media must be having a field day with no statement from the queen bitch herself. "Were you really thinking about suing for full custody?"

"No. This is Gray exercising his power over me. We threaten each other with it all the time but we never mean it. This time he just struck a nerve and I got mean." He sighs against my neck.

"You can't let him get away with this. This is damaging." Tell me something I *don't* know. What am I supposed to hit him back with, "No I didn't?"

"My PR team is on it." I quickly grab my phone and text Megan to come up with a statement. They're on it *now*.

My phone lights up with a slew of notifications. Missed phone calls, at least three dozen texts that have gone unanswered, seven voicemails from Nick. *Ugh.*

If I didn't love acting so much, I'd go off the grid. I'd move the family out to some little town in Texas and delete social media and the world would never hear from me again.

I tempt fate. No, I straight up set fate on fire when I put Nick's first message on speaker.

"Ava, call me ASAP."

"Ava. None of the parts you read for panned out. We need to take a step back. Let's talk about some pilots for some networks to get you back onto people's screens."

"Ava? I know you're ignoring me! Answer the phone!"

"What's going on with Gray? Why are you threatening to sue him for full custody of the kids? Your career can't take that hit, Ava! You're coming off as spiteful!"

"Okay, look. I'm sorry. Please stop ignoring me. Call me about the pilots."

"Jason Evans is starting rumors about you now. We need to get ahead of this."

"I'm calling the PR team."

At least he got to the PR team before I did. Brandon swipes my phone out of my hand and tucks it under his body.

"Go back to bed, baby. Put this shitty day behind you."

"What time is it? I have to go get the kids."

"You still have some time. Just relax." What a concept. I would *love* to relax, but my whole life is pulling at the seams. I hug my pillow close to my chest and allow my eyes to droop.

Nick wants me to read for television pilots. There's nothing wrong with TV. That's where I got my start, where I learned to hone my craft and find the courage to challenge myself with movie roles. I don't want to take a step back. I've worked damn hard to get where I am.

Besides, we made a life here. My kids love their friends, their school...taking a pilot would mean moving to California.

Just once I would love it for life to go my way.

"What if I can't make a comeback? What do I do then?"

"There's no point playing the 'what-if' game, baby. You're strong. You're resilient. You have a ton of people in your corner to back you up against Gray's claims. You're an amazing actress and you have the Oscars to back it up. You don't have a choice *but* to act. It's the fabric of your being, your passion in life. Set Hollywood on fire." I fight my smile. He's the perfect hype man. Yet, I have this nagging feeling in the pit of my stomach that errs caution.

I once fell in love with a Wentworth. He married me, impregnated me, and humiliated me, all under the guise of being the perfect man.

At three o'clock, Brandon decides to hold down the fort so I can pick up the kids. I call and fight with Nick while I'm in the car line. He thinks I'm being irrational for not wanting to do pilots because I don't want to move to California. When he realized he wasn't going to get his way, he ended the call on a huff and a "You're tanking your own career."

The kids are oddly quiet. Ethan watches the world outside his window. Alice, on the other hand, knows what today was. I catch her every now and then, watching me carefully through the rearview mirror.

I stop by McDonald's for milkshakes, mostly because I need a reward for getting out of bed this morning. When we pull up into the driveway, we find Brandon waiting for us at the top of the stairs. Ethan takes off in a run and a grin that stretches ear to ear. Alice takes her sweet time. She collects her backpack and milkshake and walks her green mile.

I wish I could be the fun parent. I don't enjoy doling out punishments or being the bad cop. That's not fair. Brandon and Ethan chatter away excitedly when we finally make our way inside.

Ethan shrugs off his backpack and races out the back door with Brandon hot on his heels with the football.

Alice grimaces and trudges to the kitchen table. Time to be an adult. I sit across from her and offer a hesitant smile. I can be nice. She's six. *Remember that! She's six!*

"Baby, what's going on at school?" She shrugs half-heartedly and sinks deeper into the seat. "You teacher was saying that you aren't completing your classwork. What's up with that?"

She's silent, and she shrugs her shoulders. Again. It's this unspoken rule that as a kid if you shrug your shoulders, you don't have to answer the question. Look kid, there is room in this family for only one emotionally stunted person, and I have seniority.

"You *have* to talk to me, babe. We need to figure out how to help you."

"Mitchell *always* talks. He and his family always get to do fun things and he tells the whole class! We do fun things and I want to share, but I always get caught. Mitchell talks so much and I just want to talk!"

It's funny that I see Gray in her now, yearning to be heard. Wanting to tell a story that will top everyone else's.

"What if I ask your teacher to move you away from Mitchell?"

She groans. "She'll move me to the front of the class, mom. Only geeks sit in the front of the class!"

"That sounds like a better deal to me, kiddo. I used to sit in the front of the class, and my mom never had to question me about my classwork." *Because she wouldn't have cared, regardless.* She frowns and slides her finger through the condensation on her plastic cup. "What about the journal entry about daddy?"

Scandalized, her eyes whip up to mine. "You weren't supposed to read that!" Her bottom lip wobbles and the crocodile tears well up in her eyes.

"Why do you want daddy to die, baby?"

"I don't!" She wipes her eyes, but a fresh wave of tears glaze her face.

"Was it just a story?"

She tries with everything she has to regain her composure but fails miserably. She sobs uncontrollably.

I scramble out of my chair and occupy the one next to her and hold her in my arms as she sobs. Gone is the woman who was wallowing in her own self-pity. A new woman stands before her little girl: the protector, the badass, the momma bear.

"It's not fair! He doesn't like me!"

"Baby, that's not true. Daddy loves you…"

"We *always* do whatever Ethan wants to do. We play stupid mini-golf and stupid bowling. It's the same thing every weekend. We eat the food Ethan likes, and he never asks me what I want to do. He always tells me to go to my room or play with Ethan. And he isn't even that nice to Ethan, either! He was telling the truth, mom. He was being respectful until Lucy started yelling at him for being like you!"

I stroke my twin's hair and drop a kiss on the crown of her head. She's younger than Ethan, but she's so fiercely protective.

"It was just a story, Mom. I don't want him to die…I just don't want him to see Lucy anymore."

"Okay. It's okay to tell stories, but killing people in those stories is a little concerning, sweetheart. Do you want me to talk to daddy?"

She shakes her head.

"What's the point? He doesn't listen anyway. He doesn't listen to you, either." Well, that's one way to describe my existence.

"Why don't you go outside and play with Uncle Brand and E, okay? And Alice?" She stops in her tracks as she races to the back door, "I'm going to ask your teacher to move you away from Mitchell, okay? School is important for you to be messing around." Her face falls and she solemnly nods.

One kid down, another man child to go.

Reluctantly, I dial Gray again. And lucky for me, he answers on the first ring.

"What?" He spits.

"I talked to Alice. She thinks you don't like her, that's why she wrote the story about you." I'm met with silence.

"She said that?"

"Mmhm. She also said that you never ask her what she wants to do, and you continuously do whatever Ethan wants to do. So, this is what's going to happen, Gray. When you're in town next, you are going to take my baby out on a date. Just the two of you. You'll ask her what she wants to do, eat her favorite foods, and spend quality time with her. If you can't take her on a weekend, I will gladly pull her out of school so she can spend the day with you."

He doesn't say anything else. He awaits my next rant.

"She's fun, Gray. And if you just spent longer than a minute with her, you'd learn how intuitive and *funny* she is. She has the sarcasm of a thirty-year-old man. She loves blood and gore and telling ghost stories. You're breaking her heart, Gray, and I won't forgive you for that. Fix this."

I don't allow him to get a word in. I hang up immediately and ditch my phone on the counter. I'm done talking to people today. It's exhausting giving everyone around you one hundred percent when there's nothing left for you.

Alice and Ethan's squeals and laughter can be heard from the kitchen. I peek out the window to see Brandon holding a kid in each arm and spinning as fast as he can in circles.

Brandon Wentworth.

He wasn't exaggerating when he said he was sure I'd fall in love with him. He's seen me at my worst, both physically and mentally. I'm falling hopelessly for him. He let it slip last night that he loves me. I didn't say it back.

What happens when I tell him I love him? Will the spell be broken? Will he realize what bullshit he's got himself into and respectfully bow out?

I can't risk that.

I'm forced to keep my mouth shut.

Cooking is not an option tonight. I don't have the energy. What I *want* to do is watch my kids play with the guy I'm falling for. We can order in later and eat in front of the TV.

I let myself onto the deck. The air has warmed significantly from the winter, though I can't stand out here long without putting on a hoodie. The kids are set on the ground, and they wobble around while their whole world spins out before them. Alice is the first to fall. She belly laughs so loud it echoes off the surrounding trees. Ethan tries his best to stay up longer than his sister, but ends up falling onto his back and laughing up at the sky.

Why couldn't I have met Brandon first?

He grins at me from the ground and waves. Life is not horrible for me right now. Sure, my career and reputation are in tatters, but the life I always wanted...the one with a family who loves each other so unconditionally, is perfectly intact.

The man I pretend I don't love plays with my kids like they were his biological children. My children have genuine happy smiles on their faces for the first time in weeks.

"Mom! Come down here!" Ethan shouts. Laughing, I trot down the stairs and Ethan meets me at the bottom, wrapping his gangly arms around my torso. "I love you, Mom," he says quietly so that Brandon and Alice can't hear.

"I love you, buddy. So, so much." He lets go of me and takes off chasing Alice around the yard.

"Ave? You all right?" Grinning at my boyfriend, I nod.

"Yeah, I'm all right." He pecks my forehead and laughs when Ethan trips over his long legs.

This is the day I can pinpoint as the day I was honest with myself. I was in love with Brandon Wentworth. I frequently held onto this feeling when everything went to shit. But from the way he smiled at me, in my heart, that part of him was real.

Seventeen

Now

I *wish* the audience would make some reaction. Everyone stares at me like I just told them I was Santa Claus. Brandon doesn't talk, neither does Sunny. I've never told anyone that's when I knew I was in deep shit with him. My kids don't even know that I was thinking about forever with him.

"You were only with Brandon for a month, and you found yourself in love with him?" Sunny finally asks in disbelief.

"Sometimes, I feel like my life is a giant puzzle. Gray took a hammer to my puzzle and scattered the pieces. The only four pieces that remained exactly where they were supposed to be were Ethan, Alice, Tess, and Jordan. They were my foundation pieces...the four corners to my puzzle." I lick my lips nervously and avoid Brandon's gaze. "Brandon was the center piece of my puzzle. It's a piece I could've been okay with not having if it meant the majority of the puzzle was complete. But when I was able to fit him in place, I felt this feeling of completion...of 'Oh, there you are.'"

What a fool I was.

"Brandon, did you love her at that moment?"

Don't look at him.

"Yes. I was without a doubt in love with her at that moment."

Clearing her throat and sensing the tension, she changes the subject. "So, the rumors of you suing Grayson for full custody were not true, is that correct?"

"No. I wouldn't have ever taken my kids away from their father. At the time, Gray couldn't have cared less if he gave away his parental rights or not. I was angry. We say stupid things when we're angry. Gray just couldn't help himself and chose that moment to be nasty towards me."

"Jason Evans also took the opportunity to stoke the fire. Are you still friendly towards him?" *No.*

"I haven't spoken with Jason in six years." And when he wanted to buy the movie rights to my book, it was satisfying rejecting him as my alter ego, Amelia Ross.

"Brandon, how did you *not* step into protector mode? Did you want to go to bat for her? Did you want to save her reputation?"

I drop my eyes to the floor because I know the answer.

"I made a promise to her when we decided we would explore a relationship. We keep it a secret at all costs. It was more than just her reputation on the line. It was the sanity of the kids. I wanted to go to bat for her. I wanted to pummel my brother for being a child. No matter what I could have done, it would've made everything worse."

I bravely lift my eyes to him. His gaze is still hard, still angry.

"What do you feel when you look at her now?" My heart stops beating in my chest. I'm not game enough for any proclamations of star-crossed love. I don't want it. I don't need it. I've moved on.

"Anger."

Excuse the fuck out of me?

"Anger," I repeat monotonously. "That's what you feel? Anger towards me?"

"What did you expect, Ave?" He spits. "You left. You didn't give me any explanation other than I cheated with Ellen, which isn't true. You ignored my calls and texts, changed the code to your gate and now we're playing happy memories with an interviewer who has obviously biased opinions."

Anger bubbles in my belly. The fire under my ass to get this interview over with is now uncontained.

"You are unbelievable. You abandoned *us*." I don't miss the way his body locks straight or the pulsing veins that pop in his forehead. "I saw with my own eyes you cheated with her. You're angry because you got caught. Do you honestly think I walked into this interview today wanting to talk about *this?* You yanked the heart out of my chest and strapped a grenade to it without the pin, Brand. The shitty part about all of this is that I believed you were different from Gray." I can't stop the tears from falling or the pain in my voice that shakes.

I'm supposed to be the badass carrying myself through this interview. I can't be a badass when I'm crying all the damn time.

"Are you doing this for the cameras?" His voice rumbles. It's the voice I always feared. The *I'm disappointed* voice. "This is bullshit, Ave, and I won't have you damaging *my* reputation because you regret leaving me." He stands up and looks at Sunny. "I need a break. You can continue talking to her about this if you want."

I want to shake him. I *left* him? What is it about the Wentworth's that they always think they can do no wrong?

Sunny asks me another question, but my legs do all the talking for me. I stand up from the sofa and storm off the stage. My phone is in my hand before I can answer anyone's questions.

Crew members watch me hesitantly as I storm down the hallway. I dial Gray for the eighteenth time and, of course, get voicemail.

"Gray, I *really* need you to call me back. You promised you would be here through it all! I need you!" I hang up on a scream.

"You know, I've always said you're a *brilliant* actor. I just wish you'd stop spewing your bullshit. You should've known better after what Gray did to you." I whirl around to see him leaning against the wall. I hate his stupid face.

"That's the joke, isn't it? I knew better. I knew all the signs and the red flags and I ignored every single one of them because you came off as the knight in shining armor and country boy persona. Fuck you, Brand! You *abandoned* us without a fucking care in the world! You have no idea how badly you hurt me. More importantly the kids!"

He pushes off the wall and stalks towards me dangerously.

"No, fuck *you,* Ave! The only reason why those kids are hurt is because you've been putting your bullshit lies in their heads since the night you stood me up!"

Phones are pointed in our direction, filming every significant moment and ugly word.

I wish I never called him to hang out with Ethan that night in the hospital. I wish I told him to fuck off after asking me to spend time with the kids. What a mess.

"I'm *so* tired of you Wentworths never taking responsibility for your own fucking actions. It must be so convenient for the two of you to use me as your scapegoat whenever the opportunity arises, huh?" I wipe the tears from my eyes. I'm ruining what's left of my makeup, and Russell has already left the studio. "You made me believe in love and rainbows and butterflies and all that unrealistic bullshit. I loved you, Brand. I wanted so *badly* to be the woman you thought I was. But obviously, that was never the case because you were always going to be in love with her and I was stupid and desperate to see it!"

"I told you not to seek her out!" Tess's booming yell echoes off the walls of the buildings around us. She storms over to us and grabs my wrist. "Go inside," she growls at me.

"I know you've never liked her, Ave, but you can't keep blaming your insecurities on her. She didn't do anything wrong!"

"Stop talking—both of you!"

Her narrowed, angry eyes take me aback. I shrink away to the door. She shouts at him, but I can't make out the words. I storm through the hallway, ignoring everyone. People try to get my attention, yet I don't care. I pass my dressing room and catch Jane waiting for me.

I just need a minute alone.

She calls my name. I pretend I don't hear her. Producers attempt to stop me. Not until I find the refuge of the women's bathroom. I slip inside and deadbolt the door behind me.

Deep breath in, deep breath out.

The sink is running. When I turn the corner, a new wave of grief washes over me. Ellen Wilson and I are polar opposites, personality-wise. On the outside, there isn't much different about us. She has strawberry blonde hair, I have honey-colored hair. She's an amazon, standing at five feet, ten inches, where I'm more average at just five inches shorter than her. She wears the freckles on her nose on full display where I cover mine with makeup.

She smirks when our eyes meet. She turns off the water and reaches for a paper towel.

"This isn't going well for you," she taunts. When I don't answer, she shoulder barges me and tosses the wet paper towel in the garbage can. "Ava Reid, still desperate to be loved by a Wentworth, still failing miserably. Even *I* couldn't hope for a better end result."

"He'll cheat on you just like he did on me, Ellen. Men like that don't change. Ask Gray."

She laughs without humor.

"I was always end game, *baby.* Brandon and I were destined to be together since we were kids. Some of us have to make our own luck. You were nothing but a distraction. I took you out of the equation just like I took out Kayla." She pats my shoulder condescendingly. "He's loyal. He won't be leaving me any time soon. There's too much history. Too much chemistry. You're a footnote, Ava. It's time to move on. You're making yourself look like an idiot."

She strolls out of the bathroom like this conversation didn't happen. Much to my horror, the bathroom stall door opens slowly. Kayla pokes her head out and cautiously steps in my direction.

"Ava?" *I took you out of the equation, just like I took Kayla out.* Is she behind this? Is she purposely trying to sabotage me again? "What did she mean by that?" I don't know! My moment alone is nonexistent.

"I don't know," I answer with a sob. I want to crouch down and scream, but there are too many ears. "Ask Brand." I turn on my heel and storm out the door.

I have to move forward. It's the only way I'm going to find peace.

Eighteen

Brandon

Now

Kayla hasn't been my agent for over a year. When she turned on the news this morning to watch my interview and saw Ava instead, she put two and two together and got back to work. She drove an hour to get here and was hitting brick wall after brick wall when it came to the production team. She threatened retribution.

She enters my dressing room without knocking. She rubs soothing circles on her stretched-to-the-max belly and lowers herself onto the sofa behind me.

"I appreciate what you're trying to do here, but you should go home. Put your feet up, drink some lemonade, watch some TV." She grimaces at my greeting and swings her feet onto the couch so she can lie down.

"Where's Ellen?" That's a good question. I haven't seen her in the last twenty minutes. She said she was going to the bathroom and never came back. Not that I'm complaining. I was enjoying the silence.

"I don't know."

She sighs. "Brand, you know I love you, right?" Here we go. Kayla is not shy when it comes to her two cents. She's going to tell me how she feels, no matter what.

"What's wrong? Do you need me to call you an ambulance or something?" She scoffs.

"No. But we've been professionally involved for what, fifteen years?" When I nod, she hesitates. "I wouldn't ever steer you wrong. I love you. You're my best friend in the entire universe."

"You're scaring me, Kayla…"

"Why did we divorce?" Her question takes me off guard. What is it with the women in my life today?

"Are we seriously dissecting this now? You *know* why. I wanted kids, you didn't." How. Fucking. Ironic. She nods and chooses her next words carefully.

"I was in the bathroom just a few minutes ago. Ellen was there, though I don't think she realized I was. Ava came in a few minutes later. Ellen instigated an argument. She was nasty to Ava, and she said some things…"

"She *should* be nasty to Ava. She ruined my life, and it almost cost me mine. Don't fall for this act she has going on, Kayla." Her frown deepens, and she shakes her head.

"No, it wasn't an act. Ava barely talked. But Ellen…she said quite a bit. She said that the two of you were end game since you were kids. She said Ava was a distraction, so she took her out of the equation, just like she took me out."

That doesn't sound like Ellen. That sounds like Ava talking about Ellen, honestly. But Kayla's the one telling me, and she wouldn't steer me wrong.

"Are you sure it was Ellen? It could've been anyone."

"No, Brand. It was her. I'd know her voice anywhere. I even saw her through the crack of the stall." My stomach churns. Ellen *did* talk a lot of shit about Kayla while we were together. But she wouldn't hurt me like that. She saved my life. "I'm on your side, you know that, right? I would do anything for you. I wouldn't lie."

She rocks herself upright and stands up.

"I smell fish. Something isn't adding up and I'm getting to the bottom of it. But just prepare yourself if she's behind this. I don't want you to get hurt."

I take Kayla's words with a grain of salt. Ellen *can't* be behind this. She wouldn't hurt me like this. It's almost like my words are magic because she appears beside me with a kiss on my cheek. She's no longer angry at me like she was when we were eating breakfast.

"How are you doing?" She shrugs and pulls herself onto my lap. The fabric below my ass protests, like it's going to rip right from under me and send us both crashing to the ground.

Fitting.

"It's awkward. But I've been doing some soul searching." She turns to me and grins. "We're strong, Brandon. We've been through everything together. Whatever comes out in a stupid interview she *obviously* orchestrated isn't going to tear us apart. She was a blip in your past, nothing more."

Her monologue was meant to be comforting, but with all of the conspiracy Kayla brought in here hangs heavy in the air. It makes me feel queasy.

I know what's coming next. There's going to be a lot of pain and yelling and screaming...this is hard, and I don't want to do any of it.

"Yeah. Nothing will come between us." The voice that comes out of my mouth sounds unfamiliar, foreign. Doubt has started to creep in.

Ava didn't want to tell the world about us six years ago. Why would she now?

Ellen lifts my chin and presses her lips to mine. This boldness isn't like her.

Fuck.

A knock on the door tells me I have to move my ass back to the stage. Ellen promises she'll stay in the dressing room, but she *doesn't* want to watch Ava's lies. Fine with me. I don't necessarily want to listen to her lies either, yet here I fucking am. Tess glares at me all the way from the door to the sofa.

I've never been at odds with my ex-best friend's wife. She was a sister to me. But it always seems like Ava's the one who prevails no matter if she's wrong or not. She stares down the audience, daring them to shoot another video of her. Kayla is *finally* brought a chair and is sitting next to Jane while they whisper their game plan.

Ava arrives with a fresh face. She sits next to me quietly and doesn't utter a word until we're counted in. I expect her to brighten up, paste on a fake smile, and pretend like everything is okay. But when the red lights blink on, her face never changes.

What is she thinking about? Does she think that I'm behind this?

"Brandon?" Sunny's voice breaks through my trance.

"Hmm?"

"Looks like somebody's daydreaming." The audience laughs along with Sunny, but Ava and I remain stoic. This isn't a laughing matter. This is everything we've ever worked for put on the line. "You were a part of this family unit. Was there ever a point where you thought it was too much?"

"No." I love those kids so damn much. I've only seen fleeting glimpses of them over the last six years, but no face-to-face meetings. It's understandable with Ava, but not with Gray. Did he choose her side over mine?

"You had no problem raising your brother's kids?"

"Ethan and Alice were the kids I never had. I love them. I'd do *anything* for them. They're biologically my brother's children, yes. But I spent a lot more time with them than he ever did. While he hid away in Australia, I was helping with homework. I was learning how to braid hair and I was cooking dinner so Ava could have five minutes to relax on the couch." I look at her, but her eyes don't move from the camera. She's staring down America. "I saw how much you did, Ave. I was there for the late nights and the tears and your wondering if you were doing any of this right."

How could it *not* be real?

Her eyes water.

"Did you ever confront your brother about not stepping up?"

"Yes." She ends her one-sided staring contest and whirls around on me.

"What?"

"I confronted Gray about not showing up for the kids."

"That wasn't any of your business, Brand! Why am I just finding out about this now?"

"Because when you were at that last audition, the school called. Gray forgot to pick them up." Lava erupts in her eyes.

"Tell me about that. It's what comes next in the story, doesn't it?" I nod warily. I'm not particularly proud of what happens next. But my little brother had it coming.

Nineteen

Brandon

Then

Ava has been tirelessly putting in the work for landing a role in a new movie. From what I understand, if she has to leave to be on location, Gray would be forced to be here for the kids. As much as I would *love* to watch my brother attempt to cook a meal, I'm more worried about the kids' sanity. I lived with Gray up to when he made it big. By that time, I was already in college and mom managed to take a sabbatical from the farm until she was certain he'd be okay on his own.

I want to throw my name into the ring. I know how it would go down if I offered. Regardless, I'd sleep better at night knowing they were happy at the end of the day. I play the cards I've been dealt. One day, when we go public and I can show the world that Ava Reid is the poster child of being a badass, I can be that stand-in. I'm not their father, even though I wish I were.

Ellen massages the tender part of my knee from an old injury. She talks on and on about the food she misses in Texas and how she wants to hang out in my momma's barn like we used to when we were kids.

"Hey, your phone is ringing." She hands me the phone.

"Hello?"

"Good afternoon. This is Mrs. Banks at Pleasantdale Elementary. Is this Brandon Wentworth? I have Ethan and Alice here in the front office with me. It appears it was dad's day to pick them up."

My heart sinks to my stomach

"Yeah, this is Brandon. Gray didn't pick them up?"

"I'm afraid not. Alice is a little upset if you can't hear her crying in the background." I do. She's terrified.

"Okay. I'm on my way. I'll be right there." I take my leg away from Ellen and stand up.

"What was that all about?"

"Gray didn't pick the kids up from school." I grab my keys off the counter and the hoodie draped over the barstool. "I have to go. Probably don't wait around...I have to pick up the kids and track Gray down before this becomes World War III."

She scoffs.

"You're still seeing her?"

I am *not* entertaining this. Especially not with her.

"Yes, and save your judgment because I don't care. I'll see you later." It takes me forty-five minutes to get to their school. The parking lot has emptied with just a handful of cars. I walk as quickly as I can into the office and see Ethan and Alice sitting on chairs, watching *Reading Rainbow,* and snacking on some lollipops.

"You must be Uncle Brandon. Hi, I'm Mrs. Banks, the principal." I shake her hand eagerly and fish out my wallet.

"Just out of curiosity, did you call Gray's phone?"

She glances to the kids who still haven't acknowledged my presence, and then back to me.

"I know of the circumstances with the Wentworths. We called his phone about ten times before we started going down the list. We tried Ms. Reid but weren't successful. We tried Mr. and Mrs. Archer, but they were not answering the phone either. I'm really glad you answered, otherwise I was about to call the Department of Children and Families." Good thing she didn't.

How can my brother be so stupid? I want to apologize for him, but he's never going to fucking change.

"Well, thanks for calling me and waiting around. I know this isn't exactly protocol."

She smiles weakly.

"Ms. Reid is a good person. She donates her time and money into this school. I've been around a lot of families who make things seem like everything is fine on the outside when it's really chaotic on the inside. She's transparent about what happens with Mr. Wentworth. Calling DCF was a last resort. I was afraid she was hurt."

I weakly smile.

"She's working and must not have her phone on her." I turn to the kids and call their names. Alice's face lights up and they both stand and collect their things.

"Ethan and Alice, it's always a pleasure. Thank you for helping me with lock up." Mrs. Banks beams.

"Thanks for letting us watch *Reading Rainbow* and for the lollipops, Mrs. Banks," says Alice.

"See you tomorrow." We walk in silence to my truck. If Ava finds out about this, it's going to start a domino effect I don't think she'll think all the way through. I buckle the kids up and start for Gray's house.

"Were you busy, Uncle Brand?" Ethan asks.

"Never busy for you two. Are you guys all right?" Ethan nods, but turns his attention to the view outside his window.

"I was scared. I thought everyone forgot about us and we would have to sleep at school."

"We wouldn't sleep at school, dummy. Mom would've picked us up eventually." My stomach churns.

"Don't call your sister a dummy, Ethan." Ethan groans. "I'm sorry your dad didn't pick you up, guys. I'm taking you over to his house now."

"Do we have to? He forgot to pick us up. He doesn't want us at his house, obviously." Poor, jaded Ethan. I wonder how much truth that comes out of his mouth registers in his brain.

"I'll set him straight. Don't worry about that."

Like my father, Gray believes in optics and opulence. He owns a mansion in Burr Ridge because he *has* to have a residence close to the kids' schools but doesn't skimp on square footage. Who is he trying to impress out here, anyway? His house is gated, much like Ava's. His code is his birth year, *so original.*

Once I turn the corner to reach the front of his house, dozens of cars line the driveway. He threw a party! He was more concerned with his friends and forgot all about his children? He was not raised this way!

I park behind someone's town car about a quarter mile away from his house. The kids gather their things and hop out of the truck. What do I even say to them? I'm sorry your father is a selfish prick? It's nearing five o'clock and Ava will be by soon to pick them up. I stop them and sigh.

"If your mom finds out about this, it's not going to end well." She'll beat herself up for not taking the call. She's working so hard...I don't want her to stop because my brother is an asshole.

"So...we don't tell her?" Ethan asks.

"What do you think about your mom acting again?" Ethan furrows his brow and leans up against the truck.

"She loves it. I want her to be in movies again."

"Me too," Alice adds.

"I don't like lying, but if she finds out the truth about this, she'll blame herself for not answering the call from your principal. I'll take care of your dad, okay? But maybe this could be our little secret?" Ethan nods with determination. Alice watches me warily. I worry about her. She's six years old with a passion for telling stories. It kills me to make them lie to their mother, but I don't want this to be an excuse for her to quit doing what she loves.

"I won't say anything, I promise." Okay. At least we got that settled.

We continue down the drive. The front door is propped open with a door stopper. His housekeeper sits in a chair just beside the front door texting on her phone. When our movements register in her peripherals, her face pales when her gaze lands on the kids.

Save it. I don't want to hear it.

The roar of the crowd is irritating, like nails on a chalkboard. People I've seen on TV litter the hallways and talk to each other in the living room. The kids stick close to me, afraid they'll have to talk to people they don't know.

Gray is nowhere to be seen. I'm not planning on talking to anyone. I want to find Gray for myself and give him a piece of my mind. I notice a small group on the deck. We slip out, careful not to make eye contact with anyone. Gray is surrounded by his friends. He laughs at something one of them said. Alice clings to my hand, and Ethan glares at his father.

Finally, Gray's gaze meets mine. At first, he freezes. I'm out of place. I don't belong in his world of the rich and pretentious. My presence is an annoyance. His gaze drops to the little girl who holds my hand in terror. Recognition sets in. His face pales, and he excuses himself from his group.

"Hey guys," he says cautiously.

"You forgot about us," Alice cries. Gray glances over his shoulder to make sure he's out of earshot.

"I'm sorry, Alice..." Yep. No excuses. Fuck him.

"Why don't you guys put your stuff in your rooms? I'm going to talk to your dad." Ethan ignores Gray's flaccid attempts of getting his attention and brings Alice upstairs. "What the fuck, Gray?"

"Lower your voice!"

"How can you be so selfish? You had one job, and it was to pick up your kids from school." He shoves his hands in his pockets.

"I forgot..."

"You were raised better than this. Your kids come first before *anything*. There is no excuse for doing something this stupid. Alice was terrified, by the way. She thought she was going to have to spend the night at school."

"I'm sorry!"

"You don't have the luxury of forgetting, asshole. You wanted the family, so take care of the family. Just because you don't have primary custody of your children doesn't mean you get to do whatever the fuck you want. I was all the way downtown. It took me almost an hour to get there. The principal was going to call DCF if I didn't pick up the phone, do you realize that? You're so concerned with optics, Gray. This would've looked *horrible* for you."

"It was an honest mistake!" My hands ball into fists. God, it would be so *satisfying* to just deck him once in the face. I'd pay millions for the opportunity to destroy his money maker.

"They're smart kids. They're already on to you and your bullshit. The best thing you could do for yourself is to get all of these people out of your house before Ava gets here. This is so irresponsible!"

His eyes narrow.

"You don't get to judge me, Brand. I love my kids. I forgot about today, it's not like she reminded me or anything." She did. Last night. She called him and reminded him to pick up the kids. "What's it to you, anyway? Why do you care so much?"

"You know, you sound a lot like Dad. He couldn't have cared less about us. He did shit like this all the time, so when I see it being done to *them,* it pisses me off. Momma broke her back trying to make sure we had a good life without him. You're just carrying the torch, aren't you?"

"Fuck you!" We get a few curious glances from the people around us. I don't care. Let them see the true monster he really is.

"No, fuck you! I picked up your slack, little brother. Lie to Ava, I don't care. But if I ever get a call like that from their school again, I'm going to make you pay for it."

"Get the fuck out, Brand. Don't come back."

With pleasure!

I head back into the house on a mission. I pray Ava doesn't walk in while I'm walking out. The kids sit on the stairs looking bored as hell. I sit on the first step and pull them into a hug.

"I'm sorry about today, guys. Your mom should be here soon."

"Will you be home when we get home?" Alice asks.

I nod solemnly.

"Yeah. I'm going to go start dinner. I love you guys."

"Love you," they say in unison.

I walk out of Gray's house with a heavy heart. Anger is dumb. What's even dumber is my idiot brother living out his every fantasy while the mother of his children is breaking her back trying to provide for her children.

The walk back to my truck gives me a chance to make peace with today, not that I can ever be okay with what happened. I have about an hour to change my tune before it starts affecting the people around me.

Fortunately for me, I don't run into Ava on my way to my truck or on the way to her house. I'm the first one to arrive. I got a key to her house last month, but this is the first time I've ever had to use it.

We haven't talked about dinner tonight, but I'm pleased to find she took out chicken for the four of us tonight. I decide on something simple: chicken with garlic gravy. It'll take me an hour to get everything on the table, which gives her plenty of time to pick up the kids and come home to a home-cooked meal. When I get the chicken in the oven, I make mashed potatoes and find a bag of frozen green beans in the freezer. They walk in ten minutes before dinner is ready. I brace myself for the sour mood I *know* she'll be in after coming from Gray's. She enters the kitchen with a wide smile and wraps her arms around my torso.

"This smells good." Okay, so she isn't in a bad mood.

"Good. I'm starving and wanted comfort food. How'd today go?"

"Fine, until I had a voicemail that Gray forgot to pick up the kids." Shit. "I don't know what happened, but they were ready to go when I got to his house. He picked them up eventually."

"He's unbelievable."

"That's putting it mildly," she replies with a giggle. She lets go of me and hops up on the counter. "How was your day? It looks like you were working out," she says, wriggling her eyebrows suggestively.

"I was and then Ellen came over to work on my leg."

She scoffs and rolls her eyes. Yeah, I know. Same.

"Then I just got lazy and didn't change."

"Well...I could always help you shower later. You know, help work those knots out of your shoulders, loosen up your muscles..."

Laughing at her seduction technique, I pull her off the counter and close to me and breathe in her mango scent.

"I love you, Ave." She buries her face in my chest and squeezes me harder. She hasn't said it yet, but I know she loves me. It's in the way she takes care of me and how she makes love to me. This is more than attraction or convenience. "Do you want me to spend the night?"

She nods without removing her head from my chest.

"How'd the audition go?" She sighs and lets go of me.

"I think it went fine, but I'm not holding my breath."

"Go turn on the TV. Relax a few minutes. I'll set the table and we can eat in ten." She slips her shoes off by the door and collapses onto the couch, turning on the TV. She flicks around for a few channels until she stops on her face.

"...the photo was sent to us by a source close to the Archer's. It appears Jordan Archer and Ava Reid are closer than we originally thought." She growls when the picture appears on the screen again. It's of Jordan and Ava hugging in his kitchen. I recognize the picture from the party at Jordan's house a few weeks ago.

"It's interesting," the female co-host starts, "Ava Reid and Tessa Archer have been best friends since they were children. Why would you go after your best friend's husband? What is her end game?"

My stomach sinks.

One of my brothers sent this in. For what purpose? Why would someone knowingly cause doubt in a strong relationship? She whips out her phone and calls Tess on speaker.

"Hey whore," Tess answers the phone with a laugh.

"I'm sorry. You know I'm not going after your husband, right?"

"Yeah, I know. I know who you're sleeping with." Ava groans in reply. "Don't worry about it, babe. Come over tomorrow and we can get ahead of it. We can introduce the world to our throuple and make *everyone* uncomfortable."

Ava laughs nervously.

"I'm really sorry, Tessie. This is so embarrassing…"

"Hey, it's a tabloid. Their sources are just desperate people trying to make a quick buck at your expense. I love you, sissy. I know you'd never hurt me."

"I love you. I'll text you in a little bit about tomorrow."

They hang up, but the air around us instantly changes. She walked into the house with a lighthearted mood, but now she's more defensive. Tess and Jordan are her only family, and someone is outright trying to destroy that. It concerns me that it's someone within my team.

The kids are unusually quiet at dinner. They eat without sticking their nose up at the parsley I garnished the chicken with. Ethan eats seconds, Alice picks at her green beans. Ava insists on doing the dishes, so I help with homework. Alice is struggling with math, so we sit together and come up with alternate ways to add different numbers that equal ten.

Ethan works on his multiplication, albeit silently. He asks for clarification only once. They decline dessert, but then get in the shower and go straight to bed. They've had a long day. Ava shuts off the TV and motions for me to follow her upstairs. She strips out of her clothes and leaves a trail of them to the bathroom.

I get glimpses of snow-white flesh and an ass you can bounce a quarter off of. My shirt hits the floor in a black puddle. My shorts and briefs follow suit. She fills up the tub and pours some liquid soap in, creating a fluffy, white cloud of bubbles.

It's funny that we operate on the same wavelength for only being together for a month. I step into the tub, and she follows suit. She directs the taps with her feet and relaxes against my chest.

The scalding water envelopes us. She sighs, letting all the poison from today out. The bathroom smells of lavender and sage.

"Are you all right, Ave?"

"I'm fine. I haven't been in the news for a while. It's just taking me off guard." How does she do it? How does she handle the lies the press peddles without remorse? "I can't believe Gray forgot the kids."

Yeah. I can't either, but the fucker keeps surprising me.

"He's a jerk."

"Hey Brand?"

"Hmm?"

"You know I didn't go after Jordan, right?"

"Yeah baby, I know. I don't ever have to worry about you straying. I know where your heart lies." With me. Her pulse quickens in her throat. I itch to kiss the exposed arch of her neck, but this angle makes it awkward.

She's a vision.

She's a sight for sore eyes.

She's the woman I've wanted for way long and is even better than what I imagined it would be like.

"Hey...I was thinking. Spring Break is coming up. Do you have the kids?"

"Mm, yeah, I do. Gray is supposedly in Australia for reshoots. What did you have in mind?"

"I was thinking maybe we could go to my mom's in Texas. She hasn't seen the kids since they were little. We'll have a ton of privacy, and it would be a change of scenery." Her body tenses against mine.

"Oh, Brand, I don't know. I don't think your mom would be happy about this..."

"I already told you, she doesn't hate you. And when it comes to you and me, well...I think you'd be surprised. My mom is a progressive woman."

Her fingers nervously drum against my shin while she mulls it over.

"I don't need an answer now, but I think it would be a great idea. There's so much to do and we wouldn't even need to leave the farm. The exposure would only be at the airport and optically, it looks like you're bringing your kids to visit their grandmother for spring break. And that's not even a lie."

"Yeah..."

She allows the stress to seep into her psyche, so I drop it. I massage her shoulders and work the knots out. She purrs under my touch. I could stay in this tub with her forever if I could. Here, the outside world doesn't have a say in what we do. In this tub, we're just Brand and Ave; two people who love each other and want the best for each other.

I wish we could be a normal couple. I wish we weren't plagued by fame and horrible, public relationships.

As I sit in this tub with her, and her eyes begin to droop because she's comfortable with me, I know that this will all be worth it in the end. She's beautiful and strong. She's my warrior.

Twenty

Ava

I don't think the media has ever had this many consecutive stories on me since Gray and I divorced. There was the one last week where I was stealing Jordan away from Tess, the sighting with Ben—although that was planned. Ben is always happy to be seen with me. Brandon wasn't exactly happy about it, and this new one now of wanting Gray back.

I have no doubts that were laid intentionally by Gray's team, but I have the phone records to prove that I couldn't give two flying fucks about him. The media has paid more attention to me, which means the paparazzi have been spotted in the neighborhood. And since the paps have been around, it means Brandon hasn't.

That's been harder to work around. The only place they don't follow me is dropping off and picking up the kids from school. Instead of going back to our house, we go to his. We've had dinner in his apartment for the last week and a half. On Fridays and Saturdays, we spend the night. Luckily, nobody has caught on yet.

A week in Texas is just the reprieve I need. We booked the flights separately so it doesn't look suspicious. Bev and Brandon will pick us up from the airport when we arrive. Gray doesn't need to know our plans, and it's not like he's tried calling, anyway. My PR team is aware of our travels next week, and Nick knows not to call unless he has good news.

But that's a week away. I have bigger fish to fry today. Tess and Jordan came over this morning and began brainstorming on how to address me stealing him away from Tess. Jordan is wary about who took the picture. Tess doesn't care one way or another. She just wants her family to be out of the spotlight.

We finally land on an idea. The camera rolls. I pretend to walk by the camera, but my attention is grabbed by the online article. "Tessie!" She approaches the camera and investigates it curiously. "They cut you out of our throuple again."

She gasps. "Those bitches!" Jordan approaches my other side and does the same thing. "Let's make one thing clear: we're all together, and we love each other. Stop trying to split us up." We grin as one, and Jordan and Tess turn to me and kiss my cheeks.

It's dumb, but it pokes fun. And hopefully, that gets people off our backs for a while. After filming, Jordan leaves to go work out with the team. Tess and I crack open the box of chocolates Brandon brought me last weekend and stuff our faces while watching *The Price is Right.*

"So, the four of you are vacationing next week?" Warm air, a bright sun, no paparazzi—heaven.

"Yeah. We're going to Beverly's. Do you think she's going to smack me for jumping brothers?"

Giggling and throwing a salted caramel into her mouth, she shakes her head.

"No. Everyone has seen what Gray's like. I think you're fine." I hope so. I don't know what I'll do if she gets defensive.

"So...it's going well, then?"

My smile says it all.

"Yeah, it is. He's great...he makes me happy." *And I love him.*

"That's what I like to hear. I told you he would." I ditch the box of chocolate and sigh. Ellen's name appears on my screen, declaring that Brandon won't be coming home for dinner tonight, as he has to rest.

"What do you know about her?" I ask as Tess quickly glances at my phone and rolls her eyes when she realizes who it is.

"Not much, really. I know she's a flirt. Jordo's told me there are rumors of her sleeping around with the single members of the team. She hangs out in the weight room and ogles. But...I think she has a thing for Brand."

I scoff.

"I *know* she has a thing for him. They've been friends since they were kids. I just sometimes wonder if I'm reading much into it because of Gray..." I'm *not* the jealous girlfriend. I refuse to be the jealous girlfriend.

"I doubt Brandon has the wandering eye, but I don't think you're reading much into it. Have you told him she makes you uncomfortable?" I should, but I never have. I don't want to scare him off or make him think I'm comparing him to Gray. What kind of girlfriend would I be if I told him he can't hang out with his childhood friend anymore?

That's not me.

"No, but I'm not exactly subtle when I point out that she has a thing for him." Shrugging, she steals the box of chocolate for herself.

"She's a bitch. She's *never* liked me, not that I need her to. But she has this air of *'I'm better than you'* about her and I hate it. Besides, she may tout she's a team player, but the only team she's playing on is her own and it doesn't matter who's in her way." I'm not sure if that's supposed to make me feel better, but it doesn't.

I text Brand and ask if he's still coming over tonight or if he'd rather us come over.

"Have you thought about coming out of the closet with him yet?"

I snort and shake my head.

"No. It's not the right time. I have to figure out a way to tell Gray before we do anything. I like my PR team, but I think I may have to hire someone to focus just on that fallout." He hasn't pressured me to go public yet. And while that should make me feel warm and fuzzy, I just feel guilty. My stomach churns anytime I think about it for more than thirty seconds.

Brandon Wentworth is a stellar guy. He's my dirty little secret. He deserves more than that. He deserves a woman who isn't afraid to step into the limelight with him.

Brandon: Yes :) I'll be over after I'm done working out. You should make that lemon pasta again. It's my fav.

Me: Sure thing. Creamy lemon pasta for my favorite guy. Oh, and you.

Brandon: Sassy. Keep it up.

Laughing, I set my phone down and rest my head on the couch. Maybe I should just tell him how I feel.

"Hey, looks like our video worked." Tess points to the front window. The paparazzi are packing up. There were over a dozen this morning when I woke up, but now there are only two or three hanging around.

"Good. Now we can get back to normal."

Tess scoffs. "I don't what normal is, babe. But if it gets the creeps off your front yard so you can pork your boyfriend tonight, then I say be normal and boring."

"You're disgusting."

"But you love me. I mean, you've stuck around me for over twenty years, baby cakes. What does that say about you?"

What would I do without her?

At three o'clock, she accompanies me to pick the kids up from school. Alice tries to bribe me to stop through *Wendy's* to grab ice cream, though it's not working. I have pasta to make that will probably render all of us useless tonight when our bellies are fighting off our lactose intolerance. No regrets.

When we arrive home, all signs of the paps are gone. Other than their crumpled-up water bottles, energy drink cans, and cigarette butts, it was like they were never here. I rejoice in the fact knowing that when Brandon comes over tonight, there won't be any prying eyes.

Just one more week until Texas. I just have to hold out until then.

Twenty-One

Ava

The day I've been waiting for and dreading has finally arrived. The kids were packed up last night and their tablets charged all night long. Bev called me last night just to tell me she can't wait to see me and the kids. That's a good sign. Unless she's going to kick the shit out of me once Brandon isn't looking.

You're being dramatic.

Our flight left at six this morning, and Tess was sweet enough to spend the night so she could bring us to the airport. She helped me disguise myself with subtle makeup. TSA encouraged me to ditch the ballcap and sunglasses, but once they saw who was underneath, they allowed it.

This is America.

The plane lands in the Dallas Fort Worth airport. The sun shines brightly in the window and the skies are so blue you start to wonder where the sea ends and the sky begins. We taxi to the gate and Ethan and Alice chatter excitedly with each other about the first thing they're going to do when they get to Nana's.

When everyone gets up, I allow them to go ahead of us. Ethan groans and scolds me for not wanting to get off the plane. He isn't wrong. I'm not prepared for this. I should just go home and allow them to have a mom-free week with their grandmother.

Eventually, we're the only three on the plane. Alice demands I get their carry-on baggage so we can go, and I reluctantly oblige.

Every step is a step towards more dread. I fear the judgment, the potential recognition, the unknown...

Shit.

We take the monorail to baggage claim and walk out of security. Ethan is sick of my bullshit and walking damn slow. By this point, Alice is practically dragging me along behind her. As we descend the escalator, Bev and Brandon come into view. Alice squeals in excitement and races down the remaining steps into her nana's arms.

Bev hasn't changed a bit. She's nearing her sixties, but she doesn't look a day over forty. I'm jealous of the natural glow she embodies. She has the same rainforest eyes as Brandon. She has the same sandy blonde hair as Gray but wears it in a high ponytail.

She pulls Ethan into a tight hug and kisses his head.

"Oh, I missed you two so much!" Bev straightens and grins at me. It's not conniving or mischievous like I thought she'd be. Instead, her warmth radiates through her, like she's welcoming home her daughter she hasn't seen in years.

Her hugs are curing. A million scenarios raced through my mind last night as I imagined how this moment would play out. None of them ever came this close to making me emotional. I don't get along with my mom, and Bev has always taken care of me like I was her own child.

A new body comes into view next to Brandon when Bev and I part. Ellen makes my insides twist. A victorious smirk stretches across her lips as she sidles up to Brandon.

I'm grateful for the sunglasses.

I didn't know she would be here. I mean, I know she *lives* here, but I didn't think she would be crashing our vacation. Why wouldn't he tell me? Why would he spring this on me at the last minute?

"E, stay here with Alice and Nana. Mom and I are going to grab your bags," Brandon announces. My body works on autopilot and follows a two foot distance behind Brandon. We reach the conveyor belt and wait for the thing to start moving.

"How was your flight?"

"Fine." I'm not this girl. This is not who I am. *Stop being petty!* He arches an eyebrow.

"I missed you, killer. But I'm really glad you're here. I have the whole week planned out..."

I tune him out as the belt begins to move. Ethan and Alice's suitcases are plastered with their favorite characters, so they'll be easy to spot. Mine is just plain black. And right now, I couldn't have asked for a better distraction.

"Ave? You all right?"

I'm fine. She lives here. She came along because she *likes me so much*. God damn it. I hate this.

"Why didn't you tell me she was coming?" It takes him a minute to catch up. He glances over to the kids and Bev sitting on the seats waiting for us while Ellen stands off to the side, scrolling through her phone.

"I didn't know. She was at the gate when I got through security last night...Ave? Are you crying?"

"No."

Yes.

I'm *not* letting her ruin this for me.

I spent two and a half hours on a plane with an eight and six-year-old playing the same YouTube videos over and over again. And while this occupied them, I sat with my stomach twisting in tight knots, threatening to expel its contents.

"Baby, what's wrong? Did I do something wrong?"

You're refusing to see this woman throw herself at you!

"No."

"Ave..." I grab Ethan and Alice's suitcases and set them on the floor next to me. "Baby, I'm sorry...I—"

"You say there's nothing there, Brand, but everywhere I look, there she is. I don't want to be this jealous girl...that's not who I am.

But she *throws* herself at you and you don't see it." I find my suitcase and grab it.

"Ethan, come here, buddy," he calls to Ethan. He pulls me into his chest and rubs soothing circles in my back. The disguise is working. Nobody gives us a second glance. Ethan jogs over and stares at me in concern.

"What's wrong with mom?"

"Do me a favor, buddy, take yours and your sister's suitcase. Tell Nana I'm gonna bring mom home." Ethan places his hand on my back in comfort and then disappears. Brandon grabs my suitcase and brings it over to a row of seats and sits me down. He waves at Bev and Ellen, and we watch them walk in the direction of short-term parking.

This is so dumb. I'm acting dumb.

"I'm sorry, Ave. I wasn't thinking. Honestly, I didn't know she was coming to Texas. She showed up this morning to have breakfast with my mom and when she found out we were coming to get you, she wanted to come along." Of course she did. She's operating on a level in a game I didn't even realize we were playing.

I hate her.

"I'm not this person, Brand. Jealousy is an ugly emotion and ever since Gray...it makes me worried that you might eventually realize you wanted more with her..."

He laughs without humor.

"No, baby. Nothing could ever happen between the two of us. I'm sorry for bringing her. That was stupid on my part." He kisses my forehead. "I love *you,* Ave. You're my forever."

Right now would be a good time to tell him I love him. But how can I when I know she's still lurking and planning my demise?

Fucking Ellen.

If I ever get her alone, I will knock her out.

First, I will get self-defense lessons.

Then, I will knock her out.

The kids get a head start and once Brandon declares enough time has passed, we head to short-term parking. They took two cars because he wanted to spend some time alone with me before all the chaos ensued.

Brandon gets recognized in the garage, but I don't. My disguise is iron clad for now. It's difficult to get a good look at someone who's wearing dark sunglasses that take up most of her face and a ball cap. For all they know, I could be his long-lost sister.

I snort at the thought.

Bev has been cooking all morning, according to Brand. She's making a roasted chicken and mashed potatoes. Somehow, this woman has found the way to my heart—and it's through my stomach. He stops at a *Jack in the Box* for some fries because the drive to the Wentworth estate is an hour away into the boonies.

Brandon sings along to the radio. It's surreal seeing him in his element. The wind rushes through his chestnut hair and the sun accentuates his olive complexion. The pale, white girl in me is envious of his forever tan. His smile is wide like he doesn't have a care in the world.

For one week only, he gets to be the Brandon Wentworth before he ran off to college. I'm just glad I get a front row seat.

I've been to Brandon's childhood home before. Of course, it was when I was with Gray, so I only got to see what Gray's life was like when he lived here. I'm curious to see how Brandon lived. Did he have babes taped to his wall? Did he ever bring girls up to his room?

An hour later, we pull up to Wentworth Acres. Why did Bev keep Preston's name?

"Hey Brand? Why did your mom keep his name?"

He grins and hops out of the truck. I follow suit and meet up with him at the back of the truck.

"She's a household name in farming, baby. Dad hated the agricultural life. It's why he went to Hollywood. He wanted to erase this part of his life. After what he did to mom, she kept it to show him he's still part of the agriculture, she's just better at it than he ever was."

Her truck is parked, and the suitcases are out of the bed of her truck. I stare up at the white farmhouse in amazement. Each window has a flower box with different brightly colored flowers. She grows herbs around the perimeter of her house. Horses and cattle graze in the pastures surrounding the house.

It's so peaceful.

He leads me up the front steps of the house and into the entryway. The most amazing smells permeate the air. There are garlic and lemon. The giggles of my favorite people in the world echo from the kitchen. When I turn the corner, Ethan and Alice are at the sink helping Bev peel and cut potatoes.

Ellen sits at the kitchen table cutting off the ends of the green beans that I'm certain grew on Bev's property.

"What are you guys doing?" I ask, ignoring Ellen completely.

"We're helping Nana with the potatoes," Alice informs me while pulling a whole, giant potato out of the pot so Bev can cut it.

"Can I help with anything?" Bev grins.

"I have some lemonade in the fridge, darlin'. Make yourself at home." I skip the lemonade but sit down at the table across from Ellen so I can stay close to the kids if I need to. Ellen doesn't give me the time of day. She cuts the green beans fiercely and throws them into a colander.

She has a history with this family. Gray always loved hanging out with her, and Brandon seems to enjoy having her around…it would be so much easier if she got to know me. Maybe that's her problem. She thinks I'm brother hopping.

"Are you happy to be home, Ellen?" This feels so forced, and even she knows it. She glances up at me and arches an eyebrow.

"Yeah, I am." Good talk.

"Hey." I lower my voice so we're out of hearing range for Bev and the kids. "I think we maybe got off on the wrong foot. You're important to Brand, and I'd love it if we could be friends." She drops her knife and glances over to the sink before lowering her voice.

"I don't want to be friends with you, Ava."

I raise my eyebrows in surprise. She's just so fucking blunt about it.

"Oh..."

"Brandon wants you because you were Gray's. That's how it's always been with the two of them. Gray is notorious for sleeping with Brandon's girls, and to get back at them, Brandon goes after Gray's. You're no exception. Besides, you were a disaster for Gray. What makes you think you're going to be any better for Brandon?"

This new, but questionable information hits me like a semi-truck. She *has* been around longer than I have...but it doesn't sound like something Brand would do.

I'm not taking this lying down, that's for damn sure.

"I don't know why you think that. Even if it were true, I know you're not looking out for me. I know he's an important part of your life, but don't you think it would be easier if we just buried the hatchet? We could be friendly. We could..."

I *don't* want to go shopping with her or invite her over for dinner. I don't want to be in the same room as her.

She scoffs. "See? You can't finish that sentence. I don't like you, Ava, and you don't like me. There's no point in trying to force a friendship. You're not going to last long. Once Brandon realizes you're not all that you're cracked up to be, he'll leave you. Ask Kayla."

My stomach churns. I wish I weren't the only one hearing her poison. I *wish* Brandon were here to listen to her.

"That's not true..."

"And what are your intentions, anyway? Are you just going to play happy family and wish he were Gray? He wanted children of his own, not his brother's. You're attention-seeking. You weren't invited to the Archer's party, yet you showed up anyway. The tabloids were right about you. You're a homewrecker. You enjoy the attention and you trap men to bend to your will."

What the actual *fuck* is she talking about? I want to explode. I want to punch her in the face. I want to give her a piece of my mind. But I can't do that in front of the woman I'm trying to make a good first impression for the second time or my children.

"I *was* invited to the Archer's party, for one. Two, don't believe everything you read in the tabloids. Gray asked *me* to marry *him*. It wasn't the other way around. Gray slept around because that's who he is. He wanted a divorce, so I gave him a divorce. Brandon was the one who wanted to start the relationship. I fought him on it for so long until I couldn't anymore. When did you start loving him?" Her eyes darken.

"Gray said Alice was a mistake. Is that true? It wasn't in the tabloids. That came from the horse's mouth."

"I was a mistake?" My world is kicked clean off its axis. Alice stands beside me with watery eyes. The atmosphere in the kitchen takes a dangerous turn.

"No, baby. You weren't a mistake. You were wanted, I promise." I yank Alice into me and kiss her head. My glare finds Ellen, who is clearly enjoying the chaos.

"I think it's time for you to leave," Brandon's voice booms from behind me. Ellen straightens and that stupid smirk she wore is now wiped clean off her face.

"Brandon—"

"Let's go." She stands up and storms out of the kitchen. The front door slams shut, rattling the windows.

"I'm sorry she said that, babe. People are mean when they're scared." Bev says with a sigh, occupying Ellen's chair.

"That wasn't a nice thing to say," Alice whimpers. As much of an asshole Gray is, I know he loves his children even if he has a shitty way of showing it.

"Some people get scared when the people they love are finding peace without them," Bev explains. She drowns out the shouting from outside.

"*Slut…family…homewrecker!*" That isn't the worst somebody has called me. Brandon doesn't shout back.

What a great start to our vacation.

"Uncle Brand is finding peace?" She nods and gives me a motherly smile. We haven't had the chance to talk about this yet, but I have a funny feeling that she approves.

"With you two and your mom. He loves you all so much. Ellen has been his friend since they were little kids. Ellen didn't have a good childhood, so she made a family with ours. But now she's seeing a change, and she's trying to protect her family. Sometimes people say things they don't mean when they're scared."

Oh no, she meant every word of it.

Brandon walks back into the house. He crouches next to Alice and pulls her into a hug.

"I'm sorry she said those things, sweetheart. That wasn't nice of her." Alice sniffles into his chest with a fresh bout of tears.

"Ethan, Alice, why don't you come with me to the garage? I've got some ice pops in the freezer we can snack on before dinner is ready," Bev announces. Ethan watches his sister protectively. Alice detaches herself from her knight in shining armor and follows her brother and Nana towards the garage.

"What was that all about?" Brandon asks quietly.

"I was just making conversation. I don't like being the jealous girlfriend, Brand. I was just trying to bury the hatchet, so it would make things easier. I wanted to be friends with her."

He purses his lips and steals the seat next to me.

"She said she asked *you* to be friends with her and you said no." That conniving, insensitive, rotten *bitch*.

"That's not what happened."

He wages an invisible war in his mind. Does he believe the woman he loves, or his oldest friend?

"You don't believe her, do you?" When he hesitates, my self-confidence plummets. "Oh my god. I can't believe this." I stand up and make a beeline for the door, but Brandon grabs my wrist.

"You haven't made it a secret you don't like her, Ave. I'm trying to give her the benefit of the doubt. She's not a spiteful person."

"But I am?" I rip my arm from his. "Don't answer that. Leave me alone, Brand. Don't follow me."

I put my trust in my former mother-in-law that she'll watch out for my children while I find a place to cry. Ellen's car is gone, though I wish she would've stayed around a little longer so I could smack her at least once.

I'm not a violent person.

The barn is a football field away from the house. If memory serves correct, there's a loft up there that nobody uses. I feel all sorts of eyes on me. Brandon most likely is watching me through the window, or Ethan may be running me down to save me.

Footsteps crunch in the grass behind me. Brandon has never been one to listen. So I run.

The barn door slides open with a little hesitation. The stalls are empty, but the pile of shavings is fresh and covered. I race up the rickety stairs to the loft and find a sofa and an old box TV. I ease myself onto the sofa in hopes of my weight not being much for old wood and dropping me through the ceiling.

He believes Ellen over me. He didn't even give me a chance to hear me out. She got to him first, so he believes the first story he heard.

On top of the box TV is an old paperback book. I grab it off the TV. *The Handmaid's Tale*. Gray *loves* that show. I wonder how many women have been up here. Was this Gray's bachelor pad? Did Brandon ever bring girls up here?

The couch is dusty, but I don't care. I was up early and my eyelids are heavy. In the distance, Ethan's voice calls me. For once, I don't want to be the strong one. I *need* someone to step in for me just once. I need a moment of peace.

Footsteps on the stairs have me closing my eyes in frustration. If I pretend I'm asleep, maybe they'll go away.

"Ave?" What part of don't follow me doesn't he understand?!

"Go away." He crosses the catwalk and sits on my feet.

"No, I'm not going away. I want to talk to you."

"About what? You were clear on who you believe. Do you believe I'm a homewrecker?"

"No. And stop putting words in my mouth." He takes the weight off my feet and swings them up so now they're resting on his lap.

"I don't know what you want from me, Brand. I came here hoping to spend the week with you without the fear of media, but when I get here, I'm accused of starting a fight with the woman you claim doesn't love you. I'm not a liar."

"I know you're not." He sighs. "I'm sorry. We're on the same team."

I scoff. Yeah right.

"I've played second best my entire marriage to Gray. I won't do that again."

"You're not second best, baby. You're *the* best. There's nobody above you."

Except for your best friend.

"I believe you. You're a kind person and you don't like confrontation. Ellen...she's prickly. Her parents have always been hard on her and sometimes I forget that I'm the only one in her corner."

I refuse to feel sorry for her. Everything that came out of her mouth was intended to inflict maximum pain. How dare she say my baby was a mistake *right in front of her?*

"Do you promise me that there's nothing between you two? Is there something I need to worry about?" A genuine smile replaces the worry on his face.

"I promise. I don't love her like I love you." I hope to god he's right. I haven't loved someone like this...ever.

Gray is different. I loved him because I was young and naïve. It was what we were expected to do, get married, have kids.

But with Brandon...

It's the full confidence someone is fighting the cruelty in the world alongside you. He carries my heart with extreme care while keeping a watchful eye on Ethan and Alice. It's knowing that at the end of the day, I have a chance to feel like a loved human being instead of the entire world speculating and shitting on every single relationship you've ever been a part of.

"Will you come back inside? Ellen's gone. She's going back to Chicago tomorrow, anyway."

"Yeah. Okay."

He grins and leans over to kiss my lips.

"I love you, Ave."

I love you too.

Bev is the mother I wish I had growing up. She prepares a meal fit for a king. Her roasted chicken is perfectly golden brown and her mashed potatoes are lump-free and buttery. She laughs at Alice's corny jokes and listens to Ethan as he tells her about being Mathematician of the class. Every so often, she looks up at me and gives me a reassuring smile.

Why does it still feel like I'm waiting for the other shoe to drop? After dinner, Alice announces she's going to take a nap on the couch. Ethan follows suit, but trudges up to Gray's old bedroom. Sometimes,

I feel like I'm looking at an old man trapped in a little boy's body. He rubs his eyes and licks his lips as he struggles to keep his eyes open.

"Thanks for lunch, Nana. It was really good."

"Thank you, baby. Go get some shut-eye. I have an apple pie to put in the oven for dessert later. He gives her a sleepy grin and drags up the rest of the way on the stairs. Brandon is up immediately. He makes up a fresh pot of coffee and begins putting the food away in leftover containers. "Would you like to join me outside, darlin'?"

My anxiety fires on all cylinders. Here we go.

"Sure." We wait for the coffee to stop brewing and pour ourselves mugs. I envy her for her wrap-around porch. I could imagine coming out here, watching the sunrise, and enjoying my morning coffee on my porch swing.

I park myself on the porch swing that faces the pasture directly behind the house. Every so often, we see the horses get closer to the fence.

"I'm really glad you decided to come. I haven't seen you in so long." I feel terrible. I shouldn't be avoiding her when all she's ever been is nice.

"Me too. Though...I don't know. I stayed away because I thought maybe you would've hated me for what happened between Gray and me." She brings the mug up to her lips and takes a sip.

"We've all seen what Grayson has turned into, sweetheart. Lord knows I *tried* to set him straight. When I saw that first news story about that Lucy Rodriguez woman, it felt like Preston cheating on me all over again. Only this time, I worried about you. He was following the same path as his father and he wasn't open to hearing anyone's opinions, let alone mine. When you finally kicked him to the curb, I wanted to reach out to you, but I remember trying to raise kids and being a divorcee. There's not enough time to do anything, and I didn't want to be a burden."

I weakly smile.

"If you would've reached out, I would've been so humiliated."

She shakes her head sadly.

"No, baby. I don't hate you for leaving Grayson. Honestly, I'm surprised you stayed as long as you did. I've seen many women leave for lesser things."

"I wonder about that sometimes. I stayed because I thought the kids needed us to be together. Then it was clear to me he wasn't going to change. I don't know. I was tired. Literally, figuratively, mentally..."

"There comes a point where you wonder if it's even worth it anymore."

Exactly.

I catch Brandon watching us in concern from the kitchen window. Bev follows my gaze and grimaces and shoes him away.

"I wasn't going to say this, but I always thought you were better suited for Brandon. The two of you..." She sighs dreamily, "You had the same ideals, the same philosophy on family."

I giggle and think about the moment I first met Brandon. It was in this very house. Gray wanted to introduce me to his mom to prove that he could land someone. Brandon and Kayla were here, and when I walked in, they both froze. I think I was the first celebrity they ever met besides Gray. It was sweet. Kayla hugged me and told me she was a big fan. Brandon, always the shy guy, was much more subtle. He shook my hand and welcomed me to the family. We exchanged maybe two sentences that whole trip.

"Can I ask you something?" I ask cautiously.

"Sure."

"Do you think I have anything to worry about with Ellen?"

She barks out a laugh and shakes her head.

"I promise you, darlin', there's nothing to worry about. She loves Brandon, much like you do, but he has never seen her the way he sees you. You're his lighthouse. She's just a friend he never had an interest in."

The knots in my stomach loosen. I'm not crazy!

"Anyway, I think Grayson always held a candle for her." That's laughable. That isn't the impression I got from him. He avoided her like the plague. That very first visit, she came over and hung out with Brandon and Kayla the entire time. Gray kept himself busy in the room we shared and whenever he had to interact with her, he was very short and matter of fact.

That would be an interesting pairing though. They'd kill each other.

"You have a beautiful property, Bev. I'm so jealous. I'd love a place like this to get lost in."

She chuckles.

"You say that now, but when I wake you up to help me feed tomorrow, you won't be singing the same tune." Maybe she's right, but I'm excited to turn her down. "Sorry to keep you going down this road with you, but I just want to say…I'm so proud of you."

This grabs my attention.

I don't think *anyone* has ever said those words to me.

"Parenting is hard. You have two lives to shape, and you had to do it with no input from Grayson. You have wonderful kids. They're so polite—I don't think my kids ever offered to help me cook dinner."

I assure you, my kids never have asked me either, but they love their Nana. Ethan's protection pulls Bev under his umbrella.

"How did you get through it?" My question sobers her. The smile she wore slightly fades. She taps her fingernails on the side of her mug as she thinks about it.

"I didn't have a choice. I had two boys who depended on me to make life normal. I was a woman in a man's world, and I poured my blood, sweat, and tears into making a good life for them. It's amazing what you can do when you don't have the choice to fail."

She's absolutely right. I couldn't rely on Gray for anything. He paid child support and alimony, but other than that, it was almost like he didn't exist. Except for the demanding phone calls to see the kids and cancel at the last minute.

We're badass women. We pull ourselves up our bootstraps and get the bitch done.

"One day, your kids are going to grow up and move out on their own. The best thing you can do for them is to teach them how to be happy, to find joy when it's almost impossible to. They're going to look back on their childhood and see how much you did for them, how you showed them to be responsible and compassionate. They'll find wonderful partners who only want the best for them. And that's all because of the education *you* provided. You're an amazing mother, Ava. I know you question yourself often. Hell, *I* questioned myself any chance I got—but you're doing it. You shield them from the bullshit I *know* he doles out and still tries to make him out to be a good guy."

The tears come before I even know what's happening. Nobody has ever fully understood what it was like to raise two children with Grayson Wentworth except for Bev. Sure, she had her own Wentworth to deal with, but from what I understand, he was no walk in the park either. I've never felt so *seen*.

"We're not so different. I'm not a Hollywood A-lister like you are, but the Wentworth family is well known in this town. We'd known each other since kindergarten. We dated through high school, and then our parents started planning a wedding. Preston hadn't even asked me to marry him yet. But his family was a nationally recognized name when it came to crops. My family was most recognized for livestock. My family provided forty percent of this country's meat. Obviously, it was our parents' dream for us to shack up. We'd double the income on both sides."

She shrugs sadly. She married him. Because what else could she have done?

"College wasn't an option for both of us. Preston didn't want anything to do with farming. He begged his father to allow him to go to college, but he refused. He wanted to be an actor. He wanted to see his name on the big screen. It was a pipe dream until it wasn't.

Preston's father bought more property, roughly one hundred more acres, and was preparing it for corn. He ended up striking oil.

"The government wanted in on it immediately. They offered them a handsome sum, but they refused. They wanted to keep it within the family and have control over who it went to. Honestly, it would've been better if his father sold it to the government because one summer he had a stroke. The line of succession started. We inherited a ton of land Preston didn't want, except for that one hundred acres. He turned around and sold it to the government for quadruple the price."

"How'd you feel?"

"Happy that we could finally consolidate everything. When I found out what he did, his parents were livid. We all were. There wasn't anything they could do. Preston held their livelihood in his hands. Anyway, he started participating in some plays, enrolled in the local community college. He finally had enough material to put together a demo reel. Somebody in Hollywood finally took interest and then he went to California.

"By that time, he was already done with me. We hadn't made love in years. He barely paid attention to the kids, and when he did, he was always yelling. The gossips at church would talk loudly about the affairs he had with people in town. It was humiliating."

I can relate. I know *exactly* how it feels for your circle constantly judging you for the actions of your husband.

"One week, he came home for the weekend and surprised me. He informed me he was leaving me, and I needed to find a new place to live. I lost it. I yelled at him, threw our expensive China at him—whatever was close to me was thrown in his direction. I ran out of ammo, and he got close enough to me to grab me by the throat. I could see the evil in his eyes. I knew I was a goner."

"But Brandon walked in on you, right?" I've never heard the whole story, only the Cliff's Notes from Brandon. Her smile wanes, and she heaves a heavy sigh.

"He was supposed to be at school. He claims that he had a tummy ache and turned around to come home. He just happened to be in the right place at the right time. I don't know what you believe in, Ava, but *I* believe God was with Brandon that day. He was only ten years old. He had so much growing to do, but he was able to push Preston off of me. He called the police and Preston ran. My ten-year-old little boy witnessed his father trying to murder me. That's something you don't get over."

Of course, it doesn't. Brandon isn't the kind of guy to express his deep feelings or his inner demons. He's a fixer. He wants to be there for everyone and be the hero. When will he be the hero for himself?

"Anyway, I was rushed to the hospital. The kids stayed with my parents. A day or two later, Preston finally showed up at the hospital. He paid for the visit and said he was sorry. He still wanted a divorce, but I was prepared to give it to him with my own conditions. He was terrified for his reputation. If this got out, his career as an actor would never take off. So, I used that to my advantage. I told him that if he wanted the divorce, he'd sign all the properties over to me. He was pissed, but he agreed. And then I told him he could never contact the boys ever again. If I found out he did, I would leak that story to anyone who would listen."

It's finally coming together. When I worked with Preston, the only time we interacted was in the scenes we had together. I understand why he wouldn't talk to Gray.

"Have you ever told Gray about this?"

She shakes her head sadly. "No. I told him that Preston left, and he wasn't coming back. Naturally, he blamed it on me. I dealt with my own insecurities. Was I not pretty enough to be seen with him on the red carpet *if* that ever came to be? Was my body too toned because I did *all* of the farm work? Was it something I did or said? It took me years of therapy to realize it wasn't my fault. I married a man I had no business marrying. His needs and wants were always put before mine. He didn't fill my cup. I did end up telling Gray some of it in hopes of a wake-up call. But that didn't work. I think it made everything worse, so for that, I'm sorry."

She reaches over and squeezes my hand.

"I'm sorry for what you went through. Gray never tried to hurt me physically, so I guess maybe you win. But it's the infidelity and the humiliation the hurts the worst," I admit.

"Nobody wins, babe. But you and me? We came out on the other side and live to tell the tale." She glances over to the window, but Brandon is gone.

There is so much to unpack. I mean, I can sort of understand Gray's need to have a family, but why abandon us? It doesn't make any sense.

We finish our coffee and talk about what plans we have for the week. There's a rodeo on Wednesday she wants to take the kids to. Bev isn't the kind of woman who likes to stay idle. When we go inside, the table is already cleared, and the dishwasher is running. She declares she's going down to the bigger barn to start getting afternoon feed ready.

The living room is filled with tiny snores from my pint-sized twin. She sleeps so soundly with the blanket, practically covering the entirety of her face, which I pull down slightly so I don't have to worry about her suffocating.

I'm entranced by the pictures that canvas the walls. There's one that hangs in the back of the living room of the three of them. Bev is young, probably thirty or so. Brandon grins widely and holds Gray in his lap. They wear red bandanas around their necks with small cowboy hats. It's so corny, it's endearing.

I make my way to the stairs where I'm graced with more pictures. There are hundreds. Halloweens, Easters, high school graduations, band concerts. I stop in my tracks and quickly take a picture of Brand holding his trombone. That's a keeper.

When I reach the top of the stairs, I creep past Gray's old room. Gray picked up the important things he wanted from his childhood bedroom years ago. All that's left is the bed and dresser. Bev has framed a few of his playbills from when he attended high school, but that's about it. Ethan sleeps in a ball. Unlike his sister, he doesn't snore. He sleeps with the blanket covering him except for the one leg that sticks out. I slowly close the doors and turn to the open staircase that leads to the attic.

That's Brandon's old room.

Apparently, while Brandon was in high school, they renovated the attic, so Brandon felt he had his own space away from Gray. I creep up the stairs to find Brandon lying on the bed, shirtless—*thank you, God*—and typing away on his laptop. I sidle up next to him and rest my head against his beefy arm.

"Did you and my mom have a good talk?" I smile.

"Mmhm. I know all your secrets now, Wentworth. I know about all the women you snuck up to that barn."

He snorts.

"Nice try. That was my fortress of solitude—no chicks allowed." I giggle. He closes the laptop and hugs me close. "I'm sorry for today."

"I'm sorry. I trust you. I promise."

He kisses my forehead and sniffs my hair. Weirdo. "Don't apologize. It's been a weird day. It's nothing a nap couldn't fix." That sounds heavenly. Kicking my shoes off, I scurry under the covers and hug Brandon close to me.

"Hey Brand?"

"Hmm?"

"For the record...I love you too." I've never seen a smile so big. He won't jinx it by telling me, *"I told you so,"* instead, he grabs my leg and pulls me on top of him so that I'm straddling his lap.

"Don't make a sound, Ave."

Twenty-Two

Brandon

Then

I never thought I'd have to worry about Ellen fucking everything up for me. But that comment she made about Alice being a mistake, I couldn't believe what I was hearing. I know she doesn't like Ava, but it's only because she doesn't know her. When you're around someone for as long as Ellen and I have been around each other, you pick up on each other's mannerisms.

For instance, when Ellen lies, she avoids eye contact and touches her face. She straight up told me that she wanted to be friends with Ava. I knew she was lying, but I just didn't want to believe it. I know how that sounds...

I'm not a wishy-washy person.

But why would she lie about that?

I was relieved when I caught her father on the road yesterday morning with her in the passenger seat on the way to the airport. I love Ellen like she's a sister. But I won't tolerate her breaking hearts. That's not okay. Especially when she's breaking the heart of my six-year-old best friend/niece.

The kids haven't talked about it since the moment Ellen left. But I notice how Alice has toned down her usual boisterous personality. I just hope that it's not weighing on her.

I've slept with Ava in my arms for the last two nights. My body wakes up hours before I get out of bed and I watch her sleep. It's creepy as hell, but what else am I supposed to do? Her guard is down when she's asleep. It's the only time I get to witness her as she is. She told me she loves me, so naturally, that's a game-changer. I have so many plans put in place, but still, she keeps her guard up around me.

She wasn't lying when she said she's an open book. She doesn't have many secrets, and the ones she does have are so juvenile it's hysterical. The media has told her every secret to the world. But what about her deepest, darkest desires?

Will she want another wedding? Does she want more children?

I'm scared to even bring it up. I have this nagging sensation in the pit of my stomach that if I do, she'll bolt the other way.

I'm sick of being in hiding. We've been here a total of two days so far and it has been liberating not to hide inside.

But still, I keep my mouth shut. It's something we'll revisit when we get back home.

She stirs against my bare chest. She's stark naked under these sheets. Her silky skin is icy against mine.

"Take a picture, Wentworth. It'll last longer."

Chuckling, I kiss her forehead and grope her ass. She's so sassy in the morning. "Maybe I will. I can add it to my spank bank for when we go home."

She scoffs without opening her eyes.

"Have the kids woken up yet?"

"No. They're still sleeping. My mom is taking them to the rodeo later, but I have something planned for the two of us."

Her smile stretches against my chest. "Hmm. Home alone. Are you sure you're allowed to have girls in your room when mom's not home?"

I slap the cold skin of her ass. She shudders and giggles.

"You're trouble."

"Yeah, but you enjoy it."

I do. Holy hell, I do.

"Get up, heathen. Go shower and get dressed. I'll start on breakfast." As I start turning to get out of bed, she grabs me from around the waist and holds me down.

"I have a better offer. Stay in bed with me, Brand." It's a *way* better plan.

"Oh yeah? What's in it for me?"

Her beautiful cornflower eyes finally open, flashing with mischief. She disappears under the comforter. Her hand grips my harder than a rock dick, and then her velvety mouth replaces her hand.

Holy shit.

Her tongue is sinful. It swirls around the tip until she takes me all the way to the back of her throat.

Sweet Jesus.

The good lord could take me home, now. This has been my every fantasy since I found out who Ava Reid was.

Her head bobs up and down. Heat pools in my belly. My fingers thread into her messy hair.

"Fuck, Ave," I hiss as she cups my balls with her other hand. Her lips tighten down my shaft, sending me to the brink of insanity. I search for that friction and slam into her mouth, making her gag.

When she regains her composure, she takes me into her mouth again and hums against my shaft. The vibrations make me come so close. She strokes my shaft with her hand while she focuses on the tip.

"Please don't stop," I plead. My vision gets spotty and my ears begin to pop. I hold her head in my hands and piston my hips for that sweet release. I explode in her mouth. The covers are lifted over her head. She laps up my release with a wink and a victorious smirk.

She sidles up in bed beside me, forcing me to be her big spoon.

"Okay, okay. You win."

"I told you, Brand. I don't lose."

Yeah, I know that.

"I love you, Ave."

Giggling, her slick slit brushes against my cock. "You're only saying that because I give good head." I force her to turn around and look me in the eye. I push her hair out of her eyes and press my forehead against hers.

"You give amazing head." I kiss her lips. "I love *you*, did you know that?"

She sobers at my words and gives me a halfhearted nod.

"I love you, Brand. Don't disappear now that I've said it, okay?"

"I promise you I won't disappear. I'm all in, baby. The good, the bad, the ugly. I'll be here through all of it."

It appears Ethan is a control freak. It's comical. He respects the animals at a distance. He refuses to ride a horse, but he'll feed them treats. From what I'm gathering, he understands that animals have minds of their own. He just doesn't want to be on top of a horse when it decides he's done with the ride.

I get it.

He helps my mom with feeding. Alice, on the other hand, is so involved in the day-to-day of it all. She wakes up early to help with morning feed, helps clean out stalls, and even exercises horses with mom. It's impressive.

This life is a part of them, whether Gray likes it or not.

After our romp this morning, Ava spent the morning with mom and Alice while Ethan and I stayed back to work on the hay fields. Tonight is the night of the rodeo out in Dallas. The kids have been so excited for it that mom rooted through my and Gray's old clothes and picked out a couple of western shirts to wear with their city jeans.

I wish I could be there to see their faces when they see bull riding or barrel racing for the first time. But it's risky. Ava and I are recognizable, and I'm not about to ruin a good trip with gossip.

Even if the gossip is true.

As five o'clock rolls around, I help get the kids ready to go. Mom promises to buy them cowboy hats of their own and when Ava offers to give her money, she is promptly turned down.

Once the truck is down the drive, we start to get ready. I have a friend who owns a small restaurant halfway to Dallas that agreed to close the restaurant for the two of us tonight.

I crave a night where none of us have to cook or clean up after ourselves. My friend, Garett, was my best friend in high school. So, when I offered a handsome sum just to have dinner with my girlfriend, he didn't hesitate to close for the day one bit.

By six o'clock, my lovely lady descends the stairs in a strapless yellow sundress with a pair of red heels. Her makeup is done up gorgeous, not that she needs it, and her hair is ironed straight.

She's beautiful. And I'm the lucky son of a bitch who gets to take her out tonight.

Her smile is tight-lipped. When I reach for her hand, she holds it tightly. We lock up and get into the truck without a single word.

She watches the house with a sense of longing.

"Ave?"

"Is your friend going to talk?"

My gut twists.

"No, he's not. The whole restaurant is ours for the evening. It's just Garrett and his wife who will be there, I promise."

This is supposed to be a nice evening. It's a real date for fuck's sake!

"I'm sorry...I'm just thinking of the worst-case scenario."

"Do you trust me?" Her sad eyes meet mine and she nods. "I have the place scoped out. Garrett closed for the whole day. We're parking in the back and going into a private room where there are no windows. We won't be seen, I promise."

How crappy is that? I can't even take my girlfriend out for a nice dinner and show the world how proud I am of her.

I just wish she could relax for once...and be proud of me.

It takes us an hour to reach the restaurant. The parking lot is deserted, much to my pleasure. I swing around back and find Garrett's car and park next to him. Ava takes a moment to give herself a silent pep talk through the mirror and finally tells me she's ready.

Alex, Garrett's wife, opens the door with a wide smile and allows us in.

"I'm so glad you made it!" She kisses me on the cheek and squeezes my arm. We've known each other since high school, and it's been an embarrassingly long time since the last time we saw each other.

She turns to Ava and hesitantly opens her arms for a hug.

"I'm sorry...I'm not exactly sure how to act around you. I'm a *huge* fan. And Brand here is one of my favorite people in the world."

Ava grins and accepts Alex's hug.

"Thank you so much for closing up for us. I'm sure this wasn't ideal." Alex grins and waves her off, pushing the fly-aways of her mousy brown hair out of her face.

"Don't even worry about it. Even if Brand came alone, we would've closed up for him. We're so happy that you came along. Come on back. We have a private room for the two of you. No windows, no chances of being seen."

She leads us through the dining room to a dimly lit private room. There are candles everywhere and a basket of bread on the table.

"Make yourselves comfortable. Garrett's just picking out your wine for tonight." Alex makes herself scarce, and for the first time in an hour, Ava visibly relaxes.

"Feeling better?" She shrugs nonchalantly and drops her gaze.

"A little. I thought they were going to be judgmental about us." What is the nicest way of telling her that the only person who gives a shit about how our relationship looks is her?

And eventually Gray. But who the fuck cares about him, anyway?

"You look beautiful." Her cheeks flush.

"Thank you. You look very handsome." I reach for her hand and caress the skin on the back of it.

"How does it feel? We're on a date, semi in public..." I wriggle my eyebrows suggestively. "We have the whole night ahead of us, Ave. The kids will be home late, and I still have to repay you for this morning."

Her pupils dilate and her breath catches in her throat.

"Hey now, I know I gave you the place for the evening, but maybe don't use it as your love shack." Ava's eyes widen and bursts into nervous giggles as Garrett approaches the table with a Pinot Noir. "Ava Reid, it's so nice to finally meet you. My wife is a huge fan." He claps my back with a knowing grin and places the bottle of wine in the ice bucket next to the table. "And we're happy this guy finally found someone nice."

She becomes braver the more Garrett talks "Nice, eh? What has he been telling you?"

"Not much, unfortunately. He mentioned he was bringing a special lady here but wouldn't tell us who it was." Her gaze softens. "Anyway, take a look at the menu. Brand's capable of pouring the wine himself. Just holler if you need anything. We'll be back in a little bit to take your selections." Garrett leaves us alone.

The walls she builds around her heart are impenetrable. She's untrusting and cautious. But tonight, it's different. The bricks are starting to come down, one by one.

"Brand?"

"Hmm?"

"You didn't tell them who I was?"

"I didn't think you'd want me to. I know how much your privacy means to you." She sighs and reaches for my hand.

"It's not always going to be like this. I promise I'm kind of fun when the world isn't sitting on my shoulders."

She *wants* to give herself to me. But we can't keep doing this one foot in, one foot out bullshit we've been pulling for the last few months.

"I'm here to share the load, baby. You don't have to do this all on your own." She squeezes my hand as her eyes turn watery.

"I'm sorry for all the secrecy and this weird life I've created. I never thought I'd meet someone and fall so hopelessly as I fell for you. My life was supposed to be quiet after Gray. I was supposed to raise my kids and send them off with the tools they needed to deal with life. You coming into our life has been a blessing. And I know this arrangement we have isn't ideal, but I appreciate you for indulging me."

I lean over the table and press my lips to hers. Indulging the secrecy is stupid. I hate every minute of it, and I'm angry most of the time for even suggesting it.

But it's worth the smile on her face and the quality time we get to spend together. It's the only reason why I don't regret suggesting it.

"You're worth it, Ave. I love you for being exactly who you are. I love you for being the badass mother you are, and for *finally* loving me." Her bottom lip wobbles.

"I love you, Brand. I tell you I love you, but you have no idea how much I mean it."

There *has* to be an end date soon. I'm putting a ring on her finger and I'm locking this down. There's no fucking way I'm going to live in secret for the rest of our lives together.

This is a step in the right direction, though.

"I don't want to cry tonight, Brand," she says softly. "These are happy tears, but I put a lot of work into my appearance tonight."

"And you look beautiful. You're always beautiful, even if I ruin your makeup."

Letting go of her hand, I stand up and pour her wine in hopes it will erase the heaviness that hangs in the room.

We ask Garrett to surprise us. I scoot my chair close to hers and pull her into my side. Her skin erupts in goosebumps at my fingertips dragging on the silkiness of her arm.

"Tell me a secret, Ave." She rests her head on my shoulder and sighs.

"I don't have any. I told you...I'm an open book."

"Fine. I'll tell *you* a secret." She peers up at me, expectantly for something profound. "Your snoring is terrible." She gasps and lightly smacks my gut.

"You're horrible. I don't snore."

"You're like a lumberjack sawing wood. You snore, and it's adorable." She laughs easily, covering her mouth. It lightens the mood significantly.

"You're disgusting. Women don't snore. You wanna know a secret, Brand? You're old." My chest bounces with laughter, which results into her giggling into my chest.

"That's not a secret, because I'm not old."

"You're older than me." Chuckling, I hold her left hand and imagine the rock I'm going to put on her ring finger. She'll be mine, and she'll be happy. The kids will be happy. Everything will fall into place.

"Can I ask you something kind of serious?"

She grows weary almost instantly. "Will it make me cry?"

"No, I don't think so. I don't always aim to make you cry, you know."

She smiles weakly.

Right. Get on with it.

"Where do you see yourself in five years?"

She arches her eyebrow in confusion.

"Do you mean professionally?"

"Professionally, personally...whatever. I want to hear about what you want out of life five years from now."

She purses her lips and softens her features as she thinks about it.

"Professionally, I want to star in movies that require your brain to think. I'd *love* to work with Christopher Nolan. I love his work. Personally...I don't know. I mean, I want the kids to be happy. I want...I want you still to be here. I just want to be happy."

"Do I make you happy, Ave?"

"Yeah, Brand," she murmurs, "You make me the happiest I've ever been."

My lips fuse to hers.

She's the answer to my prayers, the focus of my hopes and dreams. We walk around this life wondering what our purpose is. I always knew I wanted to help women in domestic abuse situations—that's what the Live Oaks Foundation is for. But I'm starting to realize that helping Ava learn to trust, to be in a healthy relationship and not wait for the other shoe to drop, to be loved unconditionally is the most rewarding thing I've ever got to be a part of.

I get to be a part of my niece's and nephew's life and help shape them into functioning adults and great human beings.

I was meant to be with Ava Reid. She's the final piece of my puzzle.

"What about you? Where do you want to be in five years?"

"Retired, hopefully. I don't know how many more concussions my brain can take. And personally, well, I hope I'm married to you." Her body tenses, but I think it's more of the alleged butterflies women are supposed to have. "I want a life with you. Maybe we'll buy a beach house together so we can escape with the kids for the summer."

"Or...a farm?"

She surprises me every damn day.

"Really?"

"I like it out here. Your mom's place is the foundation of my ideal life. I'd love to drink my morning coffee on the porch swing and read a book in that reading nook upstairs while a thunderstorm rolls through. It's peaceful here. It's...home."

She'd make me the happiest man on Earth if we got to move back here. I'd give her the fucking moon.

"So, you don't regret coming here with me?" She shakes her head.

"No, I'm really happy you talked me into it. The kids are happy too. I get to spend quality time with you. This is my favorite vacation, ever, Brand." I kiss her temple. I'm doing my job, then. I'm taking care of my favorite person in the entire universe and she's happy.

Garrett arrives with two plates of spaghetti.

"Pasta Aglio y olio. Enjoy, desserts on deck."

It is no secret Ava's love language is pasta. She stares lovingly at it. She devours it with her eyes, and a smile large enough to make an imprint on my heart.

"Eat up, Ave. We have a long night ahead of us."

I'm bringing her to all the places I wish I could've taken her if I met her first. It's going to be a night to remember.

Twenty-Three

Ava

Then

Garrett and Alex's place is adorable. Alex explains that after high school, they ditched Texas and lived in Italy for ten years before coming back. They learned the Italian way of cooking and brought it back to the states so they could start a family together. They end up eating dessert with us—nothing that's on the menu. This is a Garrett special that only gets shared with Brand and me.

Brandon was the guy that ruled the school. Alex describes him as brooding, Garrett describes him as aloof. It all adds up, honestly. Brandon waves them off dismissively and I don't miss the adorable blush that colors his cheeks.

"He was asked by four different girls to go to prom." I raise my eyebrows in surprise.

"Really? Who did you end up going with?" Garrett scoffs.

"Please, Brandon wasn't going to prom. He didn't want to fall into anything that would ruin his shot at the NFL. The guy was seventeen and planning out his future and nailing down all the insignificant details. Anyway, four girls were broken-hearted that he turned them down."

"He was the community service king. He had so many volunteer hours that the school had to create a new cord for him to wear at graduation," Alex brags.

"Don't you guys have anything better to talk about?" Brandon mumbles under his breath.

"What? You don't think we're doing a good job of talking you up? That's hurtful, man. I closed my restaurant for you." Alex nudges Garrett in the ribs playfully.

"*Our* restaurant," Alex scolds.

Garrett grins.

"You guys are talking about all the embarrassing shit. Tell her about my records, about that farmer I saved from a tractor fire."

"Heroics are nice, but they're not the whole story, Brand. I like hearing about what you were like back then." He grimaces like he doesn't believe a word that comes out of my mouth. I give his knee a reassuring squeeze and turn back to Alex.

"Anyway," Brandon interrupts. "Thank you again for dinner, but we have another stop to make." My stomach churns at the notion of going out in public again. My belly is full of carbs and olive oil, and the company is so friendly.

"Ah, you killjoy," Garrett jokes, helping Alex to her feet. "It was really nice to meet you, Ava." They both hug me tight. I made two new friends tonight and they don't care about my name. They just care that Brandon is taken care of. That I can get behind.

I practically waddle to Brandon's truck. I hop onto the cracked bench seat and scoot to the middle so I can be closer to Brandon while he drives.

We head back to the farm. I'm crashing fast and my eyelids feel heavy, but I don't want to miss a thing.

My first dates with everyone else have felt...foreign. Like I had to make a good first impression and set myself up so that he could feel like he had a future with me.

But with Brand, I feel like myself. I was terrified to tell him that I love him. I was terrified his friends would hate me for once being married to his brother. Tonight, there were no false pretenses. He already knows what he's getting from me. I have money, but so does he. I have a house that's paid off, but he does too. All I have to offer him is a life of happiness. Good thing he's not materialistic.

He croons songs of Tim McGraw into my ear while his hand lies on my hip. He has the voice of an angel, and I'm the lucky bitch who gets to listen to him all night long.

Bev's truck isn't in the driveway when we get home. Traversing gravel in my highest heels should be an Olympic sport. I'd suck ass at it, but I'd at least be in the running.

Sensing my struggle, he literally sweeps me off my feet and carries me into the barn, setting me down when we reach the foot of the stairs. He allows me to climb up the stairs before him on the pretense that he's a gentleman when really, I *know* my ass looks good and he wants a gander. I sway my hips with each step, giving him the show of his life.

"You're sassy tonight, Ave. You better behave or there will be a spanking in store for later."

My heart races faster at that threat. For extra measure, I pop my heel at the landing for the sake of being extra.

Spank me, Brand. I'll like it.

The loft is softly lit by at least a hundred battery-operated candles. An air mattress is set up in the middle of the loft. Brandon fishes his phone out of his dress pants and puts on some playlist of love ballads.

The music flitters in the air with a cool chill. He gently pulls my waist, inching me closer to him. He holds my other hand and sways along to the music.

"I didn't go to prom because I didn't want to go with the wrong girl." Of course not. Brandon Wentworth has had everything figured out since he was old enough to form thoughts. "But let's just say you went to high school with me—"

"I couldn't have. You're six years older than me."

He scoffs and lightly spanks my ass.

"*If* I could do a redo prom, I'd want to take you. We'd probably leave after dinner, but this is where I would've taken you. We would've danced, just like we are now. You'd wear some gorgeous gown that would've taken ten moms to get you out of, and heels that would cut of the circulation in your feet. I imagine women like their hair to look like poodles—"

"Now you're just being an ass." His throaty chuckle makes me giggle. I can't stay mad at him.

"I didn't get to go to prom and I'm okay with that. It's brought me to this moment. I'm dancing with you in my barn. We're home alone, and I get to spend a delicious," he briefly glances at his watch, "three hours with you before the kids come looking for you."

The soft light against his tan skin reminds me of some book cover or movie poster. He's the handsome hero who gets the girl in the end. And I guess he is. His words are pretty, and his promises aren't empty.

"Three hours, hmm? That doesn't sound like a long time..." His smirk grows and his eyes darken. His erection presses hard against my stomach, threatening me with a good time.

"Then I suggest we cram as much as we can in between then." He presses his lips to mine, like he can't get enough of me. His other hand fists my hair possessively. Flashes of light fill the loft, breaking our contact. Curiously, Brandon moves to the window to investigate. My heart drops to my stomach. "It's just heat lightning. It'll pass soon." He stalks towards me, unbuttoning his shirt one button at a time, until he shrugs it off and it floats to the floor.

I adore the trail of chest hair in the valley of his pecs. My fingers explore every inch of his torso, committing it all to memory, so I have something to dream about when we have to go back home.

I fumble around with his belt buckle while he pulls the zipper of my dress down. I've never had sex publicly before. And while this isn't exactly public, it's not in the comfort of my own house.

It's different.

This is Brandon's fantasy about me.

Maybe in another life, there wouldn't be much of an age difference between us. Maybe I wouldn't marry his brother because I met him first. The other life can suck it because I'm in ecstasy right now. The air cools down, but Brandon's fiery skin against mine is a mind fogging distraction.

His hot breath fans against my skin and he gasps when he realizes I wasn't wearing a damn thing under this dress. I ditch my heels, and when I pull his pants down, he ditches his shoes.

We're buck naked in his barn in the glowing candlelight and the knowledge that at some point, my former, but future mother-in-law and my children will be pulling into the driveway soon. He pushes me gently into a corner and crowds me so that the only thing I can focus on is his cologne that fills my senses, and the sweat on his forearms. He shoves his knee in between my thighs.

He feels what he does to me, my want seeping out of me and onto his thigh. He feels how ready I am for him. I want it to hurt, but only in the best ways.

His lips assault the crook of my neck. His hands roam my body, pinching my nipple while the other finds my bundle of nerves and forces me to moan in pleasure. I shiver against the post I lean against. He lifts me and carries me to the air mattress. He kneels on the floor and spreads my legs wide open.

He admires the view and dives in. His tongue assaults me in ways that give me temporary amnesia.

"Brand, please..." my voice trails off as he slowly inserts a finger inside of me. His tongue teases my clit. He sucks, he nibbles, he soothes. "Oh my god," I whimper. My breath explodes as he enters a second finger, pumping in and out.

"You taste so good, Ave. You're my favorite dessert." My head falls back onto the mattress. I fist the sheets and my control slips away.

"Brand, stop. I'm going to come!" My thighs tighten and contract. He gives me a moment of reprieve. He stops my ecstasy and forces me to stand up. I crouch onto my knees, cheekily peering up at him and smirking. I tease his shaft with only two fingers, collecting the bead of pleasure at the tip and sucking it off my finger. He tries so hard to keep his composure but is failing miserably. I close my eyes and savor his salty taste.

I take him into my mouth, all the way to the back of my throat.

"Fuck!" He growls. I start slowly, driving him crazy for how slow I'm taking this. I want this night to last forever. He fists my hair and forces me to go faster. I gasp for air when I gag on his length. Helping me up, he lifts me, lining himself up to my entrance and slamming inside of me.

I cry out onto his shoulder. He walks over to the wall and pins me up against it. He fills me up, leaving me breathless and whimpering. My fingernails score his back the harder he thrusts into me.

"You're so fucking gorgeous, Ave." He smacks my ass so hard that I still feel his hand there, even though it's now fisted in my hair.

We move from place to place, christening the barn like it's ours. We end up on the mattress. I get the upper hand and lower myself onto him, hissing as he fills me up. I ride him slow to get used to his girth. He holds and kneads my breasts, pinching my nipples, sending shivers down my spine.

My hips roll and my breath gets caught in my throat.

"Brand," I whimper. "Fuck Brand, you feel so good." He firmly grabs my hips and moves me faster. I lean forward slightly, and he takes over. He thrusts into me, murmuring my name. This is heaven. It must be. Because waves of pleasure ripple through me, setting my equilibrium off. Warmth pools in my belly and suddenly, I'm taking off like a rocket. His fingers dig into my hips and slams me once, twice, a third time until he takes his own.

I lie on top of him until I can catch my breath. Everything with Brandon Wentworth is a dream come true. He makes love as if it's his last day on earth. He loves unconditionally and without pretense.

"I love you Brand," I whimper.

"I love you, Ave." He kisses my temple. Just as my breathing returns to normal, his hand slams onto my ass and has me wet all over again. I've tasted blood and I want more. "That was for that show you put on going up the stairs." I giggle and roll over. He opens the cooler on his side of the mattress and hands me an ice-cold bottle of water. "Hydrate, killer. I have another three or four rounds left in me."

Twenty-Four

Brandon

Then

Our vacation in Texas ends way too quickly. We end up on the same flight, though that part was planned. The kids say a tearful goodbye to my mom, and more tears are shared between mom and Ava. I don't want to leave here. Not when everything is so amazingly perfect.

Ethan and I sit next to each other on the plane. He stares out the window with a solemn expression on his face. He barely speaks, mostly because he doesn't want to go back to school when he's already had the best week of his life.

Ava and Alice sit together. Alice watches a movie on her tablet and Ava stares out the window, much like Ethan. Stray tears escape from under her sunglasses. It pains me to go back to reality. Not when we had everything we wanted back home.

When we reach Midway Airport, everyone turns on their phones, except for me. I'm not ready to face the world just yet.

"Shit," Ava cusses under her breath.

"What's wrong?" She purses her lips and scrolls through whatever she's looking at.

"Gray is starting up with me again." She hands her phone to me and folds her arms across her chest.

Grayson Wentworth: How come you're allowed to go wherever the fuck you want and I can't?

Grayson Wentworth: You went to see my mom with the kids? I don't want them around her!

Grayson Wentworth: Call me as soon as you get off the plane. This was my week to spend with them!

I reluctantly hand her back the phone because I'm tempted to light his ass on fire. Ava's indulged his temper tantrums one many times.

"You're not going to call him, are you?"

"Not right away. I'll wait until we get home."

"Don't. He didn't want this week, so you did what you had to. You don't owe him an explanation."

"I have to, Brand. As much as I don't want to, he's still their father. I'll smooth things over and that will be the end of it."

"You can't keep indulging him like this. This is why he keeps torturing you." Her sunglasses shield the dagger eyes I *know* are on me right now. She thinks it's none of my business, but it is. Ava Reid and her children are my business.

The plane comes to a stop at the gate and everyone around us begins collecting their things, except for Ava. She's the queen of avoidance. She'll smooth things over with her deadbeat ex because she doesn't like confrontation. What Gray really needs is a threat.

Gray's bark has always been bigger than his bite. He's a classic bully, picking on the little guy so he feels he has more power.

We're the only ones on the plane and the flight attendants stare at us expectantly as if to say, "Get the fuck out." Ethan and I step out of our aisles and begin grabbing the carry-on luggage. Alice and Ava finally get up, though now I feel the brush of a cold shoulder.

Tess and Jordan are picking them up and bringing them home. The plan was for me to grab an uber and then drive to Ava's house to help with the unpacking and getting ready for the week. Now, I'm not so sure.

We move through the terminal in painful silence. Alice is oblivious to the tension, but Ethan isn't. He stands protectively near his mom and watching me with uncertainty. I'm the enemy because she's upset. Not that it was my fault.

Once we get through security and take the escalator down to baggage claim, we're met with huge, glittery signs that welcome Ava and the kids home. Tess wears a giant, goofy grin while Jordan prances around his wife, waving his sign around like an idiot. It forces a crooked grin out of Ethan, and Alice enjoys the hell out of it. But Ava...she's not impressed.

"I missed you all so much!" Tess exclaims, holding out for a hug to whoever gets there first. Alice launches herself into Tess's arms and Ethan gives Jordan a half-hearted fist bump. Tess presses a noisy kiss on Alice's cheek and then peers down to Ethan. "Why the long face, handsome?"

"I didn't want to leave."

Me either, buddy.

"So, it was a good trip, huh? You had a good time?" When none of us answer her, her eyes dart from me to Ava.

"Come with me to grab the bags." Jordan nudges me with his elbow. I'm grateful for the distraction. I love Ava with every fiber of my being. However, she is the most stubborn woman on the planet.

We approach the carousel and wait for the conveyor belt to start moving. I stare at the metal like it's the most riveting thing on the planet. Twenty-four hours ago, we were blissfully happy. We had a picnic in the pasture right behind my mom's house. Ava sipped on her pink wine and laughed at my carelessness with no reservations.

Chicago is a vacuum. It sucks up all of our happiness and leaves us irritable.

"Why are you all so tense?" Jordan asks.

"Gray is stirring up shit again." None of this surprises him. Honestly, if the whole world knew the real Grayson Wentworth, none of this would come as a surprise to anyone. He's a child. He won't stop acting like this until someone puts him in his place.

"That's a typical Tuesday." It's Saturday, but I get where he's going. When things get quiet, he feels the need to make a scene.

"Yeah, well…" I don't want to talk about this, especially with him. "Leave it to Gray to ruin everything. He's been a killjoy since he was born."

Jordan grabs one of the kids' suitcases and sets it by my feet.

"You know…he'd probably listen to you." Yeah, right. Gray doesn't give a damn about me. He shows up to my games, so it looks like he supports me, but is on his phone the entire time. I don't even think he knows what a fumble is. "Look, I'm not trying to be a dick here, Brand, but I think maybe it's time you and Ava went public."

Does everyone think I *like* being the dirty little secret? I don't! I'm so tired of circling the block in case of the paparazzi. I'm sick of not taking my girlfriend out for a fancy dinner or to a movie.

"Don't you think I want to?" Jordan stills at my hiss, grabbing Ava's bag and avoiding my gaze. "If she finds out we're talking about this, it's over. She'll spook about going public and I'll never see her again. So, knock it off."

"Dude, someone *we know* was at my house taking pictures of the three of us and selling it to the highest bidder. That doesn't make me feel safe!" The girls and Ethan make their way over to us, wearing similar grim expressions. "When I married Tess, Ava was part of the package deal. She falls under my protection, so yeah, this is a big deal. I love Ava, she's my sister, but Tess will always come first."

If the shoe were on the other foot, I'd want the same thing. I'd demand Tess and Jordan to come out so the press would leave Ava alone.

Her pouty lips are pursed while she stares at me through her dark sunglasses. I want to kiss the worry away and fight her battles. I can't do that under secrecy. I have to invoke my end date soon.

"Let's get going. Brand, you need a ride?" Tess asks.

"If you're offering…" she grins and motions me to follow the pow wow to Jordan's SUV. Ava and I walk side by side in silence. No eye contact, not even a brush of her hand. Ava slows her pace and lets the four of them three feet ahead of us.

"I don't love him anymore," she murmurs.

"I know you don't."

She shakes her head and sniffles.

"No, Brand. There's somewhere deep inside of you that still thinks that. I know how to handle Gray and you telling me I'm indulging him is making me sound like I'm spineless."

"You're not spineless, baby." She stops and waits for the foursome to duck inside the garage.

"I'm not. He's your brother, I get that. But he was once my husband. I need you to let me handle this *my* way."

Her way isn't working, can't she see that? He's like a raccoon. You feed him once and he keeps coming back.

"At what point do you start fighting back?" *Shut up!*

Her spine locks straight and invokes the ice queen inside of her.

"Excuse me?"

"Come on, Ave, you yell at him, threaten to take away his custody and he keeps making your life hell! You can't live like this…it's not sustainable!" Her right eyebrow arches high over her glasses.

"Gray doesn't make my life anything," she spits poisonously. "Yeah, he's an annoyance, but it's nothing I can't handle."

"And how's that working out for you?" *Keep digging that hole, Brand!* "You are so afraid of your reputation being torn to shreds that you kiss his ass and make him happy. If Gray's happy, the world is happy, isn't that right?"

Her silence is deafening.

She *needs* to hear this. I need her to know I'm on her side.

"Ave, I can share the load. I can help fight your battles, including Gray, but I can't do it under the veil of secrecy. We *have* to go public."

Nope.

"Find another way home, Brand." Without another word, she turns on her heel and storms off in the direction the Archers went.

Yeah, I'll find another way home. And then I'll get my car and drive my sorry ass to her house to get her to listen to reason.

I reluctantly turn back to the airport and find an available taxi. I pay more than I want for him to bring me home, but at least he's quiet and doesn't ask me about my trip. He drops me off at the front and am greeted by my doorman, my only friend right now.

The elevator brings me to my floor and once my front door comes into view, my heart nearly drops out of my ass.

"What are you doing here, Gray?" Gray scrambles up and dusts off his designer jeans.

"I wanted to hang." The shitty part is he seems genuine. Sighing, I open the door and allow him to walk ahead of me. "How was Texas?"

He doesn't know anything. He can't know anything.

"It was fine. The General Store expanded. It's a strip mall now." Impressed, Gray nods and plops himself down on my sofa. "Can I get you anything?"

"Beer?"

Absolutely not.

"All out." He scrunches his nose and shakes his head. That's right, asshole.

"How's..." he trails off. He wants to ask about momma but doesn't. "The farm?"

"Good. Everything's in good shape, Gray." Why is he being so awkward? And why, all of the sudden, does he want to hang out with me?

"Were you there with Ava and the kids?" Yep. I had a grand ol' time and lived out my longest fantasy of making love to Ava Reid in my barn.

"I didn't know they were going. Momma didn't say anything."

He scoffs.

"Of course, she didn't. Why would she?" This is deteriorating.

"Is there a reason why you're here?"

"I wanted to hang—"

"Yeah, I know. You wanted to hang. Since when?"

He twiddles his thumbs, contemplating the big bang theory or some shit.

"What do you think would've happened with us if I never got my big break?" Here we go.

Sighing, I sit down on the couch three feet away from him. "I don't know. I don't like thinking about the what-ifs. Maybe we would've gotten along better. Maybe you would've been so annoyed by me filling dad's role that you would've fallen to drugs or something. You got your big break, Gray. It was what you always wanted. And it worked out for you, didn't it?" And in the process, burned every bridge he ever built. He broke my mom's heart and left our relationship for dead.

He shrugs and turns his gaze to the darkened TV screen. "Did it?" He shifts uncomfortably and then kicks off his shoes. "I could've been anything, and I decided to follow Dad."

"Okay..."

"He won't talk to me, Brand. I've sent letters, I've turned up to his house, I've called his PA. What kind of father does that?"

Him. Grayson Wentworth does that.

"He's already proven he's a shitty father, Gray. He doesn't care about us. He's *never* cared about us. I don't understand this obsession to get his approval. He's an asshole, but you don't have to be!" His eyes widen.

"I don't want or need his approval."

"Then stop trying to get in touch with him! What are you going to do if he *does* pick up the phone, huh? He's not going to have any remorse for leaving us. He chose his career over us and has never looked back."

"Don't you want answers? You believe every little thing that comes out of mom's mouth—"

"I was *there,* Gray! I witnessed our father attempting to murder our mother!" I lean back into the cushions and stares up at the ceiling like it holds all the answers. Where is all this coming from?

"Did you have a good time?" And just like that, he's back to asking about the trip.

"I did, thanks for asking." He grabs the blanket that hangs over the sofa and drapes it around himself. Great. So, he's staying.

"Have you heard from Ellen?"

No, thank god.

"No. She's been pretty quiet lately." He shrugs halfheartedly. I'm done sitting around. I might as well make food if he's going to talk my ear off like this. I don't give a shit about his dietary needs, so I opt for grilled cheese sandwiches. They're quick and easy...and I had everything I need for them in the refrigerator.

Gray trudges up to the bar and slides onto a bar stool. Why is he acting so needy?

"Dude, what's going on? You never come here. The last time I saw you, you told me not to come back. You're freaking me out."

His eyes turn glassy, and suddenly this grown man is crying at my bar. What. The. Hell? I plate the grilled cheeses and cut them down the center. I don't know how to do...whatever this is. I slide the plate down the bar, and it stops when the plate nudges his elbow.

"Lucy's pregnant."

Fuck.

"What?"

"I don't want another kid, Brand. I can barely keep up with the two I have!" He can't be serious. The sandwich sits untouched as my brother cries his eyes out. He reminds me of the five-year-old Gray. He was nice, but emotional. He cried at *everything*. He was tolerable then.

"Is it yours?"

Of course, it is! He never wraps it!

"Yeah. We've been going steady for eight months now." Ava is going to lose her shit.

"Buddy, you can't turn your back on her."

"*I. Don't. Want. It.*"

"Then you should've put on a fucking condom!" He buries his face in his hands. "The deed is done, dude. You *have* to step up. You're so worried about how everyone views you, but you leaving this child out in the cold will certainly lose your friends. Lucy isn't Ava. She's not going to let you get away with this bullshit." He straightens and drops his hands.

He frowns at his sandwich and drags his short fingernail across the crust.

"This sucks for you, I know that. But imagine how she feels. You have two other kids you hardly see. She's probably scared out of her wits you're going to leave her like you left Ava." He frowns.

"You're my brother. You're supposed to be on my side."

Not a chance in hell.

"Your actions have consequences, Gray. Like it or not, the world doesn't revolve around you. We're all fighting our own demons. I want to help you, but you make no effort to help yourself."

He sniffs. He hasn't touched his phone once since I let him in. I'm itching to see if Ava ever messaged him back.

"I want to be a better father. But I want to do it on my terms." That sounds a lot like Preston Alan Wentworth II.

"You *have* been doing it on your terms. Don't you see that? What were you doing this week?"

He drops his gaze to the table.

"I stayed home."

Pussy.

"I spent the week with Ethan and Alice." Gray's eyes briefly meet mine. "I gave Alice one lesson in riding, and she picked up the rest herself. She's *so* funny, Gray. She comes up with these wild stories and enjoys scaring the life out of everyone around her. Ethan? He helped mom with the cooking all week. He was so afraid that she was lonely and put off doing everything he wanted to do so she wouldn't feel alone. This is my first time being around them like this. Your kids are *amazing*. You're missing out on something so fucking great because you can't get your shit together."

"Ava doesn't let me—"

"No. You don't get to blame this on her. It's time to start taking responsibility for your own actions. Either be a better father and be there for all *three* of your children or give up your parental rights. It isn't fair to everyone involved for you to pick and choose when you want to be a father."

Now I'm not hungry.

"I hate you," he murmurs under his breath.

"That's fine, little brother. Hate me all you want. I'm not afraid of hurting your precious feelings. I'm happy to be the one who sets you straight." The tears that once glazed his face are completely gone. His cheeks and eyes are bone dry. I look into a dark abyss of hatred.

He picks up the plate and throws it like a frisbee in my direction. I duck down just as the plate explodes against my cabinets, his sandwich flying with the shards of the plate.

"Get the fuck out," I snap. "You are a grown ass man and you're throwing a temper tantrum like a child. Get out. Don't come back." He's stunned for a moment. I'm the one who screams family values. I looked after that punk when I was the scum on the bottom of his shoe. I was the father he never had. I'm the last piece of home he has without having to talk to our mother.

His face softens and kneels and picks up the bigger pieces of the plate.

"Gray, go. I don't want you here."

"I'm sorry," he says softly.

"If you mean that, you'll leave." I toss the sandwich and the bits of the plate into the garbage can. "You're in my space. You broke my shit, and now I need to sit here in peace before I go total ape shit on you." He backs up slowly and reluctantly turns away from me and grabs his shoes from the sofa.

I sweep up the rest of his mess, just like I've done his entire teenaged life. The front door closes with force, shaking the sliding glass door.

Fucking Gray. I feel like I'm raising my own asshole child who has no compassion or empathy except for himself.

I give Gray a forty-five minute head start before leaving for Ava's house. I'm not her favorite person right now, but that doesn't matter. We need to go public. Gray needs to stop acting like a child. I just need life to go right just fucking once.

The drive to her house helps me collect my temper. It's right at the surface and we're going to fight. It's inevitable. I want to broadcast to the world that I love her and want to make her happy for the rest of my life, but she wants to keep the peace. She doesn't want to tell the world because she's scared of what everyone thinks.

It doesn't matter!

What matters is *our* happiness. The kids' happiness. Everyone else can go fuck a fire hydrant.

Darkness falls onto La Grange when I reach Ava's house. Her lights are turned on and there aren't any stray cars that look out of place. Ava's little blue Honda is the only car in the driveway.

Punching in the code and driving a little faster than I should, I park next to her and turn off the car and jump out. I haven't missed these long ass stairs just to get to the front door. I was given a key months ago, but am surprised when I turn the door handle and the door opens.

The three of them sit at the kitchen table, eating peanut butter and jelly sandwiches like they're zombies. Purple bags sit under Ethan's eyes and Alice's hair is unkempt and unruly. Ava turns slowly and glowers when she realizes it's me.

I say hello to my favorite people, though only two of them respond. I've been here long enough to know the routine. The kids look beat, so they'll probably go to bed early, but not before taking a shower. I head in the direction of their rooms and set out their pajamas on their dressers. I flick on Alice's frog lamp and get the shower going for whoever finishes their sandwich first.

Spoiler alert: It's Ethan. While he showers, I go into the kitchen and clean off the small number of dishes and stick them in the dishwasher while Ava angrily flips through a magazine. She's mad that I spat the truth.

Alice gives me her plate when she's finished and races back to her room to avoid the ugly tension in the air. I occupy Alice's seat, so I'm staring directly in Ava's face. There are no giant sunglasses to hide her now.

"I thought you would've been here earlier," she says quietly.

"That was the plan, but Gray was waiting for me outside my apartment." This grabs her attention. Her face pales and closes the magazine.

"Did you tell him?"

"No. I wanted to talk to you about it first."

She dramatically sighs and leans back in her chair.

"What was he doing there? You guys aren't chummy."

"I'm not sure exactly. He said he wanted to hang. That turned into him telling me Lucy is pregnant and that he doesn't want the kid."

She swears under her breath and pinches the bridge of her nose. "That's perfect."

"I told him he had to either step up or dissolve his parental rights." She laughs without humor.

"How'd he take that?"

"He threw a plate at me."

Her brows furrow, and she starts wringing her hands.

"Wow. He was never violent towards me."

Dad wasn't either, but he still tried to murder my mom. "Do you remember at that party when we were talking about this and I said I needed an end date?" She sobers at my words. "I need an end date, Ava. I'm not ashamed of being with you. I love you. I'd do *anything* for you. But I'm begging you to stop hiding. I don't want to hide anymore."

She scoots out of her chair and storms into the living room, starting her pacing.

"That's great, Brand. What about what *I* want?"

"What do you want?" I walk my green mile into the living room. This is where our relationship ends. She can't ever be wrong. "I'm asking you seriously. What do you want? What you said in Texas about being with me...about having a farm of our own...was that real?"

"Of course it's real!" she cries. "I can't go public right now."

"Then when?" Her eyes water.

"I don't know!" She wails.

That's the worst possible answer she could've given me. "I don't know" means there isn't a future.

"I can't do 'I don't know,' Ave. It's going to be messy no matter when we come out of hiding. The longer we hide, the worse it looks."

I feel like I'm getting divorced all over again. Even though Kayla and I had an amicable split, it still stung. I loved her.

"I'm so tired of being on everyone else's timeline. First, it was Gray, now it's you. We tell the world what we are and then I'm stuck dealing with all the fallout—"

"Whoa, that's not true, and you know it. I would never make you deal with this all on your own. You compare me to Gray, I *know* you do, but I'm not like him. I'm not going to feed you to the wolves and for you to even suggest that is insulting!"

"Do you realize what you're asking of me? You're asking me to dump my career so we can live happily ever after!"

"I'm not asking you to dump your career! Does it even occur to you how much I love you? How much I'm trying so fucking hard to stay quiet while you deal with the shit Gray doles out?"

"That's none of your business!"

"*You're my business!*" My voice reaches decibels that are only heard on the field. "It fucking matters to me when you let him walk all over you or when his children aren't on the forefront of his mind!"

"I don't let him walk all over me!"

"You're blind." The hallway remains empty and dark, save for a smaller pair of blue eyes staring at me angrily. Ethan leans up against his doorframe, glaring at me. I can't deal with this now. I turn back to face her. "Aren't you exhausted? I'm offering you everything that I am. I'll help you with Gray. I'll help you with the kids. I'll help you find a PR Specialist who can be delegated exclusively the fallout for this. I'm *begging* you, please, let's get out of hiding."

"I *am* exhausted," she sobs. "I'm exhausted from being everyone's rock. Everybody needs me for something. The kids need me to be a mom. Gray needs me to be a mom *and* his verbal punching bag. You need me to be a girlfriend. America needs me to be fucking perfect. Hell yeah, I'm exhausted. I do *not* have the emotional stamina to go public right now."

This is it then. I can't do this.

I close the space between us and press my lips to her forehead. Tears well up in my eyes. I don't want to walk away, but she's forcing me to.

"I'm gonna go. But I need you to know that I love you. Probably more than I've ever loved anyone my entire life. I'm sorry I didn't meet you first. God knows I wanted to. I can't be a dirty little secret, Ava." Her bottom lip wobbles and the tears pour out of her eyes.

"I'm begging you to give me more time." Her voice breaks and cracks. This hurts her as much as it hurts me.

"I can't. We've had months together. I just...I can't. I need more."

She sobs and wraps her arms around my torso. "I love you more than I loved anyone. I'm just sorry I couldn't make it work." She tilts her head up and stands on her toes, giving me a watery kiss. "I love you, Brand. I'm so sorry."

I force myself to leave.

I don't get to say goodbye to Ethan or Alice. I jump into my car and drive. It doesn't matter where I go. I lost everything that truly mattered to me in one night.

All because of Gray.

Twenty-Five

Ava

I just broke up with the man of my dreams. I was cowardly. I was dismissive and defensive and now I have to explain to my kids that it was mommy who massively fucked up.

I didn't sleep a wink last night. I've spent the last week wrapped in Brandon's arms, and now I'm forced to live without it. Giving up around two o'clock, I moved downstairs and cocooned myself in a blanket, and watched Hallmark movies until Ethan and Alice woke up around eight.

I'm in no mood to cook, so we head out to Blueberry Hill Café and pig out on pancakes. I'm envious of Alice's ignorance. She flits around and talks a mile a minute while I can barely finish off my one giant pancake.

Ethan pokes about his pancakes in solidarity, occasionally rolling his eyes at something Alice said. I have a whole day dedicated to laundry, grocery shopping, and wallowing. The same Hallmark movies that played in the wee hours of the morning are being replayed this afternoon. Can't miss Lacey Chabert falling for Wes Brown for the second time today.

I'm bitter.

And the one person who could make me feel better wants me to tank my career for him. I hate men!

Tess waits for us on the staircase leading up to my front door. She grins when Alice squeals in excitement that she's here, but immediately falls when she realized someone is missing from our party.

"Don't ask," I mumble as I step past her to unlock the door.

"Okay, cranky pants. Looks like someone woke up on the wrong side of the bed."

"I didn't sleep." The kids race past us into their rooms to rot their brains with TV since they hardly watched TV in Texas.

"What's wrong?" I sling my shoes off into the shoe rack and collapse dramatically on my couch. Everything. Everything is wrong.

Brandon isn't here.

A sob rips through my throat. Tess appears at my side and wipes my tears away.

"Babe..."

"I broke up with Brand."

Her dark eyebrows knit in confusion.

"Why? You had such a good week with him...he was so good to you..."

"He wanted to go public, and I didn't." She soothingly strokes my hair while my tears ruin her stockings. She's uncharacteristically quiet. "What?"

"Babe...I mean...he's a good guy."

"He's the best."

"I don't understand the problem, then. What about him repulsed you so much that you don't want to go public with him?"

"Nothing. I'm not ready to face the internet trolls or media parked out behind my gate every day while they dissect every single one of our interactions while Gray and I were married. I'm not ready to face Gray. I'm just..."

"There is this quote from Smallville that Lionel Luthor said to Lex Luthor as a child: 'You can't get anywhere with your eyes closed.' There is a big, beautiful world outside of Hollywood. And maybe that's not what you want. We're in an era of women empowerment. You can tell your side of the story, expose Gray for who he really is.

No matter what, *I* know who you are. So do Jordan, and Ethan, Alice, and most importantly, Brandon. Everyone else doesn't matter. Open your eyes, babe. Playing it safe is fucking boring."

But it's safe.

"I want to act."

"So, act. There are so many platforms out there where you can produce your own shit. Check out the indie scene for a while. Take a break, travel the world. I don't want you to be unhappy in this life just because things aren't going with the script. Deviate. Ad lib. Fuck him senseless."

"Ew." I gasp as Ethan appears in my line of vision. Tess cackles while my cheeks flush.

"Aren't you supposed to be playing a game or something? You got your mom for an entire week, and I was left to my own devices."

Ethan grins.

"Mom was crying. I just wanted to make sure you weren't hurting her." Tess's smile wanes and caresses his cheek.

"Ethan, I hope you find the woman of your dreams, and I hope she realizes the prince she has. You're a stand-up guy, baby." He blushes and pushes her hand away.

"You okay, mom?"

"I'm okay, baby. Thanks for checking up on me." He nods slowly and then backs out of the room. "What if I lose everything?"

"I won't let it happen."

"You can't always come to the rescue, you know. Jordan won't like it. He'll think you favor me over him." She rolls her eyes knowingly.

"He already knows that, dummy."

I giggle. "We should just get married."

"It's illegal in this country to have more than one spouse. I checked. And besides, I love you. I mean, if I were into chicks, you'd be the one I'd go after. Jordo's cute and has all the parts I require."

We end up in a giggle fit. If Jordan heard her talking like this, he wouldn't be happy with her.

"Why are you here?"

She shrugs.

"I wanted to hang. I missed harassing you all last week and needed to make up for lost time."

"I love you, Tessie. I'm sorry you have to deal with an emotionally stunted best friend."

"I love you, Ava. Best friends for life, no matter how big of a cry baby you are. But...as your best friend, I suggest you go to his house and win him back. You are deserving of happiness."

Tess stands up and stretches. She bids us adieu and leaves just as fast as she came.

My whole day of laundry, grocery shopping, and wallowing is getting put on the back burner. There are delivery services for grocery shopping, the kids have enough clean clothes to get them through tomorrow, and the wallowing, well, I'll find out if I truly need to later.

I round the kids up and we pile into my car. The roads are virtually empty today since half the population is at church. It takes me a cool forty-five minutes to get to Brandon's apartment. We avoid looking at the cameras, just on the off-chance Brandon tells me to get bent. At least my reputation will still be intact.

His hallway is quiet. I'm starting to wonder if he even has neighbors. I've never seen a living soul besides Brandon in this hallway. Ethan knocks on the door with a heavy hand, proud that he can still scare the shit out of a man that's twice his size.

The door opens to an exhausted Brandon. He wears similar bags under his eyes. He wears the same pants from yesterday, though he's ditched the shirt. I'm not complaining.

"Ave," he breathes in surprise. He steps aside quickly and allows us to come in. The kids race into the living room and turn on the TV. I can't turn off the waterworks no matter how hard I try. I'm an asshole.

I'm no better than Gray.

"I'm sorry," I sob. He pulls me into his hot chest. My tears soak into his skin. He plants kisses on my head until he forces me to look up at him. "I love you. I want to be with you."

"I love you, babe."

"I want to go public with you." His full lips stretch into a wide grin.

"What?"

"You're the first person who ever accepted me for who I am. I'm indecisive and argumentative. I'm stubborn and I think I'm right all the time. But you were right. I'm living my life in idle and I don't want to do it anymore."

I swear I'm about to make him cry, but not the way he cried last night.

"You won't regret this, I promise. I'll make you happy. I'll stand with you through all of the bullshit. I'm just so happy you're here. I didn't sleep at all last night." He takes my hand and leads me through the kitchen and living room and into his room. He leaves the door open halfway so the kids don't think we've left them.

He sits on the bed, and I straddle his lap. I've missed my Brandon pillow, my personal space heater.

"Let's call Kayla. She'll know a good PR Specialist. We can get ahead of everything."

"Brand...I want to tell Gray." He searches my face as if he's waiting for a "gotcha!" moment, but when he doesn't get one, he sobers.

"Really?"

"I was hoping that maybe we could keep this under wraps just for the rest of the week and we could invite Gray over for dinner on Sunday. It'll give the kids one last week in peace before the shit storm starts, and...I don't know. Things are going to be rocky after we make a statement. I just want one more week of just the four of us." He nods slowly, contemplating if he's making the right choice.

"I can live with one more week," he replies softly. "On Saturday, you guys could come over here and spend the night...we can celebrate the end of our secret New Year's Eve style."

It sounds perfect.

He kisses me deeply, cradling my face in his giant hands, his tongue dancing with mine.

When you find your *someone,* the puzzle pieces come together. I would have been content with being a single mom for the rest of my life. Love wasn't something I was good at. I had failed relationship after failed relationship. But then, Brandon Wentworth strolls through the Emergency Room doors at La Grange Memorial and becomes my knight in shining armor. He's my final puzzle piece. That annoying one in the middle of the puzzle you spend most of the day fitting into different spots.

"I don't like sleeping without you," I murmur into his ear while he devours the crook of my neck.

"Never again. Let me move in with you. I can sell this place. I can move the porch swing onto your deck..."

Giggling, I stare into his beautiful eyes. "Moving in with me already? You're getting clingy."

His hand slams down on my ass, sending me a mile in the air and stealing the breath from my lungs.

"This is what you signed up for, killer. You're not going to be able to go to the bathroom alone anymore."

"Yeah? And what happens if I lock you out?"

"I'll kick down the door and fuck the sass out of you." Goosebumps erupt on my skin at the thought.

The three V's were right. Brandon isn't the type to make slow, sweet love. He likes it rough and raw.

"I thought you loved my sass." He chuckles.

"I love *you*, Ave." His hands find my hips and rests his forehead against mine. "I'm sorry about last night."

"Me too."

His head nestles in between my breasts with his ear pressed to my chest. He breathes in my scent and listens to my heartbeat. I love this man so much.

A knock at the bedroom door pulls us back into reality. We have two kids we need to talk to. I just wasn't expecting to see Ellen peering in.

The adrenaline surges through my veins when I see her with messy hair and a long t-shirt. Did she spend the night here? I thought they were fighting...

"Hey," she says quietly.

"She stumbled in here drunk last night," he explains softly. He's a good guy and he won't turn her away. He'd do the same for Tess. But *why* does this image of her standing at his door with naked legs and a shirt that barely covers her ass make my jealousy surge?

"Thanks for letting me crash." She opens the door wider and barely acknowledges me.

"Sure," he replies curtly.

"Hi, Ava." I suppress the urge to roll my eyes.

"Hi."

"Anyway, I'm going to get going. Can I call you later?"

Tell her no.

"Ah...Ellen, I don't think that's a good idea." Her fiery eyes meet mine. I took away her best friend, and I'm not even sorry for it. We could've been friends, but she chose to be a bitch.

"I tried to be your friend," she snaps at me. I hop off Brandon's lap and take two steps closer to her. She towers over me and while she could probably kick my ass, I have enough adrenaline to at least get her on the ground, should it come to that.

"No. You told a lie and then tried to pin your shitty behavior on me. I was trying to be friends with you, Ellen. I tried to make things peaceful with us, but you chose to hurt me *and* my daughter instead." She disregards me completely and stares straight at Brandon over my shoulder.

"I'll call you later. Answer your phone." Where the *fuck* does she get off?

"Can I spend the night?" Brandon asks me when the front door slams shut. My heart squeezes at the sincerity and hurt in his voice.

"Yeah. Pack a bag. Let's go home."

Twenty-Six

Brandon

Then

This week drags. My workout regime has increased drastically, so by the time I get to Ava's house after working out with the team, I fall on my face on her couch until she wakes me up to come to bed upstairs. The only thing getting me through is knowing that on Monday, our relationship is public knowledge.

Thursday afternoon is a time where my and Jordan's schedules line up. I haven't talked to him since the airport, and I'm betting he knows the situation now. I grin from ear to ear, knowing that in two days will be the last day of being Ava Reid's dirty little secret.

"Your happiness is throwing me off. Stop it."

"Fuck you, Archer. Be happy for me." He chuckles while he spots the barbell over my head.

"I mean, it's nice not seeing you brooding for once. You finally got your dick rubbed. I'm proud of you." We set the barbell down and we move to switch, but not before I punch him in the gut, and he folds on a wheeze.

"She's supposed to be your sister, jackass. Show a little respect." He lifts the barbell off the hooks and begins pressing.

Ellen sits at a desk in the corner of the weight room sulking. I catch her gaze every so often, and I swear she's trying to kill me with her eyes.

What the fuck ever. She's judgmental and I'm not here for it.

"So, Saturday. Where are you ordering in from?"

"RPM, her favorite. Then on Sunday, we're all going to her house for dinner with Gray." Jordan winces when he lifts. "Your shoulder still bothering you?"

"I just slept on it weird." Liar. "You think he'll take it gracefully?"

"No. I'm sure it won't go over well. There's really nothing I can do about it." I haven't talked to him since that day he came over to my apartment. It sounds like he's stepping up because he's taking Alice out for their date tomorrow. I'm proud of him. People grow all the time. My brother and I have had our differences. Most of the time I can't stand him, but from what I saw the other day, he's still that scared little boy who needs guidance but is scared to ask for it. Maybe this can be our opportunity to start our relationship over.

"And Lucy Rodriguez? The tabloids are blasting her baby bump everywhere." It's not a baby bump. Honestly, it looks like she overate and is bloating a little bit.

"What about her?"

"How are the kids handling it?" Like it isn't happening. Ethan is a man trapped in a little boy's body. He also masters avoidance like his mother. He's about to have a new brother or sister, but he doesn't care. It's almost like if he doesn't acknowledge it, it won't happen.

"Ethan is pretending it isn't happening, Alice is not convinced. They didn't even hear it from Gray, which is the shitty part. Ava sat down and told them." So really, I can understand why they entirely don't believe it.

"I need to shower. I'm taking Tess out tonight." He sets down the bar, and I follow him into the locker room. "And Ava? How's she handling it?"

"All right, I guess. He's called her a few times for advice, but I think he might be looking for a way out." I shrug. "I don't know. She refuses to talk about it. I don't think she cares much for who Gray's sleeping with nowadays." She doesn't. She's more concerned about her kids, which I understand. That other child isn't hers. It's not her responsibility.

"Are you serious, Brand? Are you still seeing her?" Ellen's voice is lowered. It's only Jordan and me near the lockers, and no chance of any onlookers.

"It's none of your business, Ellen. Yes, I'm still seeing her."

"She doesn't want to go public with you, Brand! She doesn't love you like you think she does! Don't you care how Gray feels about this?"

"No, I don't! We're telling Gray on Sunday, so either get on board or keep your distance."

"This is *so* wrong, Brandon! She's your sister-in-law—"

"Ellen, shut the fuck up," Jordan pipes up.

"This isn't your business, Archer! Stay out of it!"

"Ava's my business," he hisses. Jordan turns from best friend to protector in two point two seconds. "They are consenting adults who have weighed the pros and cons. They're coming clean. They're telling Gray, and they're going to move on with their lives. They're happy, and that's all that matters." Her eyes dart from Jordan to me.

"Are you happy, Brandon? Does she make you happy?"

"Yes. You don't know her like I do. She tried to be friends with you, Ellen, but you let your own preconceived notions cloud your judgment. She's a great person. She's funny, and sweet, and would do anything for the people she loves." Jordan slams his locker closed.

Ellen's eyes shine with emotion.

"Fine. But this will bite you in the ass. Mark my words." Maybe they will. But at least we have our dreams away from Hollywood to fall back on. She turns on her heel when I have nothing left to say, wiping tears from her eyes.

I find Ava on the deck when I walk into her house. She taps away on her laptop with her earbuds in, and her concentration unbreakable. A rotisserie chicken sits on the counter, still hot, and ready for me to devour, as is a protein recovery shake that condensation coats the glass it's in.

She's supportive. And my heart skips a beat that she thought of me when she bought me my "dinner" and made my shake. The smell of the chicken makes my stomach rumble, but I want to say hi to her first.

I trip over Alice's shoes and nearly kill myself over Ethan's football. They need to get better about picking up their shit. It'll be my first talk with them as... never mind. I don't want to call myself their stepdad. It's weird.

Stepping out into the cool air, I drop a kiss on her forehead, making her jump out of her skin. Chuckling, I kiss her again and grab the chair right across from her.

"Hi."

"You scared the shit out of me, Brand!" She lifts her legs and places them on my lap, crossing at the ankles. *Make yourself comfortable, baby. I don't mind.*

"What are you working on?"

Her snow-white cheeks flush.

"It's nothing." She closes the lid on the laptop and grins.

"It's something."

"Not telling. How was your day?"

"It was fine. I got a lot done. Thanks for the shake and the chicken."

Grinning, she shrugs and drops her gaze. "I figured you'd be starving by the time you got home."

Home.

This is home now. I scheduled movers for next weekend to start bringing my shit over. It kills me a little inside every time I have to kiss her goodnight and drive all the way back into the city to a cold bed and empty house.

"I was. Are you going to be out here long?"

"Umm.... Maybe just a half hour more. I'm in the zone. I want to get some of this finished before I turn in for the night."

What is she hiding from me? It has to do something with her work...

I wish she'd let me take a peek. I wouldn't tease her. I stare at her laptop a little long.

"Go eat your chicken, Brand. I'll be inside in a little bit."

Leaving her to her own devices, I head inside and peer into Ethan's room to see both kids playing a video game quietly together, not even realizing I'm there.

I crash on the couch just for a moment as I take in my new reality. Those kids are going to be mine. And the room upstairs...it's going to be *ours*.

Literally nothing could tear me down from cloud nine.

Twenty-Seven

Ava

Then

Alice plays hooky from school on Friday so she can go on her date with Gray. She's been going on and on about all the things they're going to do. Gray's going to *love* the American Girls store.

Gray picks her up at ten, leaving me the entire afternoon to work on my newest project.

I've been acting since I was four years old. It's all I've ever known. It was the only job I ever had. Tess was right. There are so many platforms out there for me to pursue, and not just in acting.

Writing isn't new to me. I've written screenplays and scripts, never a novel. It turns out my muse is a six and a half foot man who is a dork for American History and makes my heart burst.

I'm writing a love story. An epic one. *Ours.* It's my love letter to Brandon. I'm writing under a penname, just in case it's a hot pile of garbage. At least I can hide behind the anonymity. I'll eventually give it to him. Forty years from now.

My "office" continues to change. I spent two hours on the deck, an hour at the kitchen table, another hour on the couch until it was time to pick Ethan up from school. It's definitely going to be a night of me not cooking, and Brandon isn't coming over tonight because he wants to get the apartment ready for tomorrow. Gray decided he was going to keep Alice for dinner, so it's just me and my buddy tonight.

My TV remains off for the entire day. My phone vibrates off the hook from Tess, but I ignore it. My innermost thoughts take precedent today.

Brandon bulldozed his way into my life and made himself at home. I should be angry, but I'm not. He loves my kids like they're his own and he treats me like a human being. Not Ava Reid, America's Sweetheart, child actor turned Oscar-Winning Actress.

My front door bursts open and Alice storms through the living room, face bright red and glazed with tears.

"Baby?" She stomps to her room and slams the door and, with a faint *click,* locks her door. What the hell?

Gray appears in the doorway with a somber look.

"What happened?" He shrugs and closes the door. "Well, something happened. Why is she so upset?"

"She wanted to go into the aquarium, but I told her I didn't have enough time." I glance at my watch. It's only five forty-five. I bet my ass he didn't feed her dinner either.

"I thought you were taking her out to dinner."

"She wanted to come home."

Is this the *Twilight Zone*? Why isn't he picking a fight? Why isn't he accusing me of turning her against him?

"Okay." I glance back to the hallway in curiosity. She'll tell me what happened. "Um, Gray? Are you busy on Sunday?"

"No. Why?"

"I was hoping you'd come over for dinner? I was planning on making a pot roast..." His eyes narrow. He must think this is the *Twilight Zone*.

"Yeah, okay. Can I bring someone?" Fucking Lucy.

"Sure."

"Sweet. See you then."

What the hell is happening to the people in my life? Gray leaves without another word, and I race down the hallway to check up on my baby.

Her sobs can be heard from the living room.

"Baby? It's just me. Can I come in?" She's silent for a beat, and then the door opens while the lock pings. She runs back into bed and pulls the pink comforter off her head. "What happened today, baby?"

"He's the worst dad in the whole wide world!" Well...no arguments here.

"What happened?"

"He didn't want to eat lunch at the American Girls store!" God, he just had to indulge her for just one fucking afternoon.

"Okay..."

"We had McDonald's instead."

I close my eyes in frustration. Why is being a father so difficult?

"And then he told you he didn't have time for the aquarium?" She nods as a fresh wave of tears stream down her cherubic face.

Ethan cautiously steps in to see what's going on, but Alice isn't having any of it.

"Go away, Ethan! You *always* get to do what you want! It isn't fair!"

Ethan frowns and looks at me for direction.

"Buddy, I think your sister just needs a few minutes alone. Why don't you go look through the menus and we can pick out dinner?"

"Can Alice pick? We can do whatever she wants..." Such a gentleman. I smile and nod, turning my attention back to Alice when Ethan scampers down the hall.

"We went to the aquarium, but only to the gift shop. He didn't want to pay for tickets and then he spent the rest of the time in the gift shop on the phone."

I *try* to give him the benefit of the doubt, and he *still* manages to break hearts with no remorse. What a fucking dick.

"Did that make you cry?"

She shakes her head sadly. "No. I cried because then he didn't want to go to dinner with me."

I'm going to skin him alive.

I stretch out on the bed next to her and kiss her forehead.

"I'm so sorry, baby. That sounds like a crappy day." She sobs into my chest, sending my heart into a tailspin. I pull my phone out of my pocket and FaceTime Brandon. She perks up when she reads his name, and then a wider smile when his face fills the screen.

"Why are you crying gorgeous?"

She goes into the spiel of Gray being an idiot. Ethan sidles into the room with an arm full of take-out menus and lays them out neatly on the floor.

Brandon is her hero. He's the only man who laughs at her insane stories and lets her be her wild and crazy self. They're best friends, bonded for life. I love him so much for that.

"I'm sorry you had a crappy day, babe. I wish I could come over and give you a hug, but I'm trying to get my house ready for tomorrow so we can have a big celebration for us."

"It's okay. I know we'll have fun. We can always hug tomorrow."

I can't wait to see Gray's stupid face when we tell him about us. I'm not spiteful, however, I feel like if he saw the four of us happy, he'd regret what he let go of.

"I love you guys. I'll see you guys soon, okay?" We smile, tell him we love him, and then get down to business. One of us is hurting and no expense will be spared.

When Saturday rolls around, our bags are packed first thing in the morning. We keep ourselves busy by staying in front of the TV and marking time by how many episodes of Pokémon we get in.

Brand texts me at five to check in, which gets me off my ass to start getting ready.

Brandon Wentworth: I can't wait to see you.

Brandon Wentworth: I ordered RPM, are you okay with that?

Me: My fav! Thanks, babe!

Brandon Wentworth: We're about to start the rest of our lives together. I love you so much.

Me: I love you. So, so much. Xoxo

I trot up the steps and shake my hair out of my messy bun. I iron the waves out of my hair and start on my makeup.

Brandon Wentworth: I know I said to come over at eight, but come at seven.

Good. Because I can't wait either.

I throw on a purple spaghetti strap dress, Brandon's favorite of mine, and throw it on. I'm pleased to find the kids dressed, hair and teeth brushed, and shoes on. I slide on a pair of flip flops and carry my strappy heels in my hands while Ethan helps me load the suitcases in the trunk.

Alice wears a pink dress with black unicorns. According to her, it's her *best* dress, and she has to make a grand entrance. Her words, not mine. Ethan wears a nice pair of jeans and a button-up flannel shirt.

Where did my babies go? Why did they grow up so damn fast?

Our Disney Pandora station is our soundtrack for the ride to Brandon's house. They're upbeat songs about love and happiness—something we're all feeling right now. I'm running a little late due to traffic on 55, but luckily find a guest spot close to the elevators.

I'm going to eat a lot of food that isn't good for me and celebrate our final moments of being a secret.

Yesterday, I was terrified. I thought about all of the negativity that would surround us until somebody else did something way worse. But now, the anxiety in my belly subsides. My heart races at the possibility of being able to hold hands down Michigan Avenue or eating at some fancy restaurant wearing clothes that would make him sweat.

Telling the world would be a weight off my shoulders. And who knows. Maybe Tess is right, and I'm making a bigger deal out of it than it is. Alice jams her thumb on the *up* button and Ethan insists on pressing Brandon's floor.

I don't avoid the cameras. Whoever's watching can see my dorky smile. They can leak this footage of an Ava Reid who oozes pure joy. I don't really give a fuck.

Ethan and Alice jabber excitedly to each other about what movies they want to watch tonight. We're doing this New Year's Eve style, so we're staying up until midnight.

I see a lot of Power Rangers and Teenage Mutant Ninja Turtles in my future.

Smiling, I knock on the door, only because my hands are full and I don't feel like rooting into the dark abyss that is my purse for my keys.

The door opens, and creamy white skin catches my attention.

Boobs.

Wild, strawberry blonde hair.

A victorious smirk.

My breath is stolen from my lungs while I process this wicked sight before me. The running of the shower can be heard from the front door.

Say something!

"Ellen! Hurry up!" Brandon's voice booms from his room.

My heart splinters before us.

"Just a minute, babe!" she shouts back. I want to smack that Cheshire smile off her face. I want to push Brandon off the balcony.

They were the same.

Brandon and Gray are the same and I didn't see it.

"Come on, Mom." Ethan's voice cuts through my trance. He yanks my hand and pulls me down the hallway. Brandon's door closes, though I can't make myself turn back.

He said they weren't the same.

He said they were just friends.

She knew we were coming to Texas.

He believed *her* over me.

I don't remember the elevator ride, or even walking to the car, but Ethan, my protector, gets Alice in her seat and buckled up while I stare at my car.

She was naked. They were taking a shower together.

Ethan appears before me.

"Come on Mom, we can't stay here."

Biting back a curse, I jump into the driver's seat. I peel out of the garage like my ass is on fire. I don't want to go home. I drive around aimlessly for ten minutes before Ethan starts giving me directions.

I recognize this route. It's to the only person who will let me hole up and wallow.

Tessie.

I practically throw my keys at the valet, and Ethan and Alice have never moved faster.

This is why you can't count on anyone. Men everywhere land a woman, whisper sweet nothings and empty promises until she believes it. And when she does, he realizes the weight of the situation. Throw in a couple of kids that aren't his and *poof!* He bangs her one last time for good measure and then disappears.

I can't cry in front of my children. I *refuse* to show them that he hurt me. I'm strong. I'm Wonder Woman. I'm...

Knocking on my best friend's door with a broken heart. Again.

Tess's door swings open.

I can't hold the dam up forever.

She gasps when I fall into her and dramatically slide on the floor. These heels were a stupid choice.

I hate this dress.

I hate everything about tonight.

Twenty-Eight

Brandon

The tears stream down her face and the audience panders to her idiotic attempts of trying to bury me. She's been claiming I've cheated on her for years, and none of it's true! Ellen wasn't even there that night! Kayla watches me closely, ready to pounce. She's always been able to read me. I wear my anger on my sleeve, clear as day.

Ava's face is red and blotchy. The makeup she keeps retouching is practically nonexistent at this point. It reminds me of her over the weekends. She never wore make up. She's gorgeous.

And I fucking hate that.

"You went to your best friend's house for comfort. How long did you stay?"

"I don't know. A week, I think." She sniffles and accepts a tissue from Sunny.

"You've got to be kidding me." Her jaw clenches, but she doesn't look this way. "You know, at some point, you have to stop blaming her for all of your shortcomings. You never liked her, I get that. But she wouldn't do that."

She scoffs.

"There was never a time where you believed me about her, was there?"

"Guilty! Newsflash, Ave, she's a good person! She was there when you ghosted. You never showed up and for some strange reason, you want the whole world to believe that you came over as planned, but you got cold feet and bolted. That's what you do!"

"I bet she was," she snaps, throwing the tissue onto the floor. "How long had this whole thing been going on? Hm? Because at least Gray had the decency to tell me when he was cheating on me. He had the decency to not let me walk in on him screwing some other woman!"

"*Are you serious?* I didn't cheat on you!"

"My mom's not a liar!" Cameras swing in his direction. The woman who was wringing her hands is now jumping out of her seat, becoming the momma bear protecting her cub.

"Cut to commercial," she snaps at Sunny. Nobody makes a move. Except for me, who stands and stares at this...*man* in front of me. He's fourteen.

He could be a senior in high school! Look at him! He's built like a linebacker. He's spent considerable time in the weight room.

But I still see a little boy, my little buddy.

"No, don't!" Ethan shouts.

"Cut to commercial, Sunny," she snaps again. "Stop talking, Ethan." Ava whirls around to Sunny, who cowers in her chair as if she is going to tackle her. I'm sure she would. "He is a minor, and I'm not giving you permission to film him. Cut. To. Commercial."

"They need to hear this, Mom! They need to know the truth!"

"I said no." Her voice drops into a dangerously low tone. Even I'm scared for him. "I swear to God, if you don't cut to commercial, I will walk out. You won't get the end of this story and you will never work in television again."

Sunny nervously motions for the cameras to turn off. Red lights, one by one, blink off. Ava relaxes only slightly, but the man child in front of me threatens to knock me around.

"You don't get to call my mom a liar. She isn't lying."

"Buddy..." My heart goes out to him. This is my first time laying eyes on him in the flesh in six years. I want to hug him. I want him to be my little buddy again. "This thing with your mom and I…it's complicated…"

"Fuck you, Brandon!" Ethan shouts.

"Ethan!" Ava snaps.

Tears spring in his eyes. I'm grateful for the cameras going off. He would be so embarrassed if his friends saw this.

"I was there! I saw her boobs and her ugly dream catcher tattoo! You made us look!" My heart stops in my chest. Ethan's eyes turn glassy.

What?

"You were supposed to be better than him! You p-promised!" Ava sobs, but it's not her I want to comfort. Ethan sobs harder. His pale skin, freckled face reddens as his anger bubbles to the surface. "You're no better than dad. And the worst part is that we *heard* you tell her to hurry up. Like you wanted a good lay before we all came over and didn't want to get caught. Well, you did!"

I don't even care that most of the audience is pulling out their phones and recording all of this. I have *no* idea what he's talking about. Ellen wasn't there.

"Buddy…"

"You made Alice look, Brandon. That's worse than anything dad has ever done."

My heart sinks to my stomach. Fuck, *I* want to cry right now. Ava doesn't wait for him to open his mouth again. He's already said much and the phone cameras are rolling. She steps off the stage and grabs his arm and heads down the hallway. Kayla nervously steps onto the stage.

"Brand?"

"I can't talk to you right now."

I need to talk to Ellen. I need to know *everything*.

Crew members jump out of my way while I barrel down the hallway. Much to my surprise, Ellen sits on the ugly orange couch, scrolling through her Instagram feed. The monitor in the dressing room is off.

"Why does my nephew know what your tattoo looks like?" Her phone lowers to her lap, but she doesn't make eye contact.

"What are you talking about?"

"Why does my nephew know what your tattoo looks like?" I step deeper into the dressing room and make sure she looks me in the fucking eye when she lies to me again.

"I don't know. He probably saw me swimming or something."

Nope.

"You don't wear crop tops, you don't wear bikinis. I don't even remember the last time you went swimming. You are so damn ashamed of that tattoo that you've even looked to have it removed. Stop lying to me." She licks her dry, chapped lips, and swings her long legs over so her feet are touching the floor.

She doesn't say a damn thing. She's looking to get her story straight. And then suddenly, confidence oozes from her aura. She narrows her eyes and turns to me.

"She's just saying these things to drive a wedge in between us—"

"Ethan's here, Ellen. He told me what he saw that night." Standing up and slinging her purse over her shoulder, she huffs and attempts to leave through the door, but is blocked by Kayla. "Are you behind this?"

"Are you kidding? You really think I'd do *this* to you?" Ellen snaps.

As of right now, all bets are off. I don't know. I don't know this woman who stands before me.

"You broke Ava and me up." She purses her lips as Kayla forces her way in and shuts the door.

"We need to know everything, Ellen. Take a seat," Kayla instructs, motioning for her to sit down.

"It was *always* supposed to be me and you, Brandon. From the time we were kids to *right now,* it was always supposed to be us walking down the aisle."

Bile rises in my throat. Ava was telling the truth. Everything she said was true about Ellen. I refused to listen.

Fuck.

"So you broke them up? What about Brandon and me? I heard you in the bathroom."

I almost didn't believe Kayla.

Is this Stockholm Syndrome?

"Yes. I broke you up. You were easy to get out of the picture. Brandon always wanted kids, and when he met you, he decided he didn't want kids either." She shrugs. "I asked him for sperm."

Oh my god.

I vaguely remember this.

She planted that seed when I was drunk at Gray's engagement party!

I slide down the wall and bury my face. I can't believe what I'm hearing.

"What? You asked him for sperm? And he said no, right?"

"He said no. But it planted a seed. He wanted children, and then when Ethan was born, it solidified his need for a child."

Holy shit.

"Do you understand the magnitude of shit you've caused?" My voice is shaky. I don't want to be here. I want to find Ethan and apologize. Ava most likely will never talk to me again...

I get it now.

"I love you; doesn't that count for anything?" I laugh out of hysteria.

"People who love each other don't do *this* to each other." I stand now, ready to run home and get away from her. "You manipulated me for *years.* You broke her heart...their hearts...*my* heart. Ava was the love of my life. We had a future together!" Ellen's tears spill over.

She isn't getting any sympathy from me. I refuse.

"My love for you was always real," she spits. "I've been the one looking out for you. I know all of your secrets. I'm the one who makes you happy—"

"No. Your love was conditional. As long as I followed *your* lead, your script, then you wouldn't fuck up my life. You didn't fucking care that I loved her. You didn't care that she loved me back!"

She sobs and jumps out of her seat.

"Go home. Get your shit. Find somewhere else to stay tonight. I *never* want to see you again." She pushes past Kayla and leaves the room.

Hopefully, she leaves my life forever.

What a fucking mess.

"I'll follow her and make sure she doesn't take anything that doesn't belong to her."

"No. I need you here. I—" My own tears spill over. Everything I've known up to this point has been a lie. Frowning, Kayla closes the distance between us and wraps her arms around me while maneuvering her ever-growing belly out of the way.

"Okay. I'll stay here. I can get Cassie to meet her over there. I won't leave you. I promise."

Twenty-Nine

Ava

Now

I slingshot Ethan into my dressing room and slam the door behind me. Rage is settled so fucking deep inside of me that I can't control my temper. He fights off tears, but I can't be his friend right now. He's my protector, but right now, he's in deep shit.

"How did you get here?"

"Trevor."

"Who the fuck is Trevor?" I demand.

"Jason's brother. He's a senior."

"*Who is Jason?*" I shriek.

Ethan shrinks back. "He's on my football team."

"So you got in the car with a stranger and drove into the city?" He rolls his eyes. We've just entered into this teenage phase that everything I say gets an eye roll. I expected it from Alice, not Ethan.

"He isn't a stranger. I just told you, he's Jason's brother." It's so hard dealing with a man-child. One that I want to hug because I know he's deeply hurt by his uncle.

The uncle he just told to fuck himself while hundreds of people have recorded it with their phone and probably all over social media by now.

Mother of the year.

"Why are you here, E? I want the truth." He plops himself down on my stool and frowns.

"He was being so...*dumb.* I didn't like the way he was talking to you. So I came. Auntie Tess let me in, and then I heard him call you a liar."

"Ethan..."

"Where's Dad, anyway? He's supposed to be here for support. He should've stepped in when his asshole brother was being an asshole to you."

Asshole. Word of the day. Got it.

"I don't know." I lean against the door and slide down until my ass hits the floor. "I'm sure he's livid with me right now. This wasn't how I wanted him to find out. He must feel so betrayed."

"Still. He should've stayed. I would've been angry, but I still would've stayed." Yeah, well, not everyone is as kind and noble as Ethan Wentworth. "It's not like he has a leg to stand on, anyway. He was an asshole back then." I close my eyes in frustration.

"Baby, stop saying asshole." He snickers. "Ethan, do you understand why I wanted them to stop filming?"

"Because you love me and didn't want me to get bullied? Mom, look at me. I'm almost as tall as Dad and I spend a lot of time at the gym. *Nobody* can bully me."

So humble.

"I *do* love you. But...this is going to follow you everywhere you go, do you know that? Colleges can pull this footage and they'll think this is what kind of person you are."

He considers this a moment. I want him to weigh the gravity of the situation, take this seriously. Instead, he shrugs.

UGH.

"They'll see me sticking up for my mother who was lied to about an interview and stepping up to the guy who's hell bent on slandering her."

He has an answer for everything. I wish I had his confidence.

"They might see you as a hot head who will step up to anyone and everyone."

"When I get famous, mom, I'm not going to care about what college accepted me, or what NFL team is going to draft me. There are hundreds of careers out there that I can do. I can start my own business if I wanted to. But if someone is going to judge me for stepping up to an adult who is verbally abusing my mom and not ask for the whole story, then I don't want to be a part of their organization, anyway. I'll always stick up for what's right, and nobody can change my mind about that."

Mother of the fucking year!

He's a good man. I take comfort in the fact that in four years, I'm sending a good, compassionate, and loyal man out into the world.

I wrap him up in my arms and kiss his forehead.

"I am truly amazed at what kind of man you're becoming, baby. I'm so proud of you." His crooked grin makes me forget what dumpster fire this day was.

A knock on the door telling me I need to get back up to the stage breaks through our moment.

"I'll stay with you, Mom."

"Ha! No. You'll stay right here. I'll turn the monitor on, but you aren't allowed to interrupt anymore. I'm a grown woman. I can hold my own."

"Mom!"

"You want to take Lilian Hill out for your first date this weekend, right? So if you want to do that, you have to stay put. Auntie Tess is watching." He murmurs a string of cuss words under his breath as I exit the dressing room.

Reality hits me like a freight train. I have to walk through the rest of the story *except for that one thing* and move on with my life.

Gray knows. We became friends under worse circumstances. Maybe he'll be adult enough to...

Oh god.

He's petty.

I shake the thought when I reenter the studio. The audience chatters excitedly. Sunny fans herself with her notecards and ignores my existence. How convenient. She couldn't wait to fangirl all over me when I got here. Now that I threaten her job, she doesn't want to be friends with me? What kind of bullshit is that?

Kayla and Brandon walk in together, both wearing somber expressions. He walks slowly to the stage and lowers himself onto the cushions. His face is pale, like he just saw a ghost.

Whatever.

Still no sign of Gray.

Red lights surround us, signaling Sunny to pull her act together and look professional. I sneak a peek at Brand. His skin turns a greenish hue.

"Welcome back. When we left, we heard the gut-wrenching side of the story where Ava found Brandon's current girlfriend naked in Brandon's doorway. Brandon, you claim that Ellen wasn't there and that you didn't cheat on Ava. Are you still sticking with that story?"

Ha. Let's go, Brand.

"No."

What?

The audience chatters nervously. Kayla tries to give me a reassuring smile, but I don't like surprises. I don't like this one bit.

"I'm sorry I didn't believe you." His voice is so quiet, I can barely hear him. It *barely* registers on the mics.

"You believe me because Ethan said so? So really, you believe Ethan over me?"

"Ave..." His voice cracks. "She's manipulated me for so long...I didn't know—"

"I told you what she did, Brand!" Fuck. And now I'm crying again!

"She's been a part of my life from the beginning...I didn't know why she would lie to me. But I swear, I wasn't there at the apartment when she was. I don't know how you heard me, but I swear to God, I wasn't there."

I can't believe he's still trying to pull the wool over my eyes.

"Ava, I would like for you to look at this picture." I turn my attention to the monitor. Brandon walks down Michigan Avenue with a goofy smile on his face. He pinches a white gold engagement ring in between his thumb and forefinger. "Look at the time stamp."

6:35 pm. He couldn't have been at the apartment. We arrived just five minutes before. My eyes well up tears.

"I was going to ask you to marry me. And then you never showed up." He was going to propose. "I went to your house, but Gray met me outside. He said you didn't want to see me."

Oh my god.

"I called you so many times. I texted you all night, and you never answered. I left so many voicemails—"

"I never got any of those," I interrupt. I wanted an explanation. I wanted to give him a piece of his mind. "I called you, Brand. So many times. I even went to Lake Forest to see you but Ellen said you didn't want to see me."

...Wait.

"Ava, tell me about your hospitalization." So many things happen at once. Jane meets my eyes and tries to get the producer's attention. Tess makes a scene. Warning bells and sirens go off in my head. The audience gasps and chatters about this new piece of news. And the final nail in the coffin is the ugliest picture of me restrained to a hospital bed. My eyes are purple, my skin is green.

It looks like it was taken in between two slats of the blinds.

This can't be happening.

"Shut it down!" Tess shouts.

"Ave? What are they talking about?"

I stare at the woman in the picture. My body shakes as I remember my seventy-two hour hold when my life was falling apart.

There's an elephant on my chest, suffocating me.

Grounding.

Mindfulness.

Name five things you can see.

"I, um…"

"You were hospitalized because you couldn't handle a breakup?" Sunny asks, her voice dripping in judgement.

My mouth goes numb. Pins and needles take over the feeling in my jaw.

Four things you can hear.

"Did you have a breakdown because Brandon broke up with you?" Sunny prods.

"I didn't break up with her!"

Nobody was supposed to know about this. Only Tess.

"Babe? Don't do this. It's none of anyone's business."

It takes me a moment to realize the cameras stopped rolling. Tess is straddling my lap, her cool hands on my cheeks, so I can come back to reality.

"You told them about the hospitalization?" She shakes her head, her own tears presenting.

"No, babe. I didn't. You mean more to me than this job. I didn't say anything to them." My bottom lip wobbles. "Don't do this. At what point is your reputation worth more than the state of your heart?"

I glance to Brandon, whose own eyes shine with unshed tears.

"I have to finish this. It's already out there."

"No," she shakes her head and wipes away my tears. "Let's go home. I'll make you some tea and order some pasta—"

"I have to finish. Let me finish." Tess rests her forehead against mine.

"As soon as we're done, we're suing for everything they have, you hear me? We're going to take them for everything they have, including the tacky yellow skirt suit." I give a watery laugh and find the woman in the picture again when Tess dismounts me.

I wish I could tell her that it gets better, but obviously, it isn't true.

"Ava? Were you hospitalized because you couldn't cope with your breakup?" Sunny gently asks. She's changing her approach which is...*convenient.*

"After the commercials went out about Brandon being on that dating game show, I..." I take a deep breath. "There comes a point where you wonder if you're unlovable. My dad didn't want me and took off before I was born. My mom didn't want me, but I was her meal ticket. I've had three serious relationships in my life. One was Ben, and I'm not sure if he counts because he was my first love. The circumstances didn't allow us to be together, and we grew apart. We became friends, but that's all it ever was.

"Then there was Gray. He thought being married to me would solve all of his problems, but when it didn't, he slept with everyone. And then Brand came around. And I really thought that he was my soulmate...the love of my life, but then he cheated on me. So really, you have to look at the most common denominator, and that was me."

"Ave, I didn't cheat on you."

"I didn't know that then." I want to hug the Ava in the picture. Her world was an ugly place at that point in time. "Anyway, after the commercials, I boarded the train to self-hatred. I hated myself for being unlovable. I couldn't get out of bed. The kids missed multiple days of school, so Ethan took my phone and called Tess."

"And?"

I hate the nonchalance of her tone.

"Do you have any idea what it's like to grow up in this industry? When you star in a sitcom at four years old, the world thinks you're cute until you hit your teen years. They bet against you. They encourage eating disorders. They push you to do drugs because that's the only release you get. The world is your judge. I married Grayson Wentworth because he was pretty and he was nice to me for five minutes. It's what *everyone* expected out of us. It was the next logical step for a heart throb and America's sweetheart. Then to find out I didn't matter…that I was a PR stunt…" My sobs overtake my words, and my breathing is rapid and irregular.

"You were hospitalized—"

"Because—

My chest hurts. What are the signs for women to have a heart attack? I grip the arms of the sofa tightly.

Close your eyes. Observe the thought. Let it pass.

"This is over." Tess's voice is my lighthouse. For a moment, I can't see everything around me. I'm blinded by my hysteria and tears. She pulls me into her side and walks through the hallway. "It's going to be okay. Breathe through it. I'm right here." That's my comfort. I need to get out of here.

A new presence is behind me. Strong hands rip the battery pack from my back pocket while Tess's hands work on the microphone.

"Mom?"

"Shh, sit down, baby," Tess says to Ethan.

"Ave…I'm sorry…"

"Get out of here!" Ethan shouts.

"If Ellen wasn't there…what would you have said?" Brandon asks.

I imagine he cleaned his apartment from top to bottom. The kitchen table would've been set and the food already plated. I bet he bought black, white, and gold balloons and champagne, and sparkling cider. We would've cuddled up on the couch and watched movies until midnight.

When the kids would go to bed, he'd sink to one knee, and I'd say…

"Are you serious right now?" Tess shrieks. "She can't answer that! She's having an anxiety attack!"

"While Ava and Brandon take a breather, I'm joined by Grayson Wentworth." As one, we all turn to the monitor and watch in disbelief. "What do you think about all of this?"

The camera pans to Gray, sitting in my spot with a melancholy smile.

"I'm happy the truth is out." I lick my lips and sink to the floor.

"When did you find out about their relationship?"

"Ellen told me when she came home from that Texas trip. I didn't believe her right away."

"Were you upset?"

Gray gazes into the camera, and I swear he's looking right at me.

"I'm sorry!" Alice's voice echoes down the hallway.

For. Fuck's. Sake!

Jane ushers her into the room.

"Mom, I'm so sorry!" She curls up next to me and sobs into my chest.

"What are you sorry for, babe?"

"I told him!"

"No, not right away. As I said, I didn't believe Ellen at first. I didn't think Ava was the kind of person who would do something like that," Gray replies to Sunny.

"What?" I ask. I can't focus on Alice and the TV all at once.

"That day at the aquarium...we got into a fight when he wouldn't buy tickets. I got angry and said that I wished Uncle Brand was my dad!"

"It wasn't until Alice confirmed it. So, Ellen and I got together and..." I don't listen to the rest of what Gray has to say because Brandon storms out of the room and down the hallway to the studio.

"Let's go. Get your stuff, move your asses. We're done here." I scramble off the floor and shepherd my kids out of my dressing room while we hear the audience gasp and scream. I blink away the tears.

It was Gray all along. Why am I fucking surprised?

Thirty

Ava

Now

Alice wasn't going to watch the interview, but she happened to see a video on a friend's phone and put two and two together faster than I did. She got a soda from the vending machine and poured it down her pants and went to the nurse's office, claiming it was diarrhea.

The nurse then called down the line for someone to pick her up, but we were all busy. Except for Jordan. She told him the truth and got him to drive her downtown to the studio to warn me.

"Are you mad at me?" she asks in the car, still crying.

"No, baby. I'm not mad at you."

"I don't mean about school. I mean...about telling dad about Uncle Brand." I weakly smile and press a kiss to her forehead.

"No, I'm not mad at you for that, either. We told you and Ethan you could tell dad if you wanted to." I just wish she would've given me a heads up. Jane follows us behind Jordan's truck. She wants to regroup, but I just don't have the energy to talk about this anymore.

"How are you doing, babe?" Tess asks quietly.

"I don't know." And that's the truth.

Grayson Wentworth has always been the wolf in sheep's clothing. If it weren't for my kids, I'd wish I never met him. He's toxic. He pretended to be my friend for six years only to openly humiliate me by airing out my dirty laundry.

It's time like these that I'm glad I don't pay for cable anymore.

When we get back to my house, I invite everyone in, even though I want them to leave.

Six years ago, I was admitted into a psych ward because I lost my grip on reality. Well, sort of. I was so engrossed in my reality that it broke me. In my mind, I was the most unlovable person on the planet. Ethan called Tess because I couldn't get out of bed.

Tess did what she had to do. She committed me and then watched over my kids until I was able to leave the hospital.

Those seventy-two hours were long overdue. I'm not crazy, and I wasn't back then, either. I was overworked, exhausted, and burying my pain. I was prescribed antidepressants and referred to a psychiatrist/psychologist team to sort out my shit.

They have been my greatest gift.

Ethan parks himself on the couch while Alice races to her room to change out of her soda-stained gym shorts. Tess brews coffee while Jordan stands behind the kitchen table, not knowing exactly what to do. Jane sets up shop at the head of the table and uses her big computer brain to scan social media.

"Guys…thank you for helping me out today, but I think you guys should go home."

Tess turns to me with a pained expression.

"Ava, I don't think that's a good idea," Tess states.

"I have a tool chest of coping mechanisms that I didn't have back then." I cross the kitchen and wrap my arms around her. "I need a minute to breathe. I need to cook dinner and help out with homework. I need to feel like…a regular person. Just for tonight."

"I think we need to get ahead of the social media, Ava. Grayson is dragging you through the mud," Jane adds.

I shrug. Let it. I don't care.

"I trust you to get ahead of it."

"But, you need to make a statement—"

"And I will." I sit down at the table and sigh. "My world was turned upside down today, Jane. The last six years of my—*our*—life has been a lie. I need to tend to my children's broken hearts."

I need to sink into the bathtub with the glass of rosé I promised myself this morning and just sit in the silence for a half hour.

"You'll call me before you go to bed tonight?" Tess asks warily.

"Of course. Just like we do every night." I paste on my best fake smile. "We're going to be okay."

"Okay...will you call me later too? I just want to make sure you're okay." Jane asks. I throw my arms around Jane when she stands up and walks over to Tess and me.

"Yes. I promise to call you later." The trio descends the staircase together in a single file line. Tess refuses to break our eye contact until Jordan turns his truck around.

My kids don't have to be prompted to go to bed at a decent hour. It's Friday night, and I'm almost positive they're playing on their tablets, anyway. The media flocked around our house for most of the night, finally packing up about an hour ago.

My phone calls with Tess and Jane were short and sweet. Now, I have a hot bath calling my name. I lock the back doors and stare out the glass at the fire pit. I used to stare at it with such contempt. It was where I fell in love with Brandon. It was where we had our first fight. I wanted to get rid of it but could never build up the nerve.

I get the dishwasher going and flick off the lights.

The shrill sound of my doorbell echoes through the house. My heart races and I stay put. Who would be coming here at this hour? Steeling myself with a deep breath, I pad through the kitchen into the foyer and answer the door.

Gray, and his giant black eye and tissues up his nose, pushes past me and enters the house uninvited.

Great.

The anger and adrenaline I had when the interview first started runs through my veins.

"What happened?" I know what happened, but it'll be satisfying to hear him say he got his ass handed to him by his big brother.

"Brandon sucker-punched me." Good.

"It's late, Gray. The kids are in bed and I was just heading up myself." *Plus, I don't want you here.*

"I didn't come here for them."

"I'm not in the mood for this." I turn off the rest of the lights except for the living room. He doesn't make a move for the door. I find myself close to the hallway where the kids' rooms are, just in case.

Bev's story about how Preston tried to murder her suddenly comes to mind.

Fabulous.

"I'm trying to think of *why* you continually try to hurt me, and I'm coming up blank. Is that what you wanted to talk about?"

He balls his fist and his jaw ticks.

"Did you ever think about how this would affect me?"

"Yes! It's the whole reason why we didn't tell you! But it turns out you already knew and held it in until today. Why? Why did you wait six years and why the hell didn't you come to me like an adult and tell me that you knew?"

He laughs maniacally. He's drunk. And the fact he drove here is concerning.

"I didn't think you'd wait this long to land a role." Of course. He was waiting for the biggest opportunity to bury me.

"What is wrong with you?" I plead. "Why couldn't you just cut your ties after we divorced? There's no love lost, Gray!"

"Because he was my brother!" His roar echoes off my walls. He strides towards me and crowds me against the wall. "There are

thousands of men all over the world and you just *had* to sleep with my brother!?"

"Step back, Gray."

He shakes his head.

"I'm so sick of this 'woe is me' victim act you've had going for all of these years. People cheat on each other all the time!"

I wish I let Tess spend the night. Holy shit.

"I'm so sick of you walking around as if your shit smells like roses!" I shove him back and stroll into the kitchen. I need something to defend myself with. He grabs my wrist and spins me around. "Brandon was there for me. He was more of a father to those kids than you ever were!"

His hand cracks on my cheek. Tears spring in my eyes, and the sting of his slap warms my face. He's never gotten physical before.

The monitor to the gate buzzes. But we both ignore it.

"Why did you do this?" My sobs overshadow my anger. "Why did you pretend to be my friend all this time? Why did you have to humiliate me on national television? Does it make you feel like a big, strong man? Did it make you feel powerful?"

"Shut the fuck up!"

"You've spent your entire adult life blaming me for all of your shortcomings! I loved you, Gray, Once upon a time, I loved you. Over the last six years, we became friends, just like we were when we first met. Why did you ruin it?" A knock on the door grabs his attention. He releases my hand and answers the door.

I find Ethan standing in the doorway of the hallway with his arms across his chest and his eyes narrowed at his father.

"Ma'am? We've got a call about a disturbance."

"We're fine," Gray snaps and tries to close the door. The police officer sticks his foot in the door and swings it open, knocking Gray off-kilter.

"Ma'am? Are you all right?" I wipe my eyes while one of the police officers, the blonde one with all of the tribal tattoos leads me to the other side of the room, closer to Ethan.

"I'm fine. I think he's drunk." He winces at the red mark on my cheek.

"I'll need to take a picture of your face. Does he live here? Do you have another place to stay?" I shake my head.

"This is my home. We're divorced, and he lives out in Burr Ridge." The other cop, the older one with glasses and a soul patch, cuffs Gray against the door.

"Are you wanting to press charges?"

Am I?

I look to Ethan, who glares at his father.

"I don't know…"

Too much is happening. I still can't wrap my head around the fact he knew about my relationship with his brother for six years! I can't fucking think straight.

"He'll be in holding all night if that makes you feel better. I'd change the code on your gate if I were you. We can send a patrol over this way when he makes bail."

Oh my God.

"I…um. Do I have to make a decision right now?" He frowns and flips open his notebook.

"No, though I'd advise you to make a decision sooner rather than later. Can you tell me what happened? We need to take your statement."

The cops are here for half an hour. Ethan stays up with me until we both fall asleep on the couch.

This much I can promise: Grayson Wentworth will not leave *this* unscathed.

Thirty-One

Brandon

Now

I don't know what possessed me to agree to a meeting with Ellen, but I didn't come empty-handed. Kayla sits next to me with my attorney, Mike. Kayla's ready to pop. She's officially a week past her due date and the kid doesn't want to come out.

We're meeting on my turf. My apartment. She needs to sign to take her off the lease, and Mike wants to talk to her about keeping her distance.

My stomach has been churning all morning. I don't want to see her. I don't want to hear her lame excuses.

It's been seven whole days since the interview. Gray's mugshot has been circulated all over the place. The police report was made public. He hit Ava, and I wasn't there.

The world is shitty right now. Kayla and Mike talk in hushed tones in the kitchen. I didn't bother cleaning up, though Kayla took care of that when she walked in and found beer bottles and empty takeout containers all over the place.

The front door opens, and Ellen strolls in hesitantly. She dared to use her key fob.

I want that back.

"Hey, Brand," she says softly. I won't entertain her bullshit or her come in peace attitude. I stare at the TV and watch the coverage of Gray's publicist trying to come up with excuses for him.

"Good. You're here. Let's take this to the table," Kayla says curtly. I get up and situate myself in the middle of Kayla and Mike.

Mike opens his briefcase and takes out a notepad and the lease forms. This is the first time seeing Ellen with no confidence. She's terrified, and she shows this by wringing her hands and avoiding my gaze.

"First things first. We need your key fob back." Kayla has no problem ripping into her. Mike passes over the lease separation to her. Ellen's eyes water and she finally takes the time to look at me.

"Brand, can't we just talk about this? Just you and me?"

"Absolutely not," Kayla snaps.

"There's nothing to talk about," I say. It's been a week since I've talked to a human being. My voice comes out gravelly. I've used grocery delivery services and food delivery services. I've ignored Kayla's phone calls and only texted because talking took everything out of me.

"There's plenty to talk about. I'm sorry—"

"I don't want to hear it."

"No, Brand, honestly, I'm sorry. I'm sorry I hurt you."

"You're sorry you got caught." She's taken aback by my harshness, but she shuts up. She spins the fob off her key ring and reluctantly reaches for the pen that Mike hands to her and signs the form.

"So, is this it for us? You're never going to talk to me again?"

"You ruined my life." Her eyes shine with tears.

"We'd like to avoid using a restraining order, but we will file one if we need to." Kayla steps in, taking control of the situation.

Ellen gasps.

"Brand, you can't be serious!"

"I had to pick Gray up from jail last week. He told me everything. He told me about the private detective you had follow us, the pictures you leaked to the tabloids, and this whole ruse of blocking our numbers from each other. There is no possible way you could have loved me, Ellen. A sick obsession, maybe, but I wouldn't have dreamed of doing that to Ava. You stole six years away from me."

She shrinks back into her seat.

"I don't ever want to see you again. You've ruined my life. You've manipulated me and dragged my idiot brother into it—"

"And what about him? He gets a free pass while I get banished?" I chuckle.

"No. He's not getting a free pass. I just haven't dealt with him yet."

Her eyes darken while Mike explains the new terms to her. No getting within one hundred yards of me, no letters, emails, or following me on social media. I want to erase her from my life.

If I happen to see her from a distance when I go home to visit my mom, I have two legs that can turn in the other direction.

"Are you going back to her?" Ellen's voice breaks through my thoughts.

Every time I think of Ava, I want to hurl. My attitude towards her for the last six years makes me physically ill. I can't imagine how broken she was that night when Ellen answered the door.

She was hospitalized because of me.

There's no way she'll take me back.

"It's none of your business," Kayla answers for me. "Brandon is no longer your business. You don't call, you don't write, you don't show up. His main objective is to move on with his life and you cannot be a part of it. Should any of these conditions you just signed and agreed to be violated, a restraining order will be filed, and we will pursue legal action."

She stands up on shaky legs.

This used to be her house. And while marriage never crossed my mind with her, I wonder if she would've taken this secret to the grave. Would I have gone my whole life away from my someone?

She walks out the door without another word. Ellen Wilson is officially out of my life for good. I just wish it made me feel better.

Kayla rubs soothing circles on her belly. Her phone lays on the table and a stopwatch app rolls its numbers as she breathes heavily.

"You all right?"

"Peachy." She presses the stop button, landing on thirty seconds and some change. "I need to walk." She stands up and the yoga pants she wears are soaked, as is the cushion on my dining room chair.

"Um, Kayla, you're all wet," I state, frowning at the state of my chair.

"What?" Mike examines the chair, and then Kayla's pants.

"Sweetheart, I think your water broke." Her face lights up as Mike and I shoot up from our seats and rush around the apartment. For what? I'm not sure.

"Do you have a bag? Where's the bag? Should I call an ambulance?"

"What about your birth plan?" Mike asks.

She giggles.

"Relax, guys. Take a deep breath. I don't have my go-bag with me, but Cassie does. Brand, can you bring me to the hospital?" I freeze on the spot. There are like eight hospitals nearby!

"Where?"

She sighs. "Come on. I'll give you directions. My water broke. The baby isn't coming down the pike." How can she be so calm at a time like this? What happens if she gives birth in my car?

She insists Mike doesn't need to come with us but promises to send him pictures once the little guy is born. Meanwhile, I drive on the highway on my way to Evanston, closer to Cassie and Kayla's apartment.

I'm grateful to the hospital for valet services. Kayla has to rock herself out of the car, but otherwise, she's totally fine. Her contractions are five minutes apart and not intense yet.

Cassie meets us in Labor and Delivery. Her chocolate brown hair is tied up in a messy bun. She works nights in this very hospital as a nurse, so I'm comfortable leaving my ex-wife in capable hands.

What do I do now? Other than picking Gray up in jail last week, this is the first time seeing the light of day. The Live Oaks runs smoothly without me. I get daily updates from the President of the foundation, but that's it.

My mother has called me multiple times a day, but she gets my voicemail. When she's sick of that, she called Kayla to check up on me.

I wonder how Ava and the kids are doing. I wish I had the balls to call her.

The labor and delivery waiting room is cheery and happy faces and unicorn farts. It's for people who are excited about their bundles of joy, not for cynical assholes like me. Cassie has begged me to go home since Kayla hasn't progressed any since we got here eight hours ago, but I politely refuse.

What else am I going to do?

I don't want to go home.

I don't want to go to my *real* home in Texas.

I don't want to move. I just want everyone to ignore me until the baby is born. Hell, it isn't even *my* kid. I just want to lay eyes on a human being who doesn't know this ugly world yet. At eleven o'clock, Cassie bursts into the waiting room with a giant, dimpled smile, and tears in her eyes.

"Come on, Brand." I slowly pick myself up and follow Cassie down the hallway. Babies cry, women scream, and machines beep all around me. I once pictured Ava in one of these rooms, giving birth to our child.

I swallow that memory when I turn the corner into Kayla's room and see a stocky little boy in her arms. Kayla gives me a watery grin and motions for me to come in.

"Ten pounds of all-American boy, Brand," Kayla announces proudly.

Holy shit.

"Hi, buddy. You did good, Kayla. I'm so proud of you." I sit down in the chair next to her bed while her nurses get ready to move her to her room.

"Isn't it funny how this was never supposed to be a part of our lives?" She asks.

"Um...I wouldn't call it funny." Her hazel eyes shine and crinkle with humor. "He looks good on you."

"I love you, Brand. I know you're not supposed to say that to your ex and whatever, but I need you to know that. Being married to you wasn't for us, but I don't know what I would've done if we didn't become friends afterward."

I smile weakly.

"I love you. And you, Cassie. I love you too." Cassie grins and blushes.

"Look, I was always going to ask you whether Cass agreed to it or not, but I would love it if you would be his godfather."

I straighten up. Is this the closest I'll come to having children?

"What?"

"You're the obvious choice, dummy. If something happens to us, we wouldn't want him going with anyone else." Cassie adds.

"Are you sure? I don't know how to be a godfather."

"And we don't know how to be moms. Yes. We want you to be his godfather." I sigh and nod.

"Okay. Yeah. I'll be his godfather." Kayla grins and sits up, passing me the bundle into my arms.

He looks like an angry potato. He stirs in my arms. He's swaddled tightly and wears tiny mittens on his little hands.

"Meet Cole Brandon Jenkins, Uncle Brand." My head jerks to Kayla.

She named him after me?

"We share a name, huh?" Cole's tiny lips quirk up. "I don't know what I'm doing, buddy. But I promise to teach you how to be a good man." Kayla sniffles.

"We're in this together, Brand." She squeezes my knee in reassurance.

Yeah. No matter what happens. We're in this together.

Thirty-Two

Ava

One month after the interview

"Have you gotten out of the house lately?" I snort and cover myself with the throw blanket from the couch. Peter called to check in on me and figure out my game plan.

"Other than to drop off and pick up the kids from school, no. That's what DoorDash and Instacart are for, bay-beeee." Peter chuckles.

"You still have your sense of humor. That's good."

"Yeah, well, gotta keep me sane somehow."

"You could watch TV..."

Negative.

"I could, but I won't." I sigh. "What's being said, Peter?"

He hesitates and groans.

"They're saying you called the cops on Gray in retaliation."

That's par for the course.

"You haven't come out with a statement, yet. Everyone is coming up with their own conclusions. Can I give you a piece of unsolicited advice?"

"If I say no, will you tell me anyway?" Peter's throaty chuckle brings a smile to my face.

"Your interview was biased. You were trapped and had no control of the narrative. Why don't you go live on Instagram or something? Come out with your own statement. Reach out to the people who love you and tell them the truth. All your secrets are out now. There's nothing more Gray can drag out into the open, and besides, you don't have to tell him what you're doing, anyway."

"I guess…"

"Talk to Jane. I think she'll agree."

Maybe.

"I'll think about it."

We talk about the production of the movie and what other things I'll need to finance, and then we end the call.

I would have spent the day writing, but I can't get my mind to focus. Bev has called me nonstop, but Ethan has been the hero and talks to her and makes excuses as to why I can't answer the phone. Tess has been over every day since the interview, but I think I've become more well-adjusted.

Brandon hasn't called or showed up. Even if he did, I don't know what I'd do. He believed Ellen over me. Hell, he believed Ethan before he believed me! How can I come back to that?

I can't get over how handsome he still is. I dig the scruff. He's forty years old and other than the gray hair at his temples, he doesn't look any different from when I last saw him six years ago.

And when my hospitalization came to light and Tess pulled me out of the interview, he still followed. He made sure I was safe.

I pace around my house, considering Pete's proposal. He's right. What else could go wrong?

Tess agrees with me when she comes over an hour later. She helps me set up the lighting and shows me how to go live. Jane comes over a little later and goes over the things I should touch on.

I don't have a script or some elaborate speech prepared. I'm going into this blind and hopefully, America can accept the truth as it is.

"Try to ignore the comments. Speak clearly. And…just be comfortable. If you don't want to answer any questions, don't. We're right here if you need us," Jane reassures me. I take a deep, cleansing breath and straighten up in my chair.

Going live is worlds away from going into a scheduled interview. I've never laid it all out on the line like this before.

Click.

The screen blinks, and suddenly, I'm staring at myself. I didn't have the energy to put on makeup. My hair is brushed and put into a ponytail, but I'm still wearing my pajamas. This is the best America is going to get from me.

"Hi everyone." My current viewers jump exponentially. "It's been a crazy month, huh? I know a lot of you have been questioning everything that went down at the interview, and I was hoping to get on here—without any interruptions or distractions—and explain everything from my point of view." Comments begin scrolling onto the screen.

We love you, Ava!

#AvaEmpowerment!

Divorce is a sin. You should be ashamed of yourself for going after your husband's brother!

Were you trying to trap another Wentworth?

Men are pigs!

I snort at that last one. They're not wrong.

"So, just so you're all aware, when I was cast for the role of Avery in the movie I was trying to promote, *The Love Letter,* Gray was actually the one who talked me into doing a tell-all interview under the premise of telling the world what our marriage was really like. There was a brief moment that I thought it was a good idea. You see, you never really know how you're going to be portrayed after you come back from taking a hiatus. When our marriage came to a head, where we knew it was doomed, a lot of people painted me as the woman who trapped Gray into a loveless marriage with kids he didn't want.

"That can't be further from the truth. We did love each other...very much. I got married at twenty years old thinking I was going to grow old with him. Having a family was always at the forefront of our minds. It's no secret that Brandon and Gray no longer speak to their father, and that's what Gray was trying to avoid. Except, he realized that he wanted to play the field. He resented settling so young and essentially, that's how our marriage fell apart."

Will you answer questions?

#CancelGraysonWentworth!

"Gray's relationship with the kids distanced significantly. It's like, a few months after Alice was born, he checked out of everything. Growing up, Alice hardly ever talked about him. I've soon come to realize that you can't force fatherhood on someone. We continued with our parenting plan, even though he was giving up his days with them, and that stretched into his weekends and then eventually school breaks. There was a time where he hadn't seen them in six months. We had written into our parenting plan that he had to notify me when he took a role that would take him overseas so that we could make arrangements should anything happen with me or the kids. And that's how Brandon gets wrapped into this.

"My support system solely relied on my best friend, Tess, and her husband, Jordan. That particular Thanksgiving, they were in New York to visit Jordan's family, and Gray was gone. At that point, I hadn't talked to Brandon in over two years."

I miss him.

"Anyway, we started as being just friends. He came over every weekend to help out so I can either get some work done or have some time to myself. I don't think there was a single soul, besides my best friend, who was that considerate. Being a single mother is difficult. I think, honestly, it's the hardest job anyone would be saddled with. There is so much self-doubt that plagues you."

Is Ethan being punished for his disrespect?

Hello from Tampa!

"It didn't take long for me to develop feelings for him. I pushed them as far down as I could. He was charming and charismatic, not to mention drop-dead gorgeous." I laugh to myself. Even still, at forty years old, he's easily the most attractive man I've ever laid eyes on. "Brandon has always been a person to go after what he wants. Where I'm indecisive, he's so confident in his decisions. So naturally, when he brought up becoming more than friends, I hesitated."

Taking a deep breath, I pick up my gaze to stare at the exhausted woman looking back at me.

"In this industry, your reputation is currency. It's what determines what roles, if any, you land. It determines what people will work with you. And more importantly, it is highly rated off of the public's reception of you. I was trying to make a comeback. Going public with him would've made things so much worse. It would've been the end of my career. At least, that's what I told myself in the beginning.

"I think in the back of my mind, knowing Brandon was a Wentworth was a little bit of a speed bump for me. I already knew he was so much...*better* than Gray. And I don't mean that as a popularity kind of thing. Just that...Brand had a heart of gold. He loved people fiercely. His actions spoke much louder than his words. And Gray, well, he hurt me so deeply that I questioned everyone's motives. But what if Brandon realized that I wasn't the woman he thought I was? What if he decided to see someone on the side just like his brother?"

I shrug. He wouldn't have done that. He *didn't* do that. And now I've lost six whole years with him.

"Then, Tess sort of talked sense into me. I was so worried about my future as an actress, I wasn't looking at the bigger picture. I would've regretted letting Brand go. I would've regretted not giving us a chance, but at the same time, I still needed to make sure my reputation was on the mend, which is why we kept it a secret. Well, not entirely. I also needed to make sure it was a sure thing. I didn't want to ruin my reputation if we didn't work out, which is so selfish. I get that now."

#BrAva forever!

I can't stand the way we judge celebrities as a society. We can't forget they're people!

You should've stayed married to Grayson. He's hot!

#BrotherHopper

How are you seriously justifying this? There's a code!

"The few months I had with Brand, I felt like we had a real family. He helped the kids with homework, we took turns cooking dinner, and by the way, he's an *amazing* cook, he did my yard work. When we would spend time at his apartment, he made sure the kids had things to do. They weren't left to their own devices...he played with them. Ethan and Alice loved their uncle probably more than their own father.

"And I'm not saying that to start fights. I'm saying it because it's the truth. Gray was hardly around. He would talk to them on the phone for maybe a minute each. He was going through his quarter-life crisis. And then there was the whole pregnancy scare with Lucy Rodriguez that didn't end up panning out...I'm not a perfect person. I don't pretend to be a perfect person. I was hopeful she was pregnant. I wanted to see if he would step up for her. I hoped he would." I sigh heavily. Her pregnancy was a ruse to get him to propose.

Nobody nails down Grayson Wentworth. I learned that the hard way.

"I'd been in love before Brandon, but it never felt like it was when I was with him. I've never felt so...*seen*. Understood, even. It was the first time my heart felt stable. Love is...funny. When you find that someone who clicks into place so seamlessly, it's like the roadmap of your life becomes...fuller. There are more stops along the way. More tourist traps and detours."

I weakly smile.

We were going to have a family farm in Texas together.

"I wasn't ever going to make Brandon stop being friends with Ellen. They'd known each other since childhood. It was apparent to me that she was in love with him, but he always seemed like he didn't know, or he was in denial. I had a feeling she might have been behind that picture leak of Jordan and me in their kitchen. What that picture doesn't show was that Tess was in earshot the entire time. We joke that we are a throuple, but that's not what it is. Tess is my sister. My only family outside of my kids. Jordan naturally falls into that family. I respect them, their marriage, and the sacrifices they've made to bring the three of us into their family. Ellen chose to exploit that.

"When I saw her naked in Brandon's doorway, it hurt worse than Gray cheating on me with all of the females in Hollywood. I jumped to conclusions because I heard his voice telling her to hurry up. I'll get to that in a minute. What I didn't know was that she was working her ass off to drive a wedge between us. And when that didn't work, she went to Gray."

I wonder if he's watching this right now.

"It was over between Brandon and me. There was no coming back from that. He did end up coming over one night. He wanted to talk to the kids, but I stopped him from coming inside. We had an epic screaming match outside, which led to some choice words to each other. I won't get into that. He hasn't said anything about it, and I won't either.

"But then I saw the commercials for that stupid dating show. It drew me onto this downward spiral I couldn't control. From my perspective, it looked like he never intended on building a future with me. All of the things he said to me were lies. And, well, it broke me.

"I meant what I said in the interview about my hospitalization. There were so many things that led to my emotional breakdown. Being unlovable was one, being unwanted was another. Tess was the only one who was supposed to know about my hospitalization because she was the one who committed me." I glance up to see tears streaming down her face.

"My hospitalization may have been my saving grace. It was the greatest gift anyone could have given me. I was diagnosed with depression and anxiety. And for seventy-two hours, I was able to talk about my pain without fear of it leaking to the media. I ended up calling the hospital a few days after the interview and it turned out I still had Gray listed as my emergency contact and there was a form that I signed that gave the hospital my permission to talk to Gray about my health. He took advantage of that."

That was a tough pill to swallow. I gave him all the ammo he needed to bury me. Like the immature child he is, he took it. Fucking asshole.

"I did end up watching the rest of the interview a few days after it was on air. Ellen hired a private detective to follow us while we were in Texas. She gave the photos to Gray, and they hatched this elaborate plan to break us up. Ellen recorded Brandon's voice on her phone a few weeks before everything went down. They worked together at the time, and she spent the night every so often. He was yelling at her to hurry up so they could leave for work. At some point, they had access to our phones and blocked our numbers. It was diabolical. I'll give them that. They manipulated us."

Do you still love Brandon?

Have you talked to Brandon since the interview?

What's happening with the network?

Have you talked to Gray since the interview?

Will you forgive Ellen and Gray?

"Gray was going to expose us once I landed a role in some major production. He didn't count on it being six years from then, which is why all of this is coming out now. He wanted to humiliate me, which I'll admit he succeeded. But he also succeeded in deeply hurting me, and the kids."

He'll be dealt with once I have the energy. He hasn't asked to see the kids, and I'm tempted to tell him to fuck off if he ever does. Or at least have Ethan tell him to.

"To answer an earlier question, no. I haven't heard from Brand since the interview. None of us have reached out to each other. And if I'm being honest, I don't know how to unblock his number."

The comments pop in faster and faster. It's difficult to keep up.

The network is being sued, not just by me, but by Brandon and Tess. I can't *wait* to bury Sunny Brauer. It'll be the happiest day of my life.

"Somebody asked if I still love Brand." I don't think I ever stopped loving him. I was angry at him for all this time, devastated that he allegedly cheated on me. But it hurt so much *because* I love him so deeply. "Simply put, yes. It's not something that ever went away."

Why did you call the cops on Gray?

"So, for those of you who keep asking me why I called the cops on Gray, I can't comment on it." I'm pressing charges. He can't get away with this. Brandon was right. I indulged him for far long. It ends right now.

#BrAva!

How is Ethan doing? Seeing him cry broke my heart.

"I don't like sharing much about my children. They're old enough to have their own voice and I want to respect their privacy. However, Ethan has made it clear he wants the world to see who his father really is. Ethan wasn't supposed to be at the studio that day. He was supposed to be in school, but he was watching the interview the whole time. He came to protect me. He's my man trapped in a boy's body. The interview was biased against me and he stepped in to set Brandon straight."

Though, it turns out we were all wrong about everything. Brandon didn't cheat. He was a better man than Gray. And Ellen really was trying to get with Brandon.

"Anyway. I know you all will probably think what you want. This is my truth. I didn't mean to fall in love with my brother-in-law, though in my defense, he wasn't my brother-in-law then. Brandon

Wentworth is a good man. He's loyal to a fault and sees the best in everyone. A total romantic." I weakly smile. "And just so everyone knows, I'm starring in *The Love Letter* because I was the original author."

What!?

I need to read that book!

When will it be in theaters?

"*The Love Letter* is my love letter to Brandon. It took me years to finish writing the book, but I ended it the way I think our real love story should've ended. So, this is my shameless plug. Please read the book. Watch the movie. Peter Alvarez is the most amazing director I've ever worked with. He's a genius and made my story come to life in the most magical way. I don't think I have anything left to say. This has been terrifying to do, and I so appreciate every one of you who watched. Thank you so much."

When I click the *end* button, a wave of relief washes over me. The full story is out there. I feel the world that was resting solely on my shoulders lift off of me.

"You okay, babe?" Tess asks gently.

I nod slowly. "Yeah. I'm okay. Thank you for helping me with this."

"You had a great turnout," Jane adds softly. "I'm so proud of you for doing this. You told your story gracefully, Ava. This is a new era, and you are going to *crush* this movie premiere."

I hope so. This is what I've been working towards my whole life.

Thirty-Three

Brandon

Brandon
Two months after the interview

I have a bag packed in the back seat of my truck. I haven't driven to the suburbs in forever. Metallica blares from my speakers. It's unlike me, but it fuels the anger that courses through my veins. I drum on the steering wheel and speed through the empty streets.

When I reach my destination, I jam the code into the box and watch the gates slowly inch open. I barrel through the small opening when the gates open wide enough for my truck to fit through.

Gravel flies in every direction when I speed through Gray's driveway. There's no regard for his precious lawn or whatever ugly totems he has lying around now. I drive under the portico and don't even bother knocking on the door or ringing the doorbell.

"Gray!"

I stand in the foyer and wait for my idiot brother to show his stupid face. Timid footsteps from the stairs have me jerking my head for the source.

Gray is dressed casually in linen pants and a long-sleeved UCLA shirt. He didn't even go there.

"Dude, don't you knock?" I raise my eyebrows and scare him with a few steps forward. "Okay, okay I'm sorry! Can I help you with something?"

"Yeah. Pack a bag. Enough clothes for a week." His face pales.

"Where are you taking me?"

Yeah, not telling.

"Pack a bag, Gray. We don't have time for questions." I find a familiar pair of bright blue eyes, watching me with a hint of amusement and curiosity. He sits on the stairs and watches this all unfold.

"I can't. I have the kids."

I turn to Ethan.

"Can I trust you to watch your sister until your mom gets here?"

"Brand, you can't ask that of him!"

"Yeah, I can keep an eye on Alice. I'll call Mom right now." Gray's eyes widen. Usually, about now, I'd expect him to start yelling at Ethan and bullying him into showing loyalty. But from where I stand right now, I'm almost positive Gray is scared of him.

"Pack a bag. Enough clothes for a week." He stares at me for a long moment. He's wondering if I'm going to murder him. It's tempting, but that's not why I'm here. He slowly trudges up the stairs, leaving Ethan and me alone in a room together for the first time in six years.

"I'm sorry I told you to fuck yourself on TV."

He brings a goofy grin to my face.

"It's okay." He shrugs nonchalantly.

"I thought you hurt Mom. Nobody else was standing up for her and you weren't believing her."

Sighing, I step up the stairs and seat myself on the landing, three feet away from him.

"I know. I'm proud of you for what you did. You're a good kid, E." He grins and rolls his eyes.

"I'm in football now. Did dad tell you?"

"No, but I figured you did. You look like you can mow down anyone with ease." He smirks cockily and wriggles his eyebrows.

"I joined because I knew one day I'd get drafted by the NFL. I hope we'd be on different teams because then I could beat the shit out of you and blame it on the sport."

Oh my God.

I snort.

"You didn't factor in my age."

He barks out a laugh.

"Yeah, you're still old."

"Dude, your mom is the age I was when we first got together."

"I don't make the rules, Uncle Brand." My heart leaps that he's bestowed my "Uncle" title on me again. I've missed six years of his life because of a miscommunication. "Where are you taking dad?"

"That's classified information." He rolls his eyes in response.

"Is it true you picked him up from the clink?"

"Ha! Yeah, I did. Although, I didn't know what he was in for until after he was released. Needless to say, he got a matching black eye from the one I gave him on air." That part's true. I didn't ask the officer what he was in for and he didn't tell me. Gray was the idiot who told me when I dropped him off at his stupid mansion.

"I wish I could've seen him then. I was the one who called the cops. Did he tell you that?" I grin.

"No, he didn't tell me that."

"I didn't think he would've slapped her. I called because he was being an asshole. When I heard the crack of his hand, the dispatcher kept telling me to stay put because I said I was gonna beat the shit out of him."

No child should ever have to protect his mother from his father. No father should ever put their child in that position. The parallels are sickening. Ethan is that ten-year-old version of me pulling my father off my mother. Gray is my father. It makes me sick to my stomach.

"Buddy, I'm sorry. For everything that's happened. I know this couldn't have been easy for you and your sister, and I'm sure you're holding onto a lot of anger towards me, but I want you to know I love you. I'm sorry that I screwed everything up."

He considers this a moment, but the footsteps on the stairs behind him distract him.

"Uncle Brand!" I scramble to my feet and Alice launches herself into my arms. "I'm so sorry for telling Dad. Are you mad at me?"

"No, sweetheart. I'm not mad at you. I was never mad at you." I set her steady on her feet and she joins Ethan on the stairs. "I don't know what's going to happen. I...have a lot to deal with..." I tilt my head, referring to Gray. I don't want him to hear me talking shit about him. "But my phone number hasn't changed. You both have cell phones now, right?" They both nod. Alice holds hers up to prove it to me. "Call me. Whenever you need someone to talk to or even if you just want to say hey, I'll answer for you every single time."

"Will you go see Mom?" Alice asks hesitantly.

I can't have this conversation with them when I haven't even pulled the trigger on calling the woman who still holds my banged-up heart in her hands.

"I don't know. I think that might be something we'd both need to be open to." Ethan arches an eyebrow.

I saw the live that she did. Where she said she still loved me. But loving me and wanting to be with me are two different horses. I'm a pussy for not have the balls to talk to her about it, but I just can't handle another rejection. Trying to be with her the first time ended in a blaze of misery. I don't have the mental endurance to survive that again.

Gray's footsteps come from the staircase behind me. He holds up a beat-up black duffle bag and stares warily at Ethan.

"You sure you're going to be okay? Yolanda is here if you need anything."

"I'm fine," he snaps, his nostrils flaring. "Mom's on her way."

And that's my cue to get the fuck out of here.

"Lock the doors. Text your dad when your mom gets here, okay?" He nods firmly and pulls Alice into his side. "See ya soon, guys."

We've been heading south for an hour. I've given him the cold shoulder and one stop to get snacks and drinks. We'll be on the road for a while. He sticks his nose up at Metallica and opts for Kanye West, which *immediately* gets shut off.

Our soundtrack is now the air conditioning.

Fuck him.

"Are we just going to sit here and listen to nothing?"

Yep.

But he doesn't need to know that.

"Really? You're not going to talk to me? That's real mature, Brand."

"You know what's real mature? Getting butt hurt about finding out about me and Ava and then setting up a ruse with our childhood friend that gets us to break up and then sell our business to a talk show."

That shuts him up.

Little does he know he has a full fourteen hours of silence.

Bitch.

"I'm sorry..."

"I've heard that before." Specifically, in my apartment when he frisbeed one of my dinner plates against my cabinets.

I don't have any plans on stopping. We should be at mom's house around seven tomorrow morning. He can stretch out in the back if he wants to sleep through all of it. In fact, I hope he does. It'd give me a nice quiet ride to think about how messed up he's going to be at the end of the week.

Can't wait.

"Did you see Ava's live?"

Fuckin' A.

"Yes."

"Have you talked to her?"

"How can I? You blocked her number."

Gray slams his head on the headrest.

"Are you going to be short with me the entire drive? Where are we going, anyway?"

"What the fuck did you expect, Gray? Did you think we'd all laugh about this three months later and be buddy-buddy like nothing ever happened? I have no idea how women fawn all over you. You're a child."

His silence is almost laughable. As a kid, he could never shut up. As a teen, he'd have a comeback for everything. Even as an adult, he had to have the last word. He was a make-believe god to a fanbase that didn't know his true colors.

I was the only one who saw him for who he really was: a child.

"Fine. If you're going to be an ass, I'll sleep in the back. Wake me up when we get there."

He has no clue I'm bringing him back to Texas. Mom gave the farmhands a few days off in preparation for this. Gray needs to remember where he came from. Whose hard work got him to where he is today.

The drive is uneventful. Gray's deep snores used to be annoying, but I've gotten used to them. Music makes me think of Ava, so I don't turn it on. I don't think there's any way she'd take me back.

Too much has happened.

But she still loves me. She said that for the world to hear.

My love for her never went away. She's right. I was angry, and it just meant that I loved her.

The last six years have been brutal. I'm tired of pretending everything's okay. I want to go home. I want to phone it in and just lie in bed and relive my shitty life choices.

I stop at two gas stations. One to fill up, and then a few hours later when I stopped to stock up on energy drinks. I left Gray sleeping. I would *love* it if some wacko saw him sleeping and took ugly pictures of him and posted them all over the internet. That would be fucking sweet.

It isn't much longer until I reach my mom's house. It's seven-thirty, and the sun is slowly rising in the sky. My mind flitters to that next morning when Ava and I woke up in the barn. The sky was streaked with soft pink and navy-blue hues. Her soft skin blanketed me.

I often think about that night. How adventurous and ravenous she was. She couldn't get enough of me, and I couldn't get enough of her. Her mango scent still tickles my nose and her lumberjack snoring still brings a smile to my face all these years later.

I miss her.

"Are you serious?" Gray groans from the back.

"Get up Gray. We have shit to do." I exit the truck and don't bother with my bag. I'll get it later. His door slams behind me and his hesitant steps tell me he's looking around. We don't lock our doors here. Our closest neighbor is Ellen's family, and they keep to themselves. And I'm not exactly expecting any house calls, especially since I told her I'd get a restraining order if she came within a football field of me.

No regrets.

The screen door creaks when I rip it open. I knock once and open the door to a strong whiff of maple syrup and waffles.

"Sweetheart? Is that you?"

"Hi Momma," I call out. Gray closes the door behind us and I lead the way into the kitchen. Her gray hair is in a high ponytail while she cuts strawberries at the sink. I drop a kiss on her cheek and then straight to the coffee maker to pour myself a mug of liquid crack.

"Hi, Momma," Gray says softly, like he's embarrassed that he wasn't prepared for this moment. Momma looks him up and down. Her eyes soften and she pats his cheek. No kiss for him.

"Hi, Grayson. Have a seat. Breakfast's almost ready." Gray occupies the seat he's had since he was a kid, right across from me. He glowers into the white plate in front of him.

"You couldn't have told me we were coming here?" He snaps.

"Nope."

"Great. Back to the one-worded answers."

Momma brings over the waffles, whipped cream, and strawberries. The maple and chocolate syrups are already on the table along with the butter. She sits at the head of the table, her eyes darting from Gray to me.

"The wood in stalls eight and fourteen are rotting out. I'd like to get those stalls cleaned completely out so you boys can get going on replacing that wood. I have a sand and shavings delivery at noon and two o'clock so then we can build those stalls back up."

"Um, don't you have employees to do this for you?" Gray asks timidly.

"I do, baby, but they've been working so hard, and I gave them the week off." I grin at my brother, who is terrified to tell our mother he has no intentions of cleaning out stalls.

"Is this my punishment?"

"No," I answer matter-of-factly.

"Then why the fuck am I here?"

"Language!" Momma exclaims.

"Because Momma needs help, Gray. What kind of sons would we be if we didn't come and help our mother out?"

"What if I hire Willy? He's still constructing barns and shit, right?"

"If you cuss at my table again, I'll slap you across the face." I chuckle into my coffee.

"Willy's dead. And we're perfectly capable to fix the stalls ourselves. Right Momma?"

She sighs. "Do you hate it here this much? We've had good times here."

Gray shifts uncomfortably. I'm glad I brought him here. Watching him squirm is my favorite pastime.

"He doesn't feel like he needs to do the work," I answer for him. I'm not wrong.

"That's not true!"

"Coulda fooled me. When was the last time you visited home?"

Ages. That's the answer. I'm positive it was when he brought Ava home to meet her.

"I don't know…"

"Grayson, what is it about this place you hate so much?"

"Nothing."

Liar.

Momma purses her lips and doesn't press any further. We already know the answer. He blames his shitty attitude on dad not being here.

It's the most silent breakfast either of us has eaten at this table together. Gray wolfs down his breakfast while I try to drag it out as long as possible because, hey, he drew first blood, and this is entertaining.

"I'm going to get some shut-eye," Gray announces.

"You slept twelve hours in the truck, pretty boy. Let's get this shit done before the sand gets here."

"You can't call that sleeping! Your driving is terrible and I'm sure you were driving erratically on purpose!" True story.

"Let's go, Gray. I don't have all day."

Momma grimaces at me like she knows exactly what I'm doing. I won't apologize for this. An eye for an eye may make the whole world blind, but at least he'll get to feel some sort of pain.

He watched his ex-wife squirm while our secrets leaked to the public. So now, I'm going to hit him where it hurts: bringing him home and forcing him into manual labor.

Stalls eight and fourteen are directly across from each other. We'll need to replace the shingles on the roof above the stalls before it rains again, but we can at least get rid of the rotting wood and replace it today.

I'm a son of a farmer. I've spent my whole life mucking stalls and taking care of livestock. Basic carpentry comes with the territory. You learn how to replace a few boards, you save a couple hundred bucks. That's grocery money right there. I grab a wheelbarrow off the wall along with a pitchfork and start clearing out stall number eight.

Gray puts on some music. The pop bullshit, but it's motivation to get this done as quickly as possible.

The barn I brought Ava to is just a few feet from here. I've only been inside of it once since that night. Once was enough. The memories were still raw. I still felt her skin against mine, her breath on my neck. I could worship her a thousand ways and it still wouldn't have been enough. I had her five times in that barn before the kids came home. Each "I love you, Brand" is etched in the fabric of my soul with her sultry voice.

Fuck.

"Why'd you do it?"

I genuinely want to know. I don't want the version he gave to the cameras. I want the god honest truth.

Gray stops what he's doing and looks at me warily.

"Didn't you watch the rest of the interview? I said it then."

"That's bullshit. Try again." He growls and throws his pitchfork into his wheelbarrow and bravely steps closer to the stall I'm in.

"Because that's what Ellen wanted."

What?

"Who cares what she wanted!" He rolls his eyes and trudges back to his stall.

"That's the problem, Brand. I cared. Everyone I ever cared about always seemed to fall for you. *I* was never good enough for anyone. You were clearly momma's favorite. Ellen was in love with you from the very beginning."

"You were good enough for Ava." He stills. "She tried to make it work with you when you didn't deserve it."

"If you were in love with Ava while you were still married to Kayla, would you have tried to make it work with Kayla?"

"What does Kayla have to do with any of this?"

"She doesn't. I'm just trying to show you an example. Let's just say you knew Ava your whole life. You loved her, but she loved me, and you were married to Kayla. Would you try to make it work with Kayla knowing there was a chance you and Ava could be together?"

His example is flawed. I love Kayla, but she wasn't my missing puzzle piece. Ava is the one that got away.

"Are you saying you had a chance with Ellen?"

He shrugs.

"It wasn't out of the realm of possibility."

I sigh. "I still don't understand why you outted us on camera."

"I did it because I was fucking pissed at you. I've loved two women in this life, Brand, and you took them both away from me."

I drop the pitchfork and storm out of my stall. I pin him against the wall of his stall, my fist cocked, ready to knock his lights out.

"I didn't take Ava away from you, asshole. You did that one all by yourself. You cheated on her and then tanked her career for good measure."

"That was an accident!" I drop the scruff of his shirt and let him fall onto the shavings.

"There's nothing accidental about it. You made a family with her, and you *still* chose your dick over them."

"Look, I'm sorry I broke the two of you up. When Ellen told me you were seeing each other, there was a part of me that was relieved."

A laugh escapes me.

"Why, because I always clean up your messes?"

He sadly nods.

"The kids were happy with you."

I don't know what his play is, but it isn't making me feel any better. It's making me angrier.

"Anyway, she was hurt that you kept choosing Ava over her. I just wanted her to be happy, Brand. You made her happy."

Silence falls upon us. I know why he broke us up now, I still don't understand why he had to humiliate her on camera.

"I was still mad, though. It was another woman I loved who chose you. We got close over the six years you were broken up. I, um...I asked her out on a date."

I don't want to fucking hear this.

"She said no."

Because she still loved me.

"I thought six years was enough time to move on from you. Ellen wasn't an option anymore. My relationship with the kids slightly improved...I just thought maybe this was my chance to get things right. She told me no. I pressed her on it, and she said that she was in love with someone else."

I swallow the lump in my throat. She still thought I cheated on her, yet she was still in love with me. I hate him for hurting us.

"So, you decided to humiliate her?"

"Well...both of you. I wanted you both to feel what I felt."

Mission accomplished, jackass.

"Finish up. I'm tired."

Thirty-Four

Ava

Two and a half months after the interview

I never thought it would come to this. I've cleared my schedule for the day and kept the kids home from school. Gray knows we're coming to his house, but he doesn't know what's in store for him.

Ethan has begged me to let him write his father off. As much as I want to, Gray still has rights, and knowing him, he'll scorch the earth to exercise them. It would mean the world to me if he just dissolved his parental rights. He'd do us all a favor. Unfortunately, there isn't a judge around who will allow him to do that just because I hate his guts.

So, we make lemonade.

The car is eerily silent. It's almost like if anyone makes a sound, it'll jinx this whole meeting. I'm prepared for a fight. Unlike the night of the interview where he barged in and slapped me, I have my pepper spray on my person ready to defend my honor.

There is no official meeting with our lawyers, though I *wish* there were. The kids get to tell him exactly what is on their minds and hopefully that will either terrify him into being a better person, or he'll wise up and stay away.

I'm not holding my breath either way.

I park under the portico and hold my purse close to me. The kids follow close behind, hands shoved into the pockets of their jeans and wearing matching scowls. Ethan presses the doorbell impatiently until the front door swings open, and Gray's housekeeper, Yolanda, appears in front of us.

The poor woman looks like she hasn't slept in days. I believe it. I'm sure he's working her to the bone. He's never been one to take care of himself. Honestly, I don't even think he knows how to.

"Good morning, Ms. Reid. Please come in." The kids greet her warmly. Alice even gives her a hug. Has Yolanda been my true coparent all along?

The foyer is spotless. There are pictures of Gray and the "important" celebrities he's met and worked with since his career began. The double staircase stands before us with no footsteps.

"Mr. Wentworth is still sleeping. I can make you some coffee and breakfast if you're hungry..." I sigh. Of course he's still sleeping. He's too ignorant to realize what the hell is going on.

"Thank you so much, but we need to get this show on the road. I'll go wake him up." Yolanda hesitates to stop me, but instead shrugs and heads in the opposite direction. She doesn't want anything to do with this, and I don't necessarily blame her.

This was the house Gray had me look at when we first got married. He was so impressed with the gothic fixtures inside. It was a home fit for an A-List Hollywood celebrity. It wasn't a home for a young family.

That's where our treehouse came in. When the kids were growing up, the living room was covered in toys and spilled milk. But it was *home*.

When we agreed to divorce, he was lucky enough for this house to be on the market again.

I hope it's haunted.

The kids race up the stairs and turn the corner to the ornate oak door that leads to the master bedroom. I knock once and push the heavy door open. He lies in the middle of the bed with an eye mask to block out the natural light that pours in through the red velvet curtains.

"Gray, wake up." He stirs slightly, his rapid snores cut through the tension in the room. Ethan approaches the bed and pushes Gray.

With a roar, he yanks the mask off his eyes and chucks it across the room and rises out of bed. I yank Ethan back to me and retreat a few steps.

His eyes dart from me, to Ethan, and then to Alice. He looks...horrible. His skin has a greenish tinge to it, like he's sick or something. His hair that is typically so well groomed sticks out in all directions, and he stinks of sweat and cow manure.

"What are you doing here?" he demands.

"We had a meeting, remember?"

No, he doesn't remember.

"Yeah, I remember." Mmhm. "Give me thirty minutes to get ready. Actually, can we reschedule?"

"No. This needs to happen today. Get ready. We'll be downstairs." I'm not putting this off any longer.

We leave the room, and the kids trot down the stairs to talk to Yolanda. I walk slowly down the hallway, immediately pointing out Ethan and Alice's rooms. I crack Ethan's door open a sliver, just so I can see what his life is like here.

A queen-sized bed with a black comforter and navy-blue sheets stands in the middle of the room. He has a TV, every game system, and a bookcase full of decorative books. There's a poster of Dave Bautista just beside the TV and a poster of Scarlet Johansson hanging on the ceiling above his bed.

Ugh.

Boys.

Black curtains cover the windows. The fan circulates stale air around the room.

It feels like a dungeon.

Where Ethan's room at home is filled with colorful comic books and manga and his curtains remain open and his bed looks comfortable with green bedding, his life here is dark. He's told me time and time again that he hates it here. I close the door silently and move to Alice's room.

Her room is painted pink with ballerina decals that cling to the cheery walls. She has a TV bigger than the one we have at home mounted to the wall. There is a white toy box against the wall just below the window full of toys she hasn't played with since she was six. It's a room for a little girl.

If Gray spent a little time with his kids, he'd see that they're complex individuals. They love sports. They love reading. They don't even watch much TV at home. I'm looking into two rooms of two children neither of us knows.

I shut the door and I venture downstairs and walk around the house until I find the kids in the kitchen with Yolanda, munching on blueberry muffins and answering her questions about how they're doing. Yolanda's chocolate eyes meet mine, and a wary smile stretches on her lips.

"Can I get you anything, Ms. Reid?"

"No thank you. Is it okay if I sit with you?" She motions for me to sit down at the island and I grab the vacant seat next to Alice. "How are you doing, Yolanda?"

My question takes her aback. Her eyes dart to the door to make sure Gray isn't around and then lets out a deep cleansing breath.

"I've had better days." She sets an empty mug in front of me and pours me some coffee. I've always liked her. Gray won her in the divorce, but I was okay with it because I was hellbent on doing everything myself.

Though looking her now, with tired eyes that have weathered Gray's awful tantrums, I wonder if I screwed her by letting Gray keep her.

"My oldest son is away for college, and I miss him. I'm thankful for Mr. Wentworth keeping me on while he was away. I'm saving up money so I can visit him in New York."

I have four years until Ethan goes away for college. I empathize with her. It's hard to let your children go. You hope you've raised them good enough that they'll thrive in this crazy world, that they'll be able to survive on their own.

"That must be so difficult. I bet he misses you."

She chuckles and wipes away stray tears.

"I hope he does. We Skype every Sunday. I'm happy he's made friends, and he has a social life. But part of me wishes he would stay home forever. I didn't sign up for sending him away." Smiling, I place my hand over hers and squeeze.

"I'd like to help you go see him if you'll let me. You've helped me all this time with Ethan and Alice, and I'm so grateful for you. I want you to be able to see him." Yolanda's tears spill over the dam she's built to keep them in.

This isn't a ploy to get in her favor. This is two moms trying to keep it together and supporting each other through excruciating times.

"Thank you, Ms. Reid. I couldn't. But it means so much to me that you want to help." I'll have to find a way to send her some money anonymously.

When we finish our coffee, Gray finally decides to grace us with his presence and brings us into his study. No longer green or smelly, he invites us to occupy the seats in front of his desk just as he sinks lazily into his office chair.

"So. What did you want to talk about?"

I don't understand how he can be so nonchalant at a time like this. How did he go from being a present father in the six years he tore Brandon and I apart, then go directly back to the asshole he was before Brandon?

"We need to fix this, Gray." He raises his eyebrows expectantly. "As much as I want you to just disappear, you can't. Alice turns eighteen in six years, and that's six years you and I have to get along before we can wash our hands of each other." He pinches the bridge of his nose and rests on his elbows on the desk.

"So, what? We're just going to sit around here holding hands and singing Kumbaya? Is that what you want?"

"No." Sighing, I throw my purse to the ground and swing my legs up and sit on them. This is going to be a long day. "The kids and I have talked about this for a week now, and we have some things we would like to see changed." He drops his arms dramatically and groans.

"Great," he snaps.

"I don't want to come here anymore," Ethan pipes up. I watch for Gray's reaction. He stares at Ethan like he has four heads. How could he *not* want to spend time with the famous Grayson Wentworth? How could his own pride and joy *not* want to bask in his glory?

"What?"

"I. Don't. Want. To. Come. Here. Anymore." Ethan enunciates every clipped word dripping in anger.

"Did you come up with that all on your own, or has your mother been filling your head with that shit?" Ethan crosses his arms and glowers.

"Believe it or not, Dad, I've had my own thoughts since I was a kid. Mom has been the one encouraging us to come here and spend time with you. Should I tell her all about the times you left us here with Yolanda so you could go out without us?" Gray presses his lips in a hard line. "I didn't believe you changed. You can't just be an asshole for so long and then become a good guy overnight."

"Ethan, no swearing," I hiss.

"You took Uncle Brand away from us," Alice murmurs quietly, her eyes trained on the desk. She's fearless, but she doesn't like to hurt other people's feelings.

She bravely lifts her eyes to Gray's, tears welling up in her eyes.

"He wasn't your dad, sweetheart."

"No, he wasn't. But he did things for us my friends' dads do for them. He did things you never did…"

This all sounds so horrible for someone on the outside. But sitting here and listening to my kids call out Gray is satisfying. It proves I'm not crazy.

"But I changed—"

"Until you humiliated Mom," Ethan interrupts. Ethan shouldn't be the one who has to defend my honor. I'm perfectly capable of doing that on my own. "You made us believe Uncle Brand hurt mom. When I was in elementary school, all the kids in my class had dads who would come in for career day, eat lunch with them, volunteer for coaching teams—I never cared that you didn't show up for any of it. But mom did."

Gray's hard features soften.

"Mom was there, you weren't. Uncle Brand was there, and you weren't."

"I just wanted you to love me, Dad. Ethan doesn't care about not having you around, but I *do*." Alice's voice grows shaky as her emotions rise to the surface. "Mom came with me to father and daughter dances at school so I wouldn't feel left out. But I always did."

She turns to me with watery eyes.

"I don't mean to hurt you, Mom."

"I know, baby." She turns back to Gray and releases the rest of her tears.

"You have no idea what it feels like to be teased because your dad is on every tabloid, or that my dad doesn't care about me because he's never here." She brushes away her tears. "It's not fair."

Alice falls into my side and sobs. Gray watches helplessly and frowns.

"For the record, Alice, I *do* love you." She scoffs. He turns to Ethan and winces at Ethan's hard expression. "You don't want to come here anymore, E?"

"No. I don't think it's fair for you to force me to come here either."

"I don't want us to lose touch, buddy. I know you're mad at me, but I think we can come back from this." Ethan scoffs.

"I don't *want* to, don't you get that?"

I sit back and watch the pent up feelings rain down on Gray. He frowns as he studies Ethan.

"Okay, you don't have to come here anymore." I sit up straight and stare at Gray in bewilderment. What did he just say?

It takes Ethan by surprise too.

"You're mad, and I understand that. Maybe we can start repairing our relationship. Can I take you out for dinner?"

"Um…" Ethan's voice trails off. He looks at me for direction, but I'm just as surprised as he is. He doesn't want that, but he wasn't expecting Gray to go along with this. "I'll think about it."

"Alice, do you still want to come here?"

Alice nods slowly, quickly glancing at me for encouragement.

"Yeah, but maybe not right away. Maybe we can start slow?" Gray nods and stands up.

"Okay, good start," he quips.

Not once did he apologize.

"Why don't you two go to your rooms and see if you want to bring anything home. I want to talk to Dad." They hesitate before leaving. The last time Gray and I were in a room alone together, he hit me. Giving them a reassuring nod, the exit the study and close the door behind them.

"I'm sorry for hitting you," he says softly.

It isn't okay, and I'm not ready to forgive him yet.

"Thank you for saying that." The awkwardness hangs in the room like an ugly chandelier. I'm done. I don't have the energy to make it work. "So, I think it's time we talk about what's happening with the kids."

He furrows his eyebrows.

"Didn't we just talk about that?"

"Ethan won't be coming over anymore, you're right. But how will Alice get here?" My question sobers him. I'm asking for space.

"I could come over—"

"I think it's best if we distance ourselves from each other."

"How do you suppose we do that, Ava? Our kids are still minors. We're still court mandated to see each other."

I take a deep breath and grasp for any strand of courage I can grab onto.

"Tess, Jordan, and I have come up with an arrangement. If the kids want to see you, Tess or Jordan will bring them by."

He flounders.

"Are you kidding me?"

"How did you expect this to all shake out, Gray? Did you think we'd be a big happy family after all the shit you pulled? Do you even realize how badly you hurt me? Mentally. *Literally*. What about your kids? Have they crossed your mind at all?"

He growls and crosses the room, pouring himself a tumbler of bourbon at his bar cart. All he needs now is a cigar to transform into that pompous stereotype of rich men.

"I thought we could at least *try* to be friends again. I mean, it worked back then."

Yeah, when I thought you were turning over a new leaf.

"There's no trust, Gray. I don't have the energy to be friends with you, especially if I have to watch my back twenty-four-seven. I can't ask you to waive your parental rights. The state of Illinois will never allow it, trust me. I've looked into it."

"So that's it then? I have to parent through *your* best friends?"

"Seeing you makes my stomach churn." My voice sounds so small, so foreign. "You have hurt me in *every* possible way, and I *need* to push you as far away from me as I can. I loved you. I meant my vows, Gray. But I *can't* forgive you just yet for this. So yeah. You'll have to deal with Tess and Jordan for a while. They're an extension of me until I can stomach being in the same room as you."

"Unbelievable," he murmurs.

"Why did you do all this?" His tired, drunk eyes meet mine in surprise.

"What?"

"Was it truly because Brandon and I were seeing each other?" He shrugs and sniffs. "I'm just trying to understand. Help me understand."

"It doesn't fucking matter, Ava. Do what you want."

And this was going *so* well.

"I'm going to leave. I'll email you when Alice wants to see you." The heavy chair scrapes against the hardwood floors, making Gray visibly cringe.

Good.

As I saunter towards the door, the clink of Gray's glass against the table echoes throughout the room.

I'm glad he gifted us with his absence. I'm a terrible mother for thinking that, but I raised two great kids who didn't turn out like him. I pray for the women he'll inevitably run to so he can lick his wounds and curse my name. They'll need all the patience and wisdom this world can offer.

"Ava."

I don't bother turning around at the sound of his baritone voice. I stop in my place and wait for the crushing blow. What more can Grayson Wentworth do to ruin my life?

"I *am* sorry."

"Yeah. Me too."

Thirty-Five

Ava

Three months after the interview

Geometry is the pits. Who the fuck cares about proofs? Who cares how the problem works, it just does! I don't usually have to worry about Ethan when it comes to homework, but it's Sunday night and he hasn't touched it. At one point, I burst into tears because I didn't understand the examples in the book. He said he was just going to take the 'F' and move on with his life. Needless to say, that didn't go over well.

We stayed up until we got the damn thing done. I sent him to bed at ten-thirty knowing full well he was going to be a peach in the morning.

Pick your battles, Ava.

I stayed up later than ten-thirty to enjoy the time to myself I didn't have all day. When midnight rolls around, my eyes start drooping. Knowing I have to be up at some ungodly hour to bring the kids to school, I cut my losses and begrudgingly get up, bringing the half roll of cookie dough that *was* a full roll of cookie dough before I got into it back into the refrigerator.

I start shutting everything down. The kitchen lights go off, the front door gets locked. I pad through the living room and begin shutting the blinds on the French doors until I see something that terrifies me.

The fire pit that has been dormant for the last six years is lit. Fire licks the midnight air. It would be a beautiful sight if I wasn't so terrified.

This is how I know I'd be murdered first if a horror movie ever came to life. I step out onto the deck and nearly kill myself by tripping over my sweatpants down the stairs. When I hit the solid ground below me, I stare at the fire pit and listen to my surroundings. Footsteps that trudge through the grass make me regret not bringing down a kitchen knife.

A dark silhouette stops when they catch sight of me.

"I'll call the cops."

"Well, that would kill the mood." His voice, gravelly and smooth, relax my erratic heart.

"Brand? What are you doing here?"

"Come sit with me for a minute." My bare feet crunch the grass below me. When Brandon gets closer to the fire pit, the fire illuminates his casual frame. He wears a Chicago Bears T-shirt and dark jeans. Forty looks good on him.

I drop into my seat and stare into the fire. I'm not brave enough to look him in the eye.

"You scared the shit out of me. I was on my way up to bed..."

He chuckles.

"I'm sorry for scaring you. This was kind of a spur of the moment thing."

"How'd you get the gate code?"

A devilish smile spreads across his lips.

"I have someone on the inside."

I laugh nervously. My money's on Alice.

"You left your garage open, and I thought sitting by the fire might be a good idea." Yeah, where the mosquitos are feeding on my flesh. Good plan, Brand. "Have you been crying? Your eyes look puffy."

"Yeah, well, freshman geometry will do that to you." He grins and shakes his head.

"Yeah, he left that purposely for tonight. He knew I was coming, but traffic to get here was unbelievable."

Traitors!

How dare they conspire against me! I'm only their mother!

"I read your book." My heart hammers in my chest that I feel the pulse in my ears. Is this the part where he tells me it's not you, it's me?

Shit.

"Oh?"

"Did you really feel this way about me, Ave?"

I nod, scared to tell him the truth. "I couldn't articulate how I felt about you in front of you. But I could write it. I was going to give it to you for your birthday but then…"

Everything went to shit.

"It had a nice ending." I grin.

"I wanted Avery and Brent to have a happy ending even if we didn't." He smiles thoughtfully. I sit on my feet so the mosquitos can stop feasting on my exposed skin.

"Ave?"

"Hmm?"

"I saw your live." My heart falls into my stomach. Did he hear me tell the world I love him still? "I still love you too."

Oh, God.

I can't handle this.

I need someone else to pretend to be me so they can handle this instead of me. I can't. I can't!

"Okay." *Is that the best you can come up with!?*

"I'm sorry I didn't believe you about Ellen. I wanted to see the best in her, but I was wrong."

What do I say to that? It's okay? It's not okay!

"She's not in the picture anymore. Kayla's threatened to file for a restraining order if she comes within a hundred yards of me. She's not allowed to call, write, or show up."

Good. I wonder how she's dealing with it. She was so cocky in the bathroom at the studio.

"Gray and I are no longer on speaking terms." He raises his eyebrows in surprise.

"Seriously?"

"It was necessary. I didn't want to wait six years to be done with him officially. The kids can still have a relationship with him if they want it. Alice has been the only one who's been exploring that. If they want to see him, Tess and Jordan volunteered to handle the contact with him."

"Wow." Yeah, that's the best way to sum it up.

We reach a comfortable silence. He stokes the fire, and the warmth bathes me.

"Did you love her?" I'm a masochist.

"I loved the person I thought she was. It's hard to reconcile everything in my head. She saved my life after you and me..." he sighs. "I wouldn't have been so broken up about it had she not developed this ruse with my brother."

I get it. Gray pretended to be my friend for six years before he blasted everything to the world.

It wasn't real.

"If Gray never set this up...would you have married her?"

"No." He searches my face. "I didn't love her like I love you. Marriage was never something that crossed my mind with her. I think in the back of my mind, I was hoping you'd come around."

We're brave around each other when we're outside. I don't know what it is. It's magic...it's...destiny.

"Did you see anyone while we were apart?"

"A few guys here and there. Nothing serious." He frowns at my confession. "What happens now, Brand? Are we just going to acknowledge we love each other and go our separate ways?"

"Is that what you want?"

No.

"Is it what *you* want?"

He sighs and gives me a sleepy smile. "Be brave, Ava. Tell me something nobody else knows."

Now's the time to come out with it. I haven't slept right in years. My heart somersaults and leaps every time I hear his gravelly voice. I can't spend another six years apart from him. I don't want to sleep with other men.

"I want to be with you, Brandon. No secret relationship, no creepy people following us and taking pictures. I want a life on a farm and eat tons of pasta at Garrett and Alex's restaurant. I want late nights making love to you and then stroking my hair until I fall asleep. I want the bickering, the laughing at you when you think you're always right. I want to cook dinner with you and sit by the fire after a long day. I want you to be a family with me and my kids." He stands up slowly and stands in front of me, his hand outstretched. His hands are still rough, but mine still fits perfectly in his. He pulls me up and cradles my face in his giant hands, his thumbs caress my cheeks.

"I want it all, Ave. I'll live through your horrible snoring and your wild mood swings. I'll cook you all the pasta you want." His thumb traces my bottom lip. His rainforest eyes stare deeply into mine. Our souls connect outside our bodies, uniting us for the first time in six years. "I love you so much, Ave. More than I've ever loved anyone. This is so weird, but I want to be a father to your kids." Tears fill my eyes, making him impossible to see through the cloudiness. We both giggle.

His lips press to mine. Not possessively, like he did six years ago. But slower, sweeter. His tongue dances with mine. His hands move from my face to my waist.

He pulls away from me and rests his forehead on mine. "Forever," he whispers.

Epilogue

Seven years later

Today is the day of days. Ethan and Alice are the lucky ones. They're both in college, out of state, and can escape this shitshow. Meanwhile, Sam and I are the ones dealing with Ava's meltdowns of turning the big four-oh. Sam doesn't really understand why his mother is so emotional, he's only five.

Tess was nice enough to whisk Ava away for a girl's weekend so she'd stop crying so Ethan, Alice, Jordan, and I can get our house ready for her big surprise party. I have a giant surprise for her that I *know* I can squeeze some happy tears out of her. But now we're hanging streamers and banners and all that girly shit she loves so much.

My wife is loved. I've invited everyone she loves, even that dickhole, Ben and his wife. The director she hired to direct her movie, Peter, is also coming over. Momma flew in this morning and she's taking Sam around town to tire him out so he wouldn't be underfoot the whole time.

Yolanda, her husband Daniel, and their son, Leonardo, talk excitedly with each other and then to Peter and his wife. Gray avoids Yolanda as much as he can. I'm not sorry for stealing her away from him. Yolanda and her family have become a big part of our blended family. Now that our careers are on a steady upswing, Yolanda retired her "housekeeper" title and opted for being Sam's nanny. It's a win-win, honestly. Leo is Yolanda's only child, and I *know* the baby fever was set in around the time Sam was born. She got to cuddle with a baby and give him back at the end of the day when she was ready to spend time with her own family.

It's six o'clock. Catering has already come by and set up the food for tonight. Gray lurks in a corner and talks with Alice. Things have gotten better between the kids and Gray, a little bit with Ava, and with me, well, we have some shit to sort through.

Tess Archer: I've got the goods. We'll be there in five.

So much for the ten-minute warning. I hold Sam in my arms and crouch behind the kitchen table while everyone else scopes out a good hiding spot.

"Is she gonna be surprised?" Sam whispers loudly.

"Yeah, I think she will be, buddy." Ethan crouches next to me and nudges me with his elbow.

"She's gonna love this, Uncle Brand."

Yeah, she is.

Sam laughs at the funny face Ethan makes at him and reaches for his big brother.

"Shhhh! We can't give away the surprise yet!"

The doorknob jingles, and the small sliver of light illuminates the back of the living room.

"You don't think he'll be disappointed, do you? I'm forty!"

"I don't think you have anything to worry about, babe. You landed a good one." Ethan flips the switch, and everyone yells, "Surprise!"

She screams and sends all the shopping bags she carries flying across the room. Tess laughs and steadies her balance. Sam, Ethan, Alice, and I all swoop in, kissing her on the cheek and hugging her.

"You jerk!" She laughs. "How did you get this all together? I've been home all this time!" I kiss my wife and chuckle.

"Classified information, baby." Sam holds his arms out for Ava to hold him. Sam has her pretty blue eyes, but the rest is all me. He doesn't have to go through the shit Ethan went through when he was the man of the house. He gets to live in a house full of love and an older brother and sister who love him more than life.

Tears well up in her eyes and she reached for Sam, planting a kiss on the crown of his head. His chocolate hair that is in a bowl cut, thanks to a pair of safety scissors and sexy time with my wife that left him to his own devices, hangs in his eyes.

"Thank you so much, baby. Did you help daddy with all of this?"

"No, they wouldn't let me help. So, Nana took me for a drive and we had Wendy's." Good ol' Nana.

Ava makes her rounds with Sam on her hip, and Ethan protectively at her side.

"She's happy, Uncle Brand," Alice murmurs next to me. Her arms snake around my waist and pulls me into a side hug.

She's been my best friend since she was six. She successfully snuck in three boys in high school. The last one found me waiting outside the door and nearly shat himself. Ava and I had a good laugh about it, even though I was crying on the inside.

She's bold, daring, and so fucking fearless. Alice Wentworth has been one of the greatest blessings of my life. She has a boyfriend back at school, but she's scared to tell Ava about him. He's in the drama program.

And that should tell you enough.

"You think so? You don't think she'll try to skin me alive for pulling the wool over her eyes?"

She laughs and shakes her head.

"No, I don't think there will be any bodily harm. She was dreading forty. Now she has everyone she loves in one room celebrating a day that's all about her and she has a smile on her face. You did good."

I miss our kids when they're gone. They came for her birthday party and will be back for Thanksgiving break in a few weeks, but when they're gone, I'm eager to hear about how they're doing.

I've been told by both kids that I don't need to check in on them as often as I do, but I think deep down, they like hearing about home.

Ava saunters over to me and sets Sam on the ground and kisses me on the lips.

"I love you, Brand. This is amazing. Thank you so much for going through all this trouble—"

"It was no trouble at all. Look around, Ave. You're in a room full of people who love this shit out of you. Oh, and Gray's here." She snorts and playfully hits my chest.

"I have something for you." Her voice drops a few octaves, awakening the libido that never really sleeps around my wife.

"It's not *my* birthday." She grins.

"Come on. Come out on the deck with me for a minute. I want this moment just between you and me."

"Okay, okay. Let me grab your present first." She leads the way. Nobody misses us, they're all talking away happily and eating. I grab the gift bag off the table and stroll outside. "You have to open yours first."

She groans.

"You're a killjoy."

"But you love me."

She giggles and tears through the pink tissue paper that floats to the ground. She pulls out the pack of white paper that's stapled together.

"Oh, this is that place a few miles away from your mom, isn't it?"

"Mmhm. Three hundred acres of undeveloped land, except for the five-bedroom house."

"Can we see it?"

"Baby, it's *ours*." She lifts her eyebrows.

"What?"

"I know the family who owned it. They just renovated the house, so everything's updated. We can do anything we want. We can get cattle, horses, chickens...seriously. Anything you want to do. It's ours." Her eyes water. "Baby, I didn't mean to make you cry...we can sell it if you don't want it..."

"No, it's not that, Brand." She sighs and pulls a small rectangular box out of the back pocket of her jeans. "It's perfect."

I tear open the wrapping paper to a white and pink stick staring back at me.

"You've been wanting to know why I'm so emotional, right?"

Two lines means pregnant.

"Five bedrooms are perfect. Everyone gets their own room." I yank her into me.

"How did this happen, Ave? Don't get me wrong, I'm over the moon. I can't wait to see this little guy. But I'm almost fifty...you're *forty*..."

I can't believe it. I'm adding to the family I've always wanted.

"Things happen, Tiger." She laughs so easily. She wipes the tears out of her eyes and kisses my cheek. "Are you happy about this? You'll break my heart if you say no."

"Of course I'm happy, Ave. I've got you. I've got the two older ones I want to lock in their rooms and keep them forever, we have Sam...nothing could be better." She sobs and buries her face in my chest. "I love you so much, Ave. Happy birthday."

Author's Note

I can't believe that this book is being shown to the world. I can't speak for all writers or authors, but for me, I *never* thought this could be a reality for me. This has been the most rewarding, terrifying, nerve-wracking, humbling, and exciting experience for me.

Brandon and Ava have lived in my head for years. Their story was shown to me in snippets, and they *begged* me to tell it. So, I would write. And then it would just sit on my hard drive taunting me until I did something about it.

This book has been a labor of love. At one point I lost my entire manuscript and had to start from scratch!

When I was twelve years old, all I wanted to do was read and write books for a living. Back then, I thought the only way was to be traditionally published. And then along came Amazon!

Being as introverted and tender-hearted as I am, this wasn't easy.

I wish I could visit the past me and give her a hug. I want her to know that this is our reality. We did what we always wanted to do. And you know what? There's more to come!

I hope you enjoyed Brandon and Ava. They've become my best friends, my biggest cheerleaders. If you liked it, please consider leaving a review!

Acknowledgements

It takes a village (heh) to write a book. I am overwhelmed with how much help and support I received writing *Back and Forth*. So without further ado:

To my husband Taylor, honestly, I don't know how you survive. You have been my biggest rock and cheerleader throughout this whole process. Even when I lost my manuscript, you tried your best to save the day, and then gave me the pep talk of your life to move my ass and get it done. Again. Thank you. You're the love of my life, my favorite person in the entire universe, and I couldn't have done this without you.

To Jessica Moakley, holy cow. Jess. We did it! You have been my sounding board, my partner in all of this, my friend, the shoulder to cry on, the person who has constantly told me that I didn't write a steaming pile of garbage. I can't thank you enough for standing by my side throughout all of this. Your opinion and feedback has been the greatest blessing I could've asked for, and it is *so* appreciated!

To my betas, Kara, Andrea, Scarlette, and Jessica, THANK YOU! Your feedback has helped this be the best book it could be. You were the first sets of eyes on Brandon and Ava, and you truly helped them shine!

To Kelly Chang Rickert, thank you so much for answering all of my family law questions! You helped me glance into the hell that Ava went through with Gray, and helped me understand all of the intricacies of law that made this realistic. From the bottom of my heart, thank you!

To my editor, Amy Briggs with Briggs Consulting, Amy. Holy crap. Thank you so much. You were the first person I ever spoke to within the writing community. I was nervous and navigating imposter syndrome and you were so unbelievable helpful through it all. The hand holding, the incredible and thorough work that you do, the *Schitt's Creek* memes, were a God send. Thank you so much!

To Julia Wolf, Julia, I came across your Tik Tok during one of the hardest times of my life. I knew that I wanted to be a writer, but I never thought it could be a reality for me. I was traversing the pandemic with two young children in a job I *knew* wasn't my forever. Until I found you. I was so inspired by you, and how you became an author. I emailed you out of the blue, and honestly, I never thought you'd answer. But you did. You gave me a community of authors and aspiring authors who posted their secret sauces, the true nitty gritty of what this industry is like. Most importantly, you gifted me the confidence that I *could* do this. I was ready to throw in the towel. I accepted the fact that my characters would live solely in my head without a chance to step into the sun. Thank you. You have no idea how much your reply back to me changed my life. Thank you. Thank you. Thank you.

And finally, to my family and friends who endured my constant posting of writing this book, for those who preordered, for those who called me on the phone to tell me how proud they were that I was following my dreams. Thank you! You have no idea how much your support has impacted me. Thank you!

About the Author

Dillon Bancroft is a Contemporary Romance author based in Tampa, Florida. She was always considered a dreamer, and was constantly scolded as a student to get her head out of the clouds and pay attention.

She is a mother to two crazy girls, and wife to a former Marine who has enhanced her vocabulary in the worst ways, but has supported her in *all* of her hair-brained ideas.

She is a sucker for second chances and puppies. She watches entirely too much TV and quotes very obscure lines in popular TV shows.

Looking to Connect?

Check out my LinkTree! It has all the links to my social media and website. Please make sure to sign up for the newsletter so you can stay in the know about exciting and upcoming releases!

Email: dillon@dillonbancroft.com
LinkTree: https://linktr.ee/dillon.bancroft
Website: www.dillonbancroft.com

www.ingramcontent.com/pod-product-compliance
Lightning Source LLC
Chambersburg PA
CBHW051208190726
48288CB00006B/1866